Veiled at Midnight

~ Twilight of the British Raj ~
Book 3

Books by Christine Lindsay

Twilight of the British Raj Series

Shadowed in Silk
Captured by Moonlight
Veiled at Midnight

Stand-Alone Titles

Londonderry Dreaming (contemporary)
Heavenly Haven (contemporary Christmas short)

Veiled at Midnight

~ Twilight of the British Raj ~
Book 3

Christine Lindsay

WhiteFire Publishing

This is a work of fiction. All characters and events portrayed in this novel are either fictitious or used fictitiously.

VEILED AT MIDNIGHT

WhiteFire Publishing
13607 Bedford Rd NE
Cumberland, MD 21502

ISBN: 978-1-939023-26-1 (print)
          978-1-939023-27-8 (digital)

You are precious in His sight

This novel is dedicated to my mother-in-law, Toni Schmidtke,
for being such an exemplary Christian woman
whose faithfulness has inspired me over the years,
and whose encouragement of my writing has helped me stay the course.
Thank you, Mum.

Christine

For I am convinced that neither death, nor life, nor angels, nor principalities, nor things present, nor things to come, nor powers, nor height, nor depth, nor any other created thing, will be able to separate us from the love of God, which is in Christ Jesus our Lord.

~ Romans 8:38-39

Part One

1

August 15, 1946
Calcutta

The last arrow of sunlight shot back from the train's brass trim, blinding Cam Fraser. As he narrowed his eyes, he recognized a face at the edge of his vision. A train whistle shrieked, steam hissed. A young woman in a green sari mingled within a crowd of Indian passengers. In an instant, his legs felt encased in steel. Out of that teeming mass on the platform she stared back. Her skin the color of milky tea, her hair a thick braid of silk over one shoulder. The fast sinking sun set her awash in a glow of apricot. Then crimson. She'd been looking straight at him. Then in the descending dark she was gone.

"Hadassah."

His sister, Miriam, gripped him by the elbow. "Hadassah? Cam, you said Dassah."

"I thought I saw her." He shook his head, the pain nearly splitting it in two. He squinted to see into the crowd as the rapid Indian dusk fell. Ten long years...

With her hand on his shoulder to steady herself, Miriam strained on her tiptoes to see over the throng. "It's been simply ages! Cam, are you sure? Where'd you see her?"

At that moment, whistles blew, and conductors ushered passengers aboard the night train bound for New Delhi. Miriam sent a pleading look over her shoulder. "Find her, Cam, before the train leaves."

He didn't need any goading from his sister, and while the steward urged Miriam up the steps of their carriage, he dodged passengers along the side of the train. Hundreds scrambled to their seats, more well-to-do Indians to first and second class. At least that injustice had been corrected somewhat since his childhood. The plush elegance of first class was no longer assigned to the British alone. Still, hordes of poor mashed into the cattle-like carriages called fourth. But it wasn't fourth he'd seen Dassah standing outside of.

For as long as he could remember, scrawny little Dassah had tagged after him when he visited the mission. He and Miriam had played with the muddle of orphans—Hari, Ameera, Zakir, to name a few—enjoying the usual sort of games. Soccer, rugby, marbles. But the last time he'd seen Dassah she'd been anything but scrawny. Nor had she been a little girl.

He reached the area where he thought she'd stood. Sweat soaked the back of his shirt. Blast this muggy monsoon weather. His eyes blurred. And blast this headache. No matter where he looked he couldn't pinpoint any of the slender young Indian women on or off the train as the girl he sought. Had he conjured up her image—a mirage shimmering on the hot Indian rails? It wouldn't be the first time.

He wound back through the crowds the way he'd come. As he passed a clutch of railway officials, their talk in Hindi slowed his stride.

"...Muslim League calling for a holiday to mark their Direct Action Day—"

"Shush your foolish fretting." The Conductor glanced around. "Not until tomorrow."

"The Hindu Congress is worried." Another railroad man wiped sweat from his face with the trailing end of his turban. "I have heard rumors someone might disturb the trains, such as the Muslims tried to do to Gandhi's special train."

"Disturb? *Pah*! They tried to derail it, but that was months ago, and Gandhi is not on this train."

"But many of his friends in the Hindu Congress are."

The myriad of noise echoing under the station's massive glass and wrought iron roof absorbed the conversation. Cam's headache clasped his head in a vice, but the authorities running these trains knew their jobs. Even if there was anything to worry about, they didn't need him sticking his military nose into things.

As he entered the carriage, Miriam glanced up. "Well?"

"No time. I'll have to wait until we stop." The train started to glide forward as he sat on the seat opposite her. He reached for *The Times of India*, wishing he had an aspirin—or six—and dropped the paper to his lap. He'd tried earlier to read the news, but the grinding wheels in his head wouldn't allow it.

"Do you think it was her?" his sister asked.

He didn't want to raise Miriam's hopes. "I don't know for sure if the girl I saw even got on this train."

But the image of the woman's willowy shape in the crowd was stamped behind his eyelids. Those arched brows, those eyes that were world-weary even when she was a child. So like Dassah, how she could speak without saying a word, how she trailed constantly after him and Zakir, only running away to hide when they fought.

Miriam smoothed her skirt over her knees. "You want to see her as much as I do. She's like family. Like Ameera and Zakir."

"Not quite."

"Cam, surely you don't mean that because she's Indian."

"You know me better than that." He regretted the slight growl to his tone. Really, Miriam of all people should know better than to insult him with racial bigotry. "I'm saying that Dassah isn't quite family because she left the mission. Her and Tikah. Not a word after all this time. If they thought of us as family they'd have contacted us. As for Zakir...." He rattled his newspaper open and pretended to read.

"Honestly, Cam, you've been like a mongoose bemoaning a stolen banana all day." She wrenched off her white, wrist-length gloves and fanned herself with them. "You always get that way when we mention Zakir."

His sigh would have depressed that mongoose she compared him to, but he couldn't bear to talk about Zakir. Nor had he any intention of telling her how he felt about Dassah. Then to add on what he'd heard on the platform? Certainly not. Though recent intelligence expected this crisis to blow over, the sooner he got Miriam out of Calcutta the better.

She pulled open her handbag and offered him a packet of tablets. "And there's no need to hide your headache."

He smiled as he took the medicine, and she sent him a grin much like their mother's. Miriam was rarely nosey—bless her—and thankfully didn't ask further about his headache.

Through the window, the darkening Indian countryside sped by under a green sky with a crescent moon rising. The rocking of the train lulled him, and he shut his eyes. But Dassah's face emerged from his memory. That long black braid over her shoulder. The scent of roses and lilies from the mission's balcony, the perfume of Dassah herself as he faded to sleep.

A slight hitch in the rhythm of the train gliding along the rails woke Cam. His eyes flew open. As though a change in gear...a step out of cadence. The train met a curved section of track ahead, and he could see the line of lit windows. Not a parallel line. A ripple passed through their carriage, setting the crystal droplets on the lamps to tinkle, the hairs on his arms to stand.

Their car juddered.

A thousand screeches—were they human or metal?—as the train jumped like a frenzied horse. The momentum plucked him from his seat. Flung him across the carriage.

He picked out his sister's screams from so many others.

For a moment he was suspended in air, weightless, then landed on what had been the wall, and then the ceiling as the train tumbled, turned, and twisted. Lights went out as pain, poker hot, jabbed him in his side, his head.

A lifetime passed. Human cries mingled with tearing metal. Blackness. The roar of his pulse pounded through his temples. Until the bucking of the train stopped. He counted his breaths, his heart about to burst through his chest. Where was he? How....?

How long did it take to sort out where he was? Minutes? Seconds? Was this the wall he was lying on? Yes, the train lay on its side. His head had rammed

11

against the lamp fixture.

"Miriam," he croaked. "Where are you?"

Deathly silence.

Gradually, from all directions people began sobbing, screaming, calling out, but nothing from his sister. An acrid filament of smoke entered their carriage and yanked him into new terror.

"Miriam! Where are you?"

"I'm here." Her answer, thin and muffled, reached him.

"I'm coming. Are you all right?"

"I don't know."

He didn't like the frailty in her voice. This wasn't his gangbuster sister on her way to start a new teaching position. As he stood he found sure footing on the panelling close to where the window used to be. Most of the main structure of their carriage remained intact, though their bunks had sprung open in the upheaval, and broken furnishings created a minefield of debris.

Pain stabbed his ribs, and when he sought out the reason his hand came away warm and sticky. Same with his forehead when he touched it. He wondered what had become of his cap. As an officer he shouldn't be out of uniform. It took a moment for the absurdity to sink in. He was wearing his civvies. On leave. The train had derailed.

He was standing though, with bruised ribs probably, and able to get to Miriam. Glass splintered under his shoes as he gingerly worked his way across to where he'd heard her thread of a voice. "Call out to me again, love."

"I'm here, Cam. Are you all right?"

"Right as rain. I'm coming."

"Always the hero, just like Dad, though you'll never admit it." She giggled, but it petered out too soon.

"Big brother will always come to the rescue. Shout out now."

He took more steps. It was hard to see in the dark. His knee connected with something hard and sharp, and he felt his way around what must be an upended seat. "How are you, Miriam?"

"Nothing's changed, my darling sibling, since the last time you asked five seconds ago."

"Been that long, has it?" Keep her talking, keep her talking, that was the ticket. "Am I getting closer? Warm? Cool? Right off the map?" While shoving aside their strewn luggage, he spiked his tone with the same jolly nonsense as when they were kids playing at the mission. "Miriam?"

A hand grasped him around the ankle. "Stop shouting, and for goodness sake don't step on me."

He dropped to see what pinned her down. Some broken fixture trapped her, he surmised in the total blackness, and thrust the jumble off her. Once freed, he quickly ran his hands over her arms and legs. No broken bones, uninjured, and he sent a swift thanks to the Almighty, something he rarely did these days.

"That's enough, Cam, I'm fine. Really, I am."

"You're sure?"

"Bruised. Cuts and scrapes…all minor. Shaken." Her teeth chattered. "Yes…shaken…and you?"

He helped her to stand, and together they hobbled to below the door that now opened above them. It hurt like the blazes as he hauled himself upward through the opening, pushing the door up and out so that he emerged like a jack in the box. The pain in his side shot a haze past his vision, but he managed to reach below and lift her out.

They stood together surrounded by what appeared to be a battlefield. For a moment he was back in Burma in the war, with bedlam all around him. People, like refugees, lay about, some crouched. Others staggered by in the light of flickering flames from a series of small fires, started by flying coals from the engine. Behind them, the carriages from first and second class lay on their sides. English people stumbled from the wreckage. Nearby, one man in a white linen suit and cricket club tie had lost several layers of skin on his leg. Around him was scattered the usual paraphernalia his fellow British packed for the train: thermoses, picnic baskets, bedrolls, air inflated pillows.

Not far from him, a woman in a pink frock and straw hat festooned with silk roses cradled her arm, broken in a nasty-looking fracture. One of her shoes was missing. Many of the English had begun to assist one another, so too were the Indians from First and Second.

But closer to the front behind the engine, carriages lay smashed across the rails, nothing more than a pile of splintered wood and tangled steel. Twisted rails stuck out all over, while cars and coal tender straggled about the ballast stones. Indian passengers crept out from the broken matchbox of a train, in shock, blackened with smoke and grease. He heard and understood various dialects from people speaking all at once—Hindi, Punjabi, Urdu, and several others. Many sobbed, hunched over their wounds, while one Indian woman, seemingly uninjured, stood like a statue. Her sari fluttered in the scorching night breeze as she gazed about her at nothing.

Calls for help came from within, and a handful of Indian soldiers picked their way into the wreckage. The engine was still spouting steam. That boiler could blow.

"Stay here," he said to Miriam, "safely away from the train."

"I'm coming with you."

"No you're not."

She reached for him. "Cam, I felt blood all over your shirt."

He raised a hand to his head, pushed back his hair sticky with blood, and took a swift glance at his side. The gouge was nasty, would need stitches most likely, but it wouldn't kill him. "I'll be back soon. Help will arrive from that town over there!" he shouted back at her as he ran to join the soldiers who were sifting through debris at the front of the train. "Do what you can for the injured here."

Railroad men raked out red hot coals from the engine's firebox, but cinders belched from the locomotive lying on its side. It wheezed as if it were a huge black-and-gold striped animal brought down by a hunter's bullet. Cam shook off his fanciful thinking to climb inside the wreckage. Stewards and traveling soldiers were already at work putting out a series of small fires.

Inside fourth, Indian women tore the hems off their saris, and the men tore their scarves and shirts to staunch the bleeding of their fellow passengers. Cam threaded his way through, at times crawling, while able-bodied men carried the wounded outside to the embankment. An Englishman of military bearing attempted to free a woman from a broken baggage rack as Cam reached them. This man also wore civvies, but from his tie clip Cam recognized him as a British officer from a Punjab Regiment. A glance of understanding passed between them as they counted to three. Together they lifted the rack that pinned the unconscious woman and thrust it aside.

"Can you carry her outside?" the officer asked. "I can manage in here alone for a few minutes. It's that engine that worries me."

With a nod, Cam stooped to gain hold of the woman under her shoulders and knees, and lifted. His vision blurred as he carried her outside where a makeshift triage had already sprung up. Some of the passengers appeared to be doctors and nurses. He'd seen enough war and human misery, enough for a lifetime, and perhaps it would be worse if the sight of suffering didn't kick him in the gut like it did now. If he'd become used to this, then something truly would have died within him.

In the distance, ambulance bells clanged, adding to the other wretched sounds around them. From the nearest town came civil and railroad police, fire officials. He returned to the wreckage and for a long time helped to lift the wounded from it. At last, hours later, the locomotive was under control, all fear of an explosion causing a secondary disaster subsided, but Cam's muscles cried out. The pain in his side had worsened so that it was hard to breathe. Had he done more than bruise a rib? But his thirst was worse, enough to drive a man mad.

A local man came by with a bucket of water and a ladle, offering a drink to Cam. The water went down his throat like nectar, and it would do until he got a proper drink—or better still, a bottle. He turned to survey the derailment.

Among the crowd of injured, her green sari stood out.

Her long braid of dark hair caressed one shoulder as she sat cross-legged on the ground, a child in her lap, her arm around another. There she was. Flesh and blood. A mirage did not bleed.

Those amber eyes of Dassah's in the scarce light of flickering fires were wide with shock. As she adjusted the sari crossing her chest, the veil eased back from her forehead so that he could see the extent of a gash above one brow. Cam drew close and dropped to his knees before her. With a gulp she cradled the toddler she held that much closer, and the little one whimpered in her sleep. The other child—a boy, he could see that now—sidled closer to her.

"Are they all right?" His voice sounded alien to his own ears. "Are you?"

She shivered as if she were freezing in the hot night air and lowered her gaze. Anger, searing red as coals, coursed through him. Dassah had always been reserved, even as a baby. So had Zakir, for that matter. Surely their childhood friendship deserved more than this show of Indian subservience? But then he'd thought that of Zakir as well.

Around them, the throng of people merged into one unintelligible, buzzing mass. For once, the rest of the world could take care of itself. He lifted the boy and sat beside Dassah, holding the too-quiet child. In the face of the trauma around him, all he could think was, were these children hers? A black cloud crossed his vision. If so, Dassah must be married, and the thought of a husband snuffed out a hope he hadn't known existed.

Why that should matter made no sense, when he was practically engaged himself.

2

Since Cam left Miriam hours ago, the wreckage had gained a circus-like atmosphere. Soldiers, police, railroad gangers, all worked to clear the track. Not long ago a giant crane on a train bed arrived and was lifting cars upright. A few cinders blew, red-hot fireflies against the night sky, and Miriam brushed them away. If she knew her brother, he was working himself to exhaustion. Well as soon as she caught up to him, she'd order him to sit down and let her look at his injuries, or she'd box his ears.

Sure enough, there he was on the other side of the tracks, his face black with soot, his trousers and shirt filthy, sitting in a group of Indian passengers. And he was holding a child.

She added new vigor to her stride, but stopped. A woman in a green sari sat beside Cam…Dassah. Their childhood chum hunched on the grassy embankment in the dark, clutching a little girl about two. Cam had been right. It *was* Dassah he'd seen boarding in Calcutta. Dassah with that regal tilt to her head, and those almond-shaped eyes that could melt the hardest soul.

Miriam ran full tilt toward them. Cam never let on, but the Indian girl's friendship meant as much to him as his boyhood chums like Zakir. Probably because Dassah had been born in the mission the first year he and Mum had come out to India. She'd always been Cam's little Indian sister.

"Dassah, darling, it's you. It's really you." Miriam swooped to squeeze the young woman in a hug. For the strangest half moment, she felt the Indian woman pull away, but she must have imagined it, because seconds later Dassah's eyes brimmed, and both of them were laughing and speaking at once.

"Thank God you're safe, Dassah."

"Are you well, Miri? Oh yes I recall, you preferred to be called Miriam from the time you turned sixteen."

"Where've you been all this time? Are these children yours? Look at that darling little girl fast asleep. Cam saw you, Dassah, at the station. Knew you

16

straightaway. Are you all right?" She glanced at her brother. He had that stoic look about him he used to have as a kid, when he wasn't happy and was putting on a brave face anyway.

Dassah clutched the children that much closer and tucked an object dangling on a string under her sari. That expressive dusky brow of hers wrinkled, but her soft smile was the only answer she gave.

"Are you all right?" Cam repeated in low tones in English.

Dassah dipped her head and spoke in that measured way Miriam remembered, an almost musical pulse to her perfect British inflection. "I am completely well. Praise be to God the children are not hurt either, except for cuts and bruises that will soon mend."

It was better to give Dassah time, and goodness knew with the chaos around them, they could do with a laugh. With her hands on her hips, Miriam turned her attention to the little boy, smiled, and asked him in Hindi, "And what is your name, my good man?"

"Ramesh." He grinned, showing off the charming space where his two front teeth should have been. Like most Indian children, he seemed fascinated with her hair. It never failed—every Sunday school class she ever taught, the little ones were putty in her hands because of her blond mane. While this brought attention from unwanted male admirers, she was grateful for it when entertaining children as they giggled and touched her tresses.

"Well, Ramesh, what did you think of the train going off its rails?"

The tiny boy lost some of that pasty look. "Were you on the train? Did you hear that enormous screeching?" He chattered on like a piston engine.

Miriam made all the appropriate *oohs* and *aahs*, and saw Dassah's eyes light with laughter as the little boy came alive. She too gradually lost that death-warmed-over look, thank goodness, but still…their old friend hung back. Some of the joy of seeing Dassah froze like a new bloom in an unexpected frost. Why was Dassah acting…not standoffish exactly, but as if she and Cam were strangers? Like so many other Indian people who saw them only as members of the British Raj, the so-called ruling elite. That thought brought a sour taste to Miriam's mouth.

Cam must have felt the same from the way he raked his hair off his brow. "Are you sure you are all right, Dassah?" he asked, switching to English again. "Perhaps you should see the doctor."

"I am well," the Indian woman insisted, keeping her gaze fastened on the ground.

Miriam planted her hands on her hips. What on earth was going on here? Something charged the air between her brother and their friend. Not for the first time did she wonder why Dassah had left the mission in the first place, all those years ago. If she'd told anyone of her reasons for going, it should have been Cam. Those two had been thick as thieves as children—more of a threesome, really, if you counted Zakir.

An Englishman in gray slacks, his shirtsleeves rolled up to the elbows,

17

strolled toward their little group. "You're needed, Captain Fraser. The police have requested our help with the investigation."

Cam got to his feet. "Certainly, sir, right away."

With a glance, Miriam catalogued the man as an officer, even though he wasn't in uniform. Most likely on leave same as Cam.

Her brother took a few steps away from the embankment. "Miriam, can you get one of the doctors to take a look at these three? I'm concerned over this gash on Dassah's forehead. I can leave them in your hands, I trust."

Dassah's stiff little smile faltered. "You do not have to worry about me. There are plenty of…my people about to assist me if necessary."

Cam went rigid. "Of course," he said. "I didn't…I didn't mean to offend."

Dassah appealed with open palms, as if she were the one who'd insulted him. She dipped her head, her fingers restlessly plucking at the little girl's tunic as the child slept.

Miriam forced a laugh. "Oh my word, you two! Let's try to remember that when we were playing as children at the mission we were often put down for our naps in the same cot. Goodness gracious, I think at one time Tikah had us all together in the tin washtub for a good scrubbing after we'd been playing in the *bagh*."

Cam addressed Dassah as if Miriam hadn't spoken. "I would do the same for my sister. I'd insist she see a doctor with a gash like that. Now if you'll excuse me. I'll be back as soon as I can. Please don't go anywhere. We have a lot to catch up on…as old friends." Cam started to walk away but wavered on his feet and touched a hand to his brow.

Before Miriam had a chance to reach her brother, Dassah set the sleeping child down on the grass and bolted to her feet. To Miriam's shock, Dassah—who'd always been frightfully modest—strode toward Cam, her hand outstretched as if she wanted to lift the tail end of Cam's shirt. Instead, Dassah with eyes like wide pools turned to her. "Miriam, I believe your brother is injured."

In the light of the torches, Miriam whipped up Cam's shirttail. A wound at his side gaped. A sharp breath came from Dassah while Miriam issued a gasp of her own. In the dark she'd not noticed how large the rust red patch on Cam's shirt had become.

"What is this?" Dassah scolded. "It is you, Cam, who needs a doctor." Removing her scarf from her head she handed it to Miriam. "Please use this to wrap his waist."

Miriam's voice joined with hers as she wrapped Dassah's scarf around him. "Oh, Cam, and you didn't say a word. Sometimes you make my blood boil."

Cam, instead of being suitably subdued, released a deep chuckle as he looked down at Dassah, who stood at a respectful distance.

The officer who'd been waiting strode closer. "Are you fit for duty, Captain?"

"He is not." Dassah whirled to lecture the man, her braid flinging out. "Can you not see he is more injured than he is letting on?"

Neither she nor Cam could take their eyes off Dassah. The officer didn't notice their astonishment over the woman they used to know as extraordinarily serene. He peered closely at Cam. "Good gracious, man, I'm afraid the medics will have to take you."

Miriam touched Cam on the arm. "I'm going for a stretcher straightaway, and you will see the doctor."

He reached for her wrist as she was about to dash off, his voice drained. "For goodness sake, Miri, I'm perfectly capable of walking fifty feet." He pulled himself straighter, his gaze lingering on Dassah.

Still, Miriam was prepared to ignore her brother's refusal for a stretcher when an Indian man of about forty rushed toward them, making a beeline for Dassah and the children. Dassah broke her gaze with Cam to look at the well-dressed man wearing a Gandhi cap and a tailored suit that wouldn't have been out of place on Savile Row in London. This rather handsome man had to be Dassah's husband.

Miriam was about to nudge Cam with a grin when she noticed his face fall. Surely he'd be pleased that Dassah had done so well for herself—an orphan girl married to a wealthy Hindu.

"Come, Ramesh." The man beckoned to the boy. "We must return to Calcutta immediately. Dassah, quickly, bring Padma, for I have hired a car."

Without a word, Dassah picked the child up from the grass.

One glance at Cam's expression and Miriam knew he was not going to see the doctor just yet. Cam reached out and almost touched the Indian woman on the shoulder, but pulled his hand back. Strangely though, Dassah gave a tiny, startled jump. She stopped and looked up into his face. Cam, too, stopped, his hands fisted at his sides, his stance ramrod straight while those almond-shaped eyes of Dassah's seized on him as if she were memorizing his features. Cam moved slightly toward her, and the Indian woman's lips parted as if to speak.

Miriam put a hand to her mouth.

Something invisible and bright danced on the air between her brother and Dassah. Something holy and full of a passion she would never understand. But then Dassah glanced down and away without a word, and Cam, though he didn't move, gave the impression of shrinking back. In a heartbeat, it was done.

The military officer stood off to the side, and the elegantly dressed Indian gentleman checked his wristwatch, while Dassah inched away from Cam. No one seemed to notice. The tiny dancing flames Miriam imagined between her brother and their old Indian friend winked away while night returned. It had not been simply cinders flitting like fireflies. Miriam's hand dropped from her mouth to hang limp at her side.

But, Cam…and Dassah? It couldn't be. He was practically engaged to Phoebe.

Cam glanced at the man who was obviously the children's father by the way little Ramesh wound his arms around his neck. Her brother directed his words to him. "Sir, my sister and I knew your…we knew Dassah as a child. Might we know your name? That we may call on you."

"You are most kind, *sahib*. Arvind Malik, President of the Chartered Bank of Bombay at your service. However, please, if you will be excusing me, I must get back to Calcutta." The man bowed slightly, holding Ramesh close. "My wife was seriously hurt in the derailment, and they took her to hospital in an ambulance." He inclined his head at Dassah. "Come, there is no time."

"Your wife?" Cam winged a glance at Dassah, and Miriam could feel his palpable relief.

Dassah rushed past them, carrying the little girl along the stones behind Arvind Malik. Miriam darted after her with the hope of helping, but Dassah had not gone two steps when Cam whisked the little girl from her. At first it looked like Dassah would argue. She knew as well as Miriam that carrying that child wasn't going to do Cam's injuries any good, but like Miriam, Dassah closed her mouth and hurried alongside him. It seemed Dassah remembered that Cam had a stubborn streak a mile wide, almost as wide as Dassah's own, as Miriam recalled. With Arvind leading, they all dashed to an automobile waiting on the road by the tracks.

"What are you to these children?" Cam asked Dassah.

"I am their *ayah*."

Miriam pretended not to notice the growing relief on Cam's face. So Dassah wasn't these little ones' mother, but their nanny. Still, she could have children of her own somewhere else.

By the time they reached the banker's vehicle, the short conversation between Dassah and Cam had ended. Mr. Malik set his son in the back, gesturing for Dassah to hurry and pushed her into the backseat with Ramesh and Padma. Just as he was about to get into the front he stopped and turned to Cam, his hand tapping a rapid drumbeat on the top of the car. "Yes, please visit, *sahib*. But as soon as we are able we will be leaving Calcutta and going to Lahore where one of my bank branches is located."

Cam stood with that soldierly posture she knew so well from her father, his back straight as a board, his hands clasped behind his back. "You are concerned about Calcutta?" Cam asked softly.

The banker dropped his gaze for a moment. "Are you aware there may be trouble come this morning?" He flung out a hand at the derailed train. "Perhaps there will be more of this type of violence."

Her brother tilted his head. "What makes you think this was not an accident?"

Miriam could hear the underlying steel in his voice. He was in the intelligence service for good reason.

"It was my hope to be away from Calcutta before Direct Action Day. This so-called holiday that Muhammad Ali Jinnah has called will only give idle folk a chance to make trouble."

"Give me your address, Mr. Malik, and I will see what I can do to personally protect your house."

The banker sent Cam a thin smile as he handed him a business card. "From your demeanor, *sahib*, I am assuming you are with the army. While you British remain in India, no doubt your forces will protect the peace for the time being. But if I may speak my mind…?"

Cam lifted his chin.

Arvind Malik clasped his hands in Eastern supplication. "It angers my people that after two centuries of British rule, you should decide to give us our independence with so little time for preparation. Your government wants to hand our country back to us by June of 1948. Only two years to set up a government. Already the power struggle has begun."

Miriam moved to take hold of Cam's arm. Two years was far too quick for a transfer of power. There would be trouble. Everyone knew that.

While talking with the banker, not once did Cam glance at Dassah and the children inside the car. Nor was there a word or gesture from Dassah, who seemed to be looking through the front windshield as if her life depended on it.

Well, everyone else might be walking on eggshells, but Miriam wasn't about to let Dassah go without a proper good-bye. Not this time.

Leaving Cam's side, she knelt inside the backseat and wrapped her arms around Dassah's shoulders. "I've kept you in my prayers all these years, Dassah darling. I also know that eagle-eyed glint in my brother's eye. Seems that we, too, may be returning to Calcutta. You can be sure we will be in touch very soon." She tweaked Ramesh on the nose and plopped a kiss on the little girl's head, who'd remained oblivious in her slumber.

Miriam must have got through that protective wall Dassah had bricked up, because her friend gripped her wrist. Dassah held Miriam's hand to her cheek. "It fills my soul to see you again, Miriam."

The moment was broken when Arvind Malik jumped into the car and ordered the window blinds closed. As the car drove off toward Calcutta, Miriam turned to Cam. "So much for me getting to Lahore to set up my rooms in plenty of time."

Cam released a humorless grunt. "The decorating of your rooms can wait a day or two."

"And it is obvious *our* reunion with Dassah cannot. But for now, Cam, will you please come with me to see a doctor?"

He didn't answer but started toward the medic's tent, though his pace slowed. He wasn't as tough as he thought, because halfway there he stopped, and she slipped under his arm and let him lean on her. Poor lamb, he really was in pain. That other officer was there instantly. Between the two of them they supported Cam and called out for a medic. Good thing they did, as Cam's eyelids flickered. Turning a frightening shade of white, he slumped just as they reached the stretcher.

Cam was whisked into the temporary triage tent.

Only half listening, she caught the officer's voice. "You and I haven't been properly introduced…Lieutenant Colonel Jack Sunderland, Second Battalion, Thirteenth Gurkha Rifles…will stay to make sure your brother is all right." He continued talking, but she never heard another word.

She couldn't contain her relief that Cam had slipped into unconsciousness. If he hadn't, he'd probably have insisted on plastering a mere bandage over the wound and been on the road by now behind that car back to Calcutta.

3

The sun rose on another sticky day along the banks of the Hooghly River as Jack Sunderland drove Miriam and Cam to Calcutta in a borrowed jeep. Concentrating on the undercurrents of Calcutta, with buildings as impressive as anything in London, Miriam still caught only fragments of what the lieutenant colonel was saying. Since leaving the derailment he'd been working hard to cajole her into conversation. Well, he could flirt as much as he wanted. She wasn't budging an inch, even if he did resemble that matinée idol Peter Lawford.

"To think only yesterday," he said, "I'd taken in a rather enjoyable polo match at the Ellenborough grounds. Today, if all had gone according to plan, I'd be halfway to my post in the north of India."

She glanced at her brother—sutured, bandaged, his broken ribs taped—sprawled asleep in the back of the jeep.

"I'm sure he's fine." The lieutenant colonel checked his wristwatch for the third time in the space of half an hour. "Did your brother serve in Malaya during the war?"

"Mm? Oh yes, Cam served in Malaya and later Burma." Her conscience pricked at her lack of polite exchange, and she drummed up some of her own banter. Better to placate the man. No sense wounding his ego. "Did you also serve in Malaya, Lieutenant Colonel?"

"It's Jack, if you please. And yes, quite the nasty time we had with the loss of Singapore. I fear we may be in for similar nasty business here in India. What was it last night, do you think? Accident? Sabotage?"

"I see you and Cam share the same suspicions."

"Your brother's in Intelligence, I understand. Chaps like him, raised in India, fluent in all the dialects, are the best recruits for that."

"He is in Intelligence—at least since he got back from the war."

They lurched over a bump in the road, which brought a moan out of Cam.

Jack's fingers drummed the steering wheel as silence fell, and she darted her gaze to the streets.

Within the bazaars, vendors cooked rice in vast caldrons. Saffron and cardamom wafted on milky steam, but there didn't seem to be the usual immense throng. Nor were there as many flower stalls open. Her eye caught an old woman throwing a mass of fresh marigold heads onto a cloth in preparation of stringing them into garlands. The Muslim call to prayer floated from minarets poking up through Calcutta's morning mist. But today its pleasantly haunting sound clashed with the jangle of bells from Hindu temples and brought back that awful tumbling feeling from last night's derailment.

"You know, it's quite possible," she blurted, "the train went off the rails because of shoddy equipment."

"You don't believe that any more than I do. It was aggression, plain and simple."

"But why? The British are quitting India. There's nothing to be gained by putting Indian lives in peril."

"There were a large number of Hindus on last night's train, and indications that the derailment was organized for today's Muslim League demonstrations."

She sat back with a harrumph. "I can't bear to think of them tearing at each other. Surely the derailment has more to do with our government shipping the best of the locomotives out during the war, leaving India with the poorest gear now that independence is slated on the agenda?"

His mouth twitched into a smile.

She bristled in her seat. "I fail to see what's so funny." Her father and brother were both soldiers, and they knew better than to treat her like *the little woman*. Jack Sunderland had no idea he was stomping on thin ice.

"I was only wondering," he said, "if I should stop the jeep and locate a soapbox for you. Your lecture is rather refreshing. And you are utterly charming. Has anyone ever told you that you resemble the American film star, Carole Lombard?"

His comparing her to a film actress stung after her mental comparison of him to the handsome and distinguished Peter Lawford. "No." She bestowed him with her frostiest glance. "How kind of you to mention that though."

His laughter barked. "Obviously, not your sort of compliment."

"Anyone who knows me knows that I prefer to use the brains the Lord gave me—"

"And not slide through life, Miss Fraser, eased by your incredibly good looks."

"Shall we change the subject? First of all, I'm not Miss Fraser but Miss Richards. General Geoffrey Richards is my dad, and Cam's stepdad."

"Oh yes, I know your father. Now that I think about it, you resemble him."

She softened at the mention of her father and laced her tone with woe. "I inherited his height. Thank you, Daddy. During my schooldays it was the bane of my existence, but nowadays, my height has its merits. Keeps unwanted men at arm's length." She sent him the usual delicate sniff that warned off amorous advances, and looked away in an attempt to hide her grin.

"Ah." He glanced around, seemingly at anything and everything to keep from laughing. "You must be in excellent fighting form, keeping gawky young males in their place, but your warning to me is a total misfire, Miss Richards. Mercy, you're just a slip of a girl, probably only twenty-five or so, and I've just celebrated my forty-second birthday."

"Oh my, that old?" Normally, she had no trouble keeping her distance, but bantering with Jack Sunderland was like tasting one Turkish delight from the chocolate box. She wanted just a nibble more.

"Yes, an old soldier returning to his regiment in the Punjab."

"Like my father." Laughter overtook her.

He slapped a hand to his chest. "Ouch, a mortal wound straight to my heart. But you're right, Miss Kitty Claws, I am a doddering old career man like your dear old dad."

"That was rather brutal of me. Do forgive. As for my dad, he's far from doddering. Still swoops Mother into deep embraces when he thinks no one is looking. And you're a good twenty years younger than him. Besides, there's no such thing as *just* an old soldier." Her laughter faded. "Not easy for soldiers' wives though, sending them off to work. Not at all like sending a vicar off to the church after tea and toast in the morning, is it?"

"I'm sensing that a prudent young woman like you, Miss Richards, would never want a soldier for any...ahem...romantic entanglements."

"You're a shrewd judge of character, Jack, but it's not just soldiers. I'm not interested in any romantic entanglements at all."

"None whatsoever?"

"Absolutely nil." A fresh smile tugged at her mouth. He was brave to match her at wits. Usually, men withered after five minutes of her indifference.

He let out a mock sigh. "I can't tell you how relieved I am. I know my reason for avoiding entanglements, but why is a pretty girl like you unattached? You've not decided to join some religious enclave? Veil yourself behind cloistered walls? God forbid, become a nun?"

His chuckle fell flat as she kept her eyes on the streets ahead.

Heat rose from her neck to her cheeks. "Not a religious enclave exactly."

He glanced away and seemed to curse under his breath. "I've embarrassed you, and I ought to be drawn and quartered."

Now it was her turn to feel rotten for embarrassing him. No doubt she'd laid on him that piercing gaze she'd inherited from her father, the one where she could make a seasoned soldier feel like a raw recruit. And this Jack was oh so pleasantly seasoned, all six feet of him, very fit, and rather dishy with that bit of gray at his temples. Her laughter pealed. "Oh do be sensible. For a man of your rank and... age...you really should act with more dignity and not accuse a woman of entering a nunnery just because she doesn't fall at your feet in a swoon."

"Age! Dignity! Do sheath those claws of yours." He tugged at his ear. "But you're right, a man of my rank has brought you back to Calcutta, and we must see that your brother gets proper rest. If my intuition is correct, I think he wants to make certain that young Indian woman is all right, especially if that banker's fears play out."

All laughter left her. "Cam said the army is prepared for any mischief that might arise."

"True, our military johnnies don't expect the communal feelings to run any hotter than they have these past months. So don't worry. If they did, as a British woman you'd be well protected."

As if a cool breeze blew up, she no longer felt the joviality that had spirited them into the city. All of a sudden she feared he was a pompous, biased representative of the Raj like so many men she'd met. "I suppose you think that the fact the Muslims and Hindus may attack each other, and *perhaps* not us, is going to make me feel better."

He looked at her askance, knowing very well his remark had misfired this time. "Miriam, of course the army's concerned about the Indian people."

"But are the British forces doing enough? Rioting has escalated since Gandhi formally asked us to leave in '42."

"I'm well aware, and can quote the little Indian lawyer for you, 'Leave India to God…or to anarchy.'" A tired note entered his voice. "Well, the little man got the anarchy part right, didn't he?"

"I suppose." She remained silent for several blocks. "Jack, have you noticed how few people are out this morning?"

"Yes, I've noticed," he clipped. "The sooner I get you off these streets the better, so where precisely may I take you and your brother before I head off to Army HQ?"

"I moved out of my old digs yesterday, and my trunks are on their way north to Lahore by another train, but my former roommate will take us in."

"Was your brother going to disembark in Delhi or escort you all the way to Lahore?"

"Cam is traveling with me to my new lecturing position at the Kinnaird College for Women. After he leaves me in Lahore, he's taking a long-overdue leave."

"So you'll be lecturing at Kinnaird," he sputtered. "Let me guess…English literature, Shakespeare, sonnets?"

"I teach English lit only on occasion. I have a minor in psychology, but my degree is in theology."

He blinked. "Theology," he confirmed with a pointed glance.

She flashed him her most mischievous grin. "Predominantly New Testament theology, my strength being in the Greek languages, *Koiné* and Classical."

"Great Scott! You already have a soapbox, a theological soapbox of all things. If only I'd known this when I made my idiotic joke at the expense of religious groups." He shook his head. "Forgive me for mentioning, you do not look the part."

"Why, because I'm not fifty years old and male with gray whiskers?"

"I'd say it has more to do with the fact that you are a tall, leggy blond bombshell."

A retort hovered on her tongue, but at that moment, shrieks carried over the noise of the jeep's engine. Ahead of them, a taxi stopped by the side of the road.

Several Indian men were dragging passengers out of the backseat. The passengers—a few Indian professionals, lawyers, or businessmen in English suits—cowered on the road as the hoodlums threatened them with iron rods. The assailants' dirty white *kurtas* hung down to their knees over their pajama-style trousers.

The pit of Miriam's stomach went cold.

Jack swerved to the side of the road, and Miriam cringed at the fear in the passengers' unblinking eyes. They knelt on the road with their arms up to shield their heads. *Dear God....*

Down the street another group of men raced up to the hoodlums, shouting and brandishing long wooden *lathis*. Miriam heard the slap as one of the thugs hit the driver in the face. The man landed on the road.

Jack stomped on the brake. As the jeep ground to a stop, he jumped from the vehicle, pulling his revolver from his holster. "Don't move," he ordered her.

His shoes crunched on the splintered glass of shop windows. What little traffic there had been on the road disappeared entirely. She watched him shove his way through the mob surrounding the taxi, and her pulse galloped in soundless prayer. By the time he reached the nucleus, the situation had disintegrated into an all-out brawl.

Jack raised his arm heavenward and let off a warning shot.

The echo repeated along the street, lined with buildings several stories high.

A sea of Indian faces whipped around to him, each man a hard, unyielding statue. Each set of shoulders rigid. Each fist clenched tight.

Silence reigned for a minute, and she slid over to the driver's seat, to be ready if they needed to make a quick get-away, her eyes glued to Jack.

A number of louts came to life and ran off, but too many remained to glare at Jack. Even from the jeep, she could feel their loathing for him as the unwanted, uninvited authority. Their abhorrence hissed out from bare-teethed sneers. They were men looking for blood. Sitting in the relative safety of the jeep, Miriam's veins ran with ice.

She heard the cock of Jack's sidearm and gripped the steering wheel.

In the huddle around him, not one pair of eyes shifted. Then a man in a *dhoti* stained with betel juice edged one foot in his direction. Another man moved closer. Then another. The circle shrank, closing in. They could easily take Jack down. In minutes his blood could stream along with theirs. Her foot hovered over the gas pedal. Blasted military heroes. Why couldn't Jack have been a mild-mannered missionary and driven past, knowing full well there was nothing he could do?

Jack didn't seem to show any fear though. Good thing too. They'd be on him like a pack of wild dogs if he did. She watched as he adjusted the aim of his revolver by a degree to what appeared to be the leader. "First one who moves gets a bullet in his gut," he said. "I may not be able to kill all of you, but I promise to take a few."

One man with short hair and trimmed beard held back some of the others. He put his hands together and beseeched Jack. "In two years your government has promised to give us back our country. Leave us to deal with our own disagreements."

"And let you slaughter each other?" Jack replied. "Not while I'm on duty."

The rest of the crowd shoved the younger man out of the way, inching closer to Jack, and fear spiked at the back of Miriam's neck. The sound of feet hitting the ground ever so softly behind the jeep made her swivel around. When had Cam wakened? Her brother held his revolver as he met her eyes. She started to urge him back with a heated whisper, but he put a finger over his lips. *Oh Cam, come back, you fool,* but he was already moving to stand next to Jack, and aimed his weapon into the crowd.

She tensed, as it seemed every man in the small mob twitched, ready to strike out at the two. Yet…a moment later, the Indian men wavered as a group. They slunk back, seemingly harmless, like snakes with the poison leeched from their fangs. But for how long?

The taxi passengers scrambled to their feet and assisted the Sikh driver. Without a backward glance, they scurried as quickly as they could along the sidewalk. With the escape of the passengers, Jack worked his way backward in step with Cam, the way they'd come, not once lowering their weapons. One step…

She gripped the steering wheel again, pushed her foot down on the petrol to rev the jeep, and shouted, "Hurry. Now!"

Two steps, three…

"Oh, do hurry," she muttered.

They kept walking backward until they reached the jeep. Cam practically fell into the backseat, and Jack jumped in front with her. They were barely in the vehicle when she stepped hard on the petrol, released the brake, and spun the wheel in a hundred and eighty degree turn. Jack seemed to hold on for dear life as she raced the jeep away in a spurt of dust.

"Would you like me to take the wheel, Miss Richards?"

Away from imminent danger, she laughed as relief sparkled in her bloodstream. "Certainly not, Jack, and call me Miriam. I've never been one for stiff formality when racing away from violent mobs."

After a city block whizzed past, she felt Jack's eyes on her.

"You may look like the luscious Carole Lombard, but in truth, Miriam, you are a typical English *memsahib* born and raised in India. No doubt your father taught you to shoot, golf, and dance the foxtrot with the best of them. But a theology professor? And here you are careening this jeep around corners with a speed that would put Luigi Villoresi and his Maserati to shame."

She forced a smile. In two years their English Raj would end. But in all her life, the last thing she had ever wanted to be was a typical British *memsahib*. And the last sort of man she ever wanted to be attracted to was a man like Jack Sunderland.

4

For one copper anna, Miriam would have ignored Jack and driven on, but he insisted on taking the wheel. After dropping them off at the front door of the digs she used to share with Gladys, he gave her and Cam an abstracted wave. Over the roar of the jeep revving to take Jack on to the fort, she caught his promise that he'd check on them later in the day.

"Typical military bluster, even dressed in gray flannels and a sports jacket." Miriam muttered this to no one apparently, because her brother, staggering into the house behind her, had his mind on things other than the lieutenant colonel. Up two flights of stairs to her old flat, she slumped on the divan.

Gladys, whom she'd said good-bye to yesterday, stood in pajamas, hair still in rollers, and eyes like an annoyed owl. "Great Scott, darling, what happened? More importantly, Miriam, your hair is positively ghastly."

Miriam put a hand up to her untidy mop. Of course she looked the worse for wear. It was half past seven in the morning, and she'd been up all night.

While Gladys dashed off to make tea, Cam refused Miriam's offer to attend his wounds. He entered the bathroom and firmly closed the door. Fifteen minutes later he came out with a release of steam from the bath. Once again he was the spit and polish officer with a clean shaven jaw. Disgusting how men needed only minutes, while she… She touched her hair. She would need hours to cease looking like one of those black-faced monkeys with their hair sticking out all over the place.

Her brother was doing a poor job of hiding his pain, though. He held his stiff upper lip in place while his complexion remained as white as Gladys's face cream. Miriam watched him at the sink as he raked his wet hair back. After checking his revolver, he adjusted the Sam Browne belt that diagonally crossed his tan drill shirt. "Lord, please spare me from heroic men." She groaned. "You're going to look for Dassah, aren't you?"

"Yes."

"Good." She leaned against the doorjamb. "It's the right thing to do. I'm sure Phoebe would agree."

His brows crushed into a sharp V at the mention of Phoebe. "I was sure you'd order me to strict bed rest."

"My darling sibling, as much as I prefer you stayed put for two minutes so that I could nurse you back to strength, you have my blessing to charge off on your white stallion to rescue Dassah. She is our long lost sister, after all."

His hands folding over the flap of his holster stilled. "Miri, I wish you'd stop hoisting me up on the hero's charger. I do not possess those sterling qualities."

"Oh dear, are you in a blue funk over Phoebe? Are you two on the outs again?"

"Phoebe has nothing to do with this."

A feeling came over her, of a boat tied to its slip being loosened. Of being set adrift. "If it's not about Phoebe, then what is it? You've been trying to tell me something since you got back from Burma, but you're being maddeningly vague as usual."

"I'm afraid I am. Sorry for that. It's just…"

"What?" She gripped him by the shoulders. "It's these headaches, isn't it? You've got the shakes coming back from the war, like Dad used to have. Mum told me of his bout with shell shock. Is that it?"

"Dad had his war. I had mine, but I am not like him, Miri. I wish I was." The corners of his mouth dragged downward. "Now I've upset you, as if we don't have enough worries for the moment. For now, you and Gladys should remain inside." His despair vanished with the annoying briskness of soldiers.

She reached for her bag. "I'll go with you."

"Better I do this alone. I'll find that banker's house just to make sure she—they—remain safe." With a tweak to her chin, he left the flat. How he pulled off that even stride as if he weren't the least bit injured, she didn't know.

She walked to the door and leaned her forehead on the cool mahogany planks. As her brother's footsteps grew faint on his way down the stairs, that feeling of being set adrift washed over her again. Never being one to experience premonitions, a sense of coldness lapped at her feet as though her small rowboat of life in India had just been deliberately sunk. A hole scuttled in the bottom of their lives while they were all still aboard.

Cam's headache returned with a vengeance as soon as he stepped out into the blaring Indian sunlight. He mopped his forehead with a handkerchief. The shakes had returned. He'd downed a few headache tablets that he'd found in the bathroom cupboard, grateful he'd not had to ask Miriam for any. She'd never suspect that his wretched headache was connected with anything other than his injuries from the derailment.

If she knew the real origins of his ailment, his sister would be the last to sympathize. Never did he want to see that kind of disgust on Miriam's face, if she ever discovered the truth. He couldn't bear it.

What he needed was a drink. Knock back a few stiff pegs of whiskey to ease the splitting of his head.

Last evening traveling with Miriam had been torture. He loved his sister, but being in her presence and not able to give his body what every desert-dry atom in it craved had been sheer agony. People like him didn't get hangovers after a binge. The hangovers came first. Drinking was the only thing to smooth out the shakes. Send his nightmares of Burma to oblivion. Only his shame of having Miriam know about his drinking kept him from bolting to the nearest club.

He could almost taste the alcohol on his tongue, his need for it growing, taunting him, blotting out all other thought so that he didn't feel like a man most of the time, but a slave to a harsh mistress who came in a bottle. To top it all off, that harsh mistress didn't blot out his memories.

Now there was Dassah. He couldn't go on leave without seeing her, especially if riots were on the horizon. A drink would have to wait, and he forced his steps in the opposite direction of the bar two streets away.

Cam found a tonga easily enough that took him out of the suburbs made up mostly of English residents, past gardens full of marigolds, pink zinnias, and tree-shaded parks. People here seemed to be going about their normal business. Once within the kaleidoscope of streets in downtown Calcutta, his tonga wallah let him out under a stone archway close to the bazaars.

The driver gave a ferocious waggle to his head. "I cannot be going any farther today, sahib. Not safe. The Hindus have erected barricades at the bridges to stop Muslims from entering the city for their procession."

Cam listened to the tinkling tackle as the driver abandoned him in the middle of the narrow cobblestone road. There were a few rickshaws, one or two taxis driving past. By now this entire section of the city should be a beehive of commerce, but most of the Muslim stalls were barred.

In the near distance, the jumpy wail of harmoniums and drums, the sounds of a procession, jarred his nerves. The Muslim League had announced in the newspapers that their mass meeting would take place after mid-day prayers. There'd been meetings like this before, as well as the meetings of the Indian Congress made up of predominately Hindus. But today, the back of Cam's neck prickled. Today would start out as a political rally, but as always the underbelly of the city would steal the opportunity. Looting would soon start.

On such a day as this, a wealthy banker like Arvind Malik and his household would be a prime target.

The sun had crept to its zenith. Not long before midday, Cam stood looking up at the tall mansion in the midst of Calcutta's wealthy business section. Shutters were closed, the great bronze front door locked. Not a sign of activity within the house, but he hammered on the door anyway. Several minutes later a servant cracked open the door. Seeing a British officer, he opened wide to let him in. For generations the Indian people had resented English rule, but today this servant had more fear of his Indian neighbor and vice versa.

The servant escorted him to a private parlor. Arvind Malik stood to greet him, no longer in the gray tweed suit of last night, but a blue, high-buttoned silk coat down to his knees, pantaloons, and a Gandhi hat perched on his head. The banker issued a slight cough.

Now that he was here, Cam didn't quite know how to start. How did one ask about the ayah of another man's children without tipping his hand that he was obsessed with said ayah? And he a white man at that. "I've come to see how you and your family are doing."

"We are keeping within the house until this Direct Action Day is over." The banker appeared calm, but Cam wondered at the man's paleness. "The hospital allowed my wife to come home, and our doctor tells me that we may be able to move her out of Calcutta in a few days. She is upstairs with a nurse, but I fear that if we wait until she is well enough to travel, our lives will be in jeopardy."

"You're right to remain here, rather than make a mad dash for the trains. The usual sort of riots will simmer down by tomorrow."

The banker's gaze tested Cam's sincerity.

Cam returned the man's scrutiny. "Who do you wish to take away from Calcutta? The family and servants you had with you last evening?"

"That was yesterday. My desire is to move my entire household, whatever their religion. As a follower of Gandhi I do not distinguish between Hindu and Muslim—I even employ Muslims in my kitchen—but as much as I wish us to flee, I agree that it is not safe to leave Calcutta at this time." Arvind Malik took a step closer, bowing over his hands that he placed palm to palm. "Last night I spurned your offer, Captain, but now you are here, I would appreciate your opinion on the preparations I have made."

"Last night you said you were going to Lahore. Why Lahore? The majority of people there are Muslim."

"I have much family there. In addition, many Muslim friends, the manager of my bank there for one. He is a follower of Islam, a good man. I feel we will be safer there. Have you not felt it, a growing hatred between the various groups in Calcutta?"

Cam resisted the urge to place a shaking hand to the bandages beneath his shirt. Of course he'd felt the growing hatred, but those mounting feelings simmered just as hot in the north of India as down here. He'd like to help Arvind take his family and Dassah to the train station, but even at full strength he couldn't protect this man's entire family if a hoard of ruffians came at them between here and the trains. And the man's wife shouldn't be moved.

From outside, a scream filtered through the thick stone walls. He and Arvind raced to the windows. A shouting mob surrounded a rickshaw driver and dragged him from his conveyance.

Arvind crossed his arms and rested his head in his palm. "It has begun."

Cam clenched his teeth. "It has."

The banker gained control of his emotions, his gaze darting to Cam's sidearm. "If your offer is still on the table, I gladly accept, Captain-sahib. Tell me what to do to further protect this house." He spoke as he walked to the door, gesturing for Cam to follow. "See, already all doors and windows are barred."

"Good." Cam followed. "If riots worsen, I advise additional barricades in front of those shutters and doors. Heavy furniture, large armoires, because as of this moment no one goes out or in until the present hostilities are over. I'd like to take a look from the roof."

He strode to the base of a wide, marble staircase. Was Dassah up there? What floor? Did she know he was here? Would she care? "Mr. Malik, keep your family upstairs, the shutters closed."

The banker nodded and continued to take him throughout the mansion. As they passed through each room and Cam issued a recommendation, Arvind ordered a servant to complete it. A maelstrom of activity followed in their wake. It was obvious Arvind knew how to run a successful bank with his intelligence. He didn't need Cam's British military know-how. All the same, Cam had to remain. Dassah was somewhere in this opulent house.

They reached the top and came out on the flat roof adorned by stone urns full of flowers and small trees, tables and chairs, bright umbrellas. In the center of the roof garden, the chirping of birds from an aviary almost covered the sound from the street below. A small marble pavilion square in the middle was covered in a mass of red bougainvillea, creating an oasis in the midst of the busy Calcutta skyline. The city below spread out like a map.

At the balustrade, Cam and Arvind looked down to the filling streets. A river of Muslims paraded peacefully toward the mosque about half a mile away. As soon as their prayers were over they would move as a mass to the outdoor meeting in tents and on platforms on the grassy maidan. But what would happen after they prayed? Keeping low, Cam worked his way across the rooftop and peered down to the lane behind the houses.

Sure enough, a number of Hindu and Sikh men were congregating. Not a beggar in sight. A clear sign blood would spill. The noon sun penetrated his officer's cap, setting the top of his head aflame. He swayed, reaching out to steady himself by grasping a stone urn. With a silent gesture, he set one of Arvind's men to keep watch and crouched down Indian style in the shade with his back to the wall of the pavilion.

"Are you well, Captain?"

Cam nodded, seeing stars, and shook off the grayness. He needed rest, but that would have to wait. "I'd like to see where you are keeping your family, if I may." He managed to get up without showing how much it cost.

Arvind led him down the stairs from the roof to the third floor where a line of servants waited for further instructions on the landing. Cam thought someone in the group of servants gasped when he took the last step down to that floor. He checked to see that his blood hadn't seeped through his bandages and thereby elicited that breath of shock. But no, all was well. In a stream of Hindustani, Arvind released a slew of people to various jobs, but one woman hung back, and Arvind questioned her with a glance.

In a whirl of garments—a saffron skirt decorated with a series of small mirrors—the woman turned away and hurried down the stairs. But not before Cam recognized her.

Even without the traditional garments telling him she was a woman from Baluchistan, he would have known her. He'd known her since he was a child of three, when he and his mother first came out to India after The Great War. It was Tikah. Good old Tikah who used to work at the mission. Then years later, she'd disappeared from the mission...the same night as Dassah.

The fullness in Tikah's face showed the passing of years, and a wisp of gray hair escaped from beneath her shawl. She'd reached the age when most women become grandmothers.

But there'd been no friendliness in that look Tikah threw at him as she tromped down the stairs of Arvind Malik's house. With that glare from her, a suffocating heat came over Cam. A wisp of memory...his chest heaving with sun-scorched air, his eyes straining at blinding light on sand. Here it was—another debilitating memory associated with someone from the mission.

His happiest childhood memories and his most painful nightmares, like those with Zakir, were all associated with people from the mission. Now, some of those people were in this very house. Tikah, but most especially Dassah, the girl who never left his thoughts.

5

A breath of air tinkled through the massive chandelier suspended from four floors up. Its crystal chimes were a welcome disturbance to the silence as Cam followed Arvind. If shutters on the floor-to-ceiling windows had been open, light would have flooded these dazzling marble floors. As it was, dimness cast its own oppression. Through teak doors they entered a suite of rooms facing the back garden, away from the bustling street. Here as well the shutters were closed.

Arvind sank into a circular teak chair and gestured that Cam take one of the leather settees. "My wife and children are in the next room."

A servant in white *dhoti* and scarlet sash came in and leaned down to whisper in Arvind's ear. At a nod from his employer the servant headed for the closed doors of the next room. He returned moments later with Arvind's two children and their *ayah*.

Dassah's cotton sari rustled as she moved, the white material bordered in blue creating a foil for her dusky skin. Silver anklets jingled as she crossed the room with the children. From four feet away, Cam caught the heady sweetness of her fragrance. She always had smelled of flowers.

The children should have been out playing in the garden, chattering like magpies as children did, instead of being cooped up in a stifling house. Cam pretended to steal the little girl's nose and was rewarded with a shy grin. The boy took Cam's extended hand in a solemn handshake, and laughed as he ruffled his hair, removing the last trace of British stuffiness from the room. But all that changed when shouting voices rose outside. The children withered into themselves, their eyes going wide as they nestled close to their *ayah*.

Dassah constantly touched them. She caressed the little girl's cheek, smoothed the boy's hair, patted their shoulders as they perched on the settee, but she kept her gaze on the carpet, and he longed for her to look up. *Look at me, Dassah. If you ever saw anything good in me, please look at me.*

The little girl lisped something to Dassah, and Dassah answered in muted

36

tones, still keeping her eyes lowered.

His chest constricted, but he turned to her employer. "You've done all you can for the moment. If it's any consolation, I'm convinced this fracas will settle in no time. The army has already arranged for additional battalions. At the moment the troops are confined to barracks, to be called if the police are unable to keep the peace." Arvind would never know that he shared this information so that Dassah would hear it and not be afraid.

He stood, and without glancing at her, infused his voice with casual interest only. "Mr. Malik, before I leave you alone with your family, may I have a few moments to speak with Dassah? She is like…a sister to me." He swallowed the bile at his lie. "We spent a great deal of time together growing up."

Arvind cast a heavy glance at him and then to Dassah. Cam felt a wave of self-disgust rise up. She'd become an obsession he weighed every other woman against, invading his dreams. He'd tried to put her into the past simply as a childhood friend with the rest of the Indian orphans, but with no success. With a nod, Arvind took his children and led them from the parlor into his wife's sickroom.

At last, Cam was alone with her. A clock ticked somewhere in the room.

He felt the fool, not able to speak. Or move. Her fragrance, roses, maybe lilies or jasmine—he knew nothing of flowers—clouded all rational thought. Nor could he look at her but stare about the room, taking in its luxuries. As if he cared about furniture and frippery, but his mind grasped anything that it could catalogue, something tangible, solid, a lifeline to haul him back to shore as he floundered in a sea of longing with her only two feet away.

Velvet divans here and there, cushions of satin and silk in jewel colors—ruby, emerald, sapphire—were scattered over cool marble floors interspersed with Kashmiri carpets. Brass gods scorned him from various corners. Lush potted palms quivered in the stillness like the nerve at the side of his neck. A suite of rooms, private for a man and his wife to play with their children. A private place to hold a woman.

Dassah broke the silence. "Your injuries…?"

"Nothing worth worrying about."

"I saw your blood last night, Cam."

"I'm all right."

He looked at her then, his ear relishing her perfect English annunciation as taught by his own mother when Dassah was a child in the mission. Dassah's British phrasing danced in accord with her singsong Indian rhythm.

Keeping his hands clasped behind his back, afraid to make any movement, he ventured softly, "There are bigger issues at stake than my injuries. You, for instance."

"You always were as stubborn as a water buffalo." A hint of the teasing Dassah he used to know came through, and he almost laughed. Here she was, the little girl he used to trounce at marbles. "Well I am not going to bash myself against your will," she said on a thin note. On a short pause she skewered him with her gaze. "Why have you come, Cam?"

The abrupt question cut him to the bone, but he controlled his flinch. He didn't mean to hurt her either, but he had to see her, though nothing could come of it. Nothing good. "I wanted to know you were safe."

She looked to the carpet as if it held the answers. Why did she have to bow her head in that way? He yearned to see her hold her chin high. Stare him straight in the face. Come to him as his equal so that he could pull her close and blot out all distance between them. But he dared not. He would only be swept away with desire.

Besides, she'd been born at the mission the year of the *Bagh* massacre, 1919. That made her—oh, for goodness sake—twenty-seven. She had to be married. Probably to one of the male servants in this house. He glanced at her throat. There was no *mangalsutra* strung around the base of her throat to show she was married to a Hindu, just a leather string with something tucked beneath her clothing. Nor did she wear a ring on her finger to say she'd married a Christian.

He cleared the roughness from his voice. "Miriam and I wanted to know you were safe. We had to know you were…safe." He heard the boyish break in his voice at his absurd repetition, as if he were a brat of thirteen.

With her head still bowed she started to speak in the manner of a school recitation. "I am thankful that you came. My employer and his wife are kind people who deserve your notice."

The back of his neck went hot. "I came to ensure *your* safety, Dassah. Don't misconstrue my intentions."

Her gaze darted everywhere in the room but at him, her almost oriental sloe-shaped eyes glistening. Those sensitive hands flitted upward until they fell, trembling to her sides like falling sparrows. He wanted to link fingers with her to still her unease, knowing very well that he was the reason for her agitation. "I see Tikah is here as well." Maybe it would calm her if he chatted about good old Tikah. "I caught a glimpse of her in the hall. You should have seen the scowl she sent me. Quite froze my blood." He attempted a grin.

She slanted a glance at him. "I do not know what I would have done without Tikah. She obtained work as the cook in this house many years ago, and I was brought in as her helper. When the children were born, I became their *ayah*. Being raised in the mission prepared me well." A trace of the smile he used to know lit her amber eyes. He'd been right. Talking about Tikah seemed to reassure Dassah.

He found the courage to ask the question to which he dreaded the answer. "After all this time, Dassah, you must be married?"

Her smile disappeared. "I am not married."

Not married. She wasn't married. The words sluiced through him like the first of the summer rains.

Her gaze lifted to him but just. "And you? Are you married?"

"No." An image of Phoebe tried to inveigle her way in, but he shoved it away. "I am not married, Dassah."

The floor stole her attention again, and in the quiet room he could hear her breath quicken. Did her pulse race like his? Did every nerve in her body shiver with desire to be with him? He couldn't take his eyes off her, knowing she watched him through her veil of lowered lashes. If he didn't keep his hands in an iron grip behind his back, they would reach out to touch her cheek, slide a hand through her tresses of dark silk. Draw her to him.

Finally she spoke. "It is many years since we saw each other last."

"Ten years." An edge entered his voice. "Where did you go? *Why* did you go?"

The questions tumbled from him. Inane questions. But he could no longer bear the crushing weight of not knowing. What a ruddy fool he'd been back then, twenty-one, just back from Sandhurst before joining his Indian Regiment. She'd been seventeen, a lovely, pure Indian girl brought up in the mission next to the *bagh*. And on the very night of his return, he'd done the unpardonable by breaching the racial boundaries. He'd kissed Dassah, and not a gentleman's chaste kiss. Now every ounce of his body urged him to do the same.

God forgive me. She was no Singapore doxy to be pawed, then or now. Had she feared ten years ago he would do more than kiss her? Kiss her in a land where an Englishman, a soldier in His Majesty's forces, could never take an Indian woman as his wife? He could feel her apprehension. It wasn't last night's train derailment or the unrest simmering outside today that caused her fear. It was him. Shame filtered through his body like liquid poison. Like the ruddy poison of a whisky bottle he used to blot out the memories and loneliness.

There was no lying to himself. If he kissed Dassah again, he'd be unable to stop at that alone.

Her lips parted as if to speak, but Arvind opened the door and returned to the parlor. The banker's brows were crushed together. Clearly, Cam had stayed long enough in the presence of his children's *ayah*. Cam took a step back. With the banker's eyes fixed on him there was no way to hide the mortifying heat that must be staining his face. He stood before the banker, at the ready as if to receive the chastisement of a superior officer. And rightly so.

At that same moment, a commotion erupted outside in the street. People shouted. Someone screamed, and ascending with that scream came the reek of burning rubber.

Dassah rushed the children into another room. Cam looked only once to ascertain they were safely behind that solid set of doors. One of Arvind's men stood guard, a knife tucked into his cummerbund. Cam and the banker shared one glance and rushed from the room. They had to get back on the roof. At the staircase they leapt up the treads two at a time.

Well hidden behind the stone balustrade, they peered down on an overturned car set aflame. Fires flickered in the streets already roasting from the overhead sun. Black smoke billowed like a pillar of darkness, its acrid stench choking off their breath. With the field glasses from his pack, Cam searched the streets. The same thing was happening down at the corner, and beyond in various parts of the city.

Glass splintered. He trained his binoculars on the area where the sound came from. More glass shattered. Muslim youths threw bricks through windows all along this section of Hindu homes and businesses. Midday prayers at the mosque had ended, and Cam's gut went cold at the sight of Muslim women and children carried along the congested street. If violence escalated, the innocent would be caught in the crossfire.

Then what he'd been dreading appeared. A group of Hindu and Sikh men ran around the corner of tall brick homes, rushing toward the Muslims with batons and clubs. The crowd surged forward in one unbroken wave of white clothing that within an instant was dyed by splashes of crimson.

Men in Sikh turbans used batons on heads covered by Muslim prayer caps. Hindus with Gandhi caps broke clubs over the heads of their Muslim neighbors. And the Muslims gave back as good as received, breaking limbs with their own clubs and bricks. A tall Sikh in a royal blue turban fell to the ground, bleeding. Here and there, Hindus and Muslims staggered and also fell. Even from this distance Cam could hear the sickening thud of wood breaking on bone.

He removed his weapon from its holster. At the very least he could keep miscreants below from entering this house. Then his eyes found one family. A thin, youngish man in English trousers and white shirt, a Muslim prayer cap on his head, attempted to remove his wife and children from the fray.

One of those children was a little girl with pigtails bouncing on her back. About six or seven, she was swinging on her father's arm. She was laughing, not knowing she was entering a riot. The child thought she was still on her way to play on the grassy *maidan*. Cam didn't know these people from Adam, but it didn't matter.

He descended the wide circular staircase, two or four stairs at a time, until he reached the bottom floor, and raced for the front door. Vaguely, he thought he heard Arvind shouting behind him.

Out on the street, the shouts, screams, cries, jumbled together to buzz in his ears. He couldn't save everyone, but where in this torrent was that young family, that one little girl who could have been Dassah twenty years ago?

Wading into the fray, he butted with his elbows and fists at a number of men bent on murder. Until he saw them. The young father bent over his family, trying in vain to act as a shield. Cam pushed through the crowd. "Come with me!" he yelled.

Thank God, the man recognized his army uniform as help coming in time. Cam reached them and pulled the small girl into his arms, taking hold of the man's older daughter with his other hand. The young father pushed his wife toward Cam as well, but just as Cam made it to the steps of Arvind's house, the Muslim man fell under a pile of thundering arms and hands that clutched wooden clubs.

Arvind, who must have followed outside, stood at the top of the steps to receive the family that Cam thrust toward him while he turned back into the swarm.

Somewhere over the roar of the rioters he thought he heard Arvind calling, "No, there is nothing more you can do."

For a moment the river of people caught Cam. He was being swept away, when seconds later, hands roughly grabbed him. Arvind's? Together they rammed their way back to the steps, fending off blows. Arvind practically dragged him into the house.

The banker's servants bolted the doors and, with Arvind's instructions, hauled a heavy bookcase to strengthen the barricade. A number of servants arrived with basins of hot water and bandages. Within that small clutch of servants, Tikah held out a cup of cold water to the only small family Cam had managed to rescue. The little girls and their mother cowered in the corner close to a brass table. While the Muslim woman comforted her sobbing daughters, the riots roared outside.

A trickle of blood made its way down Cam's forehead. He wiped it away with an impatient hand, sickened by this foretaste of what was to come. With the transfer of power coming in two years, who would see to the safety of innocents like that little girl? To women…like Dassah?

It was better, Dassah decided, that the children play with their toys to block out the tumult from the streets. It was too much to expect them to sit quietly in their mother's room. Bewildered, they each silently picked up a toy from the pile they had discarded yesterday. With each shout or scream from the streets they looked to the shuttered windows and at her. She folded her hands to hide her tremors from them.

Five-year-old Ramesh held a wooden train and lifted his pale face. "Are people being hurt outside like *Amma* was last night?"

"Yes, my little *sahib*, but do not fear." She could only pray that Cam and her employer could keep them safe.

"Will they come inside the house? Will they hurt my *amma* and little sister?"

"No, my love, we are in a good strong house."

Ramesh moved closer still. "Will my *amma* get better?"

She searched her mind for what had comforted her as a child. "I was told many times when I was little, that God sees even a dusty sparrow fall from a tree. No doubt He saw when your *amma* hurt her head and knows how to mend her."

But did the God of the Christians still hear her prayers? It had been many years since she had prayed to Yeshu as she had been taught in the mission. These days, Dassah was simply a woman of India of no certain calling. She had no people. Only Tikah had been like a mother to her all these years.

Ramesh's chin quivered as he dropped his train and snuggled into her embrace. At Dassah's side, his little sister sucked her thumb, her silken lashes falling in time for her afternoon nap. If only Ramesh could rest too, but he listened to the turmoil outside, a vigilant little soldier. At five he reminded her too much of the man—the real soldier—who had looked at her moments ago with passion. She reached for the string that hung around her neck, and withdrew the small, round glass sphere, cradled in a web of leather.

Rolling the glass marble in her fingers, she pictured Cam as a boy. He had always been fearless. No matter what escapade he cooked up with the Indian boys of the mission, he had waved away their misgivings with his overconfident, English smile. The memory of that smile she had treasured all this time. Little had changed in his appearance, his slender form, his broad shoulders, his European eyes as blue as the sky.

As a teenager she had wanted much, much more from Cam. For a while she had thought he would remember his promise to her, but that was a childish wish she had outgrown long ago.

The uproar from the street grew louder, and she clutched the children to her breast. She prayed for the first time in years, for Yeshu to keep this household safe. Surely this was the reason Yeshu had sent Cam to them this day. Anything else would be silly, wishful thinking.

6

A westerly sun filtered through the louvered shutters in Miriam's old room. Her slumber had been disturbed by images of the derailment, and her muscles twanged as she attempted to rise.

Gladys trod from the door to close the shutters and crossed her arms. "You'll want to know what's going on."

"What's happened?" Miriam sat up, her feet sliding to the floor. The bedside clock said five-thirty.

"The British Empire may be on its last legs, my girl, but tea first."

She followed Gladys to the parlor, wrapping her dressing gown around her and tying the belt. Her roommate sat on the divan and poured tea, adding a generous dollop of milk to the cup, and handed it to Miriam. "Your day may have started with a derailment, but I'm afraid the worst isn't over yet."

With a rattle of china, Miriam set her cup and saucer on the table. "Cam?"

"No word yet, though I telephoned Army Headquarters while you were snoring to beat the band. The natives, darling, are rioting again."

Ignoring the malignant bias that seeped out of Gladys, Miriam sank her head into her hands. "Dear Father in Heaven, not again."

"Yes, darling, again. Since the new interim government has been installed under the leadership of Nehru, Jinnah and the Muslims have become afraid of an all Hindu India. And the Hindus are afraid of a Muslim country being created on their doorstep."

"I've got to find Cam." Miriam jumped to her feet, but Gladys reached out, stopping her from leaving the stuffy parlor.

"Honestly, Miriam, the way you barge into Dante's Inferno you must think angels ride on your shoulder. Can't you smell the fires? They're looting. Your brother will be none-too-pleased if you go tearing off into the city."

Miriam moved to the closed shutters, opening the slats to sniff the air. The choking stink of burning rubber and diesel hung a pall over the city. Horns

43

honked and sirens pealed in the distance. She turned the knob on the radio to hear the news. It took several moments for the wireless to warm up, but soon the crackling voice of the announcer confirmed there were riots all over Calcutta.

Someone knocked at the door, and she jumped to open it at the same time as Gladys, and Gladys admitted a somewhat wearier Jack Sunderland than he'd been this morning. He was in uniform now and slumped on the divan across from her. His well-oiled Sam Browne belt creaked as he did, reminding her of her father and Cam. She'd always been honest with herself. Certainly Jack stirred a certain amount of admiration within her. The sooner she tamped these feelings down the better. She would never marry a soldier. It had to be the fact Eva was planning her wedding in January that was setting off this yearning for romance. That sideways grin of Jack's didn't help.

Gladys rushed to the kitchen while Jack removed his peeked military cap, no doubt grateful for the whirling ceiling fan above. He glanced up at Gladys bearing a tray of glasses and a bottle of cold orange squash.

He drained his drink in a few gulps. "We twiddled our thumbs all day while the police remained adamant they could deal with the situation. Thing is, our intelligence confirms that while the majority of Muslims were peaceful, a large number of Muslim *goondas* made for the bazaars to loot and burn Hindu shops and houses. There's already a mass fleeing across the bridge, trying to get to the Howrah Station."

Miriam slowly lowered herself to the divan. "Can the police control the violence?"

"Local Indian officials believe our military presence could be viewed as our old British imperialistic stance, so they delayed calling us in." He sent her a rueful smile and shook his glass at her as if expecting her to refill it, and not Gladys. She ignored his teasing as he continued. "As of four-fifteen this afternoon, Fortress HQ issued a code red. Our troops are picketing all over Calcutta to keep the main routes open, thereby allowing the police to control the crowds."

As Gladys filled Jack's glass with far too much enthusiasm, considering the state of affairs outside, Miriam held back a spurt of annoyance. Really! Did Gladys have to throw herself at every attractive man? Miriam stood and paced toward the windows and back again to face Jack, angry at herself—it wasn't Gladys's fault the world was topsy-turvy. Everything was supposed to be better after the war.

Jack set his glass on a small Benares table. "Look, sitting here all night alone listening to the wireless won't help. You and I are supposed to be elsewhere, but we're here in Calcutta because we can't quite bring ourselves to get on the next train out. At the same time, there's nothing we personally can do to ease the situation."

"Shouldn't you be defending the fort, Jack?" She found herself hoping from something in his answer...something she'd not allowed herself to hope for these past six years while earning her degrees.

He tugged at his ear and went a shade red. "Still not pulling any punches are you, Miss Richards? You know, you're not at all what I'm used to in—shall we say—religious people."

"Are you disappointed that I don't wear drab clothes with stout walking shoes?"

"Not at all. In fact, I'm quite enchanted that you do not talk in a terribly tedious manner. Nor do you have a frightful look of zeal in your eye."

In spite of the riots outside, his ridiculous statement forced a smile from her. "If that's your view of committed Christians, then I must say, it does sound rather frightful."

"Then I hope my association with you, Miss Richards, will correct any fallacy in my thinking. As to why I'm here, if you recall, I promised to check on you and your brother. Where is Cam, by the way?"

That momentary slice of fun went out of her. "He went out hours ago, shortly after you left this morning."

Jack's eyes narrowed. "You've heard nothing since?"

"Not a peep." She squeezed out a lighthearted note.

"He's gone to look after that *ayah*, hasn't he? Well, don't worry. Your brother struck me as a man who can handle himself. As for you and your flatmate, I'm afraid you're stuck with me for the duration. I hope you have plenty of tinned food in the pantry. I'll sleep on the settee." No matter how much he said he wasn't interested in romance this morning, he looked at her now as if she were the strawberry jam on his bread.

Though worried sick about Cam, she pretended to sputter. "Really! Don't think for one minute that I'm not able to fend off any amorous advances. Beware, Lieutenant Colonel, I'm quite handy with a cricket bat."

He answered her with a wicked leer.

But Jack was right. No banter could erase the fact that she and Gladys would be safer with him here. If she could get Dad on the telephone, she knew he'd agree. And she'd go mad simply listening to All India Radio and feeling helpless. She might as well get changed, but as she moved toward her room the telephone rang.

Cam's voice came across the line. "Miri, everything all right in your part of town?"

She squeezed her eyes shut. "Yes, and it's terribly good of you to let me know you're alive." She sent up a prayer, asking forgiveness for her sarcasm, but Cam's chuckle assuaged her guilt.

"Right, well, I'm ringing now. I'm staying at Arvind Malik's home...seen Dassah...they're right as rain. All the same, I'll stick it out with them. Can you and Gladys stay with any friends closer to the garrison?"

"No need." She glanced at Jack perched on the arm of an overstuffed chair. "It seems Gladys and I have our own personal bodyguard. Jack Sunderland refuses to be the gentleman and leave. He insists on camping out on the parlor settee. Shocking, I know—"

"Right." She could hear her brother fiddling with something as he spoke, and she recognized the click of ammunition being loaded. "Tell Jack it gives me peace of mind knowing he's there looking after you. Must dash, love. And do be pleasant to the lieutenant colonel. It's not nice to chew decent men up and spit them out before breakfast."

He rang off, and all desire to joke evaporated as she pressed her folded arms to her stomach. Cam was her big brother. Good grief, a soldier. But as much as he worried over her, she worried over him more. It wasn't that Calcutta had gone stark raving barmy. She threw her head back and stared at the ceiling, her heart going out to God in wordless prayer. There was something very wrong in her brother's life.

Jack still perched on the arm of the chair, swinging one foot, a self-satisfied grin plastered on his face. She had the sneaking suspicion that with any other woman he'd soon show he was a libertine.

The sticky wicket was, no matter how attracted she was to him, she could never marry a man who didn't share her faith, even if he weren't military. Yes, she'd certainly need her wits about her when it came to Jack Sunderland.

Twilight didn't lie far off. All last night and all of this day, rioting enflamed the city. Cam hunched low at the parapet. Between himself and Mahsud, a young Muslim servant of Arvind's, they kept watch from the roof. Mahsud, and his trusty carbine that he'd brought back from the war, relieved Cam at shifts for food and rest in the roof pavilion. Now in the copper sunset, they looked down on a street filled with overturned trucks and cars, blackened from burnt-out fires. For the past twenty-four hours, they'd watched horrified through binoculars as teashop owners, rickshaw drivers—ordinary people—were dragged from their businesses.

Carriages and rickshaws lay abandoned at grotesquely jarred angles. Broken glass from practically every window in the area lay smashed. Except for a few broken panes, this house had been left alone. Cam had his revolver and Mahsud's carbine to thank for that. Whenever any hooligans attempted to invade or set fire to the premises, they'd been able to hold the vandals off with warning shots.

Mahsud smoothed his mustache and gestured behind them. "Captain-*sahib*, you should be taking rest."

From the corner of Cam's eye, he quickly noted a servant setting up a meal in the marble pavilion, and outside of it, water cans and basins for him to wash. It had been quiet in this section for the past few hours. From the smoke on the city horizon, it appeared most of the rioting was taking place in the poorer parts, a mile or two distant. His joints groaned as he rose to his feet, and the wounds at his side and head ached. He'd be wise to get a few hours' sleep. Nighttime brought out the worst in people, and he needed to be awake then.

He washed, relishing the soap, water, and shaving gear, feeling more human as he moved inside the small marble pavilion. On a stone bench a mass of cushions were strewn, and he looked about him, bemused. In the midst of rioting, his host had issued a white linen tablecloth, silverware, crystal goblet for water, and fine china to serve his guest. Even a pot of tea with a pitcher of milk and a sugar bowl rested next to his folded napkin on the table.

It didn't feel right to be eating in such splendor, but going hungry wasn't going to help anyone on those streets below.

The bearer lifted the covering from his plate and stood to the side as Cam ate half the tandoori chicken and rice, preferring instead the sticky Indian sweet for dessert. His appetite wasn't what it used to be. He drank all the water provided and leaned back against the carved stone fretwork, savoring that last drop of tea. His head still pounded, but there was no sense asking Arvind if he kept a bottle of whiskey. Good grief, he could use a drink. It certainly hadn't been his intention, but for the first time in—who knew how long—he'd been stone-cold sober for three days.

Birds in the aviary covered up the noise of the riots in the distance. Beyond the rooftop, twilight changed from the color of a ripe mango to that of deep pink roses…roses like those in his mother's garden in Sialkot when he'd been a boy in short trousers. Or like the roses grown on the mission balcony in Amritsar, by the elder Indian Miriam, whom his sister had been named after. He could even smell the fragrance of those particular roses, all wrapped up with his memories of growing up with the orphans.

Zakir came to Cam's mind before he could stop him, the young Zakir a few years older than him, playing rugby or soccer in the *bagh*. Cam tried to fight off the memories, of how he and Zakir used to scrap with each other, and little Dassah would run and cry. Then he and Zakir would make up, the best of friends.

But the grown Zakir, an Indian officer in the British Army serving in Burma, came to Cam's mind next. That last nightmarish memory of Zakir shuffling off in the Burma jungle with his ankles and wrists in manacles. A cold sweat broke out over Cam, and he forced himself to think of the happier memories at the mission, the memories that always centered around Dassah.

Peace of mind returned as he watched beyond the edge of the roof. Light from the fast-sinking sun went out like a lamp over Calcutta. Duck-egg green shaded the sky, a backdrop to the carved white pavilion in Mogul design where the silhouette of a woman was framed by the fretted stonework.

It took a moment to realize that she stood under that arched doorway. It was the rose-like perfume of Dassah's presence he must have taken in.

7

Cam started to rise.

Dassah lifted her hand. "Please, rest."

He sank back against the cushions, and she handed a roll of clean bandages to the bearer, along with instructions to change Cam's dressing, while she remained outside. Only when the fresh dressing was covered again by his shirt did she slip inside the pavilion.

"Is everyone all right downstairs?" he asked.

"Everyone is very well. The lady of the house awakened this afternoon, but all the household is anxious because of the disturbance outside."

"And you, Dassah, are you afraid?"

"This uprising is much worse than any I have ever seen before."

"Don't be frightened, I'm here to protect you. Like when we were little."

"As you say." She went silent for a long moment, fiddling with some leather string around her neck.

He waited, hungry for her thoughts. "And the children?"

Though he couldn't make out her features in the deepening dusk, he heard a smile in her voice. "The children, though they are frightened by the noise of the riots, are full of amazement that you and Mahsud are on the roof with guns to protect them."

"Children are always the same...cops and robbers like we used to play in the mission." He chuckled. "Do you remember?"

She let out a chuckle to match his. "I also recall playing marbles."

"You became quite good at Ring Taw. If memory serves me correctly, you won my Christensen Akro Slag from me."

"I did not win your favorite marble off you." Her voice went quiet. "You gave it to me."

"Quite right. You were crying over something. It's coming back to me."

"You were going away. To England to start school at Eton."

"That's what it was. Mother got her way long enough to keep me in India till I was twelve. Much later than most lads were sent home to school."

"It was kind of you to give a small girl your prized possession before you left India for your home in England. Kind of you to try and stop her from crying as she remained…in her place."

"We played other games too, Dassah. Cowboys and Indians."

A laden sigh issued from her, as if the cadence he preferred in their conversation was out of step for her. "Yes, Cam, that too I remember. Cowboys and Indians, the other kind of Indian, that is." She inched further into the pavilion as if relinquishing herself to his train of thought. "That always confused me. Why are native people of the Americas called Indians? They do not come from India as I do."

He smiled in the dark. "How long has that pressing question kept you up at night?"

Her laughter escaped. "I have wondered about that since I was a child and your mother taught American and British history to us at the mission."

"Mother has some explaining to do then. Next time you see her you'll have to get her to straighten the record. I think it all came about when Columbus or some other explorer looking for a new route to India bumped into the Americas and thought he'd arrived. I agree, utterly confusing."

Except for the racket the birds made, the pavilion filled with a comfortable silence. The night cloaked them, but he knew she sensed his smile, as he sensed hers. As if the two of them had slipped back twenty years or more, and were children on the balcony overlooking the city of Amritsar. Nothing could feel more right than sitting here chatting with Dassah about anything and everything, even as violence raged around them. He'd expected the same sort of easy camaraderie when he returned from England when she was seventeen, until he'd ruined that evening with his impulsiveness. He daren't make that mistake again.

"Will you sit?" He indicated a spot on the bench near him.

She shook her head and stepped back. "I should leave you now."

"Don't go, Dassah. Talk to me, like we used to."

He couldn't see her in the dark, but her posture framed by the light-filled doorway was that of one longing to flit away like the cooing doves in the aviary. From the way she dipped her head she looked so forlorn, as lost as he felt. He had to ask, "Have you been happy working here?"

"I love the children. And I have Tikah."

"Ah yes, Tikah." He never could figure out why Tikah made him feel uncomfortable, but he couched his question with all the softness he could gather. "Whose idea was it to leave the mission? Yours or Tikah's? Come now, what can it hurt ten years after the fact, to tell me the reason?"

"It was my decision," she said so quietly he could barely hear her. Her voice strengthened. "Tikah found me packing my belongings that night. When she could not talk me out of leaving, she came with me."

So it had been Dassah's decision. The unwelcome confirmation sent his side and head into painful spasms. "You left because of what I did that night."

Her continued silence was the answer he dreaded. He struggled to rise, but his weariness won the battle, and he slumped back on the cushions. "I'm sorry, Dassah. It's just that when I first left India you were a little girl. When I returned and saw you at seventeen, a beautiful woman…I lost my head. There's no excuse. I shouldn't have stolen that kiss. Will you forgive me?"

The slender silhouette against the green night sky nodded. That same silhouette raised a hand to brush something from her cheek. Her voice came out muffled. "Eshana and Tikah—your mother too for a time—raised me to be a virtuous woman. What else could I do?" Her words came out in a ragged whisper as she set something down on the pavilion floor. "English officers do not marry poor Indian women, and I could not bear to share my body with you in any other way."

She waited a fraction of a moment, then turned and fled down the stairs to the house, and he was alone, listening to her departing footsteps.

If only he was like his stepfather, Geoff. But he wasn't. He kept telling Miri he was no hero. He must be like his natural father, good old Lieutenant Nicholas Fraser, a drunken blighter that hurt women instead of protecting them.

Throughout the night, Cam and Arvind watched with Mahsud as fires lit the sky orange in the north and center of the city. Strong searchlights from army tanks flickered below, and Cam recognized the various regiments. As the hours slogged by, morning light brought no reprieve. Buses and taxis charged through the streets, loaded with Sikhs and Hindus, armed with swords and iron bars, firearms, on their way to terrorize the Muslim population of Calcutta.

Sunday afternoon showed the sadness creasing the banker's face as the major work of cleaning up the dead was left to the soldiers. "Three days of unbridled savagery." Arvind sank his head. "I am ashamed. I am ashamed of my people."

Cam's tone came out curter than he wanted. "The underworld of Calcutta must have taken advantage of the demonstrations. They must be blamed for this wholesale butchery. It couldn't be ordinary people."

Arvind forced a tired smile. "Perhaps it is ruffians as you say, but I fear it is ordinary people who, as a mass, lost their sanity. No, Captain, you are trying to be cordial in a time when it is not helpful. As an Indian I must face the truth. My neighbors are turning on each other."

Cam's gut went cold. The Indians may be turning on one another, but somehow as a British soldier he felt the weight of responsibility, the growing fear they were leaving a burning ship. But he could safely leave Arvind's house now. Between the police and the army, the rioting was brought under control. Arvind's household no longer needed his help.

And Dassah was all right. Perhaps no happier than he was, but well enough. What more could one hope for in life? As soon as her employer's wife could be moved, Dassah would be on her way to Lahore in the Punjab with the rest of the household.

And what of it?

By tomorrow he and Miriam could be back on the train for Lahore too. He could get on with his life, telephone Phoebe. No doubt he and Phoebe would be married within the year, set up home in a stylish little bungalow. When India gained her independence in two years' time, they would move back to England or some other spot still flying the British flag. Phoebe had it all planned out. Get married. That's what people did, didn't they?

His pack was still stashed in the pavilion where he'd slept for a few hours last evening. He went inside to retrieve it and was about to leave when he found a small leather casing and its attached string lying beneath it, on the floor close to where Dassah had stood. It had to be this that she'd been playing with last night, that had hung around her neck.

As he opened the leather sheath, late afternoon sun slanted on to the large yellow marble inside. It was the Christensen Akro Slag, his pride and joy as a boy, one of the marbles that Dad bought for him.

He held it up to the light. The memory crept out of the fog of years. It had been shortly before he left for school in England. He'd been playing on the balcony at the mission with Dassah. He'd been twelve, she'd been nine. The balcony had been filled with stone urns of roses and lilies. He'd given the marble to Dassah because she'd been crying. To stop the little girl's sobs, he'd hugged her in a clumsy manner and pressed the Akro Slag into her tiny hand.

He remembered his words from then. "I'll come back, Dassah, stop your blubbing. Here, keep this." The thing he hadn't remembered last night, when he'd obtusely avoided discussing their shared memory, was that he'd been crying too. As a boy of twelve, he'd whispered that he loved her. That when he came back he'd marry her. That nothing would ever separate them again.

With the marble cupped in his palm he brought it up to his lips and squeezed his eyes shut at the next set of memories.

Nine years later, the night he'd come back after Eton and Sandhurst, as he said he would. That first night back in Amritsar as a man of twenty-one, he'd dropped by the mission to say hello to all his old Indian friends. For a while he'd clapped the backs of all who were still there, playfully wrestled with a few, Zakir for one. That was the night he'd encouraged Zakir to join the army.

It wasn't until later that night he'd gone looking for Dassah and found her alone on the balcony waiting for him. He remembered feeling staggered at her beauty. She'd stood by an urn of jasmine. It wasn't the fineness of her features, the trembling of her willowy frame, but her stillness of soul that fell over him as soft as the night, like silk against skin. They'd talked briefly. Too briefly for her. She'd wanted to say so much more, but he remembered putting a finger to her lips, and pulling her to him, unable to stop himself. He'd molded her shape to his and claimed her mouth.

At first he'd been gentle. But then passion ripped through his body as he'd held her slender, womanly body in his arms.

She'd struggled. To his shame that memory came back as sharp as the metal that gouged his body during the train derailment. Her pleading from all those years ago reverberated in his ears, "No, Cam, no, no, please, not this way."

Now he rolled the marble in his fingers. She hadn't given it back to him, but all this time, she'd kept it in this little packet, a treasured item around her neck. She wouldn't have kept it unless she still felt something for him. But anything between them would come to nothing. It had to.

With the marble clutched in his hand, he left the pavilion. Leaving Mahsud on the roof, Cam and Arvind took the stairs below. The banker stopped him from going down to the foyer. "I will not have you go without showing you proper hospitality to thank you for remaining with us."

"You've taken good care of me already, I assure you, and I must be going." He couldn't face seeing Dassah again, and she could very well be with Arvind's wife and children.

"What hospitality?" Arvind cajoled. "You call upstairs on our roof, a little food and drink when you could spare the time, hospitality? I think not. Let me introduce you to my wife. She is awake and as grateful as I am for your help."

Cam glanced down at his grubby uniform. He didn't feel in the least like entering a woman's sickroom. However, it would be an insult to refuse. He bowed his head, conceding defeat, and followed the smiling banker down the hallway to the same set of rooms he'd been in three days ago. With each step he feared he'd see Dassah and yet yearned for the sight of her. There was no way to fight against the social structures. They both knew that. Her last words to him tore at him. *English officers do not marry poor Indian girls.* But one last look couldn't hurt.

He swallowed through a dry throat. Who was he joshing? One last look terrified him, like looking at a bottle of whiskey when he wanted to remain sober, and everything inside him wanted the drink. One last look would undo him.

Arvind led the way. It took all of ten seconds for Cam to sum up the occupants in the bedchamber. A doctor and nurse stood near a woman wearing a plain cotton sari, sitting in a chair by the bed—Arvind's wife. A pretty woman. Her head was bandaged, but otherwise she seemed alert and smiled. Arvind strode to her side and cupped her shoulder. The boy Ramesh and his little sister Padma played on the carpet, until Ramesh caught sight of him and ran to shake hands. Cam ruffled the boy's hair, trying not to look at the corner, where hardly visible against the slatted blinds stood Dassah.

The lady of the house shyly spoke in English, and he must have given the appropriate responses. For her sake, he switched to Hindi. Throughout the short conversation, Cam had been aware only of Dassah. She'd not said a word, but stared at the carpet as she'd done the other day.

Well, he wasn't standing for it! He'd felt dead for so long, and life cried out to be lived.

He held the Akro Slag in his hand. Moving forward, he held the marble out to Dassah. "I believe this is yours."

Her eyes widened as her gaze connected with his. "No, it is not mine."

The boy Ramesh rushed to her side. "That is your special marble, Dassah. How funny that you lost it. You are never without it."

Feeling weightless, Cam dangled the leather casing before her and smiled. He must be mad, but what of it? "I recognize this type of marble. A slag. Quite the treasure. Did someone special give it to you?"

She swallowed before answering. "I do not think the boy who gave it to me meant anything by it. He owned so many."

"I sincerely doubt that." He pressed the marble into her palm and closed her fingers around it. "I'm sure whoever gave it to you knew its value. Perhaps a promise came with it?" He dropped his voice for her alone. "I have remembered. Soon, nothing shall ever separate us."

Her head shook slightly from side to side, and she sank to a chair.

Arvind waited for him at the door, smiling, as if relieved that his family conversed about something as innocent as a child's marble after three such terrible days, but it was also clear that it was time for Cam to go.

He hated to leave Dassah like this, but he had no choice. Before leaving the room, Cam looked back at each person, his gaze resting on Dassah. Her eyes locked with his until he turned and strode down the hall, taking the stairs, and out the front door to the subdued street. Looking at the destruction surrounding him, he repeated under his breath, "Nothing shall ever separate us." He must have been out of his mind to make that promise. Where on God's green earth could that ever happen? Certainly not India.

For everyone else in the house, the pall that had been hanging over it for the past three days lifted. Dassah could hear the relief in the family's chatter. The cloud did not lift for her though. Standing by the window, she looked down on the street and watched Cam stride away. Going back to his world where the lines separating the British from the Indian were clearly defined.

Tikah came to stand at her side. When Tikah had entered this room Dassah did not know, but the woman she considered her mother touched her hand. "He is the reflection of his father," Tikah murmured in Urdu.

Dassah answered back in the same tongue. "I do not see the resemblance.

Major Geoff has sandy hair."

"Not the man who raised him, but the man who fathered him."

"I had forgotten you knew his father. You were a servant in their house, were you not, before you went to the mission?"

A moment passed before Tikah spoke. "I see the way you look at him. But know this, my child. He was kind as a boy, but his true colors grew visible when he became a man. Do you not recall how he plundered you when he returned from England? Remember why we had to leave the mission."

"*Amma*, what plunder?" She waved a hand, dismissing her reaction to Cam's embraces all that time ago. For the first time she wondered, had she overreacted? "It was only a kiss—"

"Only a kiss, Dassah?" Tikah's words dashed upon her like a basin of cold water. "Cam Fraser will mean well. Of course he means well. But he will rob you of everything that is precious. If he loves you, he loves you. But is he going to take you dancing at the club or bathing at the seashore with all the British *sahibs* and *memsahibs*? And after…he loves you…he will cast you aside like a used handkerchief. What else can an Englishman do with an Indian lover?" With that Tikah left the parlor to go to her place in the kitchen.

With a shaking hand, Dassah supported herself against the wall and peered through the window. On the street below, Cam had long since turned the corner. She raised her fingers to grasp the talisman that he had returned to her only moments ago, and she remembered his kiss when he'd come home from school a man, and she a woman. The happy chatter of the Malik family all but faded as time went backward, and the memory of Cam's lips on hers brought a flutter to her chest like a kite beating with the wind.

She returned the glass sphere in its leather casing under her sari. Though she loved Tikah, the older woman's unhappy soul made her speak with bitterness. Cam could not be the way she described. Still, it would never do for her to let Cam know that she loved him, like the mouth of a great river overflowing its banks. If he ever tempted her with his ardor…again…she did not know if she would have the strength to remain virtuous like she had all those years ago.

8

Miriam wasn't sure how much of Cam was actually in her cramped sitting quarters here at Kinnaird College. His body, to be sure, but his mind? In his crisp military vernacular, Dad advised her where to hang pictures in her postage stamp of a room while casting wary glances at Cam. Standing on a chair, she concentrated on hammering a nail into the wall. Poor lamb, Cam must be still upset over the riots. Two weeks later, the nightmare of Calcutta still headlined the newspapers.

Mum sauntered toward Cam. Bless her, she still looked lovely. In her fifties her figure was fuller, a sweet roundness to her face, her chestnut hair sprinkled with gray. Dad, on the other hand, had a full head of white hair but still strolled with ramrod precision, his hands clasped behind his back. Mum added to the current conversation that up to now Cam had not contributed to. "Your father has only been insisting on Indian independence from the time we met." Mum sent a wink toward Dad.

Dad returned a twinkle of a smile to her. Cam seemed to catch their parents' playful camaraderie. A strange look came over his face—a peacefulness. At least for this, Miriam was grateful. Though not his natural father, from the time Cam was three her father had been Cam's true dad. Mum had once told her about the death of Cam's biological father. But the passing of Nick Fraser was not a subject she ever heard discussed again.

With a bit of flourish, Miriam hung the picture on the nail then took her brother's hand as he helped her down from the chair. At the same time, she caught Dad's cool appraisal of Cam, and then a glance flickering between her parents. Miriam dusted her hands with more vigor than necessary. Good gracious—the unspoken language of families couldn't be any louder.

Since Cam had returned from school in England years ago, he and Dad had knocked heads on every subject. If only he could share with Dad the same teasing manner that Miriam did. Dad had been full of unwanted advice on where to hang her picture, and she'd simply bickered back.

With the present lull in the conversation, Cam smiled a stiff smile at the other occupant of the room, curled up in Miriam's only armchair. Phoebe Anderson had come down from Kashmir to stay with her parents in order to catch up with Cam. Her brown hair feathered about her face as she looked at Cam askance from her cat-like eyes. No doubt Phoebe sensed something cool in Cam's manner too. Nothing would make Miriam happier than if Cam dumped Phoebe. Phoebe was attractive, a ripping good sport, apparently. Growing up as the daughter of a British Resident, counsel to the Crown Prince of Kashmir, she'd make some political chap a brilliant wife. But Cam?

Miriam shook her head slightly. Hoping that at long last her prayers were being answered, and Cam was seeing the light. For the moment she'd better get this tea party off the ground. "I've had enough decorating counsel for one day, and now I'm ordering you all to the foldout table."

She grabbed her brother's arm. "Cam, shoehorn yourself into the space between Mother and Phoebe. Dad, would you do the same next to me?"

They settled in, and Miriam passed the plate of sandwiches. Her brother made a face at her over the table. "I can't for the life of me understand why women think these fussy little things will suffice."

Without missing a beat, Miriam threw her napkin at his chest. "Too much of a man to be satisfied with bread and cucumber, are you?"

Mother rolled her eyes in an attempt to not grin. Even Phoebe giggled. But as Cam helped himself to a cup of tea, stirring in three teaspoons of sugar, her father asked, "Since when did you partake of so much sugar, Cam?" There was a slight rebuke in Dad's voice. "You never used to take so much sweet."

Cam set the sugar spoon back into the bowl. Miriam had also noticed that Cam took more sugar than usual, but from the glacier forming on his face and on Dad's, it was best to change the subject and fast, but Cam beat her to it. "Are you off to Delhi, soon, sir?" They all knew Cam's usage of the word *sir* was one of affection and not only of respect.

Miriam held her breath as Dad accepted Cam's olive branch. "I'm meeting with all military branches and the viceroy this coming week. Going over preliminary arrangements for independence to pull out our British troops when the time comes. In my opinion we'll need several years to leave the forces in the hands of Indian officers completely, not just two."

Cam agreed, and Dad's features softened. For once it seemed the two of them saw eye-to-eye.

"What's your feeling about Lord Wavell?" Dad asked Cam. "He's the viceroy, but I don't believe he has a clue what the Indian people think."

Cam laid an arm along the back of Mother's chair. "He's strictly old Raj thinking, certainly—*we are your mother and father,* et cetera, et cetera. I'm glad you taught me not to pay any heed to that old rot. You were a man before your time, sir."

Miriam shot a smile across the table to Mum while Dad took Cam's praise with his usual equanimity. "I simply saw the writing on the wall a decade or two before most."

Phoebe inched her chair closer to Cam, blast her for horning in on the first moment of family closeness they'd had for months. "Well I for one," Phoebe said, "don't believe the Indians will be able to stick it without us."

"Balderdash!" Miriam set her teacup down with such force she feared for the saucer. "Really, Phoebe, sometimes you say the silliest things."

At Cam's side, Phoebe bristled. "I don't think your tone is called for, Miriam. You've always been a bit…you know…."

"Gone native?" Miriam provoked.

Sending a look of apology across to Miriam, Cam patted Phoebe's hand the same way he'd placate a hissing mongoose—with trepidation. "Well, Phoebe, you must take into account that our family in fact feel a bit strongly about Indian equality."

"I couldn't very well spend time with this family without noticing that teensy detail, darling." Phoebe huffed, but at least her spout of temper had eased.

Not so for Miriam. For two *annas*, she'd like to scramble across the table and punch Phoebe in the nose. "How terribly good of you, Phoebe, to be so accepting of our opinions when I'm sure at times you may feel we are letting down *our* side."

Thank goodness Dad jumped in to save the day. "You're right to a point, Phoebe. It is not going to be easy for the Indian people to adjust to independence without some help from us, at first. In fact, I'm worried. Right now the Indian parties are in a deadlock. The viceroy must enable the Indian parties to agree to their future constitution, and all Wavell seems to do is increase the resentment between the Muslim League and the Hindu Congress."

"And," Cam added, "the League keeps pressing for a separate Muslim state."

"Quite." Dad turned to him. "I don't think Lord Wavell is the man to lead India to independence."

"You're thinking Prime Minister Attlee may appoint a new viceroy?"

"I wouldn't be surprised."

Mother got to her feet, placing her hands on Dad's shoulders. "Enough politics for now, dear. You haven't seen Miriam for ages." She turned to Phoebe. "And my dear, would you mind? I'd like some time alone with my son. Come, darling," she said to Cam, "let's explore the school grounds. Be like old times, just you and me."

The fight went out of Miriam. Good old Mum, bless her. Always the peacemaker. Now if only Miriam could develop the same attribute. Lately, she'd been sensing the Lord was a bit miffed with her desire to hammer sense into people.

Cam jumped at the reprieve Mother offered, to escape Phoebe's possessive claws on his sleeve. Those few small whiskeys he had before coming to Miriam's place were doing nothing to help his nerves. Not to mention the appraisal in Dad's eyes every time they landed on him, as in the case of the sugar bowl. It wasn't as if he could explain his need for sweets when he was craving a drink, but Dad, having lived most of his life in the military, might guess. He'd dealt with enough drunkards in his career. Better to get out of Dad's sight before he twigged on to the truth.

It was stupid of Cam to come to tea. Spending time with his parents was not the setting for deciding what on earth to do—if anything—with Dassah. Being away from the headiness of Dassah's presence was a relief too. How she made his head swim. And if Dad knew what he was considering, Cam could just hear his stepfather's objections: the impracticalities, the possible harm to Dassah, the confusion, and so on and so forth.

Outside on the grounds, he and Mother strolled the pathway where rhododendrons, towering palms, and spreading peepal trees held the recent rains. Sweet, warm, damp air filled his lungs. The red brick and stone buildings shaded them from the sun.

"We're worried about you, Cam." Mother bent to sniff a rose. "So are your sisters."

"I can't fathom how Eva has the time to worry about me while planning her wedding."

"Ah, the wedding. It'll be wonderful to see everyone. They're all coming, you know—Eshana and Jai, Laine…although, I'm not sure about Adam."

"My very point, Mother. How can Eva concern herself with me with all that on her plate? And Miriam, instead of worrying about me, should concentrate on scratching theology on the blackboards for her students now that she's here in Lahore."

Mother reached up a gloved hand to touch his cheek. "Miriam wrote us about the Calcutta riots, but you've not said a word. It's the same way you remain silent about Burma."

His throat tightened with the memories. "What's to be said about hatred among brothers whether they be Muslim, Hindu, Sikh, or Christian?"

"And also if they be Indian by birth…or Indian by choice."

"Indian by choice? What do you mean?"

She squeezed his arm. "Our family is not exactly good British Raj stuff. As Miriam says, we've done the unpardonable. Practically gone native. And I know how much it hurt you when Zakir mutinied in Burma."

He looked off in the distance. "You knew that?"

"Your father knew that Zakir was one of the officers who led the Indian ranks away to join the Japanese. Knowing you, you would see that as a betrayal."

"We were brothers."

"And you think Zakir did not feel the same?"

"Of course he didn't. Otherwise why'd he mutiny?"

"Cam, it's got to be tearing you to pieces. Please tell me."

He slowed his step. "There's nothing to tell."

"If you wish." She gripped his arm. "But Cam, so much unhappiness, I can sense it in you no matter what mask you wear. I thought Geoff and I had given you a solid foundation, but maybe I should have told you more about your father...about Nick." Her eyes glittered, but she kept all tears at bay. "I often wonder how much our childhood traumas—things we can't even remember—affect who we are."

"Mother, what on earth? Traumas?" He patted her hand. "My present muddled thinking is only because of the war and Zakir's betrayal." He regretted spewing forth, but his mother had a way of pulling on his heartstrings. He forced a smile. "Don't worry, I'm fine. Right as rain."

"And Phoebe? When are you going to tell her that you and she are not suited?" It took a moment for his mother's words to sink in. She sent him a weak smile.

"So you don't mind that I'm not going to marry Phoebe?"

"Good gracious, Cam, mind? Charming as Phoebe is, she is not for you."

He drew her with him a few steps. "I was thinking of telling Phoebe when I return from my leave. I want to go away for a bit." He stopped and ran a hand across his brow. "Sort a few things out." Things about an Indian girl he loved and didn't know what to do with. He could never tell his mother that.

"What things?" she urged him gently.

"Now's not the time, Mum, but I promise when I get back from Kashmir we'll have a long chat, just the two of us." Grinning, he took her arm.

They strolled under the shade of tall, waving palms toward the school when Mother stopped. "I forgot to ask you about Dassah and Tikah."

"What about Dassah?" He took a few paces beyond her.

"Oh, come now. Miriam told me all about it, and I'm dying for news. I was at the mission the day Dassah was born. Tikah was such a part of our early life at our first bungalow and later at the mission. I didn't want to ask when we were all together. So, now, how are Dassah and Tikah?"

Something about Tikah filtered through his mind. A flash of parched desert. A feeling of suffocation. Since seeing Tikah in Calcutta, fragments of childhood memory came back in jolts when he least expected it. He composed his expression and turned to face her. "They're fine. Dassah has a good position as *ayah* to a wealthy banker and his wife. I imagine they've moved here to Lahore by now."

"Here? So close. Oh I must drive over from Sialkot to see them."

"Do that. I'm sure Dassah would enjoy catching up with you."

She studied his face. "You seem distant again, all of a sudden." Tucking in closer to his side, she hooked arms. "Kashmir will do you good. Why not rent that houseboat that's been our favorite all these years? Make a nice place to sort your thoughts out...decide what kind of girl you really want to marry." His mother's hazel green eyes shimmered with pride in him, and his chest ached.

He bent down to kiss her cheek. Ah, mothers—they always did see the best in their children…even if it wasn't there.

9

Cam pulled his Alvis Coupe to the side of Davis Road not far from the governor's estate. Rickshaws, trams, horse-drawn *tongas* congested the tree-lined streets of Lahore. Still, this cosmopolitan city held the ancient fragrance of India—wood-smoke from nearby villages, incense from temples, cooking spices from kitchens. Not far from here was the Kinnaird College for Women where he'd taken tea with his family this afternoon.

If Miriam knew he was still in Lahore and not on the road to Kashmir, she'd insist on knowing why. His parents, too, on their way back to Sialkot would take a dim view of him sitting outside the home of a well-to-do Indian banker instead of starting his holidays.

The coupe's engine shut off, letting in the sounds of upper-crust, suburban Lahore. The tinkle of cowbells and the drifting wail from a mosque mingled with the tooting of horns and Indian music from somewhere in the park. A wall of gray stones protected Arvind Malik's grounds. Gardens and tennis courts surrounded a pink stucco mansion. Somewhere in there, Dassah was caring for the banker's children.

Cam tilted the Panama hat to the back of his head. In his civvies he wouldn't stand out from any other Englishman going downtown. A tramcar rumbled past as he got out of the car and strode toward the gates of Arvind's home, and then to the corner while he worked up the cheek to either knock on the door or send her a note. If he knocked on the door, Arvind would think Cam wished to visit him. As for a secret note—how on earth was he to get that to Dassah without attracting attention?

At the corner he stopped and considered the park. Perhaps she took Arvind's children there. Sure enough, there were nannies and *ayahs* escorting their charges to the swings, and he took up his watch on a bench beneath the boughs of a wide-spreading neem tree. A stone pavilion took up precedence in the center where a number of men of various sects sat cross-legged in a circle. Elderly

men—some clean shaven or with flowing beards depending on their religion—
sagely discussed the ways of the world. As far as Cam could see, he was the only
non-Indian in the park.

An hour passed, another half hour, but his patience paid off. There she was
in the cool of early twilight.

His chest pounded at the sight of her wearing a soft cotton sari in her favorite
shade of green, like spring grass. With little Padma on one hip, she held Ramesh
by the hand. Cam stood to his feet and removed his hat. The movement drew
her gaze, and she stopped. Her hair in its long, thick rope reached the base of her
spine. His fingers tingled with desire to unwind that coil of dark silk. He drew
his shoulders back. He'd better stop imagining her as his lover. It wasn't right to
think of her in that way...not unless she was his wife.

Dassah directed the children to the playground. Ramesh darted off to a group
of friends, and Dassah placed the little girl in a swing and set her in motion. She
kept her back to Cam but glanced over her shoulder, inviting him with those
sloe-shaped eyes, and his breath stopped.

"Have you come to play in the park like the other little boys?" she teased.

He felt his grin break as he stood at her side. "You always liked the swing.
Shall I push you?"

"I am sorely tempted. You always took such care when you pushed me."

"If I hadn't taken care, Eshana or my mother would have given me a good
hiding." He took over for her in pushing the little girl, and Dassah stood back,
leaning against the frame of the swing set, crossing her arms to watch.

"It is all coming back to me," she said. "Pushing me in the swing was one of
the few times you did take half a care. Most of the time you and the other boys
were up to such perilous antics, climbing trees and walls, racing after *tongas* and
rickshaws, that a small girl like me was left behind."

"Again, my mother would have tanned my backside if I'd let you join in on
our more exciting escapades."

Above them the swing squeaked, and he chucked the little girl on the chin
each time she swung close. Her peals of laughter increased his own smile. On
the other side of the park, Ramesh played games with his friends. Games that
Cam remembered playing in the dusty *bagh* behind the mission, Indian games
with instructions hollered out in Urdu or Hindi, when as a boy he'd waited for
his turn at bat, or his turn to make a dash for the wicket, and no one had cared
who was English and who was Indian.

Dassah's voice grew dreamy. "We spent much of our childhood together. You,
Miriam, and us children of the mission. Except for that time your family lived
in Singapore—and China too, was it not?"

"For a year we lived in Singapore. Miriam was just a baby. Later, Eva was born
in Shanghai. When we returned to India, we practically lived at the Amritsar
mission, we visited there so often."

"Until you left to go to school in England."

He eased off on pushing little Padma. Dassah's voice, reminiscing their youth, drew him back to those years encased in golden sunshine—playing marbles on the mission balcony, sharing the treat of sugarcane in winter, mangoes in summer.

"We used to play all the time." Her musical voice danced along his spine. "As well as marbles, we played tag, *latoo,* and you boys used to be so rough together in a *kabaddi* match. All the children together…you and me, your sister, Dilpreet, Ameera…Zakir." She carried on listing names, though the last name he heard was Zakir. He didn't want to think of Zakir. The last time he'd seen Zakir was up at the Red Fort in Delhi.

Not noticing his silence, Dassah's eyes shone as she hunkered down to sit at the base of the swing set, her arms wrapped around her knees, a smile on her face like the Cheshire Cat from Alice in Wonderland.

His ears caught the present-day squeals of laughter in the park around him, and he broke into her reverie. "You kept the Akro Slag marble a long time."

Her head dipped. "Foolishness, I know."

"I'm sorry, Dassah, for forgetting."

She shrugged and smiled. "You were but twelve at the time you proposed marriage."

"And I had forgotten my promise the night I first returned from school…and found you on the balcony."

"When you kissed me…like a man kisses a woman." Her breath went wispy. She lifted her hand and let it drop in defeat to the grass.

"I did forget what I said to you all those years ago, but, Dassah…" He waited for her to meet his eyes. "I'm repeating my promise now. I've come back for you." The words were out of his mouth, though he had no clue how to make them true.

Her eyes widened as she clamped her mouth into a rigid line. She jumped to her feet and lifted Padma from the swing, turning from him so quickly his head nearly spun. "Dassah?"

"Ramesh," she called, her voice unnaturally shrill. "Ramesh, it is time to go home." With that she strode toward the edge of the park.

He had to march double-time to keep up with her. "Dassah, I mean what I say. I want to be with you and you alone."

She whirled to him, the little girl straddling her hip. "Go back to your English life, your English friends. No doubt you have plenty of Englishwomen to choose from. I am not a loose harlot for you to toy with."

"Never!" He took hold of her elbow, and she stared down at his fingers encircling her arm as if a snake coiled around her limb. "Dassah…*janu.*" She looked up at the soft use of her name and the endearment *janu,* the Hindu word meaning life. "I'm asking you to be my wife."

"Now I know you are joshing." She laughed a brittle laugh.

He took the girl from Dassah and gripped her wrist. "I mean it."

"You are speaking the words of a madman!" Her fingers twirled in concentric circles at her temple to emphasize.

"My wife, Dassah."

Her eyes swam with moisture as she took the little girl back. The boy ran up to them, complaining that he had to leave his game in the middle of an inning, until he saw Cam and peered up at him and then Dassah. "You've come back, Captain. Will you play cricket with me?"

He cupped the boy's head. "Perhaps another day."

The child's countenance fell, while he and Dassah stared at each other. Cam wanted to kick himself for disappointing the boy as well. He was tired of being on the other side of the fence. English…Indian. Nothing could have made him happier than to play with the boy for a while, then go somewhere later alone with Dassah, all fair and square. But as she searched his face, unbelief written all over her features, he couldn't blame her. English society would consider him a madman for what he was asking. Marriage to him would cost her a great deal too. He was selfish to ask her to marry him, knowing the unhappiness it might bring her in the years ahead, but he couldn't hold back the words.

"I'll wait here every day for you at this time, until I can convince you that I want you for my wife."

"Want, want, want, what does wanting have to do with life?" She grabbed hold of Ramesh's hand and ran from the park without another word.

Her retreating figure grew smaller as she stalked across the cobblestone road to the banker's mansion, until she and the two children disappeared within the gated grounds. He ambled to his car in a daze. He meant what he said. But then, a madman believed what he said too.

A week later, Cam waited for her at the park, and at last Dassah came alone. He stood up from the bench where he'd been sitting, as she took tentative steps toward him. The same grass green sari rustled as she moved. Bright glass earrings dangled against her slender neck. On her wrists, glass bangles clinked. With all his being he wanted to reach for her, draw her to him, but he kept his hands in a vice at his sides. Doves cooed in nearby trees as the last shadows of the day lengthened.

"I am here, Cam. I will listen."

He'd waited for her every day for a week, and every night she'd come with the children. Each night he'd repeated his proposal, and each night she'd flashed him a stern look as if he were that crazy man she'd called him. Every night when he'd returned to his hotel room, he'd gone over a thousand scenarios of how he'd ask her properly.

Now, with her standing before him, words he'd once read in the Song of Solomon rushed out. "Thou hast ravished my heart, Dassah, my sister, my spouse;

thou hast ravished my heart." There was no stopping now. "Come away with me, *janu*. You are my life. We'll get married."

She hugged her arms around her middle, her eyes glittering with bottled tears.

"Dassah." He reached for her, glad of the sudden fall of Indian night, its darkness cloaking them from prying eyes. His hands encased her waist, and he felt the delicacy of her ribcage. "Dassah, I love you as I could never love another woman."

"But I am Indian. I am dark-skinned."

He laughed. "I'd say you're more the color of a creamed tea. But even if you were ebony, I'll thank you very much not to insult me with idiotic racial prejudice." He lifted the back of her hand to his lips. "Is the night sky that God created any less beautiful in its darkness than the lightness of morning?"

While keeping a space between them, she sighed so heavily he geared himself up for another refusal. At last she spoke in a quiet voice he could hardly hear. "I believe you, Cam, because I want with all my soul to believe you. But I fear that your ardor will be our undoing. That once it is spent, there will be nothing left, nothing to build a life upon."

"Have you no ardor for me, Dassah?"

Her face pinched with tears like it used to when she was a child. Her broken whisper reached him in the dark. "Yes, beloved *janu*, you alone are the master of my heart."

"Then don't be afraid."

"But I am terribly afraid. It is madness." She withdrew her hands from his and let them fall to her sides. "But I, too, cannot help myself. I will go with you and pray to Yeshu to help us."

They should be rejoicing. Wasn't that what people did when they agreed to marry because they loved each other? But the night coming upon them grew heavy.

In a small voice she added while turning away. "First, I must get my things from the house. I must tell Tikah."

"No!" The thought of her going back into the house and to Tikah filled him with dread. If they didn't go now, he felt in his bones they never would. "No, Dassah, she'll talk you out of it. So will Arvind."

"As they should. As your family and friends should talk you out of marrying me." The pain in her words tore at his confidence.

"Then let's not give them the chance. Don't look back. Dassah." He was aware of every breath she took. She looked over the park grounds to the house across the street. Lights were being lit on the second story. Perhaps someone else was getting the children ready for bed. And it struck him, the right words to convince her.

"Come with me, *janu*, let me give you babies of your own."

The breath she sucked in was his answer. He hadn't thought of children up to now, but the natural result of their union could produce their offspring. His and hers. The images of their babies in his arms sent warmth flowing through his veins. He pulled gently on her hand. "Come."

"I must at least leave a note, otherwise they will think someone has done me harm."

He tore a small notepad from his breast pocket and gave this to her along with his fountain pen. Thankfully she kept her missive short and to the point, saying only that she was leaving to start a new life in another city, and that she would write more fully later. He waited at the gate while she slipped into the house and left the note within.

His heart rammed inside his chest, afraid she'd change her mind. But bless her, she came running from the house, nothing added to her person but the clothes she wore and the cheap jewelry an *ayah* could afford. He grasped her hand, and together they ran…ran across the lawns and down the street to his car. He opened the door and settled her in the passenger seat while he jumped in behind the steering wheel and pushed the starter button. The streetlights of Lahore sped by as his mind raced. He'd promised her a wedding. But when? Where?

Over the past week, he'd come up with and tossed aside a hundred solutions. There was only the one haphazard plan that seemed best.

10

Dassah glanced at Cam's beloved profile in the dark. Faint light from the car's dashboard outlined the frown on his brow. "Kashmir," Cam said a few miles after leaving Lahore. "Kashmir, that's where we can get married. I've an old friend, an army chaplain who'll marry us. He's on holiday there. I'm sorry, Dassah, I've not actually contacted the man I believe will solemnize our marriage. I suppose I thought your saying yes was too good to be true."

The smile she sent him must have reassured him, for he seemed to relax, and she too tried to rest against the vehicle's upholstery. While it crushed her soul to leave Tikah, her surrender to Cam's passion was always meant to be. As a child she had been drawn to the wild and risky games at the mission only because Cam led them. And here she was again, running with him, casting all sensible thinking away, caught up like dust on the wings of a storm.

Though she missed Ramesh and Padma already, Arvind and his wife would see that their children were cared for. And she would pray for them, though she had not prayed to Yeshu since she was a teenager at the mission. But being with Cam after all these years, the words of Yeshu whispered deep in her spirit, that Yeshu cared about the smallest sparrow that might fall to the ground, and to not fear, for she was of more value than many sparrows. She must dwell on good thoughts such as these.

Now that she was with Cam, she desired nothing more than the joy of soaking up his presence so that it felt ill-mannered even to discuss the business of where they would live. Of what his family would say about their marriage. What his commanding officer would say. Her ears longed for Cam's voice. Her fingers longed to touch his face. Whenever he spoke, she swayed slightly toward him like a snake to a charmer's flute.

To ease the frown on his brow, it would be best to set aside these deeper concerns for after their wedding and talk of old friends and his family. When she directed their conversation in that vein, Cam smiled at her in relief. Only at one point in their lighthearted chat did Cam seem to grow anxious. When she asked him if he had seen Zakir, Cam's grip on the steering wheel tightened, his foot on the petrol went heavier. The car sped up. "No, I haven't seen Zakir," he said.

"How strange. I thought you might have run into him. He served in Malaya—or was it Burma during the war, like you? Is that not so?"

His hands gripped the steering wheel even tighter.

Her questions had upset him, and she berated herself silently. "I am sorry, beloved. I did not mean to bring back unhappy memories of the war."

He ran a hand down his face. "I'm sorry for being so testy. I…I'd rather not talk about the war."

"Yes, of course. It is only that I know so little of your life these days."

His voice softened. "*Janu*, Dassah, my love, this is our wedding journey." He spread his fingers while keeping his hands on the steering. "I want to talk about you and me, and by tomorrow night, be with you like a husband is with a wife."

"That is what I want too. It is only that, well…what is your position, in the army? Where do you live? I have yet to ask such things."

"Army Intelligence. I work in the capital."

She did not ask if he was billeted in a bungalow or rented a flat in Delhi, if that would be her eventual home, but folded her hands in her lap.

"Dassah," he said quietly a moment later. "Running away to be married is not what you deserve, but it's the best I can offer right now. We'll have a happy future—you'll see." He glanced at his wristwatch. "At any rate, it'll be a long while before we reach the turnoff from the Grand Trunk Road to Kashmir. Try to get a bit of shuteye."

"As you wish, my love."

The night's breeze blew through her hair, hot and sticky as they drove through the plains. If made perfect sense that he did not wish to speak of sad things at such an auspicious time in their lives. They must think of their future, not the far off future, but the immediate. Soon she would give herself to him completely and unreservedly.

Cool mountain air carried the fragrance of pines, firs, and deodar forests as they drove out of the mountains into a wide valley the next day. Afternoon sun angled through poplar trees standing like tall sentries along the road.

"I'll buy you some new clothes. Would you like that?" Cam added to the chitchat they'd enjoyed throughout the journey all that day and during their stops for picnics.

"Yes." The image of a red sari danced in her mind. She put her hand up to the marble still hanging on its string around her throat and grinned at him. Getting his smile was all she needed, though his conversation still felt like a puzzle with too many missing pieces.

Inside the city of Srinagar, her eyes could not take in their fill of loveliness. The many waterways could only be compared to photographs she had seen of Venice. Picturesque stone bridges arched over the river and canals while the balconies of wooden and fretted chalets hung over the water.

Cam parked his car outside an agency and came out twenty minutes later. "Do you mind if I keep our final destination a surprise for a bit longer?"

"I have given you my heart, Cam. You have my trust as well, *janu.*"

His face filled with light at the pledge of her belief, though the words cost her. There were so few people she trusted. But was that not what marriage meant—believing in the one you loved?

"Only one more stop, my darling." His voice grew rough, a sweet roughness like that of a cat's kiss on her hand, sending a tingle down her spine. "Once I get you alone with my ring on your finger, Dassah, it is my intention to enjoy marital bliss in complete—I repeat—complete seclusion."

Her stomach went into a wild dervish. Last night she had marred their evening with questions. Today she would show only love. No fretful questions, only trust.

He went into another shop up the street, leaving her still in the car. She did not mind when this honeymoon that he had planned so quickly was a dream of a lifetime come true. She only wished she could stroll along the narrow, winding street with him arm in arm, but perhaps it was best she wait until they were married to outwardly act his wife.

He came out awhile later with several large flat boxes and put these in the boot of the car. The smile he sent her set her pulse to tripping. Since last night when he had held her hand and run with her to the car, they had not touched, not even a finger tracing the side of a cheek. Her breath ceased. But now he was beside her, driving her to their wedding.

Her breathing resumed a normal rhythm as Cam pulled the car up to a mooring where a long, slim flat-bottomed boat waited, that Cam told her was called a *shikara*. He helped her into the *shikara*, and along with the young Kashmiri man, Cam packed the bags and boxes into the craft. The driver, Asheesh, took his position at the back. At last, Cam sank to the seat in the middle of the craft with her, a gaily colored canopy flapping above them. Asheesh dipped heart-shaped paddles into the water and pushed them forward.

Trailing branches of willows whispered along the waterway as they glided past. For the first time since last night, Cam touched her, drawing her near to rest her head against his collarbone. She breathed in the clean scent of his cotton shirt as the sun set. Snow-packed peaks around them flushed like a ripe peach as their craft slid out to the openness of an immense placid lake, dotted with lotus blossoms.

She tilted her face up. Cam filled her vision with the angular line of his jaw, the strong mouth that appeared vulnerable the closer she inched toward him.

His fresh, warm breath fanned her hair, and she arched closer as he drew her nearer, tracing his finger along the line of her cheek, the outline of her lips. "My beautiful—" His voice broke. "Sweet *janu*, I don't deserve you." He buried his face at the side of her neck, and she clung to him, looking over his shoulder, her mouth still yearning for the touch of his lips.

She stroked the roughness of his jaw where he needed a shave. "Will we be married tonight?"

He looked out to a light glimmering on the far side of the lake. In the growing darkness, she couldn't make out what it was. A house on the shore? Another *shikara*? "I hope so, *janu*. I hope so."

She snuggled close, though he had said he did not wish for touch until they were married. But his use of the Hindi endearment filled her to overflowing.

"From this day forward," he said, "nothing will ever separate us." His gaze did not waver. "Not nationality, nor country, nor people. We'll be one before God, forever."

The light across the lake brightened, the closer they drew. As their *shikara* pulled alongside a small houseboat moored at the bank, this part of the lake struck as more of a backwater, hidden, secluded. Perfect for a honeymoon…if one did not wish to be seen.

In the dimness, the craft appeared white with blue trim, a small servants' boat moored to it. A striped awning stretched over the flat deck, where Chinese lanterns bobbed with the motion of the craft. On the water side of the boat, Cam assisted her from the *shikara,* up a set of narrow steps to the main deck. She clapped her hands at the coziness of it. All very English, but wonderful. So very, very wonderful. Inside the craft she found a main parlor, a small dining room, two bedrooms off the narrow hall, and a tiny pantry.

No one was there to greet them other than Asheesh and his wife Kavita who lived in the small boat attached. Never had Dassah been treated with such deference and she spun to face Cam, wanting to throw herself into his arms. The grin on his face matched her delight. Like the day he returned from England and found her on the mission balcony, before he kissed her with such abandon.

"Are we to be married here, beloved?"

Cam checked his wristwatch. "I'd hoped so…I thought my friend would be here by now. I sent him a telegram this morning when we stopped for food."

He looked so crestfallen her heart went out to him. "It is all right. We will wait."

"Right. In the meantime, I'll have Asheesh and Kavita start dinner. I'm sure we could both use some freshening up. A bath has already been filled for you. I'll take a dip in the lake and join you soon, and uh, there are several parcels on the bed for you in the larger room." His eyes crinkled as he smiled. "I hope you like my choices."

When he left her, she whirled, clapping her hands again, and rushing to study the craft. A bath, hopefully a scented bath, was enticing to be sure, but the small houseboat was like stories from her childhood, like a boat from *The*

Wind in the Willows. She laughed to herself thinking of Mole, Ratty, Mr. Badger, and Mr. Toad. Aloud she spoke as if she were Ratty to Mole, "Believe me, my young friend, there is nothing—absolutely nothing—half so much worth doing as simply messing about in boats."

Pretty cotton curtains fluttered at the open windows that lined the inside of the houseboat. The slight musty smell blended pleasantly with the aroma of cooking spices coming from the servants' craft. Unpainted paneling rose up the walls to meet a low ceiling. She pushed through the beaded curtain to an intimate dining room, where she would share her evening meal with her husband-to-be. Or would they dine on deck?

In another whirl of rapture she returned to the sitting room. Kicking off her *chappals*, her toes felt the worn threads of a carpet, and she landed with an ecstatic flump on one of the stuffed cretonne armchairs interspersed with small wooden tables. A loose spring complained in the faded settee, but to her it was the sound of heaven. To be here with the man she loved. How good God had been to her when she least expected it.

She stood to study a small bookcase, her fingers exploring the spines, and sure enough, there was a dog-eared copy of *The Wind in the Willows.* Later, after they were married and spent a number of days learning the secret ways of husbands and wives, they might curl up together and read this. The first time she had heard the story, she had been but five or six. Cam had been there too, as his mother read the book to the mission children. But not yet, not yet. Tonight she would become a wife.

The splashing of water from outside alerted her that she had better get a move on. Cam must be almost finished with his ablutions. It would not do for her lover to wait while she washed away the dishevelment of the long drive here. She darted for the tiny bathroom. Another time she would have reveled in the zinc tub filled with water scented by roses of attar, but she hurried to wash. Leaving her hair unbound, but brushed in a sheen down to her waist, she turned to open the boxes on the bed. Her breath escaped in wonder.

Sari material in green silk, pink the color of the roses at the mission, and another in apricot cascaded in a waterfall of color over the bed. Her heart sank a fraction. No red sari, the color of joy in the East. There were English clothes though, including a frock in pale blue polished cotton. Lace edged the collar and short sleeves and around the waist. There were sandals of white leather with a bit of a heel. If she was to be the wife of an Englishman, she must dress the part.

Pushing aside the saris, she slipped the charming European dress over her head to do up the tiny buttons. With the sandals on her feet, she looked about the bedroom at the vase of flowers and added a spray of daisies to her hair. In the mirror, she saw what she hoped was a *memsahib* for Cam.

He waited for her out on the upper deck, quickly setting aside a glass he'd been drinking from, and came to her with a half-smile. "I thought for sure you'd choose the green sari for our wedding."

She glanced down at the frock. "Is it not what you prefer? I can change." She moved to return to the bedroom, but he stopped her.

"Darling, no, the dress is fine. What does it matter?" He gathered her in his arms, peering down into her face. "You're exquisite whatever you wear. Please never feel you have to act English to please me. I love you, my beautiful Indian bride." Leaning down to kiss her cheek, his breath touched her, and the smell of alcohol was not unpleasant. With another innocent kiss to her forehead, he released her and held out a chair for her to sit at the table set out on deck.

Asheesh and Kavita served them dinner with smiles. They did not appear to hold any objections to her and Cam, a couple of mixed race, alone on the houseboat. The young Kashmiri husband and wife served them a dish of chicken over rice in a savory sauce of yoghurt, ginger, tomatoes, and almonds. Dassah's nose caught the whiff of cardamom and a more subtle aroma of garlic than she was used to from the hot plains of India. Her stomach growled. It had been hours since they last ate, and yet she had not noticed her hunger while she was with Cam. He had been the entire hub of her thinking. But he, too, must have realized how hungry he was, and together they tucked into their meal.

Over small earthenware bowls they later partook of *kong firni* that Cam explained was his favorite Kashmiri dessert. She made a mental note to learn from Kavita how to prepare the cool, saffron rice pudding. As dinner came to an end, Cam filled his tumbler with more of the whiskey he enjoyed, and she smiled at his pleasure. His friend had not arrived, and that leached much of the sparkle from his eyes as the evening waned. From the small sofa in the sitting room, she watched him pace.

He had drunk more than six of the tumblers of whiskey, but it was to assuage his disappointment, and it didn't seem to affect him. There was nothing wrong with his drowning this setback tonight, a setback she shared. "It is all right, my love. Perhaps your friend is detained and we will have to wait until tomorrow to wed."

The blueness of his eyes seemed less blue. "This is not what I had hoped for, Dassah. I hoped my friend would have got the telegram that I sent this morning." He lifted a hand and let it drop to his side. "This is not what you deserve." He poured another drink from the decanter and took a deep draught from it. "I'll sleep in the *shikara*."

"You will be uncomfortable. I will sleep in the servants' boat, and you must sleep here as befitting—"

"That's not fair to Asheesh and Kavita. I'll be fine in the *shikara*." He released a brittle laugh. "I've slept in worse places."

"At least sleep on the main boat, above on the deck."

"Dassah, it's best that if we're not married, I put a bit of distance between us for the night." He placed a thumb and finger against his closed eyes and swayed. "You don't know how the sight of you weakens me. All I want to do is take…" He strode from her quickly. "Asheesh will set me up. Sleep tight, my love."

She almost ran after him to beg him to set aside his scruples. But were they not the same scruples as she had ten years ago when she had run away from the mission? He had kissed her then with such recklessness on the mission balcony, with such lack of care for the consequences that she had feared for her virtue. Now she was here alone with him but for two servants in a backwater of Kashmir.

Tikah's voice came to her from that day in Calcutta after the riots. *He will only rob you of what is most precious. Later he will cast you aside like a used handkerchief.*

She curled up in the armchair, wrapping her arms around her legs and resting her chin on her knee. She loved him. She must trust him. Surely Tikah's mistrust of Cam was unfounded. Still though, what kept this chaplain that was to marry them?

11

Sleeping alone in the skinny, flat-bottomed boat, not much more than an extravagant canoe, was not Cam's idea of a wedding night. Nor had he dreamt of waking up to whining mosquitoes, croaking frogs, and maddeningly twittering bulbuls flitting in the thicket. What little sleep he'd gotten was full of thoughts of Dassah not ten feet from him inside the houseboat. At three in the morning, for tuppence, he'd have boarded the craft, strode to the bedroom, and taken her in his arms, but he'd held back. At least he'd retained some of his Christian virtues.

It would be a while before the sun crept over the mountains, and he thrust off the light blanket to climb the steps to the houseboat. He might as well clean up and go into Srinagar. There had to be someone in that city who could marry them.

Under the striped awning that covered the open deck, Dassah lay out on the lounge as if waiting for him. Wrapped in a woolen blanket, she smiled at his approach. She'd tucked a flower behind her ear, and her braid hung unraveled over her shoulder. He hunkered down at the lounge by her side. "How long have you been out here in the damp, silly old bean?"

"Since you left last evening, *janu*."

"I leave the perfectly snug bed to you, and you choose a rickety lounger to spend the night in."

"I wanted to be near you. Like Ruth who slept at the feet of Boaz before they were married."

He squeezed her knee through the blanket. "Quite *beyond the pale* in British society."

She lifted a slim hand from beneath the blanket to touch his sandpaper jaw. Her sloe-shaped eyes followed the same journey as her fingers. With the frisson of her smooth skin against his stubble, his knees turned to water. If he didn't move soon, what little restraint he had would dissipate with the morning mist on the lake. "Now don't be a tease." What she was doing to him shoved his normal baritone down to his boots. He gave her a fierce grin and her knee an extra hard squeeze for causing him such emotional torture and bolted to his feet.

She infused her grin with the adorable ferocity she used to bestow on him when they were children. But the stakes were higher now. And they were not children.

The laughter in her amber eyes changed to molten desire. "I am in anguish, my rajah, aching for your touch."

His insides somersaulted. "Ah…my tigress." He swallowed deeply and backed away. "Here I was thinking I was the disreputable good-for-nothing at risk of taking advantage of your innocence."

She snuggled into her blanket again and spoke in a deep voice to mirror his. "Put a ring on my finger, *sahib*, and I will show you the dormant tigress who strains to be released."

He couldn't take his eyes off her, and yelled for Asheesh with mock alarm. "Asheesh, wake up my good man, we're going to the city! There's not a moment to lose."

The first thing Cam did when he reached Srinagar was check at Nedou's Hotel where Miles Robbins, his chaplain friend from the 75th Highlanders was supposed to be staying, only to be told that Miles had cancelled his booking due to ill health. No wonder there'd been no response to Cam's telegram.

With instructions to Asheesh to wait by the mooring, Cam set off. He'd ask at every single church in the city if he had to. He could arrange a wedding with the local justice of the peace but preferred to give Dassah the closest thing to a church wedding as possible. They'd both been raised as Christians, although he didn't know how deep her faith went—nor his own faith, for that matter.

As he trudged the street in search of churches, it struck him how few British there were holidaying in Srinagar compared to years past. The English and Europeans were definitely moving home. Why, this time last year these streets were packed with holidaymakers.

By luncheon, Cam's hopes dropped to mid-mast. Each minister in the city gladly took him into their study, offered him a cup of tea, but they all tried to talk him out of marrying an Indian girl. "Not in her best interest or yours," a number of them said in varying ways. With each successive disappointment, a growing hole yawned in his chest. He was about to give up and make arrangements for a civil ceremony when a small church caught his eye close to the outskirts of Srinagar, leading into the hills. One of those small missionary denominations— KASHMIRI VALE GOSPEL CHAPEL, the chipped-painted sign said.

Inside, the building was set up more for Indian parishioners, not a pew in sight. September's cool breeze blew through open shutters. A number of Indian men congregated close to the front, sitting cross-legged on the earthen floor. With them sat a tall, angular man, his black suit and clerical collar proclaiming him as a Protestant minister. He left the others to their prayers and, in his socks—one with a hole in the toe—made his way to the back of the church to greet Cam. After introducing himself as Reverend Alan Callahan, he stooped to put his shoes on and gestured for Cam to precede him outside. They stopped at a well shaded by an umbrella tree where a number of Indian women were drawing water.

Cam could feel the man's gaze. Weathered skin and dark hair graying at the temples placed the reverend somewhere in his mid-to-late-forties. By this time Cam was so fed up with so-called men of the cloth attempting to talk him out of marrying Dassah that he got straight to the point. "Look here, I've been to every church in Srinagar today. I want to marry an Indian girl that I've known and loved since childhood. What's more, I'd like to get married as soon as possible. Today would be best. Tomorrow would be satisfactory."

The reverend rubbed the side of his longish nose. "Are you always this eloquent?" His upper-crust accent came straight out of Oxford or Cambridge, and the dryness to his tone brought a chuckle to Cam, the first all day since he'd left Dassah this morning. The minister indicated Cam take a seat on the edge of the well. "I assure you, I am not in the habit of talking Englishmen out of marrying young Indian women. More frequently I'm called in to suggest they at least give the girl some form of financial support after they've got her with child. Your request to get married is an honorable one that I am inclined to take seriously, as that of a mature...military man?"

"Captain Cameron Fraser, Army Intelligence, stationed in New Delhi."

"Well, Captain, you've been gadding about to all the churches in Srinagar today? Now you've come to this lowly Indian church?"

Cam returned the parson's shrewd gaze. "I spent most of my childhood Sundays in lowly Indian churches like this. No matter where my stepfather, Major Geoffrey Richards was stationed—India, Malaya, China—we attended native Christian congregations. To tell you the truth...I feel at home here."

The reverend pursed his lips together, holding back a chuckle. "In that case, I'm all ears. So tell me—the young lady, her full age?"

"Twenty-seven."

"Not a child then. Why the hurry to the altar?"

Cam looked the man straight in the eye. "She's not pregnant, Reverend, if that's what you think. In fact, I've kept her honor, and she's waiting at a houseboat I've rented."

"I'm relieved to hear it. You say you've kept her honor? For how long will you remain this chivalrous knight, if you don't get your wish to marry her today?"

The razor-sharp repartee from this minister of the gospel was not at all what Cam expected. Most of the clerics he'd talked to today had simpered and smiled but still refused to marry him and Dassah. "Then I shall keep looking for a minister or justice of the peace to marry us. I'm not giving up."

The man gave a slight nod in acquiescence. "That determined, are you? My word, sounds like you'll try for what…a good week or two to marry her? Then what? After you're at all sixes and sevens, what will you do then? Fall victim to your passions?"

It took all of Cam's strength not to get up and walk away. "I assure you, sir, it is my intention to marry Dassah at all cost."

"Very well then. Do you have the license to marry? Permission from your commanding officer?"

The dusty ground drew Cam's gaze. "Neither. It was all rather a rush once we decided."

"All…rather…a rush, you say. Mm." The minister began to stride toward the back of the church. "Sorry, can't be done."

Cam followed. "What? Just like that? Can't be done?"

"Are you hard of hearing, man? I said I cannot." Alan Callahan's voice resonated with a rich bass that no doubt would have stood him well in a cathedral where his sermons could reach the back of the nave. How that worked in this small mud brick church with a thatched roof, Cam couldn't fathom, but this ordained minister was his last chance.

They entered a small study at the back of the church crammed with dusty tomes, and Cam watched the parson thrust various items of clothing into a pair of saddlebags, along with a Bible and several other books. "I can't perform your marriage for several reasons," he said. "I'm starting out this evening on the first leg of my monthly circuit into the hills. By tomorrow I'll be fifty miles from here in another parish." He reached behind Cam for a small leather briefcase and continued to talk rapid fire with that crisp, bass annunciation. "Marriages have to wait until my return."

"Your parishioners are Indian Christians?"

"My entire flock is Indian Christian." He glanced at Cam. "And I view my calling to serve them all with happy sincerity. However, that has no bearing on your situation. You do not have a license. Obtain one, and I will consider marrying the two of you when I get back in a month."

"A month! Would you say that to every soldier who wants to get married? The war is over. Surely you've married men more quickly than that? What about military men who have to return home on the next ship?" He slammed his hand down on the reverend's desk. "I'd have thought a man of the cloth would be more interested in helping an individual do the right thing rather than constraining him in a situation that could cause him to sin."

Reverend Alan Callahan gave him another scrutinizing stare along the length of his patrician nose. "Are you threatening me, Captain? Are you threatening to dishonor this young woman? I assure you, I am not swayed by spiritual blackmail. That's the business of Satan, and I'll have nothing to do with it."

Cam sank to the only chair in the room, a straight-backed wooden thing. "No…I'd rather die than dishonor her." He leaned forward, his head in his hands.

"I haven't applied for a license yet, knowing full well the kind of social stigma we'd both receive. And I haven't asked my CO."

"So you're willing to risk getting kicked out of the army for getting married without permission?"

"I'm hoping to keep it hush-hush until I can sort things out." His neck and cheeks began to burn.

"And where will you live? What about the children you conceive?"

A sharp little pain drove into his heart. His and Dassah's children. Little ones like Ramesh and Padma. "I don't know that either, Reverend. Where we'll live now or after the transfer of power." His head dropped further. He was a ruddy fool. Might as well be ten and in short trousers the way he was acting. "All I know is I love her and want to marry her." He went on to explain that his chaplain friend had failed to arrive, and his and Dassah's disappointment. After he finished, the drawn out silence from the minister took the last of his confidence.

Outside, the men from the prayer meeting disbanded and waved good-bye to one another. Alan Callahan left his saddlebags on the desk and strolled to the doorway to lean against it and wave to his parishioners. "All right," he said a long moment later. "Tell me how you two lovebirds came to know each other."

He turned to face Cam and crossed his arms. The kindness in his deep voice gave Cam the gumption to tell him about his and Dassah's past. When Cam came to a stuttering end, Alan rubbed the back of his knuckles along his jaw. "Answer me this. Can you, before God, tell me if there are any impediments that should hinder the two of you from being married?"

"None, sir."

"And you will promise before God Almighty that you will not abandon her or her children when your passion wanes, which it will, if only temporarily? Or when your mixed marriage causes financial and emotional hardships you had not anticipated, which it most certainly will?"

"It is my desire, sir, to love and care for Dassah and our children in the same noble manner in which my stepfather loved and protected my mother, myself, and two sisters."

"Quite the mouthful, I must say." The reverend tapped a thumb against his lips. "Well then, you shall be married. No reason under God's heaven why you shouldn't."

The shock of the minister's statement took what remained of the wind out of Cam.

"You've convinced me, Captain. It is all rather fast, I admit, but I'll do as you've so…eloquently petitioned." Alan strode to the desk and picked up his saddlebags to finish his packing. "Now then, where is this wedding to take place? It'll have to be tonight. You mentioned that you're moored out on a spot the far side of the lake. I planned on going that direction tomorrow morning as it is, so I'll ride out this evening."

Cam swept his gaze along the tall minister's clothing, the riding boots he was changing into as they'd talked. This time Cam took in the shiny, thin spots on the man's trousers, the numerous repairs to the jacket, the worn clerical collar. Reverend Callahan's voice showed his classical education, but he'd chosen a career in one of those missionary denominations. Aside from his articulate and ecclesiastical intonation, the man was clearly a maverick. "You're going by horseback?" Cam asked.

Alan sharpened the crease in the crown of his panama hat and clapped it on his head. "Only way to travel in India, far as I'm concerned. If you're as fired up to do the right thing by this young woman as you say, then I suggest we get along. Quite refreshing to meet an English gentleman who isn't taken in by all that segregation rot. You and this girl grew up together. No surprises as far as culture and customs are concerned. You'll certainly not be shocked by what she makes for tea. Although it will be an adjustment for her when you take her back to England, but you sound as though you're soldier enough to protect her from any bigotry nonsense there. You are, aren't you?"

A lump of lead landed in Cam's stomach at the thought of taking Dassah to England.

The minister's gaze narrowed. "Ah. Not quite so prepared as at first blush. You can still back out while you can. Your challenges as a mixed race couple will be twice those of anyone else, so now's the time to tuck your tail between your legs and take to the hills if you're not up to the challenge. No one will know. No one but me, you, the girl. And God."

Cam's head jerked up to glare at the man.

Alan's brows couldn't rise any higher. "Do I detect some godly spirit there? Convince me, Captain, that you're a man. Surprise me. Act like your noble stepfather whom you admire so much."

"I told you, Reverend, I will make Dassah my wife." Cam practically ground the statement through his teeth.

The minister gave him a tepid smile. "Good man. For half a second I feared I was wrong in my judgment. But the only way to winnow the chaff from the kernel is to give it a bit of a thrashing. I'm afraid that's what I've just given you—a verbal thrashing. The stuff of quality always rises to the top, and granted, while I detect you have still much to learn in spiritual matters, I also think you are a man of your word. So, Captain Cameron Fraser, I will marry you and your young lady."

The reverend started to stride from the parsonage. "And may God make you the man you'll need to be for this holy undertaking."

The mist had long melted away. The *rista kebab* that Kavita made for lunch could not interest Dassah. Cam had been away hours. What if he did not return?

Always the fear that this was a dream and she would wake alone coiled at the back of her mind, and she forced herself to take renewed interest in her surroundings.

On the bank, moss and ferns grew at the base of a giant chinar tree whose boughs sheltered the small craft. All day, sunlight dazzled as it travelled across the lake. Not until the setting sun turned the peaks of the mountains to peach and then plum did she see the *shikara* in the distance. Cam waved to her from under the small vessel's canopy as it glided toward the houseboat.

She would have wept with happiness if she had not feared ruining her face for him. He had not abandoned her. She had been a fool to think so, and she ran along the narrow edging of the houseboat to greet him at the water steps.

He reached for her around the waist and pulled her to him hard, and she felt the length of his body against hers. *Her husband-to-be.* The kiss he gave her stole her breath.

Many heartbeats later he released her. "I deserved that kiss. A reward, you might say." His breath, too, came fast and uneven. "Good news, darling. The minister's on his way. Tonight's the night."

She leaned against his shoulder, unable to speak. Her arms wound around his neck, and she breathed in the scent of him. She could feel his heart beat against hers through his cotton shirt and her sari, the one she'd come away in, not having the courage to wear the beautiful clothes he had bought. With that thought, she leaned backward over his arm that supported her, her arms outstretched behind her as though she were a dancer, and laughed up at him. "What shall I wear for our wedding?"

His arms tightened around her waist, and he swung her upright to him, their mouths but inches apart. "Whatever makes you happiest," he said in a thick voice.

"Red, the color of joy!" she squealed like a foolish child.

His countenance fell. "But I didn't buy you red."

"Beloved…." She laughed. "It is of no consequence."

"Dassah, I'm so sorry, I never thought."

She pressed a kiss against his mouth to stop him. When she pulled away, a shy stillness floated over them, broken only by the bulbuls chattering in the bushes along the bank. A few crickets started their chorus with the twilight that was fast coming.

With what appeared considerable reluctance, Cam pulled away from her and grew boisterous—she knew to cover up his longing. If there was one thing she was assured of, it was that he desired her. "The reverend will be here in about an hour," he said. "You'll need to do all the fussy things women do to get married, and I'll need a good scrubbing so as not to shame you." Laughing, he slapped imaginary dust from his trousers.

"The reverend?" She looked down at the *shikara*, for the first time wondering how this minister would be getting here if he had not come with Cam, and Cam was not taking her to church. From what she could tell, the roads on the bank where they were moored were rough.

He caught her unspoken questions. "He's coming on horseback, soon, so off you go."

She turned from him and went inside to the parlor and beyond to the larger of the bedrooms. The next thing she knew Cam started singing. The sound of one shoe dropping onto the deck came to her, and then the sound of the other. A moment later she heard a splash as he dove into the lake. From the bed, she listened to him singing in the water, the gurgle when he dunked himself and the triumphant chorus bursting from his lungs as he emerged above the surface. She recognized the hymn he sang—"Christ the Lord Is Risen Today." With the chorus drawn out—*ha...ha...ha...ha...ha...lay...eee...luu...uuu...yah....*

She sang the same hymn quietly in the room by herself. They had sung that together many an Easter at the mission. Perhaps Yeshu had not left her, if he truly had sent Cam to be her Christian husband. Perhaps she was still one of Yeshu's little sparrows.

Over the next hour with Kavita's help, Dassah took time over her beautification and adornment. Unlike Queen Esther from the Bible, she only had an hour to prepare. Unlike Lakshmi of Hindu lore, she did not have jewels, only the Akro Slag marble still strung about her neck. Nor did she have great beauty like Esther. And unlike most Indian brides, she did not even have the hennaed curlicues of flowers and birds on her arms and hands to celebrate this hour. Kavita helped her wrap the emerald sari around her body. Though she would so much have preferred red, green was her favorite and the color of fertility.

As Kavita tucked a comb with a pink lotus blossom into her hair, Dassah heard the approach of a horse's hooves outside on the bank, and a man call out, "Ahoy!"

Cam answered, and, as the visitor walked up the gangplank, the houseboat gently rocked. Kavita whirled toward Dassah, her eyes round as a monkey's when Asheesh delivered a bouquet of flowers for Dassah. They were lotus blossoms much like the flowers that filled the lake, but Cam must have had them arranged at a shop in the city. These pink and white blossoms cascaded in a waterfall that reached the hem of her sari just above her bare feet.

Her stomach flitted as with a thousand darting kingfishers as she waited for Cam's call to join him on the deck. To ease her excitement, she touched the marble that hung around her throat.

When Asheesh took her arm in the way of western men, she knew Cam had instructed him. With the young Kashmiri couple escorting her, she walked through the small parlor and out to the main deck under the awning.

Cam stood at the bow with a tall, thin man in the garments of a Christian minister. She walked forward, praying to Yeshu—who must have brought them together—that her love for Cam and her trust in him would shine through her eyes.

The ceremony did not take long. Cam slipped a plain gold band on her left hand, and the night seemed to sing. She felt she walked on air. Around her, the minister and Cam spoke quietly as they showed her where to sign her name on a clean page in a battered leather book.

A while later Asheesh and Kavita brought out food, and Cam poured drinks for himself and the minister.

He declined. "Never touch the stuff. The wretched poison robbed me of a prestigious career in a church in England. Not that I mind now. The Lord led me here to this calling, and for that I'm more than grateful."

She glanced at the man's clothing, noting the dustiness of his suit, his worn and patched state, the fact that he'd come on horseback. But no matter, she had signed her name in that thick book that must be the registry. She and Cam were married, and as this thought sent joy leaping through her, Cam and the minister's voices receded. Dimly, she heard the minister say, "And if you truly love this woman, you'll do her a favor and put a cork in that bottle. Better still, throw it overboard."

Soon the minister made preparations to leave. "I mustn't stay. You just take care of your bride." He took the gangplank to the shore where his mount was tied. He disappeared into the dark, the shadows of the giant chinar and willow trees swallowing him. She had been so tongue-tied during her wedding that she had failed to catch his name. With shining smiles and shy salaams, Asheesh and Kavita slipped away to their own small craft.

They were alone at last.

Cam set down his tumbler of whiskey and strode toward her. With tender care not to break a single stem, he took the bouquet of lotus blossoms and lilies from her and laid them on the lounger where she had slept the night before. He walked back to her as if treasuring each step. When he reached her, he entwined his fingers with hers. Moisture shimmered in his eyes. "My little Hadassah," he whispered, "I'm so afraid."

Her pulse beat at her throat. "Why, my beloved?" But she too felt fear—even yet—that she would waken tomorrow and be alone.

"I don't want to hurt you, Dassah."

She felt the heat of her blush. "Do you mean in our marriage bed?"

He raised his face to the sky and his laughter rang out. "No, sweet love. Not that. I promise to be gentle." Growing serious once more, he lifted her chin. "I don't want to cause you any heartache...but somehow I know I will."

"We cannot fail but to hurt each other at times."

He laid his forehead against hers, while her lips hungered for his. "Please remember this moment, my little love, when the time comes and I've hurt you by something I've done...or not done. Please remember that I adore you, as I have since you were a tiny girl. I want nothing to ever part us in our hearts even if we are separated by distance."

"Separated by distance? You mean because you are in the army, and must be away from me at times?" Why must her fear always lurk in the shadows?

"Yes, that...and if at any other time I cannot share the same...place with you for a time...that I am still yours and you are mine." He gripped her suddenly and held her to him. "Promise me, you'll never think that I don't love you."

"Yes, beloved. This is the way of life. There will naturally be times we are parted. Do not fear." Taking his face in her hands, she lifted her mouth to meet his and whispered against his lips, "Cam, *janu*, we have waited so long. I want to give myself to you. And have you give yourself to me."

He caught his breath. With exquisite tenderness that sent her insides into a maelstrom of yearning, he held her with one arm and stooped to place his other arm beneath her knees. She floated seemingly on air as he carried her inside the houseboat. The same floating sensation she had been feeling since he'd slipped the ring on her finger and promised to worship her with his body until death did part them.

12

To Miriam, the comfortable mahogany furniture with white doilies on the back of the chairs, along with the massive aspidistras fern, looked like any typical British *Raj* residence. These quarters belonging to Principal Isabella McNair were only slightly larger than Miriam's own cramped quarters at Kinnaird College.

Isabella had invited Miriam to tea. This short woman in her fifties, with her hair pulled back in a tidy bun, passed a plate of freshly made scones to Miriam and then to her vice principal, Priobala. In a soft but determined Scottish brogue, Isabella asked Miriam, "Now we're four weeks into the fall semester, we want to know—settling in all right?"

Miriam set her teacup down, the desire to talk with her hands too strong. "Feels like home. I adore my students." She recognized the same gleam of love in the eyes of the principal and vice principal. The students of Kinnaird College were the cream of the crop as far as they were concerned, young women from Christian, Hindu, and Muslim homes all over India and the Middle East.

Totally unlike Miss McNair, Priobala was a tall, slender Indian woman wearing a traditional sari. "How are you managing the different cultures and religions?"

"The differences have made no impact on my classes. All my students are far more interested in their studies and sports than in political or religious disparity."

"Good, good," Miss McNair said, beaming. She leaned forward, her elbows resting on her knees. In the past month since Miriam had been at Kinnaird, she'd come to recognize this small Presbyterian lady as a powerhouse of quiet dignity. "That is my desire for Kinnaird, that we forge a sense of unity."

The principal lifted the teapot. Miriam shook her head to the unspoken question of another cup as Miss McNair leaned back in her chair. "We're entering a difficult time. Where will those dividing lines be if Mr. Jinnah of the Muslim League gets his way? Will Lahore be in India or in this new country Pakistan? I'm urging our staff, Miriam, to do all they can to maintain that unity we've worked so hard for."

A tingle ran along Miriam's arms.

The principal straightened up, giving her knees a little slap. "But God has brought us here, and for as long as whatever government is in charge allows us, we will endeavor to keep love and harmony among our students." Miss McNair sent her a twinkling grin. "And I know you will be a blessing, Miriam. I've listened to you teaching from the hallway. I've heard the laughter of your students. Seen the faces of our girls looking up at you, enraptured. Both Priobala and I are convinced that God has brought you to us for such a time as we are entering."

A girlish sigh escaped Miriam, and tears pricked at the back of her eyes. She blinked them away. She rarely became misty, but her sacrifices of boyfriends and parties to burn the midnight oil on essays were worth it. This was what those years of earning her BA and MA in theology and psychology had been for, to be able to teach these vibrant young minds.

She felt God's confirmation of that fact as clearly as she felt herself breathe.

After tea, Miriam left the two heads of the college in the principal's parlor, closed the door behind her, and, hugging her lesson plan to her chest, strolled across the grounds to her quarters. Before going up to her rooms, she checked with the porter to see if she had any post. After collecting her letters, she ran up the stairs, flipping through the envelopes. One from Mother, another from Eva, another from friends she'd gone to university with, a postcard from Jack of all things.

Why that man sent her postcards of the garrison town of Rawalpindi she had no idea. Still, she chuckled at the silliness. *Oh no, Lieutenant Colonel Jack Sunderland, you are most assuredly not what I'm looking for. Though you're far too attractive for your own good, I have a calling. I am doing God's work and nothing—do you hear?—nothing will distract me.*

On entering her room, her chuckle died. Still no letters from Cam. Since they'd parted that day he'd been here to tea with Mother and Father, she'd heard not a word, though she'd written several times to the post office in Kashmir. She'd like to clip him along the ear. The cheek! Ignoring her! They'd been close growing up, even closer than either one of them had been to the baby of the family, Eva. Still, they both adored Eva. And reading the baby of the family's letter, Miriam sighed.

Her younger sister's news dripped with sensual bliss, looking forward to her wedding. Mother had helped her choose the gown and veil. Daddy was a tease about the cost of the wedding breakfast. Then—blast it all—Eva went into an endless rhapsody on her trousseau lingerie.

Miriam's hand, holding the letter, sank to her lap. Details like these were the last thing she wanted, and her eye jumped to the note about Dad's teasing. She'd appreciate her father's counsel on preserving the unity of her students. That would help shove thoughts of romantic wedding nights out of her mind.

Sitting at her desk, she toyed with pen and paper, her eye going to the postcard from Jack, where she'd tucked it in the corner of her blotter.

His garrison in Rawalpindi lay only three hundred miles north of Lahore. Too far to get together over tea, to pick his brain as a commander over British, Muslim, Hindu, and Sikh men. She drew her writing pad toward her and pulled the cap off her fountain pen. *Dear Jack*, she began, mentally praying he'd not get the wrong end of the stick. This was strictly business.

She'd admitted to herself that in Calcutta that she was attracted to him, but since coming here to Lahore, the pendulum of her desires swung to the other side. When she was with her students, the desire to sink her teeth into her full-time vocation pulled at her heartstrings. Nurturing other people's children could be as equally satisfying as marriage. Couldn't it? The elder Indian Miriam, the woman she was named after, had found her desires fulfilled in the Jallianwalla Bagh Mission.

After finishing her carefully worded letter to Jack, she was wetting the envelope when Deidre McGuiness, who taught mathematics, popped into her room to announce Miriam had a telephone call downstairs. Miriam dashed down, letter in hand, and picked up the receiver. She recognized Jack's smooth chuckle as soon as she said hello.

"Do ye have time for a wee drop 'a tea?" he asked in a riotous Irish accent.

She choked on laughter. "I do. However I should mention I'm not in the mood for a long train ride to Rawalpindi just for a cuppa."

"Charmingly elusive as ever, Miss Richards." He dropped the Irish lilt. "You'll have to do better than that to turn me down. As it is, I'm in town."

"Oh." She pretended nonchalance.

"My, my, can't you do better than that? I thoroughly expected you to give me some blistering rejection that would wound me for life."

"You are an absolute beast, saying such things to a lady."

He seemed to check something before answering her. "I'm in Lahore for precisely two hours and twenty minutes. Can you drum up the forbearance to come out with this beast of a man?" He pasted on a thick Irish accent again. "And I promise on me saintly mother's grave to not slurp me tea from the saucer or chew on the sugar cubes."

"One more crack from you in that horribly fake brogue and I'm ringing off." Sneaking a glance at herself in the hall mirror, she grimaced. "I'm not exactly polished to the nines today. It's my day to wash my hair."

"Blast! How terribly inconvenient. I'd not counted on spending time with a woman in desperate need of the beauty parlor. So stick a kerchief on your head or whatever women wear these days and hide your mop."

"Very well, but you're not winning any points for gallantry. Shall you be picking me up?"

"I shall, I shall," he added again in that atrocious Irish, then slipped into his usual clipped London inflection. "I shall be outside the main entrance to your college in fifteen minutes. Will that give you enough time to spruce up? I do have my standards you know."

"Say one more ghastly thing and I won't give you the letter I'd written you. It's here in my hand as I was about to post it, but I can easily throw it in the bin."

"Don't do that. I'll savor every line when I read it." His chuckle came over the line like warm honey. "One more thing…what is your favorite flower?"

"Yellow roses."

"Ah, I should have guessed that, my golden lovely," he said as he rang off.

Back in her room, she changed her blouse, ran a comb through her hair, added a slash of her favorite shade of lipstick, Red Velvet, to her lips, blew herself a kiss in the mirror, and darted down the stairs. She sprinted across the quad to the front of the main entrance, letter to Jack in hand, only to stand on the steps breathing hard. He'd said fifteen minutes, but as it was, she was early. Fuming with herself for letting him wind her up the way he did, she was in the midst of thinking of ways to send him into the same sort of tizzy when two of her students, local girls, Anjuli and Faiza came around the corner.

Walking their bicycles together, they appeared to be in a heated discussion. "What are you saying?" Anjuli said to Faiza. "Surely, you would not kill me to gain Pakistan?"

"Of course, I would kill you unhesitatingly to get Pakistan," came Faiza's reply.

The blood in Miriam's veins froze.

Anjuli stopped walking her bike to stare at Faiza, whose steps petered out to look back at her friend. Up to this point these two girls—Faiza, who was Muslim, and Anjuli, Hindu—had been inseparable. That is, until Mr. Jinnah's call for a separate state for Muslims. A wave of nausea welled up inside Miriam. It couldn't be. Why, only last week she'd coached them in field hockey. No two girls could have been closer as they'd tumbled onto the grass, sweaty and grass-stained after the match, in a heap of giggles. Friends couldn't turn into enemies overnight. She shook her head. Could they?

Miriam took the steps down to the drive. "Anjuli, Faiza, what's this I hear?" She tried to inject a joking tone. "I must have heard you incorrectly."

Faiza's gaze fell to the ground.

Anjuli jumped in to defend Faiza. "It is only the discussions of what is going on around us. A misunderstanding, surely?" But it was to Faiza that Anjuli implored, her brown gaze latching on to that of her friend's.

Miriam moved closer to Faiza and patted the girl's arm. "Come, Faiza, what is bothering you? You look terribly sad."

The young woman dipped her veiled-covered head. The pretty blue gossamer falling to her shoulders matched her pantaloons and knee-length tunic. Her sandaled feet scuffed the dust close to her bicycle's front tire. "I did not wish to hurt Anjuli's feelings." The unhappiness on Faiza's face was as deep as that of

Anjuli's.

"Of course you don't wish to hurt your friend, dear." Miriam put her arm around Faiza but included Anjuli with her gaze. At first Faiza stiffened, but a moment later she surrendered to Miriam's hug. When she felt Faiza relax a bit, Miriam dared to ask, "If you do not wish to hurt each other's feelings, then why say such things to each other?"

Faiza's eyes brimmed. "My people are saying it is important we Muslims have our own country."

"Does this mean you cannot love your friends who are not Muslim? Can you not continue to live as neighbors and keep your religious identity? Why, I have all sorts of friends from all sorts of backgrounds."

"No!" The shout that came out of Faiza startled both Anjuli and Miriam. "No," she repeated in a broken whisper. "This cannot be. Not for Pakistan." She glanced at her friend. "This is what I have been trying to explain to Anjuli. While I love her—she is my dearest friend—there will come a time when I will have to put our friendship aside for the dream of Pakistan. Soon the English will no longer have any say in how we get along." She said this with such brokenness, Miriam's heart ached.

She placed an arm around Anjuli while continuing to hold Faiza, with a prayer that Faiza wouldn't bolt. Thank God the young Muslim girl seemed more confused that militant. She melted into Miriam's arm while Miriam measured her words. "God forbid that the times will bring us to spill blood, Faiza. God forbid." Her own tears blended with the two girls as they hugged each other in a clumsy manner, the girls still clenching the handlebars of their bicycles.

Miriam became dimly aware of a car driving up and stopping a few feet away, but she took out her handkerchief and forcing a smile, dabbed at first Anjuli's eyes and then Faiza's. "Off you go. Would you please, for my sake, talk about this some more? Try to sort out why your friendship is precious, and how you can both remain friends no matter what happens. What about tea and chocolate biscuits in my office tomorrow after classes? We can have a nice long chat, just the three of us."

Bracketed on either side by their bikes, the two girls walked away, close together, their heads only inches apart.

"Miriam?" Jack waited at the bottom step, peering at her as she watched the girls leaving the school grounds. It was his vehicle parked on the drive. "Are you all right, Miriam?"

In a daze, she took his hand as he assisted her down the stairs and into the car. "I was just witness to the most awful thing," she said as he got into the car and started it up. He listened, his features taking on a resolute hardness.

"I'm sorry, Miriam. Bewildering how we can watch an entire city like Calcutta go up in flames, but something cracks inside us when it's brought so near to home. Do you know those girls well?"

"Two of my star pupils." She looked out at the passing city of Lahore, the red brick, white colonnaded government buildings, vast gardens, universities, theaters, museums. Why, Lahore and Amritsar, two cities so close together in the Punjab, were each referred to as the Paris of the East. Cities of enlightenment! Her breath sped up. "Only yesterday in class we discussed Acts chapter ten and Peter's vision. God is no respecter of persons. He does not show partiality. It's one of the foundations of my faith."

Her gaze settled on the bemused set to his mouth as he kept his thoughts to himself.

"I'm sorry, Jack. I do tend to get hot under the collar at times."

"On the contrary, you're rather splendid when you get up on your soapbox. Never let me be one to curtail your fervor." He reached over the seat to the back and drew from it a small bouquet which he handed to her.

She smiled her thanks for the yellow roses, her gaze winging outside again as he drove downtown. Outside Nedou's Hotel, he stopped and left the keys with the valet before helping her from the car.

"If I promise to set aside my soapbox," she said with a laugh, "will you escort me within?"

"Are you sure you don't need a moment? You were badly shaken by that episode with your students." The kindness of his rich baritone eased some of her anxiety.

"I'm fine now. Really."

His slow smile did something to her insides. Something she preferred not to dwell on. Best to get this social event on the correct footing—she reached for a measure of her usual cheekiness. "Good thing I didn't take your advice and wear a kerchief. I'd be decidedly underdressed for the occasion."

His mouth twitched as he scrutinized her plain navy skirt, white cotton shirt, and school tie. "You could wear a pair of farmer's dungarees and rubber wellies on your feet, and I'd still think you were breathtaking."

"If you don't escort me inside soon for tea," she chirped in an attempt to tamp down the feelings his smile stirred up, "I must warn you, Jack Sunderland, that you could be held accountable for the consequences."

"Consequences?"

"I'm ravenous. Rather partial to a nice roast beef. And as there are several cows meandering down the road as usual, if you don't hurry, I could set up a spit on the lawn and start a bonfire. But as this is India—"

"Not another word." He took her by the elbow and rushed her through the foyer to the dining room. "I'll not be held accountable for starting a Hindu uprising," he hissed into her ear as they waited to be seated by the maître d'.

They kept up the banter through ordering sandwiches and creamed teas, and she was grateful for his diversion from that shocking conversation at the school. "When were you planning on delivering my post?" he asked when silence landed, breaking into the thoughts that had wandered again to Anjuli and Faiza.

She dug the envelope out of her handbag. "I'm afraid it's about the very thing we've been discussing." She held back a giggle when he propped a pair of reading glasses on his nose and began to read her missive.

A moment later he looked up. "I'm afraid you're up against it, the same as the rest of us. As our army will be sent home, it'll be the job of senior officers to help the Indians take the forces under their own leadership. Hard enough to do if India were to remain one country, but if India is separated, then dash it all, it'll be downright thorny to separate the Muslim officers from Hindu officers, and then the rank and file." He held her gaze. "All I can tell you, Miriam, is to keep reminding your students that they are neighbors."

"Like the neighbors in Calcutta?"

"God forbid we see that level of rioting again."

"We could though, couldn't we?"

He reached across the table to take her hand. "I'm terribly sorry, Miriam. It doesn't feel right talking about such horrible events with a lady." His hand gripped hers a little tighter. "Hopefully you and your students will see nothing unpleasant in Lahore." His smile was somewhat forced, though.

Had he forgotten she was the daughter of a soldier, and the sister of one? She wondered what he would think of her childhood experiences—roughing it in the mission with the orphans or helping Dr. Vicky with the sick during an epidemic. It seemed Jack wanted to pretend that nothing had changed in British Colonial India.

Potted palms graced the corners of the restaurant. Fans whirled high above their heads from the ornate ceiling. Waiters in startling white pajama-style uniforms with cummerbunds and turbans served them from massive silver trays while he, the dashing solider, held the hand of a delicate British *memsahib*.

She ought to correct his mistake. She was no *memsahib*. But some romantic tune wafted from the dais where a few musicians played, and Jack played with her hand on the linen-clad table. Her eyes were drawn to the breadth of his shoulders, the strength of his fingers that gently held hers, the hard but sensual shape of his mouth. Then he sighed. "My two hours and twenty minutes are up."

His words brought the tinkling of broken glass to her thoughts, as if chandeliers fell from the ceiling. It had felt like only minutes in his company, and now he was standing, holding her chair as she rose. Placing his hand at the small of her back, he escorted her through the tables and out to wait under the hotel portico for the valet to bring his car around.

She wanted his touch at the small of her back to remain. When had that changed? She could get used to his hand holding hers. Get used to his arms around her. And why not? Romance and marriage suited a great many people in the world. Blast Eva! Why did she have to be choosing a wedding gown and lingerie, writing about every blessed-intimate-detail about lace and satin undies? As her sister, how was she, a woman bent on a profession, to withstand the normal yearnings for a husband when Eva didn't have the sense to keep those elements of married life under her hat?

"I'll be up this way again on the return trip," Jack murmured. "Can easily pop by."

"Tea would be lovely," she murmured.

The major-domo held the door open for her to get into the car. As Jack slid in beside her, he turned to face her. "What about turning that tea into dinner?"

She clasped her hands together on her lap. For a moment she'd weakened, but it was time to put some steel into her spine. She didn't want the route of marriage and children. At least not yet. Best to set out the lines for this playing field at the start. "Dinner would be fine, Jack, as long as you realize I have no intention of becoming—"

"Yes, yes, I know." He tapped his temple but smiled to soften his words. "No intention of becoming romantically involved. Old ground, my dear. And I assured you that I'm not the marrying kind. So, that ought to wrap things up for us. With you as a theology professor of a highly respected Christian college and me a confirmed bachelor, there couldn't be anything between us but the innocent love of friendship as per the Greek word *philos*. However, if you ever do change your mind, you'll let me know?"

She returned his smile. "Jack Sunderland, if I ever change my mind about romance, you will be the first to know."

He let her out in front of the college and drove off when the vice principal strolled toward her. "Miriam, you have a guest. We thought it best to let her wait for you in the staff room. I have already served her tea, as she seems very anxious."

She? Anxious! Had Anjuli or Faiza come back in an emotional state? As Miriam ripped into the staff room, it wasn't either of her students waiting for her. At first she couldn't make out the woman standing by the window, but from her stature she appeared old, a little bent. The constant wringing of her hands proved she was anxious to be sure.

Then as the woman turned, Miriam released a small gasp. Tikah.

13

Miriam held back her astonishment as she escorted the older woman to her private rooms and to her only decent chair while she straddled the stool from her desk. Tikah had always been in the background of the mission in those early days, but as a child, Miriam had paid little attention to the woman of Baluchistan.

With that huge black shawl enveloping Tikah, the only cheerful thing about her was the tiny mirrors in her saffron-colored skirt, a traditional garment from Baluchistan in the northwest of India. She was about Mother's age, Miriam guessed, trying to visualize the younger woman beneath the heavy folds of Tikah's features. Her light gray eyes were like many of the people from the Northwest Frontier and Afghanistan. She'd been a striking woman, but it seemed as if someone had taken a charcoal drawing of her face and smudged it downward.

"Would you like a cup of tea, Tikah? A glass of water?"

Still, Tikah sat quiet as death. When Miriam was about to jump in with another inane question, Tikah spoke at last, softly in the Urdu language. "You and your brother saw Dassah in Calcutta."

Miriam answered in Urdu. "You were there too, I heard. I want to tell you that I'm glad you were with Dassah all those years." She tried to cajole a smile from the woman, but a smile never came.

Tikah got to her feet and moved to the bureau where several of Miriam's framed photographs were displayed. The older woman reached out a finger to a photograph of Dad and Mum, her, Cam and Eva, but then Tikah's finger curled back as if burnt. "You have such a happy family. Your father, mother, sister, and your brother, the son of…"

There was such loss in her voice Miriam didn't have the heart to gush over the blessing of her family, but then a memory of an old talk with her mother came to mind. "I remember now. You knew Cam and Mum when they first came out to India. Of course this was all before I was even born." She forced a chuckle.

Tikah's eyes glittered like gems, or better still, like the mirrors on her skirt.

"Little Miriam, I am bringing sadness into your home. Forgive me. I should not hold you accountable for the sins of others."

Now this was something Miriam understood from a theological standpoint. "Sins? Whose sins?"

It had to be a full minute later that Tikah spoke softly. "Do you receive letters from Eshana?"

Miriam had to angle her head to catch the words. "Why yes. Eshana writes me a couple of times a year. She's doing marvelous...married...and she's a doctor still at that hospital in Vellore. But that's old news." She rattled this out at a breathless pace in an attempt to bring some light to the unhappy soul before her.

Tikah cleared her throat. "If only Eshana could have returned to visit the mission in Amritsar more than that one time."

"But I know for a fact Eshana wrote to the mission once a week. Still does." Then the penny dropped. Miriam sucked in a breath. She took in the quivering line of Tikah's mouth, the restless plucking of her fingers at the fringe of her shawl since they'd started talking about Eshana. "Is that what wounds you? That Eshana never returned to the mission? Or are you hurt that she did not personally write to you?"

Tikah turned back to the photo of Miriam's family. "It is only to be expected that people leave others behind. That is the way of the world. For a while I thought the mission was my home, that they were my people, that I shared their God. But I realized I had never really been a part of your family. Even part of Eshana's inner circle, though she, too, is Indian. Now I am a husk of an old woman." Tikah's magnificent eyes glittered. "All of my heart is wrapped up in my daughter. I would tear a mountain down with my own hands for Dassah."

A breath of cool air touched Miriam's shoulder. "Has something happened to Dassah? Stop beating around the bush, Tikah, please. Is she well?"

"Dassah...is well. You have no need for concern, and I will be leaving you now." Tikah took hold of the doorknob, but her gaze landed again on the photograph. "But I am wondering, Miriam...where is your brother?" She said this in a reserved manner that held a trace of animation.

"My brother?" Miriam's eyes followed the track of Tikah's gaze to the photograph. Tikah was not a good actress, though she'd tried to make it look as though her question was on the spur of the moment. A tingle ran down Miriam's arms. "Cam? Why, Cam is on holiday. Fishing I think, up in Kashmir. Why—?"

"No doubt he is renting a houseboat on Dal Lake like you used to do as a family?"

"Yes." She squinted at Tikah. "My, you do recall a lot about us."

"When one is poor, one takes an avid interest in the rich around them."

"Oh, we weren't rich. Dad was just a military man."

"Compared to us, you were rich, little one. We were but orphans and widows. You were our English benefactors." Though her words were soft, the truth in them couldn't help but wound.

Miriam wanted to gather Tikah close, but the woman was hurting too much and clinging to the door as if desperate to escape. "I'm sorry. You are right again. I keep forgetting you're a widow. I'd always had this impression that you never married."

Tikah waved her hand in a dismissive gesture. "The…husband of my heart died many years ago."

"You loved him dearly?"

"I gave him all that was most precious to me."

"Did you ever have a child?" She injected all the softness she could into that hard question. A question she would never normally ask.

Tikah's gaze landed again on the photo of Miriam's family. "No children of that union."

Miriam dropped the obviously painful subject. "You know, Tikah, people like us—Mum and Dad and us kids—we only wanted to help. Though we tend to forget when we spend time helping out in places like the mission that we can go home at the end of the day to our comfortable bungalow. As much as we want to feel part of the family of orphans, we're not really. I think my brother and I felt that keenly."

"Yes, your brother." Tikah's eyes glittered, still on the photograph. "When do you expect him back?"

"He's on a long leave, not due back at his post until the end of October."

"He was a handsome man. Brutal and handsome," Tikah whispered as if to herself.

"Handsome," Miriam blurted, "yes, but brutal? Certainly not. Cam's as soft as a toffee on the inside."

Tikah opened the door and spoke on the wisp of a breath. "Yes, handsome and cruel. Beautiful and brutal, like his father." She turned and left.

With an open mouth, Miriam stood at her door listening to the receding sounds of Tikah's footsteps. The sensation came over her of dark waters from the past swirling with the flotsam of sin—actual sin that caused pain—and not something academic from her lesson plan.

She snapped her mouth shut, closed the door, and slumped into the overstuffed chair. Her head swam with the juxtaposed memories and the strange things Tikah said and left unsaid. The window drew her, and she stood to watch the figure of Tikah racing away from the school. Those chilling words of Tikah's when she spoke of Cam's father… *Beautiful and brutal*.

Tikah disappeared around the far corner, and Miriam crossed her room in two strides and was down the stairs before she could think her objective through. In the foyer, her hand was on the telephone receiver, her fingers in the dial, when she replaced the receiver back on its hook.

She'd been about to ring her mother in Sialkot. But really, what could she say? That something from the past—waters that were thought long gone—threatened to rise?

14

Leaves from chinar and poplar trees—that had been green when they first arrived—had started to turn the color of a golden sunset. Dassah walked along the lake with her husband. Leaves crunched beneath her feet as Cam held her hand. Six weeks of marriage had been filled with the sweetness of kisses, whispers in the night, laughter over board games, and reading to each other in the evenings. On several warm afternoons they swam together in the lake, where he had pulled her beneath the lotus blossoms to kiss her in the blue and green depths.

She was happy, so happy tears caught at the back of her throat. It could not possibly last. So often she found Cam deep in thought, thoughts that he did not share with her.

To lift his apprehension she injected the frivolous tone that always relieved him. "We have been married six weeks, beloved. Should we not celebrate?"

"Funny, I was thinking the same." His brow lifted, though a trace of worry remained in his tone. He tucked her arm in his as he resumed walking along the path.

"I have had the most wonderful time here on the lake, but soon your leave will end." She hesitated. "Would you not take me into the city? I only had that brief look on the night we came. It is like Venice—"

"Darling little Dassah." He seemed to work hard to produce his smile. "I've already arranged with Kavita and Asheesh. We're going to have the most marvelous dinner tonight, and I've bought you a present."

She had no doubt the food would be mouthwatering, and he brought her gifts from town almost daily—flowers, satin heart-shaped boxes of bonbons, ornaments for her hair. But she did not want gifts. She wanted to stroll along the street with him. She wanted to do her own shopping and cook their meals. She wanted to clean and tidy their home.

Close to the bank, the leaves of another tree flamed red the color of the sari she had dreamed of for her wedding. A breeze snatched the leaf, breaking its tenuous hold so that it landed as a splash of crimson on the lake. Eventually, all the leaves would be parted from the tree to stand cold and alone. Cold from the snows when they filled this Vale of Kashmir, and this single scarlet leaf would be forgotten.

"Dassah." Her husband cupped her chin. "You look positively heart-broken."

"It is only the autumn that steals a moment of my joy. Coming from the hot plains, I am not used to the trees losing their leaves in such splendor. Their time of glory...so short."

"It's only leaves, *janu*, there'll be more in the spring." He held her tighter. "Are you sure that's all? You've gone quite pale."

Her shivering was real, but it was not simply the coolness that she was unused to. She glanced up at the canopy of fire above them. Fire the color of their passion. But fire burned quickly, and burned out. She wound her arms around his neck, seeking his lips with hers. "How long will you love me, *janu*?"

He kissed her slowly, cradling her face in his palms. Much later he lifted his mouth from hers. "Darling, we're married. Surely you know how desperately I love you."

To hide her tears that threatened to escape, she flung herself into his arms and spoke over his shoulder. "No woman could ever exult in the love of her husband more than I. And I, too, love you with the same desperation."

He ran his hand down the length of her spine, molding her shape to his. "Then this little depression is gone?"

She nodded.

"Shall we go back to the houseboat?" he whispered into the crevice of her neck. In spite of her secret sorrow, his lips trailing her collarbone made her yearn for the privacy of their bedroom. "We'll dance," he murmured against her throat. "You're becoming quite the seductress as a dancer, Dassah. As good as Ginger Rogers."

"But you are no Fred Astaire. You stepped on my toe last night."

His voice reached a deeper level, as it always did when he grew amorous. "Never mind Fred Astaire. Later, after dancing, will you let me show you how much I adore you?"

She squeezed her eyes shut, glorying in their love. But what would happen when the fire in their marriage dimmed as it did with all marriages? Would enjoying the same literature be enough? Would they be happy spending time together walking or playing games?

By the time he released her, the need to cry left her enough so that she turned with him back to the houseboat, drawing a shawl around her shoulders against the afternoon chill.

Kavita and Asheesh greeted them from the boat, and she and Cam walked up the gangplank to the table on deck, set with white linen tablecloth, crystal goblets, English china, and the finest of Kashmiri cuisine.

Cam smiled over the table as he poured the fruit juice she preferred and filled his tumbler with whiskey. After dessert, he wound up the old-fashioned gramophone and put on one of the records as Kavita and Asheesh disappeared with their usual tact. American Big Band music floated over the lake as leaves floated off the trees, and Cam pulled her into his arms. In her sari, she danced as well as any Englishwoman. In her conversations each day she entertained him as well as any Englishwoman. But why she must compare herself to an English *memsahib*, she did not know. Cam never did the comparing. Only she did.

He swung her around to the swirl of a clarinet as the disk played a famous Cole Porter tune, "Begin the Beguine." The bolero rhythm set her blood to thrumming, and she knew it did the same for Cam. As the music ended, he laid his cheek next to hers. Passion filled her at the same time sadness crept close. Cam set her from him and downed his most recent glass of whiskey, but in a moment he would lift and carry her to the privacy of their room.

A sliver of moon barely lit the peaks around them, and a cold breeze rustled a few leaves littering the deck. After the exertions of their dance, the breeze felt especially chilly, tempering her desire for physical love. "Cam, you have not said when we must leave the houseboat?"

He took her in his arms as if she had not spoken, tilting his head to kiss her.

"Beloved." She pulled back but kept her arms around his neck. "Where are you planning on taking me when it grows cold?"

He drew back as well. "Darling, did you ever think of picking your moments with a little more...shall we say...sophistication?"

At first he did not seem to notice that she went quiet, but a long moment later his hands at her waist went equally still. "Blast! It's me who's gone and ruined the moment." He stood back and let his hand drop to his thigh. "I'm sorry, darling, that was a stupid thing for me to say." He strode from her and poured himself another drink from the crystal decanter.

She would save her questions of where they would live for later. "Cam, why must you drink so much?"

He drained his glass, then grimaced at its emptiness. "I've been wondering when the day would come when you'd ask me that."

"Why, beloved? What is the reason you drown yourself?"

He took so long to answer. When he did, he directed his words at the deck. "I honestly don't know. Memories...maybe. One can always make war the excuse. It was vile enough. Then...old friends that one loses in war." Swallowing deeply, he looked at her. "The night we got married I told you that I would most likely hurt you." Pain laced his smile. "Has it started so soon? Have I tarnished this lovely thing between us already?"

"No, my beloved." She lunged forward to wind her arms around his neck. "You must never think that. As you said, nothing can separate us."

For a long moment, he kept his arms stiff at his sides. She reached up to cradle his face, lifting on tiptoe to press her lips against his brow, as if by pressing her lips against the lines of his unspoken anxiety she could hold back her own fear that at any moment the world would steal their happiness. Heartbeats passed, and he groaned. He did not kiss her in return, but folded her so tightly in his arms that it hurt. But she rejoiced in the pain as he sank his head to her shoulder.

She did not know how long they stood like that. At last he released her and held her at arm's length. Darkness leeched the blueness from his eyes.

"Beloved…." She placed his hands, palm to palm, within hers, and held them close to her heart. As if he were a small boy she was teaching to pray. "Beloved, when we were young we went to church together. Not once as man and wife, except at our wedding, have we prayed—"

"Don't ask me to pray with you, Dassah. I can't."

"It is all right, *janu*. But know this—I will start to pray to Yeshu again, like I used to as a girl. I will pray for you every day, my husband, that you will find the joy that we used to share as innocent children. There is much I do not remember of my early Christian faith, but recently I have been remembering that God cares when the smallest sparrow falls from a tree. And you and I are much more treasured than even these precious birds to Yeshu."

She took him by the hand. "But for now, my love, come," she coaxed. "Never mind about passion tonight. Let us show our love in a different way."

He slanted a grin. "Tired of making love already, are you? Banishing me to the cold?"

"Don't be a fool." With a smile, she softened the play slap she gave his arm. "Let us simply spend time together doing something we both enjoy—a game perhaps. Cribbage?"

"Well I suppose that's more romantic that checkers?"

Her spurt of laughter escaped. "Then we shall cross a game of checkers off tonight's agenda." Though she had lain in his arms as his wife, she felt suddenly shy. "We could read together."

His gaze held a puzzled relief. "Do you know, I am in the mood to read. Want to finish another few scenes of *Romeo and Juliet*?"

She led him to the lounger and curled up beside him, dragging one of the shawls she had borrowed from Kavita to cover them. "Perhaps later we will read more of Shakespeare, but will you read to me something I have wanted since the night we came here?" She placed into his hands the children's story, *The Wind in the Willows*.

His laughter bubbled. "If you insist."

At first he remained only slightly amused, humoring her, as they took turns reading the antics of Badger, Ratty, Mole, and Mr. Toad. But as the mountains surrounding the lake turned to gold and twilight faded, his interest in the tale increased.

From time to time he got up to make saffron tea for her in their tiny pantry inside the houseboat, and she brought the decanter of whiskey to him, even pouring him a glass when they eventually started on the next few scenes of *Romeo and Juliet*. Her heart sang as like two children they read to each other…though he had still not mentioned where they were to live when his leave finished.

The next day, Dassah stood on the deck overlooking the lake, her eye on an approaching houseboat. During the night the temperature had dropped so that November felt so close. Her fingers plaited her hair, her breath catching at the memory of last night after they'd finally grown tired of reading. Cam's hands entwined in her tresses as they shared the secrets of marriage.

But not during the day.

She tightened the plaiting of her hair. Its length was far too cumbersome, especially when she bundled up in warm clothing. And it was so much colder today than yesterday. Her eyes sought the expanse of the lake. Where was he?

Earlier, Cam and Asheesh took the *shikara* into Srinagar, and now it was afternoon. She stamped her cold feet on the wooden deck. It seemed more of the chinar and poplar trees along the lake had turned gold and red overnight. According to Kavita, they would see snow on the peaks any day, and Dassah pulled the long woolen garment, a *phiran* that Kavita had loaned her, closer around her. Traditional to Kashmiri people, this soft woolen, knee-length *phiran* was embroidered in a swirl of butterflies. Still, while the garment helped, it did not entirely keep the damp breeze away. Why, at night it was almost down to freezing, and during the day only sixty-five.

She stamped her feet again and watched the approaching houseboat draw closer. Living on the plains of India all her life, and the last ten years in steaming Calcutta, these Kashmiri temperatures were unbearable.

Kavita joined her on the main boat and began to straighten the deck. To keep herself from boredom, Dassah plumped a cushion when the puttering sound of the other houseboat's engine broke the peace of the lake. Still a distance from their craft, Dassah could make out the notes of an English tune. She fully expected the boat to take up mooring further on, but it puttered closer and closer, dwarfing her and Cam's smaller vessel. This houseboat must have at least three or four bedrooms, and a large dining room and parlor.

On that deck, several Englishwomen and two or three men chatted, partaking of drinks. One couple danced. The tranquility of this isolated spot disappeared with the intrusion. To add to her annoyance, none of the intruders seemed to feel the cold like she did. The ladies wore sweaters only over their frocks, and the men light blazers.

It would be best to pay them no mind, but apparently this was not to be. The other boat prepared to moor. As Dassah took the broom to sweep leaves from the deck, a woman called out from the other vessel. "Hello there, we're looking for Cam Fraser. Is he about?"

Dassah swung around to face the young woman with dark hair that feathered around her face. Her pretty white cotton dress with poppy red caps to her sleeves and pockets on the skirt was the epitome of sophistication. What Europeans called *chic*. The fact that Dassah was bundled in a shapeless shawl did nothing to endear the English girl to her. Instead, the serpent of jealousy coiled around her heart.

"I say," the other girl said. "Cat got your tongue? Look here, do you speak the King's English or not?" She shouted, "I'm looking for Captain Cam Fraser," as if being deaf was synonymous with lack of understanding.

"He is not here at present," Dassah annunciated quietly in perfect English the way Cam's mother had taught her.

"When do you expect him back, then?" The other girl's eyes were green like a cat's. Or a snake's.

"I expect Captain Fraser to return shortly." A tiny spurt of perverseness held her back from saying, "My husband." She would take such pleasure in watching this woman's face when Cam did come home and introduce Dassah as his wife.

Not in the least dismayed, the girl called out to the others dancing the American jitterbug on deck. "He's not in at present, darlings. We'll start celebrating without him."

"All right, Phoebe," one of the men answered. "This spot's as good as any to wait for your tardy fiancé."

Dassah stood rigid. *Fiancé?* Had Cam once been engaged to this girl, and the other girl had failed to let her friends know the engagement had ended? Dassah sank to the lounger. Why had Cam never mentioned he had been engaged before? But then there was so much that Cam did not tell her.

The music from the other boat bounced off the surface of the water to disturb the leaves on the trees. They loosened and fluttered to the surface of the lake, drifting away from her.

In the distance coming across the lake, Asheesh and Cam in the *shikara* parted the mist. At last he was coming. From where he sat in the narrow gondola, he couldn't miss the larger boat, and she could not wait for him to arrive to set these intruders right. But it would be best if she was dressed appropriately and not in Kavita's castoffs when he made the announcement that she was his wife.

Inside the houseboat, she discarded the Kashmiri wool and stood shivering in the bedroom wearing only thin muslin undergarments and a chemise. Should she wear the English dress that Cam had bought for her? She would fit into Cam's world quicker if she wore it, but in her Indian garb she felt more confident. She was still trying to decide when she heard the bump of the *shikara* pulling up to the houseboat.

Moments later, Cam stood in the bedroom doorway. "You'll catch pneumonia in those flimsy things, as much as I enjoy seeing you in nothing but."

"What should I wear to meet your friends?"

"Have you introduced yourself yet?"

"I thought it best to wait for you to introduce me, *janu.*"

"So you haven't talked with them at any length?"

"A little."

He came toward her, put his hands at her waist, and rested his lips against her brow. The smoky odor of whiskey fanned her face. "Did they say anything to hurt your feelings?"

"Only the usual way that *sahibs* and *memsahibs* speak to one such as me. As if I were a piece of furniture."

His shoulders went rigid. "Oh they did, did they? Well, the sooner I get them to move on the better."

His admission erased much of her fears, and she wound her arms around his neck. Her lips trailed the roughness of his chin and then his mouth again. His responding kiss almost obliterated the uneasiness that had settled on her since the other houseboat arrived. "What do you wish me to wear to meet your friends, *janu*?"

His kissing stopped with an abruptness that left her cold. With a light touch of his lips to her forehead as if she were six, he shut the closet door. "No need to worry about that."

"But will it not offend your friends if we do not visit?"

He stooped to the bed, and, taking the soft woolen Kashmiri garment, he lifted it over her head and bundled her in it. "You feel the cold, Dassah. Better for you to stay here in our little love nest by the charcoal brazier."

"And you do not feel the cold?"

"What cold?" Smiling, he reached for one of the shawls she'd discarded and placed that around her too. After tying the ends of the shawl in a knot at her chest, he tweaked her nose. "After spending my school years in England, this is nothing more than a crisp fall day. Quite warm actually. I might even take a swim later."

She shoved him playfully in the chest. "Swimming indeed. It is freezing."

The sound of his chuckle turned her insides to warm pudding. "I assure you it is not. You can't even see your breath on the air. It's only your hot Indian blood that can't take a bit of a chill."

Standing before him wrapped in bulky clothes, she was sure she resembled one of the black bears they had seen prowling the woods. With difficulty, she put her arms up to draw him into her embrace. "If you do not wish to visit your friends, then…there is another way you can warm me."

His eyes narrowed with a twinkling smile. "You saucy little thing. In the middle of the day. I'm shocked!"

"You are not shocked. Only two days ago—"

"I tell you I am shocked, appalled, quite taken aback. Being propositioned in the middle of the afternoon, by an alluring minx intent on the ruination of my schoolboy innocence, is scandalous to say the least." He smacked her on the backside, which she hardly felt through the layers of clothing.

Together they landed in a heap on the bed, and he proceeded to kiss her soundly. She kissed him with more passion than she felt at the moment. If she could keep him here by the allure of her body… But far too soon he untangled himself from her arms and stood by the side of the bed, his head brushing the low ceiling. He straightened his tie and slipped into a tan wool sports jacket with tweed patches at the elbows.

She leaned up on one elbow. "Must you go?"

"As you say, *janu*, it would offend them if I don't at least drop in for an hour. Leave it with me and they'll be gone by tomorrow."

"Why can I not accompany you?"

He leaned down to kiss the tip of her nose. "My darling Dassah, I've thought long and hard, when is the best time to announce our marriage and to whom. Those people out there are not those whom I wish to honor with that first announcement. You're too precious—like those blighted sparrows you're always talking about—too precious to expose to those particular people. They won't understand. I don't care in the slightest what they think of me, but to have them disparage you..."

"I see." She shifted to a sitting position. "Perhaps if we tell your parents soon we will not have this problem in the future. Once they see that your parents accept me as their daughter-in-law. Oh please, beloved, when may I write and tell Tikah?"

"Tikah?"

"Yes, Tikah. She has been like a mother to me."

He turned from her, his hand on the door. "Can we not simply savor the time to ourselves for a while longer?"

"But your leave finishes in days. Surely marriages are something to shout from the rooftops." Her voice came out small, though her pulse pounded in her ears. "You are ashamed of me, Cam. It is because I am Indian." She bit down on her lip to hold back tears.

He whirled to her, dropping to his knees at her feet where she sat on their bed. "My darling wife, never, never think that. I am not ashamed of you. I'm proud of your heritage. But there are many fools in the world, and I don't want them hurting you." Taking her hand, he kissed her palm and closed her fingers around the place where his lips had been. His eyes, blue as the sky, pierced her heart. "I would die for you, *janu*. Trust me, please."

She ran her hand around the side of his head, feeling the crispness of his hair against her fingertips. "All right, I will accept what you say about these friends of yours."

"They're not friends. Just people I know."

"One of them said..." Her voice trailed off as she looked out the window, their beautiful view of the lake hidden by the other houseboat. "One of them—a man—said to a girl, Phoebe, that you were her fiancé." Unable to look at him, she kept her gaze fastened on the other craft.

Little waves blown up by a breeze slapped against their boat. He cupped her chin in his fingers. "*Janu*, I swear, you are the only woman I have ever asked to be my wife."

"But was their some unspoken communication, something to give this Phoebe the wrong impression?"

The softness in his voice disappeared as he got to his feet and towered over her. "Blast Phoebe! Blast them all." He ran his hand around the back of his neck. "Dassah, I'm only going to say this one more time. You are the only woman I have ever asked to be my wife. And I am making preparations for where you will live. In fact, that's what I've been doing in town all day. Telegraphs back and forth, but I've finally got it sorted."

"You have! Where?" Her heart lifted, a kite taken up with the wind.

His brows pulled together. "Blast it all again! This is not the way I wanted to share this news." He played with the silk of her green sari that sat folded on the bureau. "I've been thinking of renting a little house for you, darling. In Delhi. Where I can visit you daily."

"Visit me?" She felt the need to be sick. "Will I not live with you?"

"The flat I share with the other officers won't work, *janu*. But we'll talk about that when I get back. I'll tell Kavita to make you something to eat, and I want you to stay here where it's warm. I'll be back soon, I promise." He kissed her on the forehead with that same abruptness as earlier.

Moments later, his footsteps rocked the houseboat as he strode down the gangplank. She heard him call out to the other boat, and his voice grew muffled as he joined the group of people on that vessel. But she would no longer stand for this. The slight wave of nausea disappeared, and she jumped to her feet to run out to the deck where she would be visible to the other boat.

Music on the other craft drowned out the conversation of the occupants, so she could no longer pick out Cam's voice. Just as her view of the lake had disappeared from the bedroom she had shared with her husband, so too did the peaceful sounds of croaking frogs and twittering bulbuls. Clenching her fists, she slumped to the lounger where they had sat together last night. She would remain here so that Cam could see her if he happened to glance her way. She was his wife. She would not be hidden away like some woman in purdah.

Twilight ended. A crescent moon rose over the mountains. Was it only last night she and her husband had read books together in each other's arms? From the moment he slipped the ring on her finger six weeks ago, she had not spent an entire evening alone. Now, all night, music blared from the other boat. Lights blazed. Somewhere around four in the morning Dassah left the deck, and inside the houseboat she climbed into their bed to pull the covers over her head.

She had been correct. As the leaves drifted away on the surface of the lake, so too had her honeymoon drifted away. It was over. And was a wife truly a wife, if no one else knew?

15

Heavy mist concealed the lake by six the next morning. Cam had not returned from the other houseboat. Dassah paced the deck of their small craft while Kavita prepared her a cup of hot saffron tea and offered her *Kander Czout*, the Kashmiri bread, for breakfast, but Dassah could not eat. The other craft at last lay silent. Its revelry had finally shut off an hour ago, but its lights still glowed behind the drape of fog.

She could not bear to cross to the other vessel to look for her husband. Her mind conjured up images of him in the arms of that Phoebe and her sophistication. All night long, thoughts of betrayal tormented her. Why should Cam be satisfied with a poor Indian wife? But by eight in the morning she'd had enough of sitting and waiting. Though lacking the courage to march over to the other boat, she at least had the audacity to defy Cam in one other area. She would go into town.

At first Asheesh demurred, but between her and Kavita they convinced him that Dassah should take this little jaunt to Srinagar for shopping. Kavita sat next to Dassah under the canopy as Asheesh paddled the *shikara* across to the busy shore. Sunlight strained to penetrate the mist until a breeze pulled apart the heavy veil of fog, and the golden trees circling the lake became visible. The air sparkled with sun-drenched moisture so that the morning shimmered like gold.

Kavita pointed out the Maharaja's palace on the far shore, but thoughts of the Hindu ruler of Kashmir meant nothing to Dassah. Kingfishers darted, and herons either stood on spindly legs in the shallows or lifted on wide wings to swoop over the lake. The closer they came to the city, more and more of the small wooden gondola-like boats glided out, filled to the brim with wares for sale, creating a floating market. Carved wooden knickknacks, Kashmiri shawls, paper-mâché boxes. Other *shikaras* drifted with vegetables—radishes, lettuce, potatoes. Or gardens of flowers, roses, lilies, and pansies.

Asheesh paddled the small craft under one of Kashmir's many stone bridges and moored at a spot to allow Dassah to disembark. They waved good-bye, saying they would return for her in an hour.

Dassah had no idea where to go in the sprawling city of boulevards and gardens. Though it was autumn, flowers still tumbled from wooden balconies with their highly decorated fretwork and steeply peaked roofs. As she strolled through the streets, she stopped at each church to speak to the minister. She had been so overcome with joy at her wedding that she had not really heard the reverend's name. Nor could she remember the name of the church that Cam gave her. Or had Cam even mentioned which church? She wasn't sure if she wanted to speak with this minister for comfort…or for the other question that lay unformed in the pit of her stomach.

She went as far as the edge of the city and found a small native church with a thatched roof. Its wooden sign had fallen to the ground, KASHMIRI VALE GOSPEL CHAPEL, half covered by creepers. Peeking through the open door, she saw a Kashmiri man leading a prayer meeting. The minister of this church was clearly not the man who had married her and Cam. One more church to strike off her list, and she headed back for the shore.

At the edge of the lake, Asheesh and Kavita stood by their *shikara*, but instead of Asheesh waiting to assist her into the small wooden boat, he hurried toward her. "At the place where I take tea with my friends, it has been said that there is a woman looking for you, by the name of Tikah."

She placed a hand to her chest. "Tikah."

"This woman is known to you?"

"She is my *amma*."

Asheesh's brows rose. "This Tikah has left a message that she will wait each day in the Kehawa Teashop from noon." He pointed. "Close to the water…down there."

She looked at the rickety place of unpainted boards and a narrow dock that jutted out onto the lake. Numerous Kashmiri people sat within or outside on their *shikaras* smoking and drinking tea. "Will you wait for me, Asheesh?"

He glanced back at his boat. "It will be better if I return my wife to the houseboat so that she may start cooking the mid-day meal. Will three hours be enough?"

"I will be here then." She hurried from him, along the shoreline cluttered with *shikaras* jutting here and there at all angles. Rubbish floated in the water, and a faint odor soured the air, but it disappeared when she reached the teashop. The fragrances of cinnamon, almonds, and saffron cleansed her senses. At the back of the shop, the owner stood at a rough-hewn table and made tea in a samovar, but before she had a chance to search the shop, a voice cried out, "Dassah!"

The next moment, Tikah rushed to her from a corner table and held her.

The misery of last night's loneliness, the uncertainty, the hurt that she could not live in the same house as her husband, the joy in the loving embrace of Tikah, released all at once like the sudden summer monsoons.

Tikah hurried her outside to a private place beneath a willow. They sat on a dry patch of grass. "Hush, my little one," Tikah murmured in Urdu as she wiped Dassah's tears with the corner of her shawl. "I am here now, my beloved light of my eyes, do not cry so."

Wrapping her arms around herself, Dassah brought her weeping to an end. She had always been able to control her despair, and she would do so now. Though her face stung with drying salt, her gaze took in the comforting image of Tikah, the saffron skirt and all its wonderful mirrors that Dassah had found her face in as a child. "*Amma*." She smiled with the title and role that Tikah deserved. "How did you find me?"

"It matters only that I did." Tikah stroked Dassah's cheek and chucked her beneath the chin. "My heart spills over that I found you. I have been searching since you left the house of our employer."

Dassah dropped her gaze. "I should not have left in that way. How are the children? Was Mr. Malik angry?"

"I left the house soon after you did, comfort of my heart, to look for you. Of course the children are well. And, yes, Mr. Malik was very angry. Your sneaking off in such a manner caused everyone to think there was some reason for shame. Only I knew better."

"But I did sneak off."

"Yes, though I knew that you were tricked. It is not your fault that you were tempted to give away your virtue. You are not the first girl of India to be deceived by an Englishman."

Her happiness had bubbled over to see Tikah again, but now she shook her head. "*Amma*, Cam did not deceive me. I went with him willingly."

Tikah made a face as she glanced away, the skin of her neck going red and blotched with white. "I understand how you willingly gave your body to him. When you are under the sway of a man it is hard to refuse, but he will cast you away." Tikah's last words took on a shrill note.

"That is not so, *Amma*. Cam and I are married. He has not...cast me away." Or had he? She was a fool not to have stormed over to the other boat and demanded an explanation like a proper wife. Her lack of uncertainty grew like a lump of yeast in her stomach.

"Comfort of my heart, what makes you believe you are truly married in the eyes of the authorities? Were you married in an English church?" A sliver of hope shone from Tikah's eyes. She repeated her question with urgency. "Were you married in an English church like a proper wife?"

Dassah's throat closed. The sensation of the gently rocking houseboat came over her as if she were still standing on its deck in her green sari. At her inability to speak, the hope faded from Tikah's eyes.

"So you were not married in a church. An English court then? A justice of the peace?"

It was hard to project the words, "On a houseboat." Then the memory of the minister's clothes came to mind. The shabbiness. The worn and patched suit. She had never before seen a Christian reverend riding from parish to parish on a horse, but then she had lived most of her life in large Indian cities.

"Were any proper papers signed?" The defeat in Tikah's voice added to her own that was growing moment by moment.

"Papers?" Her voice cracked. "Yes, I signed a book, but I do not know what kind of book."

"Were other marriages listed in this book?"

"It was…a fresh page." She shook her head. What Tikah implied couldn't be. But the image of Cam's face as he put the ring on her finger, his declarations of love, his asking her to trust him, echoed in her heart. "I am married, *Amma*. I know I am. The minister has his church here in Srinagar. That church must be close by."

Tikah gave her a smile, heavy with sadness as she stood with difficulty, her knees stiff from sitting on the ground. "I will search the city with you, every church, every building, my beloved child, until we find this man."

Dassah had no money for drink or food. Tikah had little, but they could hardly afford a rickshaw. They went first to the agency where Cam rented the houseboat, and she learned the names of all the churches in the city. Dassah had already been to several, so that it took only the afternoon to visit the rest. How strange that she had begun her tour of the town with this search. What other premonitions of hers were true? Still, Cam's declarations beat in her mind with every step she took. He had asked her to trust him.

But other declarations followed, what he'd said on their wedding night. *When the time comes, and I've hurt you by something I've done…or not done… If I cannot share the same place with you for a time… If I ever have to go away. I am still yours and you are mine.* Was it possible he always meant to keep her as his mistress only? His wife in body only? Keeping her in a house apart from him, like so many men kept their harlots until they left India to return to England?

Her head ached with thoughts that would not give her rest. *I will not believe he could do such a thing.*

Three hours passed like a blur. Churches, streets, boulevards, parsonages, pastors, reverends, priests, who all smiled kindly but were not the man who came to the houseboat that night. It was already past the time that Asheesh said he would return to the shore to take her across the lake. Would Cam still be on the other boat? Though Tikah never complained, her *amma*'s face was gray with weariness.

"I cannot find the minister, *Amma*."

"No, my child, you will not find him." Tikah wobbled on sore feet to slump on a bench outside the last church. With a heavy breath she patted the bench for Dassah to join her. "It is time I told you all."

Amma's steady gaze and words held the ring of truth. Dassah did as she asked, as if a heavy metal door were about to swing closed. For a while, they watched the last of the afternoon sun dance on the lake. Soon, the sun would dip behind the mountains, the peaks would blaze in golden glory, a glory she could no longer view with joy.

Tikah's voice began low. "I was born a Muslim, and though for a while I considered myself a Christian while I lived in the mission, I sometimes dwell on the Hindu belief of reincarnation. I fear Cam Fraser is the image of his father—"

"Like his father! No, *Amma*, I refuse to believe in reincarnation, but how do you know these things about Cam's lineage?"

"I know this because his father, Lieutenant Nicholas Fraser, took me from my mother and my father's tent when I was a girl of fifteen. I swooned like you did for a man."

She hid her wince from Tikah.

"My beloved child, how could I not swoon? He, a British cavalry *sahib* on his charger, his sword at his thigh, said he wanted me for his wife. This is why I do not think ill of you. I know the trickery of a man."

Her mother glanced away, as if looking down the long corridor of the past. "We went that very night to a writer of letters in the bazaar. Nicholas signed his name on a paper as I did. For many years I acted as his wife. Then one day, after The Great War ended, a woman and a small boy came to the bungalow where I lived with…my husband. That woman was Abby Fraser, and her son, Cam, the son of my husband." Her voice broke like the tinkling of glass. "The piece of paper I cherished was nothing more than a trick. In the eyes of my people I was a harlot. I was a woman without a home, without a husband, without even a child of my own."

Sitting in the shelter of the church with the setting sun before them, Dassah went cold. Tikah took her hand. "Dassah, light of my eyes—" Her voice dropped. "—he looks so much like his father. Dark, crisp hair that curls when it is over-long. Eyes the color of the sky."

Dassah shook her head. Cam was not his father. He was like Major Geoff, his stepfather. "What happened to this Nicholas Fraser?"

"He died." At that Tikah leaned back, weary of the story.

When she had first seen Tikah at noon today, Dassah had wept bitter tears. Now with all that Tikah said, she should be weeping more bitterly. *Amma* would have no cause to make up such a tale. "What will I do, *Amma*?" she whispered.

"Leave him. It is kindest to him as well. Do not forget, I have known Cam since he was three. I always thought that he wished to be Indian, that the ways of the British Raj embarrassed him. A boy of great kindness, but he is British. He must get on with his true life, find joy in the arms of a British wife, because they say in a few years all of the English will leave India."

At Tikah's words, she stood. No tears, only the coldness that went deep into her marrow. Cam must have returned to their houseboat by now. Had he despaired over his foolishness when he found her gone? Did he wring his hands and pace the deck? Perhaps he had come with Asheesh in the *shikara* and searched the shore? She suspected this of him. He was kind as Tikah said. And tonight when she did not return, would he beat his breast? Would he weep bitter tears?

Reaching down to help Tikah up, she said, "Come, *Amma*, it is time we found a new home. From now on, wherever I am, you will be also. Never again will I be parted from you."

As soon as Asheesh had returned to the houseboat after lunch, Cam, in a shaking voice, ordered him to turn around and take him into Srinagar. For hours the two of them searched the sprawling city. In the fading sunlight, the stone in his chest growing heavier all the time, Cam beat the shoreline for Dassah. Not only did Cam inwardly curse the diminishing light, he cursed himself. The word *fool* wasn't a harsh enough slur. At least a fool might be forgiven, because most fools had no idea they were foolish. But he had known. *Dear God Almighty, he had known.*

In all good intentions he'd planned on staying only an hour on the boat with Phoebe, Frank, Carly, and the others last night. But like a dog returns to its vomit, he'd spent the night drinking, smiling like an idiot when someone opened another bottle, and another.

Phoebe had been of no interest to him. Though she'd tried, one thinly veiled insult from him and she'd left him alone. No, his mistress was that wretched amber liquid in a bottle. So much a mistress, he'd forgotten his wife sitting alone all evening in the very next houseboat.

He had no idea when he eventually passed out. Birds woke him around ten while the rest of the boat's occupants lay in unconscious states. When he staggered to his own craft and found Dassah gone, even then the fear didn't hammer in his head as it did now. She had to be doing the little ordinary things a wife did. The things he'd stopped her from.

Asheesh called to him now. "Captain-*sahib*, come back to the teashop where that woman was waiting for Dassah."

Cam raked his hair back. They'd already talked to the owner of this teashop hours ago. He'd already heard the man's story, and deduced that Tikah had met up with Dassah. But until this moment, he'd not allowed himself to entertain the thought that tore at his insides. They had to still be in the city. Yet the truth bore down on him as he trudged the path to the ramshackle shop. Dassah did not want to be found.

With little preamble, the owner said that while he and Asheesh had been scouring other parts of the city, the older woman had returned and left a letter addressed to Captain Cameron Fraser on the houseboat operated by Asheesh.

Cam's hands trembled as he held the envelope. He recognized Dassah's perfectly formed script as she'd written his name. His heart in his throat, unable to breathe properly, he slit the envelope open. She'd written a full page, full of kindness, understanding, forgiveness even. But she had left him with the belief that she was not truly married to him, that he had taken her body on a lie. Within the envelope she had returned the gold wedding band.

You must get on with your true life now, janu. Marry in true faith to an Englishwoman.

No physical pain could hurt more. He wished something would hit him.

At last a physical sensation. His throat closed. His chest burned. Somewhere deep inside a black loneliness grew like a cancer as he staggered out of the teashop and walked to the end of the dock to overlook the lake that defined his honeymoon.

With one last flash from the setting sun, gently veiling the valley in a gauze of gold, the sky turned a verdant shade of grass green. A crescent-shaped moon hung on the horizon as it emerged over the mountain peaks. One bright star penetrated the dusky end of twilight.

And Cam cursed himself. She was gone.

Part Two

16

Two months later—December 1946
Amritsar, Northern India

The rails leading out of the Amritsar station caught the last vestiges of setting sun and quivered in two molten lines of steel. Miriam tapped her foot while fanning herself with her gloves. Her brother was late. He never used to be so tardy. Really, couldn't Cam be on time for once? It was more than frustrating, having the sense that he not only hid things from her...but could he be lying to her as well?

Now twilight haunted, the beginning of the end of a day, heavy with the sense that everything was passing, quickly. And the unasked question thumped in her mind. Why with all her so-called theological education did she not have the gumption to confront her brother? But what did she know of the passions and brutality of life? What could she say that wasn't the mouthings of an academic? And...so what if he liked a drink now and then?

But the usual loud, smelly, gaudy cacophony of Indian train stations pulled her from her worries. Venders of tea, flowers, and food squawked and hollered. Porters piled carts high with baggage. Whistles shrilled and steam shrieked. The shifting mosaic of humanity tugged a smile out of her, and yet, behind this fluid screen of people she kept expecting Dassah to emerge, the way she had back in August on that steaming Calcutta platform. Wearing that pretty green sari, her hair a braid over one shoulder, those glorious almond-shaped eyes smiling.

Miriam's gaze pulled back from staring into blank space when she spied her brother standing on the platform. The base of her stomach went cold. He'd lost more weight. He had to be unwell. "Ah, there you are at last," she sputtered, fearing if she mentioned his weight or pallor, he'd sink into that awful silence of his. "How terribly good of you to remember when my train came in."

"I'm only twenty minutes overdue, but I am sorry." He raked the hair from his brow and leaned forward to kiss her cheek. The tang of peppermints on his breath didn't quite cover up the odor of whiskey. So he'd stopped for a drink or two.

"Twenty minutes late? Try forty-five. I wrote to you how excited I am to rendezvous with the family at the mission. You know I'm dying to see them all again. How are they? Eshana? How's my darling Laine? Is Mother coping? Eva?" Maybe if she bombarded him with their usual nonsense she might elicit a smile from him.

"May I squeeze a word in?" He produced a wan smile and bent to pick up her suitcase. Taking her by the arm, he maneuvered her out of the station. "Mother is far more collected than you, at least when I saw her this morning. She and Eva are at the club in Sialkot decorating the banquet room for the wedding. Dad had the sense to disappear with his mount. Steeple jumping over a few canals might work the kinks out of him. I'm not sure he's thrilled about giving his youngest daughter away."

She meant to keep their conversation light, but couldn't resist observing, "At least Dad didn't remain working in Delhi until the last minute like you. I wondered if you were coming at all."

"As father of the bride, Dad is man enough to take all that female chatter on the chin. As for me, I wish Eva would keep in mind what her favorite Jane Austen had to say in that blasted *Pride and Prejudice* she's always quoting."

She laughed and they quoted in unison, "No lace, Mrs. Bennett, no lace!"

"As bad as all that?" She grinned, enjoying this repartee like the old days.

"Atrocious! I swear, Miriam, if I hear one more word about veils or the train of Eva's gown, I may do something desperate."

"Murder?" she quipped.

"If I did snap to that extent I'm sure I'd be exonerated by my peers. No, I'm more likely to commandeer Dad's mount and take off for the hills until the blasted wedding is over."

"Will you stop blasting things?" She squeezed his arm that was tucked through hers. "You can escape our sister's nuptials only if you commandeer a horse for me too. You shouldn't assume that women are exempt from dreading weddings. I, too, am in complete agreement with Mr. Bennett. Please, no more talk of lace, satin, chiffon, and especially no mention of frilly undies. Count yourself lucky—as her brother, Eva has mercifully excluded you from the more excruciatingly intimate details." She chuckled but glanced up at him when he failed to reciprocate.

In fact he'd gone quite pale. He stopped beside a car to place her suitcase in the backseat, tossing a coin to the young man he'd hired to guard it.

"Good gracious, Cam, it's a Rolls-Royce."

"A 1924 Silver Ghost, to be precise," he added dryly. "Dad borrowed it from one of his chums on the viceroy staff. How else would you expect me to transport three—or is it four of us—from Amritsar to Sialkot?"

She had to look this glorious car over before getting in and walked around it, running a finger along the vehicle's smooth bonnet. "Dear Dad, such an old softy, bringing the family to his daughter's wedding in style. He's doing her nuptials up proud." Her besotted sighs increased as she investigated the rest of the Rolls. "Not shabby at all, Cam. Not shabby at all." Until his silence pulled her up from studying the storage boxes on the running boards. The thinness of his face tore at her heart. This was the last straw. No longer was she going to pretend all was well. "What is it, Cam? Please tell me."

"We should get going," he clipped as he swung the car door open and got in the driver's seat.

There was nothing for it but to get in next to him. She held her tongue while he drove out of the red-bricked train station. In moments, the lengthy Rolls purred through the rabbit warren streets of Amritsar.

"I haven't seen any of the others yet," he said as they passed the Hindu Temple, obviously with no intention of answering her question. "I arrived in Sialkot last night by train and brought the car down today at Dad's instructions, going straight to the station to pick you up."

"I see." *Dear God, help me ferret the truth out of him.*

Nothing further issued from him. Only his gripping the steering wheel tighter told her the truth.

"You can't hide it from me forever, you know," she added.

He took his time to answer. "I know, Miri. In time…but for now, would you be the dear old thing you always are? Leave me to my thoughts?"

Her heart turned over. "All right, brother dear, I'll not badger you to spill the beans. But if I don't see any lifting of your dark cloud within a reasonable length of time, I will tackle you for answers. Next time, I will not be so easily thrown off the scent."

A smile cracked the tightness around his mouth. "Agreed," he said softly.

"Have you seen or heard of Dassah?" She held her breath.

The car lurched. In an instant, he had the Rolls prowling again at a sedate speed, but his slip-up on the petrol said volumes. "No," he croaked. "Why, have you heard from her?" So there it was—Dassah was the reason for this brokenness, or at least part of it.

"Not a word," she measured out carefully, as if he were a wild buck ready to bolt. "I told you about Tikah's strange visit to me in Lahore back in September?" Pieces were starting to come together, and she reined herself in from jumping on him too soon.

"Yes, you told me."

"But you never laid an eye on Tikah during your holiday in Kashmir?"

"No."

His one-word answer sent a chill across her shoulders. "It's all so terribly odd." She sat back, crossing her arms, wishing her pile of theological tomes held the answers to this kind of human heartache. Thank God she would soon have time to talk with Eshana and Laine. "Tikah seemed awfully worried about Dassah when she visited me."

"So you mentioned in your letter."

She watched him from the corner of her eye. "I told you I also dropped by Arvind Malik's home, and they told me that both Dassah and Tikah had done it again—flown the coop like they did from the mission ten years ago."

His knuckles on the steering wheel whitened. "I dropped by on Arvind as well. He has no clue where they are, or why they disappeared."

"But you know...don't you, Cam?"

His mouth went as tight as a clamshell. Glimpses of the Golden Temple in the openings between other buildings flashed by as Cam turned the massive Rolls into the narrow, cobblestoned Bazar Lakar Mandi. They stopped outside the four-story building, the mission that the elder Miriam had developed over thirty years ago—the Jallianwalla Bagh Mission.

He shut off the engine and faced her. They only had a moment before the household realized they were here. "Yes, I know why Dassah disappeared again."

His hands shook. Her poor brother, but she held back from taking his hand like she wanted to.

"I can't talk about it now, Miri. Please leave it alone. I promise, after the wedding—"

There was no chance for him to finish anyway. The faded turquoise door of the mission burst open, and a river of children poured out. Teenage boys with brash grins jumped into the backseat, girls with shy smiles opened the passenger door for Miriam and took turns hugging her and exclaiming over her frock and hat. Toddlers squealed and jumped up and down on the pavement, eyes bright in the hope of sweets. Scrambling children, dusty from playing in the *bagh* behind the mission, hooted and hollered and ran around the vehicle. The darlings always did get keyed up whenever company arrived. But it had been far too long since she and Cam visited.

Miriam allowed herself to be drawn inside the mission as if on a wave of laughing children, her arms around as many as she could. Laughing over her shoulder back at Cam, she saw him lift one little lad onto his shoulders, and grip another under his other arm like a sack of rice. The rest of the boys clamored around him as if he were India's favorite polo star.

She yelled back at him over the deafening din when they got inside. "Take a sniff, Cam." Then stabbing the air with her finger as she identified each scent, "Garlic, cardamom, mustard oil, and carbolic soap."

"Right you are, clever puss. And roses and lilies." The grin he sent her eased some of her worry.

But the sight of Laine—darling Laine—waiting at the rattan table out on the patio overlooking the *bagh* was her undoing. Whatever Cam was saying behind Miriam flitted away as she burst out to the sunlit patio, the children following like a swarm of noisy parakeets.

From the time she and Cam were children, it had been Eshana for Cam and Laine for her. Of course, they loved and were both loved back by these two dear friends of Mother's, but a special auntie relationship had been feathered for each of them. And right now Laine bolted toward her. "Eshana, Jai!" Laine shrieked with ecstatic joy in Miriam's ear, holding her close. "Oh good show. You're here at last."

Their arms around each other's waist, she and Laine turned to watch Cam make his way to the patio with the children hanging on to him. Whatever was bothering Cam, surely there was no better place to sort it all out than the mission. *Oh thank you, Lord, we're home. Now you can make him happy again. And me... help me to...oh I don't even know...but you know what I need.*

Cam was grateful that Miriam went ahead of him to the patio, before she noticed his brief flutter of joy drain away. Home—the concept snuck up on him as the aromas and fragrances of this house lulled him.

He could never think of this place as home again, though. Not without his wife.

For Miri's sake and the rest of *The Family* as she called them, he forced a smile, and gently pulled one of the new orphan boys down from his shoulders. Many lads he knew from recent years were either hanging about his waist or attempting to wrestle him to the floor, but strolling toward him now was the present administrator, Dr. Victoria Owens. Dr. Vicky, her gray hair done up in a roll, struck him as elderly now.

With Dr. Vicky came the tall Sikh, Eshana's husband, Dr. Jai Kaur, looking as impressive as ever with his royal blue turban and dark, trimmed beard, now sprinkled with white.

Dr. Vicky, kindly and oh so firmly, tut-tutted and clapped her hands. "Boys, let our guest catch his breath. Perhaps later Cam will join you in the *bagh* for a soccer match." Cam nodded, and Dr. Vicky smiled as she extended her hand to him. "Off you go to play, boys, and those of you who have chores, let me remind you that time waits for no man."

A chorus of half-hearted moans rippled through the group, but at a stern bird's eye look from Dr. Vicky and another sweet smile, the children reluctantly disbanded.

Jai grasped Cam's hand and clapped him on the back, while Laine barged toward him and swooped him into a firm hug. A little plumper, white at the temples, but there never had been anything tepid about Laine. He often wondered if Miriam developed her exuberance from Laine, who was no blood relative. Dad had such a quiet humor. Mother, always a gentle lark, whereas his sister and Laine were absolute hoots. For a moment in the company of these warm people, he felt alive again. If only Dassah were here.

Thank goodness Miriam claimed their attention, waving her hands about and telling Dr. Vicky and Jai about her students. He allowed his mind to flow effortlessly along with his sister's voice, when Laine drew him to the side. "I want to catch up with you too, before we leave for Sialkot, but Eshana is waiting for you at the top of the house, in the prayer room."

"Shall I pop up there then?" he asked in low tones.

"Eshana wants a visit with you in private and thinks there won't be a chance once we're at the wedding. We flipped a coin—who'd get you first. Naturally, she won." Laine's impudent smile wrapped up the tender moment with a slice of nonsense.

He kissed her cheek and started to move inside again.

"Cam…" Laine called him back, her wide smile dimming a little. "Eshana's not alone." He questioned her with his gaze, but she waved him on, her eyes going a tad moist. "Never mind. You'll find out soon enough. Now up you go. Your former *ayah* awaits."

Making his way up the four flights of stairs, he found the various floors where the children slept, where he'd often slept tucked between orphans. On the nursery floor, one or two babies wailed but were quickly picked up and cuddled, bringing back memories of Dassah as a toddler. Having first come here with Mother when he was three, he couldn't remember a time when the mission wasn't part of his life. But then came the fragmented memory of someone lifting him from the room below…taking him away from the mission…away from his mother. Of Tikah's dusky face rocking him and singing to him in the back of a car when he was so hot…thirsty…the sensation and image of hot sand and blinding light rushed over him.

He raised a shaking hand to his raging temple. A sudden headache. Every time he came to the mission, a slew of memories either wooed him or assaulted him. He needed a drink, but there was no chance of that anytime soon.

The closer he got to the top of the house, the memories softened, dappled with a gentler light, scented with the perfume of lilies and roses. These memories were no less painful or confusing, for their reminders of Dassah and them playing on the balcony as children. Then of the time he'd come home from England at twenty-one and kissed her there like a degenerate.

In Kashmir, he'd done the right thing at last—taken Dassah as his wife—but he'd drawn a line in the sand that said she was different from him because of the color of her skin. What other interpretation could be put on the reprehensible cover-up of his marriage?

Perhaps it was best she'd run away from him. He didn't deserve her. Alan Callahan agreed with him in that respect. The reverend's blasting tones tolled in his ears still.

He'd gone to see Alan the day after Dassah disappeared in Kashmir. He'd told him his deplorable story, thinking the reverend, knowing everyone in the vicinity, would be able to locate Dassah quickly. The minister, while saddling his horse to start searching, gave Cam a sound verbal thrashing on the vice of drunkenness. Cam had cut him short by grating out, "I'm willing to do anything to get my wife back."

"Quite. You're just not man enough to make your marriage public to your British peers." As Alan swung up into his saddle, he clapped his Panama hat on his head and glared down at Cam. "What's more—are you willing to give up the drink? I tried to warn you. I too used to be a drunk, but we'll talk more of that when I return from putting the word out to my congregations."

Though Alan had done his best—called out the parishioners of all his flocks in the hills to keep their eyes open for Dassah and Tikah—after all these months, no one at all had seen a thing.

Now, months later, Cam reached the top floor of the tall, narrow house. Inside this room he'd find Eshana, his beloved *ayah* from when he'd first arrived in India as a boy. He'd missed Eshana dreadfully when she'd moved away to the south where she'd become a doctor and married Jai. Perhaps talking it over with her, she could help him blot out the pain of losing Dassah. Not that he would tell her the truth. If he couldn't stand to see Miriam's disappointment in him, seeing that in Eshana's eyes would be far worse.

The door opened easily, and he stepped into the sun-filled upper room that used to be the living quarters of the elder, Indian Miriam. Since her death in 1919, the staff of this house had kept the room in her memory. Eshana, his mother, Laine, all those who helped in the past caring for the widows and orphans, and later Dr. Vicky, used this room as a place to pray.

Nothing had changed. The oyster shell coating of the walls captured sunlight, turning them to apricot. Glass doors stood open to catch the warm December breeze. Scattered, colorful wool carpets invited people to sit on the floor or kneel in prayer before a simple reed table and a Bible in Hindustani script.

A wisp of indrawn breath pulled his gaze to the corner of the room where two people sat cross-legged on one of the carpets. His beloved Eshana, a little thinner with graying hair, but still with that gentle smile, rose up from the carpet like a lotus blossom unfolding. She ran to him, her arms outstretched, the end of her blue sari streaming behind her.

"Cam, heart of my heart, my princeling," she whispered as she reached him.

How could one's heart sing and crack at the same time? With his old *ayah* in his arms, his heart did sing. But in looking over her head to the other person in the room, he could almost hear the splinter of another unwanted memory. Shackles on brown wrists and ankles of Indian soldiers after they were arrested for treason against Great Britain.

Zakir sat on the carpet. His stare as sullen as Cam's, and as unforgiving as the harsh Indian sun.

17

Cam sat on the carpet, Zakir across from him, Eshana between them, their mutually safe, no-man's land. His beloved *ayah* had to be aware that he and Zakir avoided each other's gaze, but she cheerfully poured creamy chai from the teapot. Her sandalwood fragrance sweetened the air.

"Here, light of my eyes," she said to Zakir as she passed him a cup. To Cam she said, "And you, comfort of my heart," passing a cup to him. Cam sipped from the spicy, hot brew, flicking a glance at the man who once was his closest friend. Instead of sipping tea, he'd have preferred to take Zakir by the scruff of the neck and thrown him to the ground. Knock him senseless for his act of sedition. But for Eshana's sake, he held his tongue and his fists in check.

His supposed-old-friend narrowed his eyes to study the contents of his cup. The brooding Zakir no longer wore the uniform of the British Army. That had been torn from him after he'd been taken into custody for siding with the Japanese. As if that dishonor had happened to him personally, Cam flinched. By the time Zakir had been arrested by British Military Intelligence, his khaki drill shirt and shorts had been in tatters anyway…the way Cam, as one of the arresting officers, had seen him that day. A shudder ran through him at the memory—Zakir, malnourished, in filthy rags, only his boots holding together, shuffling out of the jungle in manacles.

Bile ran up his throat as he looked away from Zakir and through the window to the skyline of Amritsar. Cam could no longer pretend to drink tea and set it down on the carpet.

What he'd seen when he'd helped to free the POW camps at the end of the war…what the allied soldiers had suffered at the hands of their enemy brought back the remembered reek of suffering. As the mist cleared the morning they liberated the first of several camps, they'd come across a community of bamboo huts filled with skeletons…men so thin. He'd thought at the time, *those soldiers have to be dead.* Then those skeletons had come to life. Tried to stand. Salute.

They stumbled toward their liberators, weeping with joy.

Cam's fingers sank into the deep wool pile of the carpet as he reached for equilibrium, a way out from the living nightmare to flounder back to the present. To think that the Indian soldiers had somehow been treated worse by the Japanese…

A waft of sandalwood cleansed his thoughts as Eshana moved slightly beside him. "Cam, my princeling, are you unwell?"

When Cam opened his eyes, he could have sworn—for half a second—that he saw a ghost of sympathy in Zakir's gaze, as if they shared the same nightmare of the war. That moment dissolved, and Zakir hardened his mouth and looked out over the skyline of Amritsar and directly below to the Jallianwalla Bagh.

Thank the good Lord, Zakir was not wearing the prison garb from the Red Fort that he'd last seen him in several months ago. Today, Zakir was dressed much as he had been as a boy, white *dhoti* down to his ankles, long white shirt. The addition of a Muslim prayer cap on Zakir's head was new though. As boys, they'd worshipped together in the native Christian church a few blocks away. A touch of green tinged Zakir's brown skin, that pasty, telling stamp of one who'd been recently incarcerated. Again, Cam winced. They couldn't go on like this. Eshana, thrusting them together, obviously wanted peace. "I heard in Delhi that you'd been released," he said.

Zakir spat back, "I have been given my freedom, but I am sure it is your wish that I remain behind bars for the rest of my life…to rot."

Eshana gasped. As for himself, he wasn't surprised by Zakir's response, but his nausea increased. Zakir only spouted the truth. He had wanted him to remain in prison.

"The only reason the government released me," Zakir continued, "is because it is expedient for the viceroy to keep India peaceful while they transfer power to us in the next few years. But I am sure, Captain-*sahib*, that you think it foolish for Indians to rule India. Like many of your British Raj, you consider your white skin better than our brown."

"Never!" the word burst from Cam. How could he sit here and make peace if this was the attitude that greeted him? But a warning glance from Eshana held him in place.

The material of her sari rustled as she reached forward. It wasn't Cam's hand she seized in order to comfort, but Zakir's. "Cam would never want you to remain in prison, beloved." She turned her gaze to Cam. The supplication in her eyes kicked him in the belly. There was no way he could do what she silently asked. He had no forgiveness to offer this traitor.

But the stone-like features of Zakir seemed to crack. An emotion, more human than what he'd been extending to Cam, softened his face. "Auntie, why do you concern yourself with what is between me and…the captain-*sahib*?"

Eshana's bangles tinkled as she caressed his cheek. "We are knit together not by flesh and blood but by the Spirit of the Living God. The love of Christ and the love of the founder of this house held us together, no matter our skin, or where we came from. When you were both boys, I washed and fed you within these walls. The children of this house are brothers and sisters."

Zakir's gaze shot to Cam's. "Yes, brothers—and sisters…like Dassah." There was something in his tone. Insinuation? "It is many years since I last saw Dassah. I remember the night she left this mission. The same night the captain-*sahib* came home from England. You would not remember, Auntie, you had long since moved to the south. But I have never forgotten." His gaze grew dark. "Cam visited with us young men, then came up to this room to visit with Dassah. Later, I heard her crying, and the next morning she was gone."

Mesmerized, as if a cobra swayed before him, Cam couldn't look away. Zakir somehow knew of his shame, of his forcing his kiss on Dassah.

Eshana's hesitation lasted far more than a few seconds. Eventually she spoke, softly as always. "Dr. Vicky wrote to me about Dassah leaving this house. But that was ten years ago, Zakir. Why do you bring up that unhappy incident?" Her voice took on new energy. "Unless, you have news of Dassah and of Tikah who went with her that night? Do you?"

Cam's headache pounded. Zakir couldn't know where Dassah was. He'd still been in prison last September. But could she have read of Zakir's release in the newspaper? Sought out refuge with his old enemy?

Not once since Zakir brought up Dassah's name had he removed his gaze from Cam.

"Yes, Zakir, have you seen Dassah?" he added to Eshana's question. Surely the Indian man was seeing through to his soul.

When Zakir finally spoke it was with defeat. "No, Auntie, I have not heard from Dassah in all these years. I had hoped, though, that…someone here… had." He looked away at last. "I loved her, you see. I had hoped to make her my wife, but bided my time too long. Then she vanished with no word." His gaze narrowed back to Cam's. "After you came back to India."

So this was how a bug felt pinned to a paper? Why had he never guessed that Zakir also loved Dassah? Yet she talked of Zakir only as a brother. Still, if he had left Dassah alone that night ten years ago, maybe she would have found comfort in marriage to Zakir and not be someplace now—God only knew where—thinking that Cam had tricked her into giving her body to him only to discard her.

An uneasy silence settled. Eshana, deep in thought, linked and unlinked her fingers. "I had hoped, Cam, that you would know where Dassah was since you seem to be the last of us to see her. Your mother wrote and told me that you were reunited with Dassah for a time in Calcutta, and Miriam wrote that Dassah had moved to Lahore. I had hoped…"

Black dots swam in front of Cam's eyes. A breeze blew through the open balcony doors bringing a sweet coolness. *Dear God, where is she?* He couldn't bear much more of this.

Nor it seemed could Zakir, who scowled and jolted to his feet. "Respected

Auntie, do you not see that it is torture for me to sit here with a British *sahib*, one of the many who lorded it over us for centuries? I turned my back on England during the war, and I feel no shame. I tell you, I feel no shame! This man is my enemy."

Cam's head snapped back as if he'd been given a clout on the jaw.

"Enemy?" Eshana rapped in the tone she used when they were boys and done something dangerous. "Enemy? I will not listen to such words. In these rooms, too many prayers have been cast heavenward on behalf of you both." Rarely did Eshana show anger. She turned her luminous brown eyes on Zakir. "I understand your desire for an independent India. How can I be a daughter of Hind and not hear the complaints of our people? But, perhaps, heart of my heart, you chose the wrong path to reach a worthy goal?

"And you, my princeling." She turned to Cam. "Perhaps you fail to understand what it is for us as Indians. Should you not have compassion on the one who has committed treason? Have you forgotten whose sin nailed our Lord to his cross?" She pointed to Zakir. "His sin nailed Yeshu to that cross." Her arm dropped to her side. "And my sin and yours."

Eshana's rebuke left welts on the raw patch that used to be Cam's self-respect.

Zakir's face contorted from where he stood. Cam's stomach twisted as his gaze dropped to the hands of his former friend. As a boy, Zakir's brown hands used to swing a cricket bat like no other during their matches, but as a man, those brown hands had aimed a gun in treason against the very army that trained him. As if Zakir read his mind, he sent a rancid smile to Cam.

Eshana rose to detain Zakir, but he stalked to the doorway and stood at the top of the stairs. "No, Auntie, though I love you as much as I love the mother of my heart, I cannot and will not repair that which is divided forever." Zakir turned to the stairs, but Eshana's cry stopped him.

She beseeched him with open hands. "If you must go, Zakir, go with my love and my prayers, but think of the mother of your heart, Miriam. Our founder brought you into this house when your mother died." With a shaking hand Eshana pointed outside to the dusty parcel of ground. "Our beloved Miriam was with you that day in *bagh*…when you were only six." Her voice wavered. "The day the soldiers came, Miriam, lost her life in saving yours. What I want you to remember, light of my eyes, is all that she taught you from her knee."

Zakir flinched and bowed over his hands that were palm to palm. "Yes, beloved Auntie. How can I ever forget that day? Or her?"

Tears shone on her cheeks. "I know you remember that day, my son, you remember it very well, but please remember what Miriam taught you." She took his face in her hands. "'For I am persuaded, that neither death, nor life… nor powers, nor things present, nor things to come…shall be able to separate us from the love of God, which is in Christ Jesus our Lord.' Whatever happens to you or to our country, Zakir, hold to this truth."

An island unto himself, Cam watched Eshana and Zakir embrace and Zakir turn away to stumble down the narrow staircase. His beloved *ayah* held a tight fist to her mouth as she supported herself at the banister, until Zakir's footsteps were no longer heard below.

Feeling the intruder, Cam hung his head as Eshana passed by him to stroll to the open glass doors and out to the balcony overlooking the Jallianwalla Bagh.

Cam got to his feet, shaken from the ugly scene. Or was it that he simply needed a whiskey? He walked out to join her. The scent of roses and lilies in the clay urns tormented him with memories of Dassah. As he stood next to Eshana, her sandalwood fragrance soothed his anguish somewhat. Something he once heard about that essence rippled through his mind. *A true Christian is like sandalwood, which imparts its fragrance to the axe which cuts it, without doing any harm in return.*

"Do you see down there, my princeling?"

"What is it you want me to see, Eshana?"

"Many years ago, Gandhi inspired the people of India to begin a trust fund for a monument to be erected."

He looked down at the large parcel of land below. No monument stood there. "For those who lost their lives in the 1919 massacre?"

"You were only three at the time, Cam, but Zakir recalls the day as if it were yesterday. All you boys were playing in the *bagh*. Then the soldiers came. Led in by that foolish English general. Hundreds of innocents were killed that day. The Indian people have much to forgive England for. And now England has cause to forgive India as well. But our history together will not be unraveled. Our combined impact on the world will remain a tapestry of two different types of wool."

Her bangles jingled as she looked up at him. Her sandalwood filled his senses. "In my prayers for you, Cam, I wonder how the traumas from your early childhood have affected you, just as Zakir's affect him."

He went stock still. Mother said something similar in Lahore during their walk in the college gardens. Of course he couldn't recall something that happened when he was three. Yet fragmented images…hot sand…blinding light…Tikah's brown face and brown hands when he wanted his mother, and before all of that, he *had* heard a long stream of gunfire. But he must be confusing his memories from the war with the fuzzy memories of childhood.

He ran a hand around the back of his neck. Pain gouged the center of his brain. Dear God, he needed a drink to blot out this blasted nonsense of his so-called childhood trauma.

"Light of my eyes." Eshana clutched his arm. "There is truth to my fears, is there not?" Her voice went ragged. "Beloved son of my heart, I will say the same to you as I said to your brother. 'Nothing shall be able to separate us from the love of God, which is in Christ Jesus our Lord.' Because in my soul I feel you are in torment, Cam, separating yourself from all that is good."

She took him by the shoulders and shook him. As small as she was, he barely felt it. "I am not blind, Cam," she implored. "Nor is there anything wrong with my senses. Tell me…why do I smell whiskey seeping from your pores, like it did from your natural father?"

The truth hit him like an artillery barrage. His beloved *ayah* saw clear through to his soul. He was just like his wretch of a father.

18

The next day in Sialkot's regimental club, the bride and groom chatted with guests before they were to leave for their honeymoon in Kenya. They were flying out of Delhi tomorrow. Miriam squinted to avoid the blue nimbus bouncing off the regimental silver in the glass case behind her sister and her husband. Indian Cavalry swords, crossed high up on the whitewashed walls, ballroom floors polished to a gleam with coconut oil, copies of *The Midnight Steeplechase* and other such paintings were but snippets of two hundred years of British Colonial history.

One day soon, all this grandeur would no longer belong to the English. These fine military establishments would be left to their Indian counterparts.

She'd be the first to toot the horn for Indian independence. Still, a trace of homesickness fluttered. Mum and Dad had always planned on retiring in Kashmir like most of their army cronies. Now, they too were making plans to retire in the British Isles. Dad's cousin in Ireland had left him a house.

Where would that leave her? Eva, now married to an English soldier, would go wherever her husband was posted, Africa most likely, and somehow Miriam had the feeling Cam wasn't going to remain with the army much longer.

Her father's voice reached her where she stood, flanked by a sandstone pillar and a potted palm. With his hands clasped behind him, back straight as the spine of a book, Dad chatted with Major General Pete Rees by the tea trolley.

"Our Indian Army's a million strong," Pete Rees said to her father. "Counting Muslims, Hindus, and Sikhs, it will be one difficult organization to sift apart."

Her father confirmed in a low voice. "And what's this I hear? Rumors there might be a new viceroy?"

Pete Rees dropped his voice too. "Wavell hasn't been able to do the job. After all this time, still unable to gain a consensus between Nehru and the Hindu Congress, and Jinnah and the Muslim League."

"Gandhi can't get them to agree?" Her father put a hand on Pete Rees's shoulder, and they turned away but stayed within her hearing.

"Gandhi?" Pete scoffed. "Not a chance. Even though Nehru worships the old man, he too thinks Gandhi's ideas are archaic—wanting to take India back to a golden age that perhaps never existed. Might be the only thing Nehru and Jinnah agree on."

They stopped close to where she stood, hidden behind the palm. "So who do you think will be the next viceroy?"

Pete Rees's voice took on a jovial bounce. "My guess is our old friend from the war, the supreme allied commander of the South East Asia command, no less. Apparently, Nehru has suggested Lord Louis Mountbatten for the job."

Her father's face lit. "Just the ticket, no one more suitable for the job of last viceroy to India than Dickie Mountbatten."

Their voices faded as they moved out the French doors to the garden. For a moment, her father's excitement stirred something in Miriam too.

But what was she to do when the night did come, and a new day dawned with no British India? Should she move to Great Britain like her parents, a place she'd only visited once? That feeling of being set adrift came over her. Perhaps that's what bothered Cam. Maybe he drank a bit too much because he didn't know what to do when the life they knew was coming to a close.

But right now her feet were screaming from standing in these new pumps all day. The tulle frill at the top of her bodice chafed. As far as weddings went, the event had smoothly rolled off the rails. Yesterday, Cam had driven the family up from Amritsar to Sialkot as per schedule. With everyone helping, Lieutenant Harry Braithwaite in his dress uniform and Eva in silk and satin looked terribly handsome.

Any minute now, Mother would give the signal for Miriam to come and help her sister out of her gown and into her going-away suit, a sweet little thing in pink linen. Looking at the bride standing there—small and soft like Mother, the groom tall and straight like Dad—Miriam's throat thickened. She dabbed a handkerchief to her eyes to soak up the annoying moisture, letting her gaze track the reception room.

From his stance by the massive fireplace, Jack latched eyes with her and raised a champagne flute. A series of fizzy bubbles popped all the way up her spine. Dad insisted Jack be invited to the wedding to thank him for doing his bit to protect Miriam during the Calcutta riots. During the reception, Jack had proven more than proficient at the rumba, foxtrot, and the one or two waltzes he'd danced with her, as well as that American jive he'd danced with Laine. Well, sore feet or not, the night was young. She'd get Eva changed into her honeymoon trousseau and personally stuff her into the Rolls that Dad had borrowed for the occasion. Once rid of the bride and groom, she'd spend the rest of the evening dancing with Jack.

He sauntered across the room to Miriam's side, in dashing regimental uniform, and another fizzy pop went off at the base of her neck. "I saw you mopping up with a handkerchief. Getting misty? Couldn't be. Not the young woman who stoically abhors all that is romantic."

"I confess, wedding fever has struck even me. I can recite every detail of my sister's gown in soft ivory satin embroidered with roses, high neckline, long sleeves, tailored bodice, and short train. Nor have the orange blossoms and lilies escaped my admiration."

"Noticed them myself," he bantered back. "There's enough jasmine here today to fill a parade ground."

She gave him a rap on the wrist with her bridesmaid bouquet, sprinkling a few rose petals on the floor. "I couldn't be happier for Eva. Harry is going to be an outstanding husband." A man of strong faith, the sort of chap her father would like to see her with. Certainly not this man standing next to her, whose brown gaze was making her midsection do cartwheels.

Undeterred from her disciplinary thump, Jack folded his arms. "Wonderful occasion. Why, I even found myself humming along with the soloist during the ceremony. I'll never forget how her charming purple gown strained as she trilled 'I Love You Truly.' Stout little woman, isn't she?"

That did it. Sentimental sniffles vanished while Miriam choked on laughter, only to have tears stream down her face. "Say one more beastly thing and I really will wallop you."

"Promise? Will you, Miriam…promise?" His dark eyes turned slumberous, and all laughter left her.

She took her time straightening the bent rose stems in her bouquet. It was all too obvious he was becoming interested in her. And he—each time she saw him—made the adrenalin in her body gallop. "I'll have you know, Mrs. Benson-Watson is one of the kindest ladies I have ever known. She was my Sunday school teacher, leader of my Girl Guide troop, and largely instrumental in my choosing to teach theology as a profession. You should not speak of her with such impertinence. It's unkind."

"Ouch!"

She smiled to soften her scolding. "Well what do you expect when it was you this time, unsheathing your claws to take it out on poor Mrs. Benson-Watson?"

He had the decency to look abashed. "Quite right. It was me acting *Mr.* Kitty Claws this time." Then he spoiled it all by the ridiculous grin spreading over his face. "If I behave, will you introduce me to this paragon who shaped you into the remarkable woman you are?"

Her sigh came from the bottom of her aching feet. "Do you ever speak with seriousness other than in the middle of a military crisis?"

She carefully avoided another of his ravishing smiles, which were increasingly turning her into jelly. At any moment, she just might take him by the arm, drag him out to the rosebushes, and demand that he kiss her. Then, through the crowded room, she saw her brother.

Cam stood by the gift table, wearing an expression that would frighten off even the most brazen thief loitering too close to the wedding presents. Jack may be exasperating, but her sibling topped the list. Cam's despondency sapped all joy from her. She was getting tired of worrying about him.

"I adamantly refuse to converse with any seriousness," Jack countered her earlier remark. "Don't believe in hashing over somber twaddle. Life's far too short."

Life *was* short. Her heart turned over for her brother's sadness. Why? Why? She softly uttered to herself, "Sorrow is better than laughter, for by the sadness of the countenance the heart is made better."

"Spouting Ecclesiastes to me this time, are you?" Jack's gaze traveled to where hers rested. "Ah, I see." He let out a sigh. "You're correct to worry about him, Miriam."

"Oh, he's all right." Miriam could tell that Cam's veneer was slipping. He'd had a number of glasses of champagne. A larger man would have been three sheets to the wind long ago. Still, he just needed rest, a good talking to, and he'd be right as rain.

"Your brother is not all right, Miriam. Far from it." Jack's brow creased the way she'd seen it during the Calcutta riots. So he really could become grave when it suited him, but with that gravity focused on her brother the fizz went out of her entirely.

Jack stood in front of her, blocking her view of Cam. "I know that to knock Cam off that pedestal you have him on isn't going to win me points in your regard." He took her hand. "But, my lovely, charming girl, I have to say it. Your brother is drowning in alcohol. He's no ordinary Saturday night drinker. He is a man with a serious problem."

She dropped his hand. "What utter rot."

"Miriam, please, I'm trying to help."

"Help?" She came to within an inch of his face. "How can insulting my brother help him?"

"Because he listens to you. So I'm taking the bullet with my teeth in an attempt to open your eyes to his predicament."

Perhaps she did need to tell her brother in uncertain terms to shape up, but what Jack was implying was off the mark. "You think you're helping by calling my brother a drunk?"

"No, darl—" He flushed to the roots of his hair. "No, Miriam, only you used that vulgar term. Maybe because you already know deep down how badly your brother is doing, but is your father aware of Cam's capacity for inebriation? Because I can assure you, Cam has an astonishing tolerance for alcohol. He's not only drunk several bottles of champagne today, but has a flask containing whiskey secreted within his uniform. He'll soon be looking to refill that flask." Though his voice remained at whisper level, the intensity in his tone flayed her.

She was about to tell him to go jump off a short pier when he added, "Open your eyes, Miriam. Returning from war is not straightforward for a lot of men. Take your pious little blinkers off and put that religion of yours to work!"

How dare he? A shiver ran through her insides, and it had nothing to do with the cool December breeze blowing in the French doors. Her face went hot. It had to be as red as Jack's. The band wound down. Dancers meandered toward their tables. Glasses clinked, and still she and Jack skewered each other with their gazes. So what if Cam drank a bit? She didn't like it, but that didn't make him any less a Christian. But Jack might as well have called *her* a Pharisee. Take her religious blinkers off indeed!

A movement at the corner of her eye pulled her from Jack's glower. Mother was trying to get her attention. With a slight indication of Mum's chin—the secret signal—it was time to take Eva to a back room. At the same moment, Eshana reached her. "Your mother is asking for us, Miriam."

"I'm coming," she answered, working to settle her breathing. Her gaze dropped to the floor and to Jack's highly polished shoes, travelled up his precisely creased trousers and tunic decorated with medals, to his face, now apparently contrite. She wasn't going to let him off the hook though, and turned her back to him.

Eshana glanced past Miriam to Jack, and then to Cam beyond. Eshana's eyes welled, but she hooked her arm with Miriam's to cross the banquet hall. Like a teddy bear with all its stuffing knocked out, Miriam went with her. Jack could stay where he was for all she cared. She'd go ice-skating in the tropical south of India before she'd talk to him again.

But something was different with Eshana. She leaned on Miriam, tired. At the moment Miriam wished for the old days when she could lean on Eshana, but in all truth, Miriam was so angry she had enough steam rising in her to run several locomotives. "Are you all right, Eshana?"

The voice of Cam's old *ayah* went rough. "It is only that I know my princeling suffers. And you see it too."

It was to be expected that Eshana would notice that Cam was in a blue funk. She squeezed Eshana's arm. "He'll be fine. He's still sorting things out from the war. Just like Dad did after The Great War. Mum told me about his shell shock—"

"I was there during your father's battle with shell shock, Miriam. Do not forget, I have known your father for longer than even your mother has known him. This despair of your brother's is not the same as your father's."

"You talked with Cam a long time yesterday at the mission. Did he say anything to explain this misery—whatever it is—to you?"

Eshana shrank a fraction. "He did not, though I asked him pointblank." They had reached the hallway to the room where Eva was to change. Eshana touched her hand. "We must not speak of it now. This is your sister's wedding. After we send Eva and Harry off with joy we must talk as a family." She patted Miriam's hand. "Then we can concentrate on the light of our eyes."

So Eshana was worried about Cam too. Somewhat in a daze, Miriam went with her. Still, Jack was off the mark by half with the things he said. To think she'd been tempted to flirt in the garden with him. Kiss him! Not all the heaviness she felt had to do with Cam though. She didn't like this ripple disturbing her dalliance with Jack, no matter how minor their flirtation.

She and Eshana found the room set aside for the bride at the back of the club. Mum and Laine were already removing Eva's veil. As soon as Miriam and Eshana entered, Eva jumped up from the stool she was sitting on. She hugged Eshana, then Miriam. "Thank you, darlings, for helping to make my wedding so gloriously happy." She turned to include Mum and Laine. "It's been wonderful to share this day with you, my mother, my aunties, my sister."

"Darling," Miriam drawled, "as a family we could hardly *not* send you off in proper style."

While Mother and Laine folded the veil and packed it into a box, Eva took Miriam's arm and pulled her to the side. "Not everyone's happy. Cam most certainly isn't."

Miriam smiled a tight smile. Oh, not Eva too. "Don't worry about big brother—"

"Miriam, don't stop me. I've only got a few minutes. I'm worried sick about him. Cam's been wonderful, terribly helpful all day. He's joked with Harry and Dad, played with all the children to keep them from becoming bored, although he refused to dance with anyone. Phoebe Anderson is in a snit, I can tell you. Otherwise, Cam's been as sugary as Indian sweets, he has. But, Miri, he's absolutely miserable underneath." Her voice dropped to a whisper that Miriam barely caught. "As if he can't wait to get away from my wedding."

Eva's observations sent a drizzle of cold along Miriam's arms. She'd assumed Cam was only joking yesterday about not wanting to be at their sister's wedding, as she had been. But she now realized he'd meant every word. Maybe Jack was right. Cam must be drinking to excess today because…he hated this beautiful gathering, one of the holiest and happiest of family milestones.

She'd spied him herself, this morning in church, flinching when Dad gave Eva away. As Eva came down the aisle on the arm of her husband, Cam glanced away, out the window, as if their sister in her wedding gown and veil was painful to him.

Since that strange visit from Tikah in her rooms at the college, she'd not been able to stop thinking about what Tikah said, *handsome and brutal.* She'd been referring to Cam's natural father, but could it be true? Was Cam like his natural father, Nick Fraser?

That feeling of being set adrift came over Miriam again. Of a loosened tether floating on the water as a ship drew away from the shore, as though she drew away from all she knew to be sure.

19

Cam woke. His head cleaved in two, it hurt so much. To his blighted regret, he still breathed. He squinted at his watch. Late morning. The day after the wedding. Eva must be on her way to her honeymoon. God bless her. She deserved happiness. And Harry was a chap worth having as a husband. Good man, Harry, twice the man Cam was.

Staggering to his feet, he stuck out a hand to steady himself. The bar where he'd bought the homemade booze was only a shack of coarse wooden boards where patrons slouched or lay out cold like he'd been on the mud floor. The rancid stench of stale beer, whiskey, and sweat, along with the lingering reek of hashish, soiled the air. Any decent person would gag. He did not. Blast him to Hades, he was used to this.

Putting a hand to his head, he peered outside, wincing at the sunlight. He must have walked here last night. It came back to him now. Last night after the reception, Jack had done his best to wheedle Cam into getting sober, but he'd quickly given Jack the slip and spent the rest of the night in a bar in this seedy section in the native town. He'd slept the hours away, with his mistress curled in his arm—an empty bottle of homemade poison that he'd purchased from the bar owner. He'd not cared if the alcohol would kill him or not. He wished it had.

Outside the shack, the sun splintered his skull, and he strained to see through a blur. He'd prefer to take a taxi back to his parents' home, but when he checked his pockets, his money was gone. He might have known. Now he'd have to walk clear to their bungalow on the outskirts of the Sialkot garrison, if he could. With any luck, he might sneak into his old room, have a bath before they noticed he was back. Before they started in with questions.

There was nothing for it but start to walk the two miles. White light blinded, so that he kept his gaze on his feet, trudging along the dry mud path out of the native section toward the military cantonment. Every time he sobered up, flashes of memories assaulted. Now, grenades of images exploded behind his eyes. White sand, sun-burnt desert, a woman's brown face, brown hands, Tikah.

And Dassah…beautiful Dassah.

Her big brown eyes when he'd come back to their houseboat that day. The way she'd begged him not to go to the party on the other craft…but to stay with her.

As if out of his living nightmares, a mob of voices raised in anger shouted. Another of those blighted parades like he'd seen in Calcutta. Here in the north of India, Muslims and Hindus paraded alike. A crowd of fifty or more strong marched past him, carrying banners of grass green
silk, a crescent moon in the center and a single star above it. The marchers chanted, *"Pakistan Zindabad! Pakistan Zindabad!"*

The uproar from the incensed throng increased his nausea. The fools wanted to rip the country apart. He turned to them, kicked at a stone, and in his mind yelled at them, but his throat was too dry to utter a sound. "What good will that do you, you mad idiots? Go to war against each other then! Go on and see what it's like when littered corpses fill your dreams and when long after the war every backfiring car makes you leap five feet as if you've just been shot at." He sank to his knees. "Have at it if you haven't got any better sense. Go on, kill each other."

The memory of Zakir slogged past with a stream of prisoners, from a night two years ago when the Indian defectors were brought back to India. An arc of light had lit them in the darkness as they wore their gray prison garb. And then again, the glare in Zakir's eyes the day before, at the mission, that look that said they were no longer friends, never mind brothers.

The soothing balm of Eshana's voice came over him too. *Nothing shall be able to separate us from the love of God.*

He bent over from the weight of his disgust, his face not two inches from the dirt. Not true. Not true. If Jinnah got his way, India would be parted in two. Zakir plainly wanted to separate from all his British friendships of the past. And Cam's own debauchery did separate him from God. The revolting way he'd treated the most precious of women separated him from God.

Why couldn't he have died in the war like many a worthy man had? Why the blazes did he still walk the earth, taking up space when so many others would have used their life to a better end? *Dear God, why don't you just finish it? Lay me out in the dirt where I belong.*

Bile rose up his throat. It wasn't as if he hadn't tried to stop drinking. Since Dassah left him, he'd tried to take the pledge of sobriety. Went an entire week once. Just when he thought he could win, he'd gone into a shop for shaving cream. As if his hands had a mind of their own, he'd scooped up several bottles, leaving the shaving cream on the shelf. At home, he'd blacked out, started the day over again. Got cleaned up. Put on the uniform. Went to Army Headquarters and put in a day's work. Then went home, closed the door of his room, and drank till he forgot.

Tomorrow he'd start fresh. But tomorrow always got moved along to the next day.

The crowd of marchers turned a corner. Their outcry faded. Kneeling in the dirt, bent in two, his fingers razed his hair back from his forehead. There was nothing within him to weep. His sockets dry, every pore in his body dry—or like Eshana said, reeking with stale whiskey. He was no different than his natural father.

Dear God, do me a kindness...here in the dirt where I belong.

"Cam!"

Cam's forehead sank to the ground. The desire to be sick grew stronger.

"Cam...Cameron!" a man's voice called.

He lifted his head and squinted through eyes that strained to focus on a large black sedan glinting in the sunlight. A soldier stood by an open car door. *Oh dear God...Dad.*

He was wrong. There was something left in his wretched sockets. Hot liquid forced out of his eyes, scraping like sand. His father remained where he was by the car, looking down at the ground as if he too might be sick. A long moment later, Dad came toward him.

Cam lifted his hand up to halt Dad from coming closer. "Leave me. I'm sorry." His vision blurred as he felt his father's strong grip on his shoulders.

Dad's grip hurt, as it was meant to, and his voice cracked. "Being sorry is only a place to start, son. Now get up. Remember the man I raised you to be."

Yesterday her parents' bungalow had been a madhouse in preparation. Bridal bouquets strewn hither and yon, gowns over this chair and that, hats and gloves laid out in rank and file on the hallway table. Now Miriam practically tiptoed through the whitewashed stone house that stood on an acre of garden. Today the bungalow felt more like a hospital ward with the smell of antiseptic soap and hushed tones.

As soon as Dad's car arrived back before lunch with Cam inside, Jai, Eshana, and Laine raced out of the bungalow ahead of Mother, down the veranda, and began rapping out their low-toned medical jargon to one another. They relieved Dad of Cam, supported him under his arms, and whisked him to his bedroom. All three medical valises—without which none of them traveled—were opened, and instruments removed as if Cam was at the point of death.

Mother and Dad offered to help but were lovingly and firmly told to let their two visiting doctors and nurse do their job. Jai and Eshana checked Cam's vitals while Laine rigged up a saline drip. Thankfully, her brother was conscious, but weak. There was nothing to do but pray. But pray about what exactly?

After a while, Jai left Eshana and Laine with Cam and joined Miriam and her parents in the front parlor. Sitting on the cretonne-covered sofa, he held the look of a physician today, and not just that of her dear Indian uncle. For a moment, he studied the Kashmiri carpet, the brass Benares table. Was he about to say something awful, like Cam had a cancer, developed tuberculosis, or contracted typhoid? Miriam's hands formed fists as she waited.

"It is alcohol poisoning," Jai said. "As we have been suspecting, Cam is an alcoholic."

"Alcoholic!" she barked. Her parents and Jai turned to her sitting in the corner of the settee, clutching a cushion. "You practically carried Cam into the house. He's seriously ill, not simply under the influence of a few too many drinks."

Jai smoothed his mustache with his thumb and forefinger. "You are correct, Miriam. Cam is seriously ill. Aside from the immediate threat from poisoning, there are long-term concerns. There is research being done into alcoholism. Is it simply a social concern, a religious matter of sin? Or is it a disease? There is also the issue of Cam's mental health. He is clearly suffering from depression. This was evident the other day when he came to pick us up in Amritsar, though he hid it well."

She hugged the cushion closer. "Of course he's depressed. I've been trying to get him to talk to me." This was all sounding far too much like the nonsense Jack spewed yesterday. "I will not accept that Cam is an alcoholic."

Mother, her eyes bright with tears, got up and perched on the arm of the settee beside her. Taking Miriam's hand, she turned to Jai. "Go on. How far has the drinking affected him?"

Jai nodded at Mother's calm acceptance of his analysis.

"Cam is somewhat jaundiced. A blood test will tell the extent of liver damage, if any. At the moment I am concerned about his blood pressure. It is far too low. And his heart is beating erratically."

His voice came softly moments later. "In simple terms, withdrawal from alcohol poisoning is a shock to the body, and surprisingly can be more fatal than withdrawal from narcotics. Over the next twenty-four to forty-eight hours we must watch him carefully. A hospital stay—or if you wish, Eshana and I can treat him here. We were planning to remain here for the week anyway."

The only sound in the parlor came from the ticking clock on the mantel.

Poisoning. Erratic heartbeat. They couldn't be saying these things about her brother. Not in peacetime. All the while he'd been in Burma and Malaya, she'd worried sick over him. If Cam died in battle, she'd have had the strength to accept that. But hearing this diagnosis from Jai…. She shook her head. This couldn't be happening.

Dad stared down at his hands clasped on his knees. Mother blinked back tears and, for some insane reason, kept staring at her, as if it were she who was ill and not Cam.

Though she felt wooden, Miriam managed to speak. "Dad, say something. Cam, possibly dying from alcohol?" The image of her tall, handsome brother, lying in the gutter like other poor souls she'd seen lying drunk by the roadside didn't tally.

Her father's gray eyes pierced her through. "We've all seen it. Surely you have too, Miriam."

Her jaw dropped. Then it was Mother speaking, at first a mere buzzing in her ears. "Miri, I know you idolize Cam, but it's true. We should have talked about this more openly, when we first saw the signs, but I kept hoping, praying he'd change." Her mother rummaged in her frock sleeve for a handkerchief to wipe her eyes.

Miriam couldn't believe her parents and got to her feet to pace the parlor carpet. "Do further tests, Jai. You must be wrong."

Her father stood and took her by the shoulders. "Do you know where I found Cam this morning? Out at a filthy shack, lying in the dirt, barely able to stand." Dad's voice halted. "When I helped him to his feet, he fell down…on his backside."

She shook her head. "His drinking can't be as bad as you say." She pulled away from her father, needing to get out in the fresh air. Behind her she heard Mother say, "Let her go, Geoff. She needs time."

Outside the bungalow, Miriam paced from the patio to the edge of the garden, hugging herself around the middle, gulping in air with the hope it would settle her hammering heart. Her soul would bleed for Cam if he was ill from something. But if it was the drink—the idiocy of alcoholism—that she could not accept. He wasn't some poor orphan who'd never had a chance. He'd had a loving childhood, an education, the best of parents. He had Eva and her.

Flumping down in a deckchair, she let her prayers rise without articulation. But the attitude of prayer didn't come to her spirit. How could her brother waste the life God had given him?

Her gaze, after a while, rested on Mother's rose-beds that stretched from the bungalow to the end of the property, where it dropped off at the edge of a crag. A feast of color and perfume danced in perfect rows. When they first returned to India from Singapore, Dad had a waist-high wall built on the edge of the property to protect the children from falling below. She and Cam, Eva later too, would sit on that stone wall, dangling their little legs, and looking out over the violet foothills of the Himalayas cresting in the distance.

Now her brother's life was sliding off the rails. He'd kept his shameful secret. And that was the part that hurt the worst. It had all been so furtive. But then, he'd given her a hint months ago. The day after the train derailment, he'd tried to tell her. *Miri, I wish you'd stop hoisting me up on the hero's charger. I do not possess those sterling qualities.*

Jack's words came back to taunt her too. *Take your pious little blinkers off and put that religion of yours to work.*

She'd not wanted to listen to Cam, and he'd never explained, probably knowing how she'd react. Too cold, too pious to approach? Her throat thickened, but, still frozen with anger, her tears remained locked, stinging the back of her eyes.

A while later, Laine came out of the bungalow and took the deckchair next to Miriam. "Cam's sleeping. Eshana's with him, and Jai's talking to your parents," she said, though Miriam had not asked.

"Apparently, you're all afraid he has alcohol poisoning." To say it out loud hurt, and Miriam squeezed her eyes shut.

"Until the other day, Miri, when we met up in Amritsar, I'd no idea. Jai thinks he's been drinking for years." Laine stretched out her legs encased in white slacks, a cardigan around her shoulders. Christmas had just passed, and a winter chill lingered. Laine tilted her head back and commented in a desultory voice. "Eva and Harry must be halfway to Kenya by now."

"I expect so." She bit down on her lip. How could Laine be so unruffled? Was this a nursing trait that normal human beings didn't have?

"And Jack? Left early this morning, didn't he?" Laine coaxed.

"Took the train for Rawalpindi." To think, Jack had been dead on target about Cam. She shot upright in her deckchair. "Do you know, Laine, last night Jack had the gumption to corner me. The only one to face the lioness in her den." The witticism didn't sound all that funny to her ears. "With all the theology books lining my shelves, and me supposedly being someone of wisdom to teach young minds, I had to have this tremendous character flaw in my brother pointed out to me by a...by a rogue like Jack Sunderland."

"He's a rogue, is he?"

"Never mind about Jack, Laine."

Laine played with a pulled stitch in her cardigan. "If Cam were sick from something else you wouldn't bat an eyelash but would delve into easing his suffering. Too bad Adam had to remain at home looking after a batch of sickly mango trees. I'm just plucky old Laine who for years ignored God. It wasn't until I'd gone a few years of not being able to have a...baby...that you might say I decided to dive headfirst into the swimming pool of faith."

"Oh, I know all that, Laine. I've believed in the salvation of Christ since I wore ankle socks to Sunday school."

"Have you, Miri? Yes, you've got it all up there." She pointed to Miriam's temple. "Maybe you just need to lie back on those promises and commands of God, like you would lie back on a hammock on a hot summer's day. I'm not saying turn off your academic brain, but there is no way you can map out your brother's life, or your own life. People fail. People sin."

Thank goodness Laine got stopped in the middle of her sermonizing when Mother came to stand on the veranda. Something was going on in the house, and she beckoned to her and Laine. "Because you both have trains to catch tomorrow, we thought we'd gather together in the front room now. Jai feels the time is right for us to talk to your brother."

Feeling light-headed from the strong waft of jasmine that swathed the veranda pillars, and from what her mother said, Miriam sputtered, "You mean gang up on Cam as a group?"

Mother's face pinched. "Jai and your father have been discussing it all afternoon. They have come to the consensus that talking to him as a group will be beneficial."

"Come, luv," Laine said to Mother. "We'll trust in God for the healing he needs."

"Is it a sickness, Laine?" her mother cried out to her old friend. "Or is it simply sin?"

"What does it matter, Abby? What I learned in Sunday school at six years old still stands. God sent his son to heal the sick and forgive us of our sins. Period. Now, let's go in and look after the boy."

By the time they all assembled in the parlor, the rain started. Silver streams dashed at the windows, turning the colors of the garden outside to a wash of liquid hues. Twilight snuffed out, and Dad's bearer Hakim lit the lamps just as Jai walked Cam into the parlor and settled him in a comfortable armchair. Eshana tucked a woolen blanket over his knees. Cam was clean and in pajamas, though a day's growth of beard blurred the lines of his jaw. But Miriam couldn't bear to look at him after a cursory glance.

Before Hakim left the parlor, he patted Mother's shoulder, and for a moment she reached up to cover his hand with hers.

Mother's eyes smiled bravely as she took the chair next to Cam, with Eshana on the other side. Jai stood by her father at the window. Dad had that stoic look, tempered with his faith that had gotten him through many conflicts, including two world wars. With an elbow propped on the fireplace mantel, Jai sagely nodded his head wrapped in his royal blue turban. That left the sofa, and Laine took a spot on it. Miriam took her favorite corner of the settee and pulled a cushion over her lap again. They all seemed to be trying not to look at Cam.

Miriam's jaw ached from clenching her teeth. Seeing Cam's head bent in shame didn't help either. Such selfishness. Maybe there was some truth to what Tikah said, *handsome and brutal.* Why would her brother torment the people who loved him by seeking the contents of a bottle instead of them? A young man just past thirty, blessed with good health, blessed with so much, but weak enough to succumb to stupid drink. She didn't know whether she wanted to hit her brother or hug him. Cry with him or yell at him? Or throw this blasted cushion at his head?

While Mother held his hand and Eshana laid a hand on his shoulder, it was to Miriam that he looked across the parlor as if begging for her forgiveness. She turned her gaze away from him to glower at the painting above the mantel, that of a British Raj woman from a generation ago, standing under a feathery tamarind tree and holding two straining leopards on a leash.

Since Dad had the floor, he began, looking Cam square in the eye. "Son, we are your family, and we love you enough to tell you that we can no longer tolerate what you are doing to yourself. Nor will we pretend that you are fine." Her father stopped, put a fist to his lips and cleared his throat. Whatever little speech he'd composed dissolved with the rain hitting the windows. "What we want to know, what I need to know, Cam, is—are you willing to stop drinking…if we help you?"

Something inside Miriam cracked. To see her tall, military Dad hurting this way…it wasn't right. She kept her profile to Cam, but from the corner of her eye knew that he was boring a hole in her head with his pathetic gaze. She shivered. How long could she keep up this tough facade before she broke down?

Jai took over from his place by the mantel. "Cam, I am recommending temporary or permanent leave from your current posting in Intelligence. For starters, a few days for your vitals to return to normal, then a number of weeks, six or eight to recuperate quietly. I must return to the hospital in Vellore in a week's time, but Eshana has elected to stay."

"What?" Laine questioned Eshana with a glance.

Eshana remained where she was, sitting in the chair next to Cam. "It is true. For some time now Jai and I have been discussing our permanent return to Amritsar. It seems fitting that I remain here, and wait for him to join me in a few months. But we will speak of this later." She cupped Cam's shoulder. "I will be your doctor through the first stage of your healing."

"Stage?" Miriam let the word hang on the air. "Can't he just stop drinking?"

Mother reached over to touch her on the arm. "Your father and Jai have come up with a plan, a sort of mental and physical convalescence."

"Yes," her father added, "a plan, but I know what you are saying, Miri. I too wish he would have simply stopped a long time ago." Dad seemed to have the same problem as her, a difficulty in addressing Cam directly. And his hand shook. That tremble only occurred when he was deeply distraught. He turned to Cam and sat down on a straight-backed chair close to him.

"Your life has become an unmitigated disaster." Again Dad couldn't seem to finish. It felt as though the room held its breath. "Are you willing to change, Cam?"

Her poor father. And Cam, her handsome six-foot brother, a British Military Intelligence officer, hanging his head low and wiping his eyes with a shaking hand. His voice quavered. "If I don't change, Dad…I'll die."

A sharp pain drove into Miriam's chest. She lifted her gaze to look at him through a veil of tears. Her stupid frozen tears had to thaw now? But oh dear Lord, her brother was suffering. He looked ready to collapse.

Dad nodded and gripped Cam by the knee. "Then why, son? Why? Why have you not reached out to God before this to restore you?"

Jai intervened. "What your father is saying is, there is healing, but it can only come through the power of God."

Rain drummed on the windows.

Please Cam, please Cam, she pleaded silently, feeling sick that earlier she'd been so angry. *Believe. Reach out to God, Cam. Come back to God…come back to me.*

At last her brother lifted a weary hand and let it drop to his lap. "I have nowhere else to turn."

Her father straightened in his chair. "If only you had come to me sooner. I would have done anything to help you." A long moment later released a sigh. "All right, all right." He turned to Jai. "Would you...?"

Jai stood before Cam. "What we as a family need to know is, will you make a decision, a promise, to turn your life over to the care of God to gain complete and constant sobriety?"

Cam's face grimaced to hold back tears, but they came anyway. He wiped his dripping nose with the handkerchief Mother passed him. No one moved closer. No one spoke, or cajoled as his shoulders shuddered, and he coughed on his sobs. The clock struck and Cam nodded, gripping Mother's hand and meeting Dad's eyes. "I want with all my heart to turn my life over to God. If he'll have me?"

Her father's voice ground out in a shaking bass, "He will have you, Cam, and so will I. Your drinking has angered me. Frightened me, but tonight you give me hope."

Miriam used the cushion to soak up the wetness on her face.

Eshana slipped to the floor to kneel at Cam's feet. "Beloved princeling, what did I tell you the other day? Nothing can separate us from the love of God. Not even your own sin."

The spirits of everyone in the room seemed to lift slightly. Only Cam seemed to shrivel more into himself. His tears stopped, but some inner pain twisted his mouth in a harsh line. "God might forgive me for my drinking." His gaze encompassed everyone in the parlor. "But I'm not so sure he—or any of you for that matter—will forgive me when I tell you what I cannot forgive myself for."

Eshana tilted her head as she peered up at Cam. "Are you speaking of what is between you and Zakir? If so, please do not—"

"No, beloved Auntie, while I admit I have hurt my brother...I have hurt our sister far worse."

"Dassah." The name burst from Miriam's mouth in a harsh whisper. All eyes flew to meet hers.

Cam turned to her, anguish lining his face. "So you've guessed, clever puss."

He'd hinted and hinted about his drinking, and she'd not listened. He'd also tried to tell her something about Dassah. *Dear Father in heaven, it was all starting to make sense.*

20

At the end of January, it was still nippy outside, though it grew warmer each day. Mother's rose garden was doing well, but one could look at the flowerbeds for only so long. Cam came in from the garden to the breakfast nook. The room was still empty, but he could hear the noises of his parents and Eshana preparing for the day, and he helped himself to a cup of tea at the sideboard.

Surprisingly, the quiet of his parents' whitewashed bungalow helped at first. After Miriam went back to Lahore and the house was empty of wedding guests, Mother and Eshana fussed over him while Dad went back and forth to the Sialkot Regiment. Though the house was as silent as a tomb, Cam wouldn't have wanted it any other way. Two days ago, Mother received a telegram saying Eva and Harry had returned from their honeymoon but gone directly to Harry's station in Quetta. At least Cam had been spared a visit from his youngest sister and all accompanying emotions. Family didn't quite know what to do. Console him as if he were sickly, smack him across the head, or give him a good stiff sermon. He rubbed his jaw now as if he felt that deserved smack.

He picked up the morning mail from the table and found a letter from Alan Callahan in Kashmir. Cam had started to write to Alan that first week of his convalescence. The minister had spoken openly of his battle with the bottle. With the routine of the house taking Cam back to his boyhood when he didn't have the life and death of others weighing on his hands, his parents' house created a good place to take stock. And writing it out in letters, confessional in a way, helped him look into the moral mirror, something that had been nigh impossible for a long time. Prayer helped too. Something else he'd not had the courage to do for a long time.

Alan's first answering letter came quickly, followed by one or two per week. His voice was as erudite on the page as if he stood beside Cam, staring out at his mother's rose-beds. He encouraged Cam to study chapter eight in the book of Romans. "There is now no condemnation to those in Christ. But our flesh

141

is weak," Alan wrote. "Why, all of creation groaneth and travaileth in pain. Still though, we are the firstfruits of the Spirit…waiting for the adoption…the redemption of our body."

As Alan shared his struggles, his long creeping crawl to sobriety, to a life pleasing to God, Cam bared his soul too. In his last letter to Alan, Cam mentioned he'd not needed a drink these past weeks. At least not yet. Perhaps the rotgut he'd drunk after Eva's wedding did the trick. He'd like to think it was his turning down the fork in the road of God's choosing.

But in Alan's letter today, he'd written that Cam's current sobriety probably had more to do with the abhorrence of ever again being that ill. Cam could almost hear the wry humor in the minister's voice as he dished out that cold dose of reality.

A bedroom door closed, and Eshana's footsteps pattered up the hall. Still no sign of his parents. The quiet of the bungalow had certainly helped him convalesce. The ticking clock in the parlor. Winds soughing from the Himalayan foothills and into his mother's garden stirred the need to get moving. Start again to find Dassah, although Cam couldn't fathom how. When she first left him three months ago, he'd spent days hunting all over Srinagar for her. He'd driven like a madman to Rawalpindi, Lahore, scores of towns and villages in between. Not one sight of her.

Today, as he waited for Eshana or someone, anyone, to join him at breakfast, he ran his hands through his hair. Dear God, he needed to do something or he really would need the army psychiatrist's couch.

At last his parents darted into the breakfast room and joined him at the table. A moment later, Eshana did too, letter in hand. "Dr. Vicky wishes to retire earlier than expected, her mother in England is ailing," she said, perusing her post. "The board wants to instate Jai and myself as administrators of the mission."

Mother reached across the table for Eshana's hand. "After all these years, your heart's desire."

Eshana gave her a wan little smile. "I am at sixes and sevens. Now the day is here, my prayers answered, I am breathless with the goodness of God."

Dad raised his teacup in Eshana's direction. "Congratulations, little sister, I never doubted the day would come. Our beloved old Miriam must be looking down from heaven, pleased as punch you will fill her shoes."

Eshana's bangles jingled as she stuffed the letter into its envelope. "Jai must come as soon as arrangements are made. I must leave for Sialkot immediately." She turned to Cam. "And you, my princeling, are doing much better, but I think it best you make your transition back to your occupation in stages. Why not accompany me to Amritsar and help me in the mission for a few weeks?"

Cam pushed his empty breakfast plate away. The fear of failure sat at the back of his throat ready to choke. It had been bad enough talking about his alcoholism, but that first night after he'd told the family about Dassah and his marriage, they'd stared at him in silence for heart-wrenchingly long minutes. Still, he couldn't hide in his parents' house any longer. The quiet was slowly driving him mad. "If you feel I'm ready to do something, Eshana, then I'd rather get on with my search for my wife."

His mother put a hand to her head. "But where? As well as you're doing, Cam, I believe you need more time. You're not quite..."

Dad, dressed in a precisely pressed uniform, spoke at his side. "Not to mention, Dassah may not be ready to take you back. She, too, may need proof that you've changed."

If Mother's reverting to treating him like an infant wasn't bad enough, the way Dad said, *she, too,* made it all too clear that it was he who needed evidence that Cam had changed. From the table, his stepdad looked through the window to the Himalayan foothills, his jaw set. He was still angry over the way Cam had treated Dassah, and Cam could only agree. These days he and Dad were talking even less than they used to.

Mother piped in. "Well then, Geoff, working at the mission might be the very thing. Help him prove he's really stopped drinking and he—"

"That he'll what, Abby? Prove to be a husband worthy of that young woman? You of all people should understand my abhorrence of the mistreatment of a wife." A muscle ticked at the side of Dad's jaw. "Isn't that why Tikah did that monstrous thing she did all those years ago? Tearing off into the desert with—" He cleared his throat. "And now, history has an uncanny way of repeating itself. All because some men can't embrace their responsibilities."

Cam forced himself to not wince. The dose of cold reality in Alan's letter had been bad enough. Dad's words went clear to the bone.

His father stood from the table, letting his napkin drop. A moment later he softened his voice. "For what it's worth I agree with you both, Abby and Eshana. Honest toil at the mission, doing something for others, has always been the best medicine. I'm not sure if you are requesting my blessing or even need it, Cam, but I offer it anyway."

The rest of the table remained quiet as Dad took a few steps away, preparing to leave for the garrison. He returned seconds later and cupped Mother's shoulder in a tender squeeze. With obvious difficulty he faced Cam across the table. "Before you leave, I hope you'll consider the suggestion I made the other evening. You can't remain on medical leave interminably, and the offer from the viceroy staff is still on the table. They're willing to take you on as aide-de-camp. Quite an honor, considering."

Yes, considering that in Dad's opinion he was still nothing more than a drunk—but of course the viceroy staff didn't know that. They only knew that he was the son of Geoff Richards, and that was good enough for them. But Cam's stomach lurched. He wasn't sure he wanted to remain in the forces. Now that war was over, it was easy enough to be decommissioned.

But he, too, couldn't get away from the fact that this man with the steady gray eyes had raised him as his own all these years. As much as he wanted to search every alleyway, every hut in India for Dassah, the task was hopeless without God's help. *Looking for a diamond on a sand-filled beach.* Perhaps it would be better to bridge the chasm between him and his parents first, some small attempt to make Dad proud of him again. And as much as he loved her, to stop that blasted out-of-character-fussing on his mother's part.

Cam stood to meet those steady gray eyes. "I can't thank you enough, Dad, for recommending me for the post. I'll send a telegram today that I accept and will join the staff when my medical leave ends. As for the next few weeks, I would consider it an honor to assist Eshana." He turned to Eshana. "So, yes, please give me something to do."

His attempt at a smile must have worked because Eshana rewarded him with a bright grin. Mother exhaled with relief, and for the first time in…Cam didn't know how long…Dad's eyes softened toward him as he tucked his briefcase under his arm and left for the garrison.

Only the sound of the houseboy washing dishes in the kitchen broke the silence. Cam took his seat, not able to meet the gazes of either Eshana or his mother.

"He doesn't mean to hurt you," Mother said.

"He's livid, Mum. I broke one of his cardinal rules—never abuse the people you're obligated to protect."

"As long as you understand he's not angry because you married Dassah—but, oh Cam, the world is so harsh toward those who step out of societal bounds. He just worries."

"Don't you think I know how cruel society is?" As he got to his feet, he scraped his chair across the floor. "I'm sure Dad would have been happier if I'd been a man and left Dassah entirely alone. It would have been kinder to love her silently from afar."

"Don't be stupid."

Cam sought his mother's eyes. "For the past weeks I've felt it, something Dad said just now. How you of all people should understand his abhorrence of the mistreatment of a wife."

Eshana made a small sound of apology and started to get up to give them privacy, but his mother fluttered her hand for Eshana to remain. "Cam, just keep looking forward, don't look to the past. Become the man God wants you to be. Find your wife and hold her close."

With that, Eshana got to her feet. "Cam, light of my eyes, why not try to think simply, as though you were standing before God, who is the only one who matters. You are British and you married an Indian girl. So?" She spread her hands, palms up. "To my thinking, you and Dassah were two people unprepared for a marriage between two races. Stop making mountains out of a pile of dust, and leave your future dilemmas to Yeshu. Life is already very difficult."

She adjusted the end of her sari over her shoulder. "Now, come, heart of my heart. We have packing to do. We must not be tardy in our obedience to God."

From the front stoop of the mission, the din of *tonga* bells, honking horns, and discordant Indian wailing reached Cam. At all times of the day and night, these bustling sounds and the natter of millions of people wafted on air scented with over-ripe fruit, dust, and diesel fumes. Today was no different as he kneeled at the front door to scrape off several decades of turquoise paint. For all his life, this door had been this color, and Eshana wanted a fresh coat applied.

He wiped the sweat from his forehead with the tail of his shirt. For the last five weeks he'd been Eshana's willing slave. He slept in a matchbox of a room off the nursery, one he'd shared a few times as a child with an ever-changing assortment of orphans. If he was lucky enough to get a night's sleep without being wakened by the wail of at least three babies, he would clatter down the stairs in the morning with a mob of laughing, squealing, or in some cases grumpy, children.

After a simple breakfast of *chapattis* and lentils, he would start his tasks, laying flagstones outside, chopping and hauling wood for the kitchen stoves, carrying in forty-pound bags of rice. As a slave driver, his beloved Eshana was disgustingly cheerful as she doled out his orders. He scraped and painted. He repaired broken furniture. But not all his tasks were manly. He even diced vegetables, plucked chickens, and cooked cauldrons of the rice he toted in.

At night, he fell exhausted into his string bed, thanking God that Eshana was not his CO in the army.

But no matter where he looked in the mission, he saw Dassah's face—when she was three and peeked around the clay urns to giggle at him as he played marbles with the other boys. When she was six and he nine, she'd insisted on sitting beside him on the floor to eat her dinner, pushing away two other orphans in the process. And when she was seventeen....

By his count, he'd been sober sixty-two days. Twice a week, he and Alan traded letters as Alan mentored him toward a life of sobriety. Cam added new vigor to scraping the old turquoise paint from the worn front door. Surely he was becoming the man his parents hoped. Surely he was becoming the kind of man Dassah deserved. In a matter of days, Jai would arrive to join Eshana, and Cam would be ready to leave the mission to take up his new position at Viceroy House. And then, with God's help, if Dassah was found, he prayed she'd take him back.

He'd reached an especially hard patch of paint that refused to budge with his scraper when a pack of boys from six to sixteen years rushed out of the mission. They'd finished their schoolwork and demanded he join them in a cricket match. Eshana came up behind the youngsters and, with a gleam in her eye, nodded him off.

Cam didn't even have to stop to put his tools away or gather the bats and wickets. The boys had it all and dragged him by the hand through the mission and out the back. He remembered when he was little they used to have a rope ladder to climb the ten feet down to the *bagh*. A number of years ago, new steps had been carved to allow access to the two hundred yard, oblong-shaped parcel of dusty earth. People still came here for horse fairs and the sale of livestock. Visitors still slept on the ground.

The boys set the pitch up far enough from the well so as not to disturb people lounging in the shade of the peepal trees. There were enough lads from the mission to make up two teams, and a few extra. The first bowler, a boy of twelve, smacked the ball into his hands with style as good as a professional, delivering the ball to Cam as first batsman up. Cam hit the ball away from the fielders and ran to the opposite end of the pitch. The game was on.

Many of the boys grew downright grubby, running or sliding in the dust. A few grazed knees were earned, one smacked eye, but overall as the afternoon waned, tired smiles lit the boys' dirty faces. To Cam it was sheer heaven listening to their whoops and hollers, their loud complaints in Hindi and Urdu when the other team scored.

Late afternoon sun slanted as they neared the end of the second inning. He hunkered down to sit on the back of his heels. Their match stirred up the dust, an ochre yellow cloud. A man sat nearby on the rim of the well in the center of the *bagh*. The man had been watching the cricket match, but jerked his back straight and stared. Then he rose and strode toward Cam. Cam knew him first by his gait. He'd played too many cricket matches with Zakir not to know him.

At last Zakir came to stand but three feet from Cam, glancing up at the stone wall protecting the mission. "I had heard in the city that Auntie had become the new administrator, but I had not known that you returned with her."

Not wanting to be at a disadvantage with Zakir looming, Cam got to his feet. "Don't let my presence stop you from visiting Eshana. She'd be delighted to see you. Besides, I'm leaving in two days."

Zakir scuffed a sandaled foot in the dust. Behind him, the boys went on with their game. Cam was no longer needed, and the match would soon end. Perhaps it was seeing their own past acted out by these younger boys that softened the harsh lines to Zakir's face. "It is no matter whether you are here in Amritsar or not. You may jump into that well behind me, if it pleases you. But nor is it my intent to stay in Amritsar, but to find a place where as a Muslim I will feel at home."

Cam's eyes shot to Zakir's prayer cap. "This used to be your home. You have every right to worship as you wish and where, but will this idea of Pakistan give you what you're looking for?"

"Pakistan is no idea. It is a land whose time has come."

"You're one of those marching the streets, shouting, '*Pakistan Zindabad.*'"

"If I am?"

Cam slapped dust from his trousers. "Then I pray you have compassion on those who choose India and not Pakistan for their homeland when the time comes."

"You speak harshly of us, *sahib*. It was one of your English generals who marched troops into this very *bagh* and trained rifles on innocent people, killing hundreds." Zakir looked back at the well, at the people sitting peacefully in the shade. His voice dropped to a dry husk. "I remember standing by that well. Bullets whizzed past my head. People collapsed. Blood soaked the *bagh*. And then Miriam—whom I loved as my mother—ran to me."

The image of Zakir as a boy came over Cam. He remembered the times they'd come in from this patch of ground, played out, covered in dirt, stinking with sweat. "I may not remember the day of the massacre, but my father told me in detail of the atrocity when I was old enough to understand. Many British people feel shame for that event."

"You agree an Englishman treated my Indian people with great cruelty. Yet you would curse me for joining the National Indian Army."

"At the time you joined the NIA it was treason. What would you have me think?"

Zakir sliced a hand through the air. "It is of no matter. I am a free Indian now."

"You always had that freedom. I only ask you to be compassionate as India is given her independence because I've seen what comes over people in the hysteria of political fervor. I was in Calcutta during the riots last August."

Zakir took a moment to study him. "You have changed. You act like a horse that is finally broken. In days gone by if I had stoked your English ire you would have shown your temper." He chuckled. "It gives me satisfaction to see this attitude of submission in you. Now I can take your leave, and keep this picture of you in my mind—Captain Cameron Fraser, a cowed man. A broken man, I wonder?"

"Not cowed. Surrendered, bridled, and saddled, the reins held in the guiding hand of God." Yes, he wanted a drink right now. Desperately. But he would fight it. For Dassah. For himself. He'd make it to sixty-three days of sobriety.

"Bridled, you say." Zakir pursed his mouth. "If that is the case, then I will not spit upon this transformation of your spirit." He made a quick salaam. "This does not change the fact that you are, and always will be, my enemy."

"Zakir." Cam stopped him from turning away. "Enemy or not, before you go, I wish you God's blessing…but I must ask you one thing. About Dassah."

Zakir swung around. "What of Dassah?"

"There's something you need to know. She and I were married in September."

The tall Indian man before him went dreadfully still. He'd expected a reaction, but seeing Zakir take it badly didn't please him. At the same time a perverse sort of pride pushed forward. Dassah was his wife, and he didn't care for that proprietary disgust in Zakir's face as if Cam had snuck into the rajah's harem and stolen another man's bride. Dassah was his.

"You married Dassah." Zakir's fists hung at his sides.

Cam stood his ground. "She and I were married in Kashmir."

Zakir bowed his head, breathing heavily. "Then would you give your…wife my blessing upon her. For *her* good health."

"That's the issue." He regretted bringing up his and Dassah's marriage now. He looked down at his feet. The boys were packing up their cricket paraphernalia. Older lads were leading the younger ones up the stone steps and into the mission. He hated having to beg Zakir, but he needed all the irons in the fire he could get. As many eyes out there in the vast kaleidoscope of India as he could gather. "Thing is, Zakir, I…it is not easy, a mixed race marriage. I'm afraid Dassah is under a miscomprehension…."

"What are you saying, man? Is something wrong with Dassah?"

"Not that I'm aware of."

Zakir's eyes narrowed on him. "You do not know?" His former friend gave him a sham of a smile. "Do not tell me, Englishman, you have lost your wife."

Cam wanted to punch the lights out of Zakir, at the way the Indian man laughed. "As I said, she is under a misunderstanding. I love her with all my heart. She's my legal wife. I am only telling you this…if in your travels you happen to see her, I'm begging you…please tell her I want her back. To love and to cherish. That as you have seen, there has been a transformation of my spirit. I'm a new man." His mouth went dry.

Cam hadn't noticed the length of time they'd stood talking. Twilight was long gone. A few early stars struggled to shine. Lights flickered on in the houses surrounding the *bagh*. Cooking fires were lit, and the aroma of garlic hung heavy in the evening air.

Zakir lifted his head. He was the same height as Cam, yet at this moment he seemed taller. He smiled. "You have given me proof that there is a god, a god of vengeance. To see you defeated. I rejoice. I rejoice. I *will* find Dassah. And you can be assured I *will* give her a message, but not those futile words you sputtered. Dassah is a woman of this land. India! More likely Pakistan, not a woman to be wasted as the consort of our conquerors."

An iron hand gripped Cam's gut. A few months ago, he would have sought the nearest club to blot out the sort of anxiety that Zakir inflicted on him now. Blot it all out with drink. *Dear God, help me make it to sixty-three days*, because he could almost taste it on his tongue. Feel the buzzing in his mind that repeated the same message over and over. *You need a drink.*

21

At the cedar bench outside the chalet that was reserved for resort employees, Dassah blew on her frozen fingers. The journal she wrote in fell to her lap. She looked out over snow-covered grounds edged by an evergreen forest. These Swiss-style structures with steeply pointed roofs and scalloped wooden eaves were similar to the houses by Dal Lake, only twenty or so miles away. Close, and yet so far. Down in that valley she had been a wife for a time. Or so she had thought.

Sometimes the hurt felt as distant as steaming Calcutta. Other times the sorrow loomed as close as these Kashmiri peaks. So near, as if she could reach out and touch the glistening blue glaciers that would surely burn her flesh.

Last night, winter winds whistled over the crags and brought clean snow to the Gulmarg Ski Resort. That wind crept through the cracks of the small room at the top of the employees' chalet where she and Tikah lived, and she woke many times in the night wishing for another blanket.

She tucked her hands into the sleeves of the woolen Kashmiri coat and shivered, thankful for the knee-length *phiran*, that soft woolen tunic embroidered in a swirl of butterflies that she continued to wear. She had been unable to return the garment to Kavita as yet. Woolen leggings and thick fur-lined boots kept her feet warm...almost. She still required an extra shawl around her shoulders. Though the cold penetrated her bones, sunlight dancing on snow brought her a fresh delight, a small joy to soothe the wounding of her soul. When she closed her eyes, she pretended she was far away from India, in another country, far to the north, far from the memories of Cam.

After five months, the weight of leaving him continued to crush as if it were the very day she left their houseboat. Only Tikah's company, and this snow-covered mountain, gave her some joy. She had started a diary a few days after they left Srinagar, on October eighteenth, and it kept an accurate count to today.

The day after she left Cam, they had been brought to Gulmarg by car. That journey would have been one of enchantment if her heart had not been shattered, as she wondered if Cam searched for her. In October, the fir-covered valley glowed with a golden hue, and roads were bordered by rigid lines of poplar trees, straight as sentries. Villages they passed would not have been out of place in a book of fairy tales. As the car climbed the mountain to Nedou's Hotel nestled near these Himalayan peaks, she had found some solace, as if entering a dream.

Tikah found work in the kitchens, and Dassah had cleaned the guest rooms for a time.

But in December, she began to feel ill, so that only her *amma* earned their keep. It was also in December that Dassah touched the snow as it began to fall and found in its tingling cold the reassurance that life would bloom in her heart again one day, just as life bloomed in her womb. Perhaps she would rejoice when the snows melted, when Gulmarg ran with crystal streams and surrounding meadows burst with flowers, when she held Cam's child in her arms.

But for now this new season and these new surroundings gave her a glimpse into another aspect of God. Though she missed birdsong, she felt the quiet companionship of the Lord in the silence of these snow-covered mountains. Pine and deodar-scented woods, emerald and jade, against a blanket of pure white brought to her mind a Bible verse she had learned as a child. "Though your sins be as scarlet, they shall be white as snow." That comforted her soul but did little to stop her tears in the night when she fought to weep silently.

She had not realized she was unmarried when she allowed Cam to take her to his bed. The happiness of being in his arms was now stained with shame. Soiled. She should have known. But even if that sin were not her sin—but his—she still yearned for the grace of Yeshu. Her heart reached for the teachings from her mission childhood as never before.

Pulling her hands out of the warm sleeves, she blew on stiff fingers and put her fountain pen to the journal. In these pages she found renewed strength as she wrote the expressions of her being, of how she related to the Almighty. But who this journal was for, she did not know. Herself, perhaps? Her baby? For Cam—to send to him in the post one day—so he would know about the days his child grew safely beneath her heart?

Tikah came around the corner of the building and under the overhang where Dassah sat. Shaking snow from her boots and leggings, Tikah shivered and *burrrred*. She adjusted her thick Kashmiri shawls around her shoulders. Though this mountain village—a favorite holiday spot for the British—suited Dassah, it did not appeal to Tikah.

Without a greeting, she touched Dassah's forehead and cheeks, murmuring, "Have you been ill since I left you this morning?"

"Only once, *Amma*."

"Better than yesterday, but the day is still young. Have you been able to keep anything down?"

"The broth. Some bread."

"You need more fruit." Tikah sat on the wooden bench. "If only I had not listened to that Englishwoman, and taken you back to the Punjab instead of letting her bring us in her car to this bitter place. What foolishness. Wealthy Indians and British sliding down snow-covered hills on skinny wooden sticks."

Her *amma's* comment brought a smile to Dassah. "This place is not bitter. Frozen, yes, but exquisite. As though we live in the clouds." Her thoughts had taken such poetic turns of late. *In God I live and move and have my being. I am more than a precious sparrow in his eyes.*

Tikah tut-tutted. "Are you sure you are not speaking from fever?" She felt Dassah's forehead again. "At least down in the plains we could be sitting on jute *charpoys* under the mango trees, enjoying the monkey *wallahs* and eating sugarcane instead of bundling up in so many clothes. It is more icy here than the Baluchistan desert at night."

"Stop, *Amma*, you bring me fruit enough." She placed her hand on her abdomen. Surely this sickness would soon pass.

Tikah had enough of looking at the snow. She had only two hours to rest before she returned to the kitchens for the evening meal. She got to her feet and reached down to help Dassah rise. "Come, you need to eat. The paths have recently been cleared but are slippery. Lean on me." She tsked-tsked. "What are you thinking? What if you had fallen?"

"I am all right, *Amma*."

As they crept along the wall of their lodgings, they could see the main entrance for the resort. Skis and ski poles were propped on the veranda against the cedar walls. British people, fresh-faced from being out on the slopes all day, strolled inside the main foyer. So too did a few wealthy Indians. Their clothing seemed outlandish to Dassah when she first came here, nylon pantaloons and jackets, heavy woolen jumpers, scarves and toques.

Tikah clucked her tongue. "I am not pleased with your lack of appetite. We will have the doctor visit you again."

Dassah tugged on the woolen sleeve of Tikah's heavily embroidered tunic. "We do not have the money. Besides, the doctor will only tell me what he told me last week. To rest."

She reached the door to their own quarters and climbed the stairs to their room. The log walls did not reflect much light, but Dassah savored their fragrance of cedar and pine. In their room at the end of the hall, Tikah opened their door, and Dassah moved quickly to the cot by the window and sank upon it.

Tikah's frown creased deeper. "Are you faint?"

"A little."

In a whirl of her heavy Kashmiri skirt, Tikah turned to make tea at the brazier. Dassah removed her coat but wrapped her shawl around her shoulders.

Tikah brought her a cup of saffron tea with honey and placed a plate of *bakarkhani*, Kashmiri bread, beside her on a rickety table. Dassah had come to relish this bread that was thinner than *naan* and sprinkled with sesame seeds. Perhaps if she ate very, very slowly, she might keep this down.

They sat in the quiet of early afternoon, but after a while Dassah noticed the lines between Tikah's brows were deeper than usual.

"*Amma*, is something troubling you?"

Tikah lifted her hand and let it drop. "It is best you know. I have seen her again."

"Who?" Though she asked, they both knew there was only one *her*.

"Phoebe, the one who brought us here. She has come up to ski with her friends."

If Phoebe was here with friends...? A shiver ran through Dassah's center. She swallowed deeply. "Is he...?"

"No, beloved, I have already ascertained. Cam is not among them."

Her sudden fear—or was it exhilaration—of being discovered by Cam faded. Her head swam from her thinking. For one wild minute she hoped he had come looking for her. But nothing would change. Yes, he would gather her close, take her home and kiss her through the night. But in the morning she would still be what he had made her, his mistress. The temptation would have been strong to resist, to take what crumb of affections he had for her. Except there was now his child.

Tikah sat next to her on the cot. "Have you bled since last week?"

"*Amma*, you know I would tell you." Her sickness had been worse than normal, and there had been bleeding on two occasions.

"It is only that I fear. I have never known the joy of pregnancy, but from caring for mothers at the mission I know that by this month you should be feeling better. You worry me when you go outside."

"All right, *Amma*, as you wish. I will remain inside until we are sure I will not lose the baby."

The features of Tikah took on the softness that transformed her from a tired old woman to a vibrant one in her fifties. Though Dassah's baby was not her grandchild by blood, this infant was her grandchild by reason of the heart. Tikah gently patted Dassah's tummy. "Of course, comfort of my life, we must do all we can to protect the little one." *Amma* released a sigh. "Being with you, as you bear this baby, my beloved daughter, it is as though God has heard my prayers. At long last I will be a grandmother when my very name means *barren*."

Dassah took up Tikah's hand and held it to her cheek. "It is so, *Amma*, not only are you the mother of my heart, it is the will of God that my child be laid upon your lap like Ruth laid Obed upon the lap of Naomi."

Tikah's eyes shimmered bright. "You would bless me in the way of the Christian's Holy Book? I, who have turned my back on Yeshu?"

"Yes, *Amma*. For though we for a time separated ourselves from Yeshu, the understanding has been renewed in my heart that he has never left us. Now rest. You must be tired." Her *amma* grew silent in gentle weeping, and Dassah watched her slip into peaceful sleep. For a time, she watched the rise and fall of Tikah at rest.

Sunlight on the snow pulled her gaze to the slopes outside, to hotel guests swooping down the mountain, but the sesame seed bread lost its flavor. Her hot saffron tea changed to merely warm, flat water. Phoebe and the rest of Cam's friends were here. But as far as she was concerned, these English people could ski the slopes of the Gulmarg until the snows melted. Or dance the nights away in Srinagar. Or drink themselves to forgetfulness. Nothing of the British Raj and their amusements mattered any longer.

Even if Cam were here, she would not seek him out, but as Tikah continued her deep sleep, the desire to learn how Cam was doing would not leave her. Would it not be best to let him know about his child, for medical reasons? He could afford the best of care....

And Phoebe was here. She must have news of Cam.

A soft snore broke the silence. She glanced at Tikah's sleeping form. *Amma* should remain in sound slumber for at least an hour. What would it harm to ask a few questions?

Dassah eased off the *charpoy* and dressed in her coat and boots. Closing the door behind her, she slipped into the hallway, down the stairs, out to the grounds between the employee lodgings and to the main part of the hotel. As she crossed over to the shoveled paths for the guests, she thought back to those days when she first left Cam in October.

She and Tikah had been waiting at the bus station in Srinagar—hiding from view in case Cam saw them. But it was that woman, Phoebe, who found them. At first Dassah had recoiled from her approach. Phoebe was the last person in the world she wanted to see. Nor did she believe Phoebe when the Englishwoman explained that she just happened to see them by accident as they stood waiting in line for the bus. Phoebe's words had the ring of a lie. The way the woman had pouted, it was evident that somehow—as women know these things—Phoebe guessed that Dassah was far more than a servant to Cam. Phoebe in her jealousy had rightly ascertained that Dassah was his...mistress.

It was Tikah who, in listening to Phoebe, decided that it would be wise to accept her offer to bring them to this place where they could find employment. Tikah reasoned they could afford to be insulted by this woman since Gulmarg sounded as good as any place to start over again. And they would have the comfort of a car instead of the crowded, smelly bus.

Though it sliced deep at her heart, Dassah agreed to come here in Phoebe's vehicle. Phoebe left them here that day, after convincing the hotel owner, a friend of hers, to hire them.

The wind blew off the mountain, picking up the white crystal powder, throwing a cloud of it against Dassah's hot face. Perhaps Tikah was correct. She did not feel well. Overheated now. A wave of nausea. But the strength of her need to hear something about Cam goaded her on. Dassah glanced up the path, filled with guests trudging down from the slopes with their skis and poles balanced on their shoulders. Their laughter and chatter bounced off her. Phoebe was not among them. She might already be inside the hotel, taking tea.

Dassah followed a group of English people inside the hotel foyer. Normally she went through the doors at the back for employees. She must find Phoebe before the manager saw her and sent her from the guests' lounge.

In moments, she found her. Phoebe perched on the end of a settee, close to the window with a group of male and female friends. They sipped from cups of tea at a low table, chatting, laughing, just as the people on the hills outside did. People, wealthy in their opportunities to take a holiday.

And then Dassah saw him. Her love. Her heart turned over. Tikah had told her Cam was not here in Gulmarg, but there he was. Heat enflamed her cheeks. He would see her...if he but turned. Surely, he would sense that she was here? Surely, he would want her? *Yeshu, I am not strong.* No matter what little Cam could offer her, she wanted to be with him. Even if she was his wife only in *her* heart.

But his back was turned to her, he was facing Phoebe. Why must this woman steal her love? The world turned dark.

But he turned. It was not her beloved's profile. Only a man who looked like him from the back. Her heart eased only a little. Or was it that it broke again so she felt only numbness?

Phoebe must have sensed her stare and looked up. A pout like that of the time she found Dassah and Tikah in Srinagar spoiled her mouth again.

Trembling, Dassah dipped her head, a silent gesture asking for a moment of the young Englishwoman's time. From the hard line to Phoebe's mouth, it was clear she had no wish to talk to Dassah, but she rose anyway and wove through the crowd of hotel guests. She strode in front of Dassah, leading the way outside to the wide cedar veranda. Taking shelter from the wind behind a carved pillar, she crossed her arms and swung around to face Dassah. "What is it, Dassah? I got you these jobs, what more can you possibly expect me to do for you? I don't have much money."

"It was most kind of you to offer your help, but if you will recall correctly, it was you who approached Tikah and me in Srinagar. We did not ask for your help." She folded her arms across her middle too, so this woman would not see how her rudeness affected her.

The Englishwoman's complexion flushed to the shade of her pink scarf. "You're quite right. I'm sorry. Very well, what can I do for you?"

"I will keep this brief. I wish to know if you have seen Cam...if he is well."

Phoebe glanced at the powdery snow swirling at their feet along the veranda. "Now really, what can the business of a *sahib's* life be to you?"

The pain of that statement drove deep. A sharp knife in the center of her being. It took many heartbeats to regain her breath. "I think you surmised that I was more than a mere servant to Cam. Is that not why you helped me leave Srinagar without his notice?"

The woman's flush deepened. "I got you out of Srinagar because the situation isn't good for you, or him, or when he marries someday." She met Dassah's gaze. "Especially as I will be his wife."

Dassah placed a hand at her abdomen to ease the pain from these wounding words. "When will…your happy occasion take place?"

The other woman let out brittle laughter. Her mouth no longer pouting, but pulled downward. "Darling Cam is a hard man to pin down, but our wedding will be as charming as his sister's, I'm sure."

The swirling snow within the deodar trees drew Dassah's gaze, giving her a moment to regain her voice. "You were invited to Eva's wedding?"

"Of course. Been friends of the family for years. But then, you knew them from their mission work, didn't you? Well, I can tell you Eva was absolutely heavenly. Harry almost as handsome as Cam, and Miri was her usual…well, you know Miriam, a bit of a bossy know-it-all."

"And his parents?"

"Charming as ever."

Dassah's throat thickened. "I will leave you now."

"Is that all you wanted?" Phoebe's voice rose as Dassah took steps off the veranda and to the path. "Dassah, I don't mean to be cruel, but really, this is better for you…and Cam. These things happen." Her voice grew fainter as Dassah picked up her pace. "I'm sure Cam never meant to hurt you in this way, Dassah. But it can never be. You see that, don't you? Better to find a nice man of your own kind. I do wish you well."

Phoebe's voice faded completely. She must have gone inside the hotel. A buzzing filled the air. But how could there be locusts in this place of winter… and cold?

Phoebe had been to Eva's wedding. The buzzing in Dassah's ears grew louder. Her eyes stung. All of his family would have attended that wedding. Those who were important to the family, invited. A pain in her abdomen stole her breath. There would have been at least one banquet. Perhaps many banquets like in Indian weddings. His mother and father—they would have stood up with their daughter, pride shining from their eyes. Miri and other relatives—Cam, too—must have laughed and danced at his sister's wedding. Danced with Phoebe.

In the lower center of her body, a stabbing brought her to her knees. Her fingers gripped the snow. So cold. She lost all feeling to the rest of her body. Only the terrible ache where her baby slept. A terrifying wetness between her legs.

Someone called her name, "Dassah!"

Dassah rolled to look where she had been hunched in the snow. A small spatter of blood created a crimson pattern against the white, sparkling powder.

Hands took her. Tikah's hands. Others came running, speaking in rapid Kashmiri. She was lifted…and blackness overtook….

She had been dreaming of birds singing, sparrows and little bulbuls when the scent of lemons teased Dassah from the darkness. The perfume of saffron tea. Tikah's voice and that of a man speaking low. Cedar and pine, the smells of the walls in their room filled her senses. She murmured.

"Heart of my heart," Tikah said, rushing to her side to sit on the cot.

"*Amma*?" She shielded her eyes from the lamp burning on the table. Rising on her elbow, she looked through the window to the night. "How long?"

"You have been unconscious for close to an hour."

She recognized the man talking as the doctor.

"This can happen with emotional distress. No more gallivanting on the icy paths outside—"

"My baby?"

"You have not lost the child." He stopped when he saw her tears. "It is all right, but again there was bleeding, so I am ordering complete bed rest." He wrote on a paper and gave it to Tikah. "See that she takes this tonic to build her strength."

Dassah could not look up, only weep for gratitude that her child was still with her.

The doctor stood over her. "Your *amma* tells me that your husband is dead. I am very sorry, but I must also say to you, try to keep your heart from breaking. Anguish can cause your baby to be delivered before it is time."

Tikah let the doctor out and returned to sit on the edge of the cot. "Will you do as the doctor has said? I saw what you did. You talked to that woman."

"Yes, *Amma*, I am sorry."

"It is lucky for you that Phoebe did not notice. If she had seen you fall, she might have been curious to discover why. What if she put two and two together and told Cam? He might come for the baby then, and take our baby away." Tikah's voice pitched to a raw height.

"He would not take my baby from me."

"Do you know anything about a *sahib*, really? He has already fooled you once, like his father fooled me. Like all men, if the child is a boy he would want to raise him, casting you aside. Perhaps letting that other woman take him for her own."

Though the blankets around her were warm, Dassah went cold. No. No. Cam could not...would not. "You say Phoebe knows nothing of my condition?"

"I found you as I saw her going into the hotel. Then you fell. For the sake of your baby you must put all thought of English life away forever."

"Yes, *Amma*." She scrubbed away scalding tears. No more. She would not risk her baby's life by yearning for what could never be. Though Cam could provide the best of medical care, she would not give anyone the opportunity to steal her baby from her. And no matter how much she loved him, she could not be his mistress.

22

Delhi, March 20, 1947

She must have been stark raving bonkers to agree to join Dad and Mother for the Swearing In. But when Miriam brought it up to Principal McNair, Isabella insisted Miriam join her parents and report back with her firsthand impressions for the student body.

Delhi was a raging kiln in March, and the cheering crowds deafened Miriam. The open horse-drawn carriage conveyed the new viceroy and vicereine past, but she caught hardly a glimpse. Too many bobbing heads in the way with crowds, six people deep, lining both sides of the wide Parliament Street leading up to Viceroy House. All Miriam saw was the top of Mountbatten's military cap and some stylish little hat that presumably belonged to his wife, Edwina, as the carriage rolled past.

So much for capturing photographs with her own Brownie. Still, Miriam sighed. She always grew misty over the Sikh Regiment sitting their steeds, their gorgeous uniforms, elegant turbans with regimental insignia, lances pointing skyward. Or was it the Celtic wail of bagpipes from the Scots' Fusiliers that brought on this sentimentality? The crowds went mad, as usual, even though violence was breaking out like a pox over the entire country, especially in the north. The Indian people loved nothing better than a good show. And no one displayed pomp better than the English.

Perfect lines of mounted Indian Cavalry followed the carriage, and a number of black sedans. No doubt one of those official vehicles contained her brother, and she strained her neck to see. As one of the new aides-de-camp to Mountbatten, Cam must have been out to the airport to greet the new viceroy.

Hemmed in by a wall of bodies, she attempted to snap some more photos before a burly British sergeant squeezed in front and she gave up. Better to shove her way out of the crowd. She mopped her throat with a handkerchief.

Like any properly dressed British *memsahib*, she wore her wrist-length gloves and stockings with this linen frock, but Miriam wished she could go back to the hotel, rip these clothes off, and dive into the hotel pool.

Not once had she and Cam talked since she left Sialkot after Eva's wedding. In Mother's letters, Miriam had learned he was still sober. Aside from the weekly stilted missive she sent Cam, and his dutiful weekly return, they'd barely scratched the surface. How did one go about asking, "Well, Cam, do you think you'll fall off the wagon? Become a drunk again anytime soon?"

After that evening in their parents' parlor, hearing his abysmal story that he'd secretly married Dassah and not told a soul, she had to get up then and there, or she'd have hit him. Better for his health she'd left Sialkot the next day, and now she was here in Delhi, and so was he. Time to drum up the courage to face him.

Thing was, she missed him terribly.

Behind the crowds lining the road, she started walking in the direction of the hotel. When she reached the hotel's drive flanked by parallel rows of king palms, a man called out, "So there you are. Had enough already?"

She looked up to see Jack in civvies, leaning against the trunk of one of the tall palms. "Don't you ever work?" she asked.

With hands in his trouser pockets, he sauntered in her direction. "I haven't seen you since December and you assume the whole time I've been on holiday. I'll have you know I've had the old nose to the grindstone. I'm here for the festivities."

She got into step with him. "Are you attending the garden party after the Swearing In?"

"Managed to wangle an invite. I assume your name is on the guest list. So how do you feel, Miss Miriam Richards, about our first kiss taking place in the Mogul Gardens of the viceroy's palace? Under the moonlight. I could slip you away. Dip you over my arm. Lean you back—"

"Take liberties before I say you may, Lieutenant Colonel, and you will end up losing your head." But a tiny shiver danced its way down her spine.

Though he strode at her side, he tilted his head to see beneath her hat. "Your words may say *no*, but your bewitching lips say otherwise."

"Watch these lips carefully, Jack. I am here on official college business."

His sigh would have put a dying man to shame. "Ah yes, the students and the prim theology professor. Will you at least let me buy you a cup of tea?"

She was dying of thirst. Before she had a chance to refuse, he offered his arm and hailed a rickshaw. Sitting next to him as the streets of Delhi whirled past brought the illusion of a breeze. They left New Delhi behind with its monumental government buildings and headed for the old section of the city.

The narrowing streets were crowded with people. Stalls overflowed with food, silk, and flowers. Animals—goats, cows, and a few scrawny dogs—meandered among the bazaars. She snapped a few pictures before stowing her Brownie in its carrying bag. "New Delhi is impressive, but I love Old Delhi, don't you?"

Jack leaned far too close, looking over her side of the rickshaw so that if she moved two inches her mouth would meet his chin. "Miriam, darling, while I agree Old Delhi is much more colorful, it is terribly crowded, and there's always that inevitable odor of dung."

"You really know how to woo a woman. How is it you're still single?"

"It took me till now to find the right woman." He didn't bother to wait for any repartee on her part, but called out to stop the rickshaw.

She wouldn't give any weight to his idiotic statement as he helped her down. Jack seemed bent on romancing her and tucked her arm in his. They strolled along the bazaar, past cauldrons of cooking rice, vegetable stalls, silk merchants with reams of shimmering rivers of ruby, emerald, amethyst. The scent of cloves and sandalwood filled her senses. So too did the clean smell of his soap.

He stopped by a stall piled high with masses of marigolds and jasmine, their combined sweet and musky perfume making her dizzy. "Are you still angry with me, Miriam, for what I said about Cam? You haven't responded to any of my letters."

"I've quite forgiven you, Jack. Besides, you were brave to tell me. And Cam is doing very well, thank you."

Crowds eddied past them as though they were a stone in the middle of a stream. His voice dipped to bass as he leaned closer. "Am I forgiven enough to seriously court you?"

"Court me?" The image of Eva's trousseau filled her mind.

"I believe a woman of fervent Christian faith like you may prefer the old-fashioned mode of doing things. So, yes, court you."

That little shiver dancing down her spine turned into the tango. "Why would you wish to…court me?"

"Because, Miriam, I'm going to work very hard to become the man you want to marry."

Her dress was sticking to her back. The dizzying fragrance of jasmine muddied into the overpowering musk of marigolds, and she caught a trace of the refuse in the air. Any pictures in her mind of silk and satin and Jack's kisses popped like soap bubbles. A man shouldn't have to work hard to become what a woman wanted in marriage. They should simply fall in love. Shouldn't they?

From where Cam stood with another of the ADCs, he could see his parents take their seats in the throne room. Outside, a monumental throng waited, along with a crowd of reporters from around the world. Members of the armed palace bodyguard kept the population a safe distance from the steps carpeted in crimson, and leading up to the pillared columns into the Durbar Hall. If anything it was even hotter this morning than when Mountbatten arrived two days ago. But in this marble room with domed ceiling there was an illusion of coolness.

The Mountbattens didn't need to come by car or carriage today. Already installed in the palace, they merely had to walk from one end of this imposing bastion to the other. Brisk exercise that. A good ten minutes to walk from the bedrooms assigned to the new viceroy to the dining room. Today, it might take fifteen minutes for Lady Mountbatten to walk from her room to the Durbar Hall in heels and gown.

A signal from the head ADC let him know that the viceroy and his wife had arrived and waited outside the closed bronze doors.

Inside, the room echoed with the buzz of hundreds of hushed human voices. British in impeccable suits, dignitaries from around the world, Sikh leaders in European suits with silk turbans, Indians in Rajput coats, Gandhi hats, Muslim prayer caps, all seated on plush velvet and gilded chairs. Gandhi was not in attendance, being unwilling to leave Calcutta where his presence kept some peace. As for the rest, whatever their religion they all seemed to hold their breath, waiting for the man they hoped, they prayed, would guide India to self-government without them tearing themselves apart.

From the top of the roof outside the palace came the shattering blare of trumpets.

The doors of the Durbar Hall opened, and the tall, elegant form of Louis Francis Albert Victor Nicholas Mountbatten, 1st Earl Mountbatten of Burma, began to walk up the carpeted aisle, his wife at his side. Cam's throat closed. If only Dassah were here to share in his pride over this historic moment for India. The last viceroy, wearing his dress naval whites, his array of orders and decorations covering his chest, and his dark blue ribbon designating him as a Knight of the Garter, was someone—representing something—to be proud of. Nehru himself had requested Mountbatten for his diplomacy and personal knowledge of India.

Lady Mountbatten matched her husband's stride in her long, simple gown of white silk. She wore a tiara and a ribbon crossed from shoulder to waist that held the New Order of the Crown of India, and her own array of medals earned during the war for her humanitarian work.

The two walked side by side up the aisle toward the gilded thrones waiting on a low dais. Behind the thrones, rich red hangings hid lighting that cast the hall in superb dignity. This was British India. The country Cam called home. Not that small green island—England—thousands of miles to the north, but this massive dusty, vibrant mosaic of a subcontinent.

But soon the two hundred years of British rule over India would be finished, a mere flash in the pan of history.

God help them came his wordless prayer. And God help Mountbatten. Shortly after joining the viceroy staff, Cam became aware that Mountbatten's task was impossible. The country stood on the brink of the volcano.

Keep her safe, Lord. Keep her safe until I can find her.

As the sun set, the vast geometrically laid out courtyards drew Miriam's eye. Yesterday she'd taken a number of photos to show her students, and for herself. She'd never been to Viceroy House before. Mother and Father plenty of times, especially these days when Father was closeted with Pete Rees on preliminary discussions over separating the army next year.

So much to do by June, 1948. She'd heard that date uttered over and over since Mountbatten arrived. "Not possible," everyone said. "Too little time to transfer power of full government." That would be something to add to her talk during the student assembly. Many of her students were worried already how the handover would affect their young lives.

But tonight the extensive Mogul Gardens with their pools and channels, roses, lilies, jasmine, every exotic Indian flower she knew, led her thoughts in another direction. As she'd dressed for the evening, she'd told herself to be sensible. *He's a bit old for you.* And what did she really know about Jack other than he excited her like no man ever before?

She turned to survey the garden party in search of him, though he'd yet to arrive. Swarms of servants wove through hundreds of guests, balancing trays of cocktails, fruit drinks, hors d'oeuvres. Lights shimmered in the garden foliage while Indian ladies shimmered equally in silk saris. Englishwomen held their own in the latest from Paris and London. Her own mother and father were a distance away nattering with military bigwigs. But the royal stars of the show, the Mountbattens, looked wonderfully chic, along with their young adult daughter, Pamela.

Music played from somewhere, a combination of modern tunes and classics, Indian music too. Whether it was the excitement of the illustrious occasion or that Miriam was dressed for once in something terribly stylish, a mass of fireflies was doing the jitterbug in her stomach. Her knee-length cocktail dress molded to her figure in diaphanous stuff like cobwebs made from starlight, giving her a sensual feeling she was not used to at all, and she gave a little laugh.

"Utterly charming." Jack's voice held a strange huskiness from where he stood not three feet away. She hadn't seen him arrive. In his precise dress uniform, epaulets on his shoulders, military cap on his head, he held a single, long-stemmed yellow rose.

She felt the heat flame in her cheeks at his perusal. *Get thee to a nunnery* ran through her mind.

"Miriam," Jack murmured. "You have the look of a scared mongoose."

"And you're the cobra."

"If that's the case, keep in mind it's the mongoose that kills the snake." He took her by the arm, his smile slipping a tad. "Really, can't you think of nicer analogies for us?"

She'd hurt his feelings. As they hurried through the paths of gardens, she interjected a laugh. "You started it, Lieutenant Colonel, by saying I looked like a frightened mongoose. And must we do the hundred yard dash?"

But they continued to scurry, dodging guests and servants. She was practically out of breath by the time he stopped near a group of trees out of sight from others. From here the music floated in discordant waves. But in all honesty, it wasn't the pace he'd pushed her to, but something else, that elusive sensual somersault in the pit of her stomach. A weakness in her knees from the look in his eyes. A hunger she'd never felt before when her gaze studied the shape of his mouth.

The bark of a tree brushed her bare shoulder. Jack put out a hand to brace them both, so that she was in his arms. His mouth landed on hers before she could think. She could no longer feel her feet on the ground. Only his arms around her, the strength of his shoulder that he nestled her against. The warm, steady, moving pressure of his lips on hers.

She wound her arms up over his shoulders. There was nothing else in this world...nothing.

He set her from him. "Miriam." His voice was breathy but nothing like what was going on inside her, her heart beating like a hundred village tom-toms.

"Had to do it, Miriam. Planned to woo you. Stroll the gardens, but when I saw you twaddling about like a girl at her first fancy dress ball I lost all sense of decorum. I want to marry you, you beautiful, nose-in-a-book schoolmarm."

"Marry? But only the other day you asked to court me."

"I know, but put me out of my misery. At least let me know there's a chance."

The man was in his forties, yet he stood there like a gauche boy straight out of military school. He'd been through the war, probably dallied with any number of women—she just knew that in her bones—and yet he wanted to marry her. And all she wanted right now—prim theological professor—was to get back into his arms and let him kiss her senseless. But marriage? She hadn't even got her mind around courtship.

From her lack of response he took the cue. "It's not a matter of the cat's got your tongue, is it?"

"Marriage...such a big step."

"I've never wanted to marry anyone before." He ran a hand around the back of his neck. She wanted to take him by the hand and tell him yes, they'd be married next week. But that would be madness. What did they really know about each other? Where would Jack go after Britain quit India? Did she want to live in England, another British colony like Kenya? Did she want to be the wife of a soldier?

He took her hand. "Come on, darling, you're taking far too long to think about this." Slowly they retraced their steps back to the larger gathering. Before they were in sight of her parents, he lifted her hand to his lips and gently let it drop. All spark of laughter had left his eyes.

"Jack, I need time—"

"Usually it's me who mouths words like that." He let out a bitter little laugh. "Dash it all, I never knew how statements like that could hurt." The next thing she knew he was making his way through the guests and was gone. The whole episode must have taken only twenty minutes. And she stood there as if every nerve in her body had blown a fuse and the lights went out.

"Miri?" Her brother laid a hand on her shoulder. "Miri, love, are you all right?"

A sniff came out first. Then a muffled howl as she turned to his shoulder.

Cam's arms came around her. "Oh, clever puss." He drew her to a quiet spot, not unlike the one Jack had just taken her too, pulled out a large hanky, put it up to her nose and told her to blow.

"Better now?" he asked a moment later.

"Oh, Cam, a perfectly wonderful man just proposed to me."

"Normally a cause for celebration."

"Yes, normally, but you and I seem to be a couple of dunderheads when it comes to romance."

"Speak for yourself. I happen to believe I made the right choice. I was just so ruddy stupid that I failed to announce it to the world."

"I could kick you in the shins for being such an idiot."

"I can think of far stronger words than idiot to describe me, but I'll not sizzle your ears with profanity. So, is it Jack Sunderland?"

She nodded.

"A good chap that. What's the problem?"

"I'm not sure. He certainly makes me feel—"

"No need for details, my gangbuster sister. I'm thinking you've awakened to your passions about ten years after the average person does."

"My darling brother, if you're insinuating I'm immature in that department, I'm not sure you're any wiser."

"Terribly astute of you, old girl. Have we been riding too long on our parents' coattails when it comes to the wisdom of life? This is really your department—theology and all—you of all people should know better, but have you just discovered that you desperately need God?"

She pulled back to study him. "Where on earth did that pearl of wisdom germinate?"

"The oyster of pain, I suppose." He slanted her a wry grin. "It wasn't until I planted my face in the dirt with my blasted drinking that I understood. I need Christ to live, to breathe. He's the only one who can disinfect my disgusting soul."

"Good gracious, Cam. You've become a Christian."

"I believe I have. I'm glad for my sake of course, but mostly I'm glad for Dassah. With God's help I want to become the man she deserves for a husband."

"Working hard at it?" she asked, thinking of what Jack said to her the other day. I'm *going to work very hard to become the man you want to marry.* She placed her hand on top of Cam's where it lay on his knee. "It's time for me to say how

163

proud I am of you. Not easy to give up the crutch of alcohol."

He looked down at his feet. "No." He rolled his shoulders back. "But never mind me. You, my almost perfect sister, must decide what you'll do with this proposal. Marry this highly decorated and respected soldier? Of course that will mean leaving India."

Her gaze searched the garden party for Jack, though she suspected he'd left. All her life, people had been talking about Britain leaving India. But now that the event drew near…how could she do it? How could she possibly leave India?

23

The khaki-colored north of India wavered in the heat. It hadn't been this hot in India in seventy-five years, they said. That insignificant fact in the face of genocide stuck in Cam's head. His feet, encased in military boots, stirred up ash as he stumbled through chards of broken bricks. He followed Lord Louis in his green khaki drill, and Lady Mountbatten in her official Red Cross relief uniform, also in jungle green. They made their way through the maze of crumbling buildings. As far as Cam could see, ruined roofs, missing walls, and jagged pieces of windows were all that was left of the village of Kahutal. A few survivors sat silently in the dust.

Lord Louis stopped ahead of Cam and stared around him at the extent of the violence. "It's hard to take in." He gestured to the town flattened by riots. "This entire Hindu-Sikh part of the Punjab is an absolute wreck."

"As if it had been subjected to an air raid," Cam murmured.

Mountbatten narrowed his eyes at the scene. "Quite right, Captain."

The vicereine turned away. Though she'd seen much suffering in Burma and Malaya, Lady Mountbatten's long silence said it all. A moment later, she cleared her voice. "Is it true? A large number of Sikhs and Hindus forcibly converted? Children kidnapped?"

"Young women abducted and openly raped," Cam added. A vision of Dassah being ravaged assaulted his mind. A knife seemed to slide through his heart.

Pockets of violence were spreading in size all over India like a bad rash in response to the idea of partition, whether for or against. Hindus and Sikh against Muslims. Muslims against Hindus and Sikhs. Whole towns wiped out.

In conjunction with her husband, Lady Mountbatten began to issue sharp orders as she conferred with local civil servants. Standing in the midst of the charred remains of this village, she arranged for medical help for those few who had escaped the slaughter, those terribly wounded who amazingly still breathed. Food would be flown in, outdoor kitchens set up to feed the multitudes of displaced people trickling in from other villages.

While it was true that in only one month the new viceroy had done what previous viceroys had been unable to do—break the deadlock between the two main political parties—Partition, now with a capital P, was becoming a reality. Bloodshed in the north had escalated to a pitch Cam had seen only in war. The word *Pakistan* was slashed in green paint on the doors of houses of unearthly quiet towns with its lives and voices snuffed out.

Like the mother and child half buried beneath that pile of blackened bricks two feet away from Cam. A few clay toys were strewn around, close to the child's hand where her rag doll lay filthy in the ashes.

That image, not the sun bearing down on Cam's cap, wrapped a tightening band of steel around his head. Dassah could be in any small town like this. He could only pray with heat-scorched breath that she was safe in some quiet backwater, if there was such a thing in India these days. Or that she wore a cross around her neck. Some said that pretending to be a Christian might save an Indian's life right now. *Dear God, let that be true.* But then, so small a part of the population, the Christians and other minorities were just pushed aside by the greater swell of hatred. With only a year to go, everyone worried on what side of the new borders their town or city would lie. *What will Pakistan look like? What will be the shape of India when all is said and done?*

Lady Mountbatten picked her way through the rubble beside her husband and their entourage of ADCs, bodyguards, soldiers, the governor of the province, and various military and political personnel. Ahead of Cam, the Mountbattens were doing what they could for this town. Refugee camps were springing up everywhere you looked—camps of thousands who stared with wild eyes as if the world was coming to an end.

On Wednesday, the viceroy and his daughter Pamela prepared to fly back to Delhi in the York aircraft while Cam arranged for Lady Mountbatten's briefcase to be taken to a separate car. He would carry on with the vicereine for the rest of her tour of the Punjab.

Cam closed his own briefcase, placed it in the boot of the car, and checked his revolver. After she said her good-byes to her husband and daughter, Lady Mountbatten slipped inside the backseat of the car and sank against the upholstery. Cam got in the back next to her. Her bodyguard sat in the front beside the driver and turned around to address him. "All accounted for, Captain. Both cars are ready to leave on your word."

"Then let's be off," Cam ordered with a sideways glance at her ladyship. This morning her complexion was a bit gray. One couldn't act as her aide-de-camp and not notice she suffered from headaches, though she hid it well.

Edwina Mountbatten was an unusual woman to say the least. She hated the fuss and standing on ceremony of her husband's British royalty. The fact that Lord Louis was the great-grandson of Queen Victoria did not impress her. The morality of her private life wouldn't bear much scrutiny, nor, Cam suspected, would Mountbatten's. An odd marriage. Nonetheless the vicereine was tireless in her relief work here in India, as she'd been during the war—one small thing to be thankful for. All around him, people were suffering in ways that made him shudder, and him a seasoned soldier.

As they headed down the road toward Lahore, she adjusted her Red Cross cap and traced one finger along her temple.

"Madam, are you sure you should continue? I can't help but notice you are unwell."

She gave him a tired smile. "Dickie relies on my assessments."

"Your husband is wise to depend on your observation skills."

She laughed at him. "So he says. Frequently. But yes, we're a good team. He'll get back to work hammering out the details with the politicians in Delhi while I get on with the medical and social welfare organizations. They need to be ready when we make our exit."

He settled himself back in the seat. The miles to Lahore would give them both a bit of a rest. This past month they'd run on little sleep to keep up the unceasing pace for meetings, visiting orphanages, hospitals, and refugee camps. "I was rather hoping that Gandhi could have drawn Nehru of the Hindu Congress and Jinnah of the Muslim League together."

"Don't count on it, Captain. The two days of Gandhi's visit to Viceroy House were wonderful. He even ate his habitual goat curd in front of us. Offered some to Dickie. Quite the honor, I assure you, but even Gandhi's last ditch efforts to stop Partition have come to nothing."

"I was as surprised as the rest of the staff that Gandhi had asked Nehru to allow Jinnah the place of prime minister of India, if it would keep unity."

Her eyes widened in admiration. "Nehru was wise enough to decline Gandhi's request to step down in favor of Jinnah. He knows Jinnah won't settle for anything other than running his own country. An obstinate man, that Jinnah, he wants his Pakistan carved out of India."

She closed her eyes to the mustard yellow countryside passing by. "Tell me something pleasant, Captain Fraser, anything to take my mind off the chaos and tragedy we've observed this past week. Any word of your wife?"

His heart did a little thump at the question. Edwina Mountbatten was like that, interested in the smallest details of all her staff. "Nothing yet, your ladyship. It's very kind of you to ask."

"Nothing of the sort. Do keep me informed, Captain. You mentioned that you were getting copies of your wife's photograph for the police in the areas we'll be touring? An excellent idea. If I can be of any help, let me know."

"Thank you, madam. I was able to obtain the photographs. I'm putting a lot of hope into the fact we're going to Lahore and Amritsar next."

"You mentioned that your former nanny runs a medical mission in Amritsar. I'm assuming she'll be interested in joining the relief coalition I'm organizing."

He chuckled. It seemed weeks since he had. Probably since the night he and Miriam chatted at the garden party after the Swearing In. "You will find Eshana to be as unflagging a relief worker as yourself. No doubt, my mother as well."

"Your mother is the wife of General Richards? Why yes, she and I have compared notes already, and added to what you've told me of your former nanny."

"If I know anything of Eshana, she has probably already set up a relief center in the *bagh*."

"Excellent. She's on my list. But Captain, as shocked as Dickie and I are to see the extent of this violence, our fear is growing that as we British leave India, the carnage could become far worse."

"Yes, madam, India is being ruptured as we speak." He turned to watch the passing countryside for a moment, his gnawing fear for Dassah creeping up again.

She watched him carefully. "Forgive my impertinence, but I must say I admire your open-mindedness in this part of the Empire that is known for its nauseating bias. How refreshing to find a British officer taking a stand such as you have—to marry an Indian woman for love. Makes me hope for a better world. Especially now in the face of…" Her brow knit. "I do hope you find your wife soon, Captain."

A number of students brushed past Miriam's desk so that a pile of marked exam papers slid to the floor. One of the girls knelt to pick them up. The group—ten, fifteen… no, more like two dozen students—crowded into Miriam's classroom, most of them from her Christian theology course. She noted Anjuli among them, except that today Anjuli was not accompanied by her best friend Faiza.

When most of the students made it inside the room, Anjuli began to weep. On closer inspection, most of the students were crying. Miriam stood from behind her desk and put an arm around Anjuli, who shoved her face into the crook of Miriam's shoulder and wept. "Now the semester is over," Anjuli said, "my father is saying I must finish my schooling in another city, one farther south. He will not let me return to Kinnaird in the autumn."

Shyla, a student from Bombay, clutched at Anjuli's sari. "Do not cry so hard, it is the same for all us Hindus. My father wanted to take me from Lahore weeks ago, but I begged him to let me finish this semester. He was right, though. I cannot believe what is happening."

All the girls started talking at once, all with the same story. They did not want to leave Kinnaird, but their faces were pinched with fear...and with something else. Clenched fists spoke of another emotion that could very well spiral out of that fear.

Shyla thrust the end of her sari over her shoulder. "I do not understand why these Muslims are killing our people. As if they are the only ones who want independence. Since I was a child, I too have wanted India to be free of British rule. My high school was a hub of nationalist movement. Why, I was the school's Head Girl, and copied down the statements of our Indian leaders in the school newspaper."

Another girl, Manvi, spoke up from the back of the classroom. "And I proudly wore my *khadi* uniform to support Gandhi's freedom movement." Manvi seemed to realize then who she was speaking to, a member of the so-called Raj, a British woman, and her cheeks flushed. "I mean no disrespect, miss."

"You have no need to feel embarrassed, Manvi. I'm in full support of Indian Independence. I hope I've made that clear in my talks with you."

Thankfully, the majority of the girls relaxed, so that Yogita, a chubby girl from Delhi, hooked her arm with Miriam's. "Most of us joined in marches in front of government buildings singing 'Vande Mataram' and 'Jana Gana Mana' in protest against the Raj. Our Muslim friends marched at our side. Never did we think that independence would lead to the division of India. Never did I think our neighbors—our fellow students—would try to kill us. It is unbelievable."

Shyla's voice rose shrill above the others. "Now we know that Muslims were never our friends." She took her eyes off Miriam and stared down every frightened girl in the room. "How many Hindus and Sikhs have been killed these past few months? Tens of thousands? Should we sit back and allow the Muslims to slaughter us? I say we should retaliate like Hindu men are doing already."

The classroom erupted with shocked murmurs. Anjuli stared at Shyla, her face no longer flushed but pale, her mouth trembling. Miriam held both Anjuli and Yogita close and sought the eyes of the rest of her students. "You speak of retaliation, but who picked up the first brick to throw? A Muslim? A Hindu? Who first set whose house on fire? And how can you douse a fire by adding more flames?"

Shyla glared at the floor, but most of the students hung on to Miriam's words until a noise from the hallway drew their attention.

Faiza stood at the threshold, her brimming eyes seeking those of Anjuli's. Unlike the sari that Anjuli wore, Faiza was dressed in the more northern tunic and pantaloons, her scarf covering her head.

"Faiza," Anjuli whispered. "Do you hate me because I am a Hindu?"

"No, my beloved friend," Faiza choked out between sobs. "Do you hate me because I am Muslim?"

Anjuli sent her friend a damp smile. "No, Faiza, you are my best friend."

"Lies! Lies!" Shyla wailed. "We Hindus need to protect ourselves. I say we must fight back. *Jai Hind!*" she shouted the counter slogan to that of *Pakistan*

Zindabad. Her hysteria was rising.

"Faiza," Miriam said over Shyla's panic, "come in and close the door." With the door closed, the classroom grew stifling, but it seemed to hold the world at bay and kept the hatred outside. Miriam gave them a few moments to settle before she spoke. A number of them wiped their wet faces and looked to her.

Young women, barely out of their teens, hungry for education. Bright minds, every one of them. Several had the makings of doctors, professors, politicians. *Dear God, what do I say to them?*

She was about to speak, but Faiza beat her to it. The young Muslim girl, her head covered with her scarf, quivered like the strings of an Indian sitar, but she stood tall. "As your fellow student, your sister of this college, you have my promise that I will do all I can to protect you. Yes, I am Muslim and you are Hindus and Sikhs, but our fellow Christian students and…me…will protect you, hide you if we must."

A gentle tap at the closed door interrupted Faiza. The door pushed open a crack, and another of the Muslim girls peeked around. "Faiza, we are here to support you." A wet sheen on the new girl's cheeks caught the light. She pushed into the classroom with a number of the Muslim girls behind her, and behind them, Principal Isabella McNair and Vice Principal Priobala. They must have been down the hall waiting, gearing up their courage.

Isabella came to stand beside Miriam. Her soft, gentle face brought a flutter of quiet breaths to the classroom. "I know you all are frightened. We will be addressing this in assembly tomorrow morning, but I'm glad you sought out Miss Richards for comfort. This terrible time has come upon us. India, Pakistan too, will need you students in the here and now, and in the years to come. I have always said I want our Kinnaird graduates to be as much at home behind a desk as behind a stove."

Each young, womanly face surrounded with sleek brown braids or hair hidden under a scarf concentrated on the small, determined Scotswoman as she continued. "You young women—not we your teachers, but *you*—will be the leaders who will help your communities come to grips with this severing of your land."

Her brogue thickened as tears glistened in her eyes. "There are hawks and doves in all sects. Let us band together, as Kinnaird sisters to protect one another, no matter what our religion. Let us safeguard one and all."

Glimmers of smiles flit over faces, easing those pinched looks. The girls reached out to each other, put arms around one another. Miriam watched Faiza comfort Anjuli.

Hawks and doves in all sects and communities. These educated minds would prove to be doves, of that Miriam was convinced. But if Kinnaird College in the city of Lahore ended up in the soon to be created Pakistan, someone needed to remain to protect these girls. Women like Isabella and Priobala and other teachers who weren't afraid to remain.

Maybe even a woman like her. But how long would Jack remain in this part of India? Or after Partition, where would he be posted? Would he be willing to be one of the few British who elected to stay on in India?

Lady Mountbatten had finished speaking to several groups of charitable organizations, and Cam escorted the weary vicereine to her guest rooms in the governor's mansion. It was late in the evening, but he could at last steal away for a few minutes. He'd sent Arvind Malik a telegram several days ago, telling him he would be here in Lahore tonight. There was no time to catch up with Miriam at her college, tomorrow he'd see Mother in Amritsar, but now he rushed outside to meet the banker.

The man he'd first met in Calcutta last August was considerably different from the man standing under a light on the wide steps of the mansion's portico. In August Arvind had overflowed with confidence. Tonight, though he still wore a dapper suit of light English tweed, his restless pacing gave him away. So too did the fact that he'd lost several pounds.

They shook hands, and Cam got right to the point. "Have you received any word of Dassah?"

"Dassah?" Arvind went ramrod straight. "After all these months, you ask me about my children's *ayah* who abandoned them? And then her *amma* left us too. What of my family, Captain? What are you British going to do to protect the innocent Indian people during this disaster? I met with you because you are now on the viceroy's staff, otherwise I would have left Lahore by now."

Cam strove to keep his own emotions under control. Their brief encounter during the Calcutta riots had proven the caliber of the man who stood before him. In another place they could have been friends, but the months since then had scraped at both their composures, shearing off the tolerance they would normally convey. "I'm sorry, Arvind. You are quite right. Tell me what is on your mind."

The banker seemed to deflate. "I am also sorry for my rudeness. You told me once that you knew Dassah as a child. Of course you would be concerned for her welfare."

A number of passersby studied them as they stood close to a sandstone pillar, and Cam gestured that they move out of earshot. "You are leaving this area then?"

"Yes, Captain, I have taken all my money and transferred it to my Bombay branch. I am leaving nothing here or in Calcutta but the bricks of my buildings, for fear they may end up as part of Pakistan. It was a mistake coming here, thinking I could trust my Muslim friends."

"But you used to believe as Gandhi did, that you cared not what religion a person was. I admired how you employed servants of all religions in your

Calcutta home."

"One changes when one sees their neighbors murdered in the name of Islam."

Without a word, they strolled close to the edge of the gardens, where Cam stared at the ground. Under the garden lamplight, petals of some red flower were loosened by the hot breeze and fluttered to the grass.

Arvind let out a deep sigh. "Many Muslims I have known have turned their backs on Hindus. Given the chance, I fear I will return that gesture of hatred. But I will do my best, Captain, to retain my tolerant nature that you admire, because you see, I also admire you. From the moment we met in the rubble of that derailed train, you struck me as, not simply the typical *sahib* with the English love of order and good deeds, but a person who appreciates the true India."

For some reason the red petals on the grass held Cam's gaze. She'd wanted a red sari. "Yes, Arvind, I do love India. This has been my home." He turned to look the banker in the eye. "In fact, it was my honor and privilege to take a woman of India as my wife. That's why I am asking if you have had word of Dassah? She is *my* family."

Arvind shut his eyes briefly. "I was afraid you had feelings for her when I saw the two of you together last August. Is this why she left us without explanation?"

"Yes, and I told her to keep our marriage secret. I'm sorrier than I can say for that now."

"But why are you asking me for the whereabouts of your wife?"

In the face of the current dangers, embarrassment was a luxury Cam couldn't afford. "Dassah mistook my desire for secrecy to mean that I was ashamed of our marriage. She left me in Kashmir, and I have no idea where she is."

The banker grasped his forearm. "I am indeed sorry to hear this."

The dismal truth weighed down on Cam's shoulders. "So you have heard nothing of them?"

"Nothing. I am sorry, Captain. Nor can I remain here to help you search for her."

His last hope, that Arvind had heard something from Dassah and Tikah, went up like cinders flying on hot smoke. On his own, he was already doing all he could to search for her in his position as ADC, and Dad too with his connections. But how could they search for one woman in a land where a tidal wave of people was surging both ways? Nor did Arvind seem to expect an answer from him. The compassion in his face said all too clearly what he thought of Cam's chances at finding Dassah.

With heavy steps he turned back with Arvind, leaving the garden behind.

Arvind stopped him at the end of the drive. "Captain, as a man who has lived most of his life in India, I am sure you are as used to the black outline of India's shape as I am. That shape of India from as far north as Afghanistan to the tip of Sri Lanka—like that of an elephant's head and long trunk—has been a silhouette on lamps, tobacco tins, the letterhead of my bank. With the imminent creation of a Muslim state here in the northwest, and another in the east near Bengal, it appears as though that India with its shape like an elephant's head will have its two ears severed. It is for all of us that I fear."

There was nothing more either of them could say. They shook hands hard and parted. Arvind to flee south to Bombay with his family, Cam feeling hollow, to his allotted room in the governor's mansion. In his mind's eye, all he could see was that shape Arvind described, his mind racing. If the shape of India was severed, the elephant could live without ears. But what of the places those ears represent? Could Pakistan and East Bengal live without the elephant? Could Dassah survive?

A voice niggled at the back of his brain. *You failed her. You are a failure. There is nothing to hope for…all is lost.*

24

The next day in Amritsar, Cam assisted the vicereine from the car outside the mission. His temples throbbed, the roof of his mouth felt like sand. But Lady Mountbatten was keen to meet Eshana and the relief center she'd set up in the *bagh,* and he worked hard to strum up enthusiasm. The last people he wanted to see right now were his mother, and Eshana and Jai. One small mercy—Dad was in Delhi.

As the usual mob of children darted out of the house and stood gawping at her ladyship, she laughed. "I fear some of the little girls are disappointed," she said to him in an aside. "They probably expected me to arrive in evening gown and tiara, not khaki drill jacket and skirt, a pair of stout walking brogues on my feet."

"The older girls understood though," he said quietly. "Look how they stare at the Red Cross insignia on your sleeves and cap."

The boys were more interested in the accompanying bodyguards and the cars in which they arrived, not in some thin, tired Englishwoman in drab clothing. The clean, sweet innocence of these children lifted some of the heaviness from him. Maybe there *was* hope, even if all last night he'd paced, tossed, and turned with the constant refrain in his mind that there was no such thing.

Eshana, wearing her working sari of crisp yellow cotton, threaded her way through the orphans that bottlenecked at the mission door. Mother hurried out on Eshana's heels. In her quiet way, Eshana welcomed the vicereine into the house with the same grace she would welcome the poorest beggar. His unwilling smile fought for control, and for a moment he let it win.

Apparently his mother, also in a cotton sari, had been put in temporary charge of the orphans. This was to free up Eshana to oversee the relief center. With only a darting glance at him, Mother clapped her hands and gathered the children into orderly groups, allowing a parting of the ways for the vicereine to enter the mission. "Welcome, your ladyship," she said only to be echoed by the choir of children's voices. "Welcome, your ladyship…ship…ship…ship…."

Edwina Mountbatten waved a hand and smiled. "Not too much formality please, Mrs. Richards. I've only come to see how you're all getting on." Her warm smile included the orphans, and she patted many a head.

As a small sea, everyone flowed after the three ladies into the house. Mother shooed the younger children to play on either the patio or large inner room so that Eshana could converse in some peace with their visitor. With a chorus of groans they obeyed. Like every other stop at orphanage, hospital, or refugee camp, this was no pleasure visit. There was no time to sit down and have tea, only for the vicereine to assess their work and collate the efforts of all charitable groups in the province.

Eshana took Edwina to the surgery where Jai had just finished operating on a Muslim man. "My husband's patient had been cut deeply by a Sikh knife in an altercation here in the city," Miriam explained. "We are keeping this Muslim here under protective guard, and not outside with the main trauma center for fear the Sikhs and Hindus will retaliate. With the recent Rawalpindi atrocities, we are afraid they would tear him apart."

Cam felt the wince Lady Mountbatten shared with Eshana. "I am so glad you are doing what you are for the benefit of all sects."

At that moment, Jai came out of the surgery, drying his hands on a clean towel. He had already removed his white lab coat and rolled down his shirtsleeves, before bowing his turbaned head to Lady Mountbatten. Although his English-style trousers were impeccably pressed, Jai had not noticed the top of his leather shoes held a spatter of his patient's blood. One tiny thing to indicate that this charming, brilliant physician was doing all he could to hold back the Armageddon these March riots had birthed.

And yet, in spite of Jai's caseload, Cam could almost read his thoughts through his assessing smile. *You're not looking well. Are you still sober?*

But Jai had no time to grill Cam, much as he may want to. Instead, he and Eshana escorted the vicereine along with her bodyguards and female companion outside, a string of older girl orphans in their wake. Standing at the stone wall, the entire entourage looked out on the large, dusty parcel of land, the Jallianwalla Bagh.

Cam listened for a moment as Jai explained that their little mission currently cared for close to a thousand Sikhs and Hindus. Their mission had become an overflow from the thousands of displaced people being looked after in the Golden Temple nearby.

Displaced, ill, and wounded people sat on the ground, others on blankets or newspaper. Various canvas shelters had been set up as temporary clinics and kitchens. Only a few months ago, Cam had played cricket with the boys on this piece of ground and afterward talked with Zakir. Now, volunteers from the local Christian church hurried about, caring for the wounded and ill under the hospice of the mission. The vicereine's staff—as well as Jai, Eshana, and the older girls—took the stone steps down into the *bagh*. Cam started down with them.

Lady Mountbatten turned back to him. "Not you, Cam. You've looked terribly under the weather all morning. I insist you take this brief opportunity in our schedule to privately catch up with your mother. I insist," she said as he started to object. "There will be plenty for you to do this evening."

His duties held little time off with the growing hostilities. And this wretched queasiness had not abated. As though he walked a tightrope and might fall at any moment. Having not seen his mother since the garden party a month ago, with a grateful smile he acquiesced.

"How are you, dear?" Mum asked with a ghost of a smile as she joined him at the balustrade looking out at the large group going down into the *bagh*.

"What you want to know, Mum, is am I still sober?"

Her eyes filled, but no tears dropped. "All that obvious, am I? Sorry."

He removed his cap. "Why sorry? Far as I'm concerned you have every right to ask. I suppose now that all's out in the open, it helps. Frankly, I'm terrified of disappointing you. So, as embarrassing as it is, keep me pinned with the high beams. Don't let me wriggle away into the dark." Did she hear the desperation in his banter?

Her voice dropped to a whisper. "If it helps then…all right. Though it rubs me the wrong way to be so invasive." But she squared her shoulders. "Are you tempted to start drinking again with all that's going on?"

"Good gracious, Mum, British Intelligence could certainly use your talents in grilling the enemy. Give a man a moment to think, won't you?"

Her mouth clamped closed.

"All right, Mum. I'll not insult you by acting the fool."

"Well?"

"Of course I've been tempted—"

"When?"

"Every blessed hour of every blessed day, Mother." He regretted the sharpness to his tone, but she seemed to know that it wasn't her that made him feel this raw.

She took a fraction of a step closer. "Why? Why?"

He shook his head. "Because the country and its people that I love are being ripped in two…not to mention I can't find my wife…the usual run of the mill sort of thing."

"But you haven't given in yet? You haven't taken a drink?"

He let the question linger. Last night had been so close after talking to Arvind. Even now his tongue yearned for the saturation of whiskey, his mind longed for the forgetfulness that came with inebriation. "No, Mum. I haven't fallen off the wagon, so far at least. Must be God giving me the strength to not open a bottle… but next time…what if I don't have the strength?"

"Then get the strength!" She moistened her lips after her retort. With a little nod she croaked, "If you don't want to disappoint me, then don't. Just don't, Cam." She folded his hands in hers, her voice going soft. "You'd have told me right away if there were any news, but still I must ask. Dassah?"

Words stuck in his throat.

"It's all right, Cam. You will find her, and when you do, you'll spend the rest of your life making it up to her."

"If only I was as sure."

She squeezed his hand. "At times like these all you can do is cling to God... pray that he will keep her safe. I know this to be true. That's what I had to do when you were taken from—"

"And if God brings Dassah back to me, how can you be sure I'll be a good husband? How can you be sure I'll make her happy?" Something his mother said ricocheted in his head, but he'd cut her off. *How she'd felt when he'd been taken from...*

"I know you will make Dassah happy because I know you, son."

"Do you, Mum? Did you know I would become a drunk like my natural father? Do you know for sure that Dassah will be safe...with me? Isn't that what Dad asked, if I could become a husband worthy of my wife?"

A few squeals of laughter pealed from children outside and from within the house. Someone dropped a pot on the stone kitchen floor. A rubber ball bounced down the stairs from the nursery inside and rolled out to the patio. His mother took a step away, taking her eyes off him to study the *bagh* and the mass of people populating it, at the vicereine being escorted around Jai and Eshana's relief center. "I'll admit I was not surprised when I saw that you struggled with alcohol."

"Then you knew I'd be like *him.*"

"No. I don't believe it was a foregone conclusion you would take after him. But Nick was your flesh and blood...so I watched. I prayed."

"What other ways am I like him, Mother? I need to know, because somehow I know there was more to your misery with him than simply his alcoholism."

His gaze tracked to where hers followed Jai and Eshana showing Lady Mountbatten their endeavors among those who were suffering from losing all— their homes, their families, in many cases every single one of their loved ones. Cam's insides filled with that dark hollowness that disturbed him all last night. In a way it felt right that he understood some of the pain of these displaced people. As if losing Dassah gave him a modicum of authenticity as a citizen of India.

His mother broke her silence. "You have the right to know, Cam, although I had hoped to spare you. Nick was physically and emotionally cruel to me... and to another...."

Something Dad said to his mother rang in his mind. *You of all people should understand my abhorrence of the mistreatment of a wife.* "So that's it. Nick was physically abusive to you...a wife beater." *Oh dear Father in Heaven, am I like Nick in this too?*

"Nick would have been a wife beater to me, if I'd let him." Mother's voice took on added strength. "Only once did he strike me. But I—"

"You stood up to him, didn't you?" His weak smile felt good at this moment when he teetered with the hints that were starting to stack up.

She turned to him. "I have Eshana and the founder of this mission to thank for that. Here in this house." Her gaze lifted to the ceiling and he knew where her thoughts took her, up to the prayer room that used to be the elder Miriam's room. "Miriam and Eshana made me see who I was through the eyes of Christ. Not an invisible victim, but a cherished daughter of God, that a mere man like Nick dare not misuse."

His mother took him by the arms and shook him, her eyes wide, her mouth a straight line of despair. "You are not your father. You are not Nick. Cam, wake up! Who are you?"

Who was he? Geoff Richards's stepson? Or the son of Nick Fraser?

Mother wilted a bit. Feeling equally wilted, he led her to a cane chair. Children played around them. Together they looked out on the mass in the *bagh*. The memory of his recent conversation there with Zakir came bursting back like the rapid fire of a machine gun, of what Zakir had said about the massacre of 1919. A fuzzy memory of fireworks crackling went off in Cam's head. Or did he remember the gunfire that happened that day? "Mother, you once said, you wondered if my childhood traumas affected me."

"Yes, last summer I merely wondered, but now with India ablaze, Dassah missing...and with Tikah."

The back of his neck prickled. "Tikah? Why should the fact that good old Tikah is with Dassah be of concern and not relief?"

His poor mother looked as if she were about to pronounce a death sentence.

The tingling in his neck ran down his arms. *Dear God, what else?* He slumped back in the cane chair. "You'd better tell me all, Mum. Don't hold anything back. If you do, that would tip me over the edge, and I just might run to the nearest bar to get flat-out plastered for all time."

"Don't even joke about that," she rapped. "It's as if you're trying to give yourself an excuse, and I won't have it!"

She glanced over the stone wall to ascertain Eshana and Jai were still busy with Lady Mountbatten while his heart pounded like the booming shots from a tank. With his pulse swooshing through his ears, he was sure he could hear grinding tank wheels roll over him, burying him in a muddy ditch. *Dear God, what else? What else?*

At last she started. "Tikah and I share much more than simply our experience in this mission and our friendship with Eshana." She glanced at him. The nervous way she danced around the issue was making him break out in a sweat.

"Mother, don't dillydally," he said from between gritted teeth.

"I was not the only woman in Nick's life. After you and I first arrived in India, I discovered that your father...had kept Tikah as his mistress and had been mistreating her for years before I came on the scene."

He squeezed his eyes shut for a moment, hardly able to imagine—his father and that dowdy old woman he'd grown up seeing in this mission? "Go on."

"Naturally Tikah hated me. In her eyes she was Nick's wife. He'd tricked her, you see. And I was threatened by her presence in the house. We were far from friends at that point. Then came the day of the massacre...in the *bagh*."

"Yes 1919," he croaked. "I don't need the history lesson."

"Do you have any memories of that time?"

"No," he lied. The memories he had were vague, but he remembered the stench of cordite as he was rushed inside the mission along with a group of orphans. They'd been playing outside. He'd been crying that his cricket match had been abruptly ended, and he had to come inside to sit quietly in a circle with the others. Then later...waking up sick in the back of a car. Tikah holding him close...wiping his tears as he cried for his mother.

"Tikah and a man kidnapped you, Cam, together for different reasons."

He had difficulty swallowing. "This man?"

"Of no concern. I only mention him because Tikah didn't come up with the idea herself. In many ways she was as much a victim as I was. As you were."

"You sound as if you feel sorry for her."

A tear trickled down her cheek. "For a long time I hated Tikah. She was jealous. Wanted Nick's child and could never have one. It was Eshana who helped me realize that Tikah had been duped by Nick, my husband. In this mission, Tikah and I both became Christians, and for years afterward she worked here with the sick and the orphans. She adored Eshana. Tikah and I became friends too, or so I thought. Then she ran away—that first time—taking Dassah."

"No, Mother, it was Dassah who ran away and Tikah who went with her, but never mind that for now. How does the *Bagh* massacre play into this?"

"Tikah used the confusion after the massacre to slip into the mission and kidnap you. She took you to—"

"A desert place." He stared blankly, seeing his memories rather than the present. He'd been warm up to this point. Now the dry raging heat of a desert almost fell over him. He'd been in the backseat of a car. So thirsty. Tikah gave him frequent drinks from a canteen.

His mother slanted a look at him. "You do have some memory, don't you?"

His eyes felt gritty as sand. But he remembered Geoff calling out to him, and him running to Geoff, but stopping. Sand whirled around him. He couldn't get to Geoff. Someone held him in a tight grip, and he remembered looking up into Tikah's face. Sunlight flashing on a knife she held high in the sky. Then she released him and thrust him away. Toward Geoff. A wild trilling noise of grief had come out of her as she dropped to her knees in the sand.

Mother looked down at the paving stones on the patio. "It was Geoff who found you and Tikah. He brought you both safely back to us. Nick may be your biological father, but Geoff is your real father."

Voices from the *bagh* were coming clearer. Eshana and Jai were on their way back across the dusty parcel of ground to the mission. Now that his fragmented memories were explained, a new fear squeezed his insides. He lifted his head to meet his mother's eyes. "You're afraid Tikah has reverted to her old jealousy.

That she'll paint me with the same brushstrokes as Nick."

His mother gave a helpless shrug.

He released a bitter laugh. "If Dassah learns what that blackguard Nick did to Tikah, she'll only come to the same conclusion as me—like father, like son. Blast him! Blast me!"

"No, Cam," his mother said on a sob.

He stood as the vicereine made her way up the stone steps from the *bagh* to the mission patio. His throat thickened so that he couldn't speak, only nod to her ladyship in greeting.

To think that seven months ago he'd been dousing himself in Dal Lake on his honeymoon. If only he could close his eyes now. Rise through the green waters to surface among lotus blossoms and hear his beautiful wife laughing at him from the deck of their houseboat.

Instead, it seemed the flames of Hades flickered around him. If Dassah survived this holocaust that was broiling here in the north of India, she wouldn't run to him for safety. She'd run in the opposite direction, straight into those flickering flames.

Later that night, Cam closed the door to the small room allotted to him for the vicereine's staff at the home of the British Resident in this area. The room's regular occupant, a Lieutenant Bradley, was on leave but had left a few of his belongings behind. Cam sank to the edge of the bed, alone at last with his thoughts. With shaking hands, he stood and paced from the window to the closet, to the window again. He'd failed his wife. He'd put her life in danger.

Last night the refrain in his mind had kept him awake. That niggling voice at the back of his brain returned with renewed insidiousness. *There is no hope. All is lost.*

No hope...*oh dear God.* He raked his hair back. Surely there was hope.

But the voice in his brain whispered. *No hope. You are undeserving. Why should God help you? You are nothing more than a drunk! There is nothing for you but fear...fear.*

The bile of fear rose up the back of Cam's throat.

There is only one way to rid yourself of fear. Blot it out...forget. You know where it is.

Yes, he knew where *it* was. Cam turned to face the closet. He'd seen the possessions of Lieutenant Bradley when he'd stowed his own kit in the closet earlier.

You need a drink. Just one drink. No one will know. The niggling voice switched from his brain and seemed to come from the closet. *What else can you do...but give up?*

He needed, yes he needed to blot out the fear. Where was she? Was she even still alive?

The door swung open easily, and he found the case of whiskey at the rear of the closet. He bent to retrieve a bottle, unsealed it and had it open in seconds. Lowering himself to sit on the bed, he raised the bottle to eye level to study and savor it. Light from the lamp flickered through the glass, showing off the amber liquid as if it were swirling, fiery tongues. The barely discernable memory of Alan's voice, and of Eshana and Jai died away. So too did his mother's pleadings from today. And he stuffed down deep the memory of Dad's gray gaze.

Instead all he heard was that voice at the back of his mind, calling out to him, to blot out all that tormented him.

With shaking hands, he poured three fingers of whiskey into a glass and lifted it to stare into its depths. He'd gone more than five months without a drink. He'd almost succeeded.

God is not here…you are alone. Drown your fears. Deep in the glass the swirling amber turned to flames, and Cam felt himself falling…falling into the fire of his cremation, as if he saw his future. This was the way he would die in India, and there was nothing he could do to stop it. Cam lifted the glass up to rest its rim against his lips, and let the sensation of falling take him to his grave if need be.

A bird sang.

A moth fluttered against the lampshade, and Cam cursed the distraction. Outside the open window in the darkened garden, a bird trilled again. The memory of a scene from *Romeo and Juliet* that he'd read with Dassah darted into his mind. Dassah had read Juliet's part: "It is not yet near day. It was the nightingale, and not the lark that pierced the fearful hollow of thine ear…"

Then he had read Romeo's part: "It was the lark, the herald of the morn…no nightingale…I must be gone and live…or stay and die."

But Cam knew it was neither the nightingale nor the lark. He scrubbed his face hard with his hand. It was nothing more than a simple dusty sparrow, a sparrow whose song pierced the darkness when it had no business being awake in the middle of the night. The sweet notes sang again, and with trembling limbs, Cam tried to stand but sank to his knees with a thud. The glass dropped from his hand, its vile contents spilled on the floor.

"You are here, aren't you?" he whispered on a hoarse breath.

I am here. I will not let you fall, for you are my son.

Truth burned hot in Cam's chest. He scoured his face with his hands again and choked on his words. "I'm not worthy to be your son."

No, but I am worthy to save you. Let me lift you.

Cam had no strength of his own. As fragile as the moth fluttering about the lampshade, he hung his head. He'd almost taken that drink, almost destroyed the months of sobriety so many people had prayed for and hoped for. He'd almost failed Dassah again.

Stand, my son. Stand like the man I want you to be.

Outside in the garden, the sparrow sang in the dark. Along the sides of Cam's torso, the sensation of a thousand moths fluttered. He lurched from his knees, planting one foot on the floor. The flitting moth sensation swirled along his spine, and, setting his other foot on the floor, he stood and looked out on the night. Raising his hands, palms up to receive, he savored the name that Dad had taught him to love so long ago. Dad pronounced his name as Jesus. Dassah called him Yeshu. The fluttering sensation of moths along his torso disappeared and was replaced by a feeling of lightness. Earlier, Mother had asked him who he was.

Cam leaned against the window frame and rested his forehead against his arm. Hope, confidence, even joy stirred within him. "Now I know, Lord, now I know who I am. I belong to you—a new man."

25

Birds started singing so early this morning. Early or not, Miriam clung to their song of hope long before a line of gold lit the horizon. With a breaking heart, she clung to this display of God's glory, the rising of the sun so commonplace, yet a reminder of the daily miracle of the Lord's presence. And the uncommon, that celestial chorus from the sparrows, so blessedly early when she needed the Lord. And oh, how she needed him right now.

With her back against the trunk of a large umbrella tree, she sat on the circular bench surrounding it. Her tan slacks were grimy. So too was her bush shirt with the Red Cross armband, and the dear old Indian woman she held wore only a tattered and filthy sari.

Miriam had been trying to get this almost catatonic woman to talk for most of the night. Now, Miriam stroked the woman's long graying hair, and her arms absorbed the woman's shuddering sobs. An hour ago the woman had finally opened up and told her story, a story that dropped stone by stone into Miriam's consciousness like that of pebbles being thrown into a deep well. Even yet, she'd not felt the full horror of the old woman's experience.

Faiza, wearing a white sari with the Red Cross insignia, hurried across the schoolyard lawn. She gently released the old woman's grip on Miriam to relieve her, and with a few soft words, Faiza escorted the bent old frame across the grass and into one of the classrooms set up as a temporary ward.

Normal classes had stopped before end of term for the students of this school. This space was needed to treat the traumatized at a distance from the main refugee camp. Camps had been set up in various spots all over the city, camps to care for Muslims, totally separate camps for Hindus and Sikhs. The only thing the differing camps shared was their mutual suffering at the hands of one another, and the cities of Lahore and Amritsar caught in the middle. And also caught in the middle, people like her and Faiza, among others.

A few weeks ago, Miriam had elected to stay nights as well as days at this

183

trauma center. When she'd confessed this over the telephone to Jack last night, he'd growled a bit. "I'll soon put a stop to that. Keep this up and you'll need psychiatric therapy yourself."

Before ending their call last night, he'd insisted on driving down from Rawalpindi to see her this morning. Miriam had tried to talk him out of it, but to no avail. She calculated he was on his way. He said he'd be here by dawn, and it was nearly six. There'd be no time to change into fresh clothing.

Hugging her middle, she wished she'd kept her tears to herself, but she'd needed a shoulder to cry on, and even over the telephone Jack had been wonderful. In spite of everything, she couldn't wait to clap eyes on him. He'd be a ray of sunshine in a world gone dark.

The distant squeal of grinding brakes outside the front of the school jerked her out of her thoughts. Could that be Jack already? She should get up and prepare to meet him, but she couldn't move. Her mind was bound, as if she were hiding in the depths of a well, listening to pebbles dropping…dropping, until the memory of the birdsong cut in—so long before dawn—and she grasped at that memory as a lifeline.

She wasn't sure how long she'd sat with her arms around herself, but as heavy footsteps landed on the flagstones, she looked up. Morning sun slanted through the banyan trees, and Jack removed his military cap as he took steps out to her. "Darling. I'm here," he said.

"Jack? Oh Jack." With a little gulp she ran and threw herself against him. His arms tightened around her, hers around his neck. His scent, a trace of sweat, of soap, of just Jack, added to her light-headedness.

He rested his lips against her hair, her forehead. She pressed her face into his shoulder as he supported her head. "It's all right," he said. "Cry it out."

She didn't speak for the longest while. He rubbed her shoulder, probably expecting her to cry, but she couldn't. They both became aware of the intense silence of the courtyard, as if they were being watched from the classrooms whose windows looked down on them, as if the happy sight of a man embracing a woman was too painful to look at and strangled all articulation.

Miriam freed herself, took him by the hand, and led him inside the school.

"You've been up all night, haven't you?" A frown accompanied his question as they walked through the halls.

"Apparently so have you," she teased in a vain attempt to lighten the mood.

"Quite right. I signed the jeep out at 0200, and with my driver and an armed guard in the back, we flew like bats over two hundred and thirty miles of dark road so that I could see you, my dear."

His booted feet clipped on the linoleum floor. She watched his expression as they passed the first set of classrooms where female patients were lying on jute *charpoys* being cared for by nurses with Red Cross armbands. That halted him. He glanced down at his army drill, his Sam Browne belt crossing his chest, the revolver at his side, and then at her.

"It's all right," she assured him. "Knowing these women's situations, one would think seeing one of our British soldiers would send them into a frenzy, but it won't."

They continued down the hall, but a woman's shrieking from somewhere in the building startled Jack to another abrupt stop. Miriam was getting used to the wild, trilling keens, but Jack's throat muscles moved as he swallowed convulsively. As a soldier he'd seen his share of death, but the woman's cries drained him of all color. This school, which should have resounded with the voices of noisy children running to and from classes, felt more like an asylum.

She'd lived with these images day in day out for a few months now, but with Jack sharing it with her, she worked to hide her grimace. A bin sat outside the door, filled with bloodstained bandages and torn clothing. He'd recognize the metallic odor, the smell he would associate with war. Sure enough, when Jack moved past the bin, he stopped to draw breath and rested a hand against the wall next to the notice, TEMPORARY MORGUE IN THE GYMNASIUM. And that one female voice still keened.

That single wailing seemed to be the anomaly this morning. Most of the women sitting Indian style on the floor looked out of vacant eyes, silent. One woman pulled her thin cotton veil over her head to hide her face entirely, quivering, a ghost shimmering in diaphanous muslin. Seeing it all through Jack's eyes, Miriam felt his embarrassment, and the sudden clamminess of his hand in hers.

She led him inside the classroom she used for small group discussions. A row of windows overlooked the schoolyard, but the room was empty. Blackboards lined the walls, the smell of chalk dust filled the room—such a happy smell. Wooden desks and chairs were set in a circle facing inward, but no one sat in them at the moment. In the middle of the space that the desks faced sat the large urn of yellow roses. She'd placed the blooms there as a ray of hope. Now she sniffed their sweetness, the only sweetness in the entire school at the moment.

They sat in a couple of straight-backed wooden chairs, staring into the circle and the bright yellow roses. "You did that," he stated rather than asked.

"Anything but the color red."

"I understand." He ran a hand across his brow. "Walking through these halls with you triggered a memory of the painting *Charon the Ferryman of Hades*, who carried the newly deceased across the River Styx that divided the world of the living from the world of the dead." He cursed under his breath as he reached for her hand. "This is what happens, Miriam, when religion gets out of hand."

His curse word added salt to the rawness she already felt, but she didn't have the strength to point out that these hostilities in the name of religion had nothing whatever to do with God.

"Miriam, my love, soldiers endure the hardships of war by picturing the women they are fighting for, safe at home. It isn't right that war should be directly waged upon women, and it isn't right that the woman I love should see firsthand the results of genocide."

She patted his knee. "Jack, I know you're upset—"

"Upset! Miriam, I'm more than upset. A refined lady like you should be heading up committees if you wanted to help. Women sit at tables over luncheons and write badgering letters to politicians. You shouldn't be on the blasted front lines offering psychological council to victims of horrendous violence. I intend to get you away from this godforsaken place immediately."

She was so tired, only one thing he said penetrated. "Dear Jack, God has not forsaken India."

"I beg to differ. Oh Miriam, you've yet to give me hope, but marry me, please. Let me take you home to England safe and sound. You can take up a teaching position in some posh school for privileged children, you can lead Bible classes at the local church if you must. After all, I believe in God too, but there are limits to what even God expects, surely." He tucked a loose strand of her hair behind her ear, working hard to infuse a smile on his face. "As for this place, it's time for you to leave. I'm surprised your parents haven't ordered you out already."

"What *are* you saying?" she whispered. She'd not had the strength to discuss his marriage proposal yet again, but his asking her to leave the trauma center cut through.

"I drove here through the night to tell you." He drew his arm from around her chair. "Forgive my commanding tone, it's obviously mangling the sentiments I want to express. What I'm trying to say is, there are plenty of other things you can do to help."

"I'm not as fragile as you imply, but thank you." Her tone had taken on a trace of steel, and from the sudden stillness to his expression he seemed to have twigged on to that fact.

His voice softened. "Aren't you fragile, Miriam? You've got circles under your eyes that would make a black-eyed monkey jealous. When was the last time you had a proper meal?"

"I eat with the patients—"

"More like you just spoon the food into their mouths."

"And, your point being?"

"Nothing, my beautiful girl." He jutted out his chin. "Of course someone must care for these wretched victims. My heart goes out to them. But, Miriam, I'm already doing my bit to help. Out of the two of us, as a couple aren't we giving enough with me serving, in my role?"

Her gaze dropped to the roses. How could she express what she wanted to say without hurting his feelings? "You are doing a lot, and knowing you, Jack, your military aid would probably be enough for most couples, most families, but we're not family yet. Are we?"

"That can be remedied as soon as you say the word."

"I'm not sure—"

"Miriam, I love you. I want to protect you from all such sadness, from every deplorable event for the rest of my days."

Protect her. She smiled, but it was really more of a wince. He had no idea that he'd just said the wrong thing.

He squeezed her hand. "Just answer this—do you love me?"

"Yes."

A ripple of joy lit his eyes. "Then...?"

She gave a sudden shake to her head and gripped her hands together so tight her knuckles whitened. "I can't...I can't think about our life right now. How can I make decisions about my own happiness with all this going on?"

"Of course not, but if you love me, it's only a matter of time. We will get married."

Her gaze slid away from him. His voice faded. A cold clamminess came over her. At first she stared into space...and then the plopping sounds of a pebble being thrown into a deep well echoed in her mind. She swallowed at the memory of what the old woman told her this morning just before dawn broke.

Jack's voice and his hands on her shoulders dragged her back from the images the old woman's story conjured up. "Miriam, come back to me. I can see it in your face—you mustn't carry their pain of this ruddy—"

"Dante's Inferno," she suggested. Her eyes filled, but still not one tear fell. "An old friend once said that I like to barge into Dante's Inferno, as if I had angels on my shoulder. But I don't, really, Jack. I'm not a flippant person, but I can't leave them to suffer alone." She tapped her temple. "I've seen the inferno...through their eyes. This morning before you arrived, I heard one woman's story." She released a bitter laugh. "All the women's stories are so similar."

For the first time this morning, Jack had the sense to sit quietly. From the tight way he held his mouth, he probably knew something of what she would share. He'd seen the atrocities firsthand while she had only heard about them and seen the results.

"This old woman," she went on, "had a daughter...and a baby granddaughter. They were trying to run away when the rioting started in their town. She's Hindu. She stopped her daughter from jumping down a well like many of their female friends were doing, preferring to kill themselves before suffering dishonor. She and her daughter hid in the cow byre of their family farm. From there they watched her husband and son being slaughtered by their Muslim neighbors... people they'd known for years." Her breath grew rapid. "But, Jack, the baby started to cry. They were discovered."

Another curse slipped from Jack's lips, and she cringed. It was his way of expressing emotions he didn't know what to do with, but for her the cursing only added to the shredding of her thin composure. "They killed the baby." She put the back of her hand against her mouth, silencing herself. A long moment later, she continued, "They raped and mutilated the old woman's daughter, who died at the main camp this morning of blood loss."

"And the old woman," he prompted. "Better get it all out, and then I'm taking you out of here."

"They raped her too. How could they have done that, Jack? How...?" Even to her, her voice sounded weak and thready. "The old woman tried to run away from the main camp this morning. With all her family dead, she wanted to kill herself. They brought her here."

"And she's in good hands now with these nurses and staff—"

"Staff!" Her tone sharpened, her back going rigid. "What staff? One or two professional nurses. They have no psychiatrist. I telephoned Cam. He's relayed this need to Lady Mountbatten, and apparently she's trying to round up some psychiatric professionals. Of course there aren't enough to go around with the whole country in an uproar."

He grasped her by the shoulders. "But this is going to scar you mentally. I know this firsthand, and so does your brother. Remember what your brother's war experiences did to him. I simply can't have that. I must insist that the woman I love—"

"Don't say it, Jack." She stood so that his hands dropped from her shoulders. "I love you, I'm thinking about marriage like I said I would, but don't ask me to stop helping. Besides, I've already promised Lady Mountbatten that I will remain." She giggled, and it came out off-key.

He raised an eyebrow in alarm.

"Don't worry. I'll admit to feeling a bit dotty at the moment, but I'm sane enough to keep going. What I find terribly funny is that right now, I'm the only one with enough psychological knowledge to assist the only two nurses they have. Me! Apparently earning a minor in psychology is all that's required in a crisis like this. And the volunteers...a number of them are my students."

Her voice hit a higher pitch. "Those two girls I told you about months ago—Faiza and Anjuli—they're here. Other girls, students who should be vacationing with their parents, who should be relaxing in preparation for the coming autumn courses at Kinnaird, are here doing what they can to help the victims. It's them I'm worried sick about. How will this scar *their* young minds?"

He tried to take her in his arms, but she stepped aside, waving a hand toward the window. "They had to close our college." At this bald statement, juxtaposed in the midst of all the outstanding horror, tears sprang and clung to her lashes.

"I'm sorry, Miriam, but there will be other schools."

She wiped her face with a rough hand. "Principal McNair will reopen as soon as the crisis is over. A skeleton staff has elected to stay on." Though her hands trembled, she widened her stance and lifted her chin.

As he studied her, he seemed to mentally tally that she was not as vulnerable as he thought. The furrow between his brows creased, his shoulders slumped ever so slightly. She had her moments of weakness—that's why'd she'd needed to talk to him last night—but with the singing of the birds so early this morning, she'd felt...a flutter of their strength. Silly, fragile creatures going about the specific business God gave them to do, no matter what.

But Jack looked so sad. "Miriam, I'm not sure your beloved college will have much of a future. If Partition goes through by next year then Lahore might actually be in Pakistan. What then?"

"Principal McNair says we'll stay. We'll build from the few teachers and what students we have. Maybe there will be no Hindu or Sikh girls, but there will be Christians. The Muslims don't seem to mind Christians, as we're followers of The Book. And the Lord knows the Muslim girls will need education as much *after* Partition as they did before. Perhaps more so."

His voice sharpened now too. "For the moment the Muslim population doesn't mind the Christian minority. As for the years or decades ahead, one can only hope."

She lifted a hand and let it flop to her side. "Jack, I don't know the future, but I do know that I want to stay with Kinnaird. Even if it does end up in Pakistan."

He spread his hands. "But don't you see? Once power is handed over in a year's time, all our British troops are leaving. I'll probably be posted to Kenya or quite possibly home."

"England?" With the word *England*, it was as though a cool breeze shifted a door shut.

"Yes, England. Your parents will retire there, won't they?"

"They're retiring to Ireland."

"Near enough." He inched closer and took her in his arms. She laid her cheek next to his as his low baritone wafted over her. "Don't fret, my love, it's a whole year before the transfer of power. Stay and help if you must. I'll wait patiently for your answer to marry me. I just wish your father would convince you to do something else."

She laughed, an honest laugh this time, and snuggled into his arms, if only for the moment. "While my father's busy working day and night with the viceroy staff, he's in full support of Mother helping in Eshana and Jai's relief center, binding up the most atrocious wounds and helping to serve thousands of meals each day. Cam is working nearly twenty hours a day with Lady Mountbatten coordinating relief efforts. Newly married Eva is doing her bit up in Quetta." With an unabashed grin she finished. "Dad would be the first to give me a brisk nod and tell me to carry on at my assigned post."

"Quite the family, aren't you?"

Loosening her embrace, she leaned back to stare at him. "Do I detect a note of censure?"

He chuckled, but his face went red. Drawing her close again, he kissed the tip of her nose and laid his cheek against hers. "Of course not, it's simply that you're all rather more than the average representatives of the Raj. Rather more missionary stock than military."

She let his rather telling statement go unanswered. There wouldn't have been time anyway to wade into that minefield of discussion because Anjuli called to her from the doorway, "Miss. Many apologies, but you are needed."

Miriam pulled gently but quickly from Jack. He let her go, and she felt the void immediately but still strode to the threshold where Anjuli told her the old woman was in great despair. Her stomach went cold at what the woman must be feeling. Jack, and all his arguments and proposal, had to wait. Everything had to wait. She heard again in her mind the dropping of stones into that well...and then the memory of those silly little birds singing their hearts out.

She swung around to him with a hand on her hip. "I'm sorry, Jack. When this catastrophe has ended, we'll have more time." She began to walk with Anjuli down the hall to the triage room.

"I'll come down from 'Pindi to see you as much as I can, darling." He'd injected a light tone, but there was no time for further discussion, even if he did follow her and Anjuli.

Still she glanced back and managed to drum up a smile. Anjuli entered the room while Miriam waited. With her hand bracing her stance at the door, she sent Jack a long, lingering look, trying to convey that she did love him, but now was not the time.

She wove her way through the *charpoys* while nurses changed bandages and held gauze to fresh bleeding on one woman who'd just arrived. But the small voice of the little woman she'd cradled before dawn reached her. Miriam dashed to a cot by the back wall and lowered herself to sit beside her elderly patient. The woman's long gray hair hung over her face as she rocked back and forth, hugging her knees and wailing. Miriam unwound the hands that captured the arthritic knees and coaxed the frail old body into her arms as if she were a child and Miriam her mother. Stroking the long mass of gray hair, Miriam started singing the old Sunday school chorus, "God Sees the Little Sparrow Fall."

The woman's keening turned to sobs as she repeated over and over again "*bíbá*," the Punjabi word for baby. As Miriam rocked her, the woman sobs subsided to hiccupping moans like that of a babe herself.

The backs of Miriam's eyes stung, and she lifted her gaze to see that Jack watched her from a crack in the door that she'd failed to close completely.

His soldierly stance gave no clue to his emotions. Only the tight lines between his nose and mouth etched his dismay. Poor Jack. Maybe when all this was over, the passion they shared would be enough, but for now...a deeper passion called. Maybe later, there would be time for Jack and marriage. For now, there was God, and there was India.

Part Three

26

June 2, 1947

"In Him I live and move and have my being." Dassah whispered the Bible verse she'd written in her journal. From the wide, flat vale surrounding Srinagar, she stood on a shack's porch looking up at the peaks and the long ridge of Apharwat. Those heights had become her friends during the cold months. In April she had shaken off the heavy Kashmiri *phiran* and woolen shawls as birdsong filled the air and melting snows became murmuring streams. Now flowering grasses and purple blossoms unfurled like a carpet on meadows down the steep mountainsides.

Down in the sprawling city of Srinagar once more, long gardens lay out like colorful saris drying in the sun. Through it all, Yeshu embraced her with his love. Her child too lived and moved and had his or her being in Yeshu, and as her Lord embraced her, soon she would embrace her babe.

When the ski season ended in Gulmarg, Tikah had been offered a better paying position in Nedou's Hotel branch in Srinagar. Along with other employees, they were bussed down to the city and set up a new home in this courtyard at the back of the hotel. At least the rough pine walls were sturdy, and the roof leaked only a little. Cooking spices—saffron, curry, ginger—as well as fretted wooden designs along the eaves of roofs, reminded her she was still in India and not in a Swiss village she had seen in a picture book as a child.

She hugged her arms around her body in full bloom with Cam's child. How she loved Kashmir, this paradise on earth of mountains and lakes. A kick from her baby drew a sharp breath. She smiled over at Tikah, who banged a paddle on their wet laundry to wash it on the cement courtyard.

Tikah replenished her wooden bucket from the communal well. "He is awake then?"

"How do you know the little one is a he?"

"I know. That is all."

"Do you also know, *Amma*, if you can be happy here in Srinagar?"

"Too much snow. I prefer the dry cold of a Baluchistan desert. If I must be rained upon then at least let it be during a warm monsoon when it is a pleasure."

Dassah's sigh matched Tikah's. "There is little rain in Baluchistan. How is it that lately you hearken so lyrically on the deserts of your youth?"

"It is as good as any place to call our permanent home. Before I met Nicholas Fraser and he took me from my homeland, my youth had been a most happy one. It would please my heart to raise my grandson there. The deserts will make him a tall, strong man like Zakir."

"Not Zakir." Dassah huffed. "If my child is a boy, he will be tall and strong because that is what his father is."

Tikah's smiled dimmed. "Most assuredly, beloved, but more importantly, it is best for us to move to the land of my youth because no one from these parts will find us in the city of Karachi."

She brought Tikah a glass of salty pink tea with almonds and laid a hand on her *amma*'s shoulder. "I do not understand your reasoning. Karachi has its millions, Calcutta its many millions. Why, pick any city in India and it is easy to become lost in its teaming throngs."

"My daughter, how can you be happy here with the memories in this place?" Tikah nodded in the direction of Dal Lake, though it was not visible where they were tucked between streets behind the hotel.

Dassah rubbed her tummy to caress the infant beneath her heart. Another six weeks and her baby would be here. But *Amma* was wrong. It was true remaining in Kashmir made the hollowness of missing Cam swell within her. Yet being here reminded her that at least when their child had been conceived, their baby had been knit together in love. For her, love for Cam would last eternal. For Cam, it would naturally fade since his love did not have the depth to produce a proper marriage in the first place. Still, loneliness was a constant companion even with Tikah, who only left her side to go to work in the hotel laundry. And now Zakir, too, had become her shadow since he had shown up three weeks ago.

She was saved from answering Tikah's question about leaving Kashmir when Zakir strolled up the worn path flanked with tall purple and white irises, jasmine, and roses gone wild.

He had found them shortly after they had moved down from the Gulmarg. He said he had been traveling since he had been released from prison. He said he wished to see various parts of India, but she had the strangest feeling his arrival in Srinagar was not as serendipitous as he made out. He had always been a man of action. What was in Kashmir to attract Zakir that he dillydallied here for weeks on end?

And the way he looked at her—as he sat on a *charpoy* under a chinar tree, looking at her with the eyes of a besotted water buffalo, and she, heavy with another man's child. Such foolishness.

The Zakir she remembered was more of a brother from their childhood in the mission. He leaned back now on the *charpoy*, his legs crossed and his hands clasped around his knees. A handsome Indian man in long white *kurta* and *dhoti* down to his ankles, a prayer cap on his head. He sent a teasing grin to Tikah. "Well, Auntie, have you talked her into going?"

Dassah's hand that had been caressing the mound of her child stopped in mid-stroke. "Talk me into what?"

"Kashmir is not a safe place," he said. "The population is Muslim, its despot of a ruler Hindu. Like all the princely states that formerly had an agreement with Britain, they will be swallowed up by either India or Pakistan. Mark my words, with its bordering neighbors Afghanistan, Russia, and China, the strategic value of Kashmir is a keg of dynamite ready to ignite."

"But Kashmir has not had unrest in the streets as bad as that taking place in other Indian provinces. We are safer here, especially with so many English about."

"There are less and less English every month. They are sailing away on ships. As for those other provinces, things will settle down as soon as these blighted English leave our soil. It is them who are causing our people to be anxious so that they strike out at each other."

She shook her head. "Foolishness! The British colonization has brought about much of this current dilemma. Still you cannot blame the English for our offenses. It is our own Indian people who choose to settle their differences with murder—but then, you made your feelings for the British clear when you turned your back on them in the war." No matter how much Zakir considered his wartime treason toward England an act of loyalty for independent India, she could not agree. His disloyalty in Burma must have caused the deaths of English and faithful Indian troops.

"And I do not understand why you defend the English, Dassah. You of all people should..." He hung his head, but she had no pity for his embarrassment.

When he first arrived in Srinagar several weeks ago, her pregnancy was so advanced it would have been laughable not to speak of it openly. Naturally the question of who the father was hung as strong as curry on the air, until she with a trace of pride announced that her child's father was Cam. Zakir hung his head in shame for her that day too.

He stood and, tapping his fingertips together, paced the courtyard. "As Muslims we will be safer in areas that are sure to be included in Pakistan."

"I am not Muslim!" Her voice rose to the lower boughs of the tree. Tikah stiffened beside her, glancing around to see if any of their neighbors heard her, but Dassah went on. "Zakir, since I was a child I believed in Yeshu as the Son of God. I am a Christian. Do not paint me as something I am not."

"I want you to be what you are, Dassah, a woman of India. Not some convert, coerced into a belief that is not of our culture."

The hairs at the back of her neck stood. "I do not know you, Zakir. You are not the son of Miriam of the mission where we grew up. You are not the son of the woman who nursed you at her knee on the teachings of Yeshu."

He took a step back as if struck.

"How can you be so foolish, Zakir? Did not Thomas, one of the Lord's disciples, come to India centuries ago and be martyred for bringing the truth of Yeshu to us?"

Beside her, Tikah dipped her head. Her *amma* must make up her own mind, and not be coerced by anyone. All winter long she and *Amma* had talked quietly of spiritual matters up at the ski resort, veiled from the rest of the world by snow and ice.

Zakir paced from them to sink upon the *charpoy*. Lifted his hand in surrender. "All right, Dassah, I will give you that. I was wrong to suggest the Christian faith does not belong to India."

At last *Amma* spoke. "From my birth I was nursed on the teachings of Islam." Zakir lifted his head to listen.

"Many years later," Tikah went on, "I believed in Yeshu at the mission in Amritsar. Then when Dassah and I ran away to Calcutta, I did not believe that God chose any particular form, but that he was a nameless entity…who did not care. My heart turned bitter, because I thought that Eshana who taught me about Christ had abandoned me. That she had cast me off as coldly as my husband had done." She glanced at Dassah, saying without words that they shared the same abandonment from a husband who was not truly a husband. Like father, like son.

Zakir stood. "And now, Auntie?"

"Though I may have been parted from my dear friend Eshana, I believe that Yeshu never left me. I choose to follow him."

"Why, Auntie?" Zakir's voice strained. "I revere you as one of the women who raised me in the mission—like a mother—why do you worship the god of our conquerors?"

"Because Yeshu does not seek to conquer us, but woos us with love, like the mother of your heart, Miriam, loved you. Because of the holy giving of Yeshu's life to save others from the pollution of their sins."

Tikah squeezed Dassah's hand. "While I understand love and sacrifice, it was the lack of love that wrought evil things in my heart. Many years ago, the hunger for my husband's child created a bitter stream in my soul. I tried to steal the child of his true wife. Only when I laid my broken heart out to Yeshu did I receive my heart's desire." She gripped Dassah's hand tighter. "Just as the Almighty gave Ruth as a daughter to Naomi in the Holy Bible, the Almighty gave me a daughter… and soon a grandson."

Dassah returned Tikah's smile. "Whither thou goest, I will go…where thou lodgest, I will lodge."

Zakir stomped a few feet away to glare at the massive trunk of the chinar tree. Moments later he returned to sit on the stone lip of the well. "I cannot argue with your Christian devotion. My beloved Miriam taught me such things from her knee. I remember her sweet voice singing me to sleep when I feared the dark." His voice broke. "I remember her sacrifice, dying when she saved me from the massacre in the *bagh* that day. Often I think of it...like the story of Yeshu's sacrifice."

He clasped his fingers and brought them up to his lips in the beseeching manner of the east, then let them drop, the sentiment of the previous moments melting away. "Believe what you will, Auntie. But know this—the lines to divide India will be drawn on a fresh map, and Kashmir will most assuredly be an area the dogs will fight over."

Dassah sat straighter. "But there is time."

"No, Dassah. I believe we should get to Muslim strongholds as soon as possible."

"We have just told you we are Christians."

He softened. "As Christians in Pakistan under my protection as a Muslim, you may worship as you wish. I promise you this, Dassah. I will build you a house. I will provide for you." He glanced at Tikah. "I feel we should go to Baluchistan. To the city of Karachi."

Dassah's heart jumped. Zakir was wise in these matters, of this she was confident, in his own way a very decent man, and she needed someone to watch over them for the sake of her babe. She needed a home to raise her child. Provisions....

Her mind soared and swooped with the speed of a kingfisher. "But Baluchistan, Karachi! I have grown to love Kashmir, with its lush beauty. Karachi is more dusty and hot than Amritsar where we grew up. At least Amritsar was perfumed with roses—"

"There are roses in Karachi." Zakir hunched down at her feet. "I will plant you a rose garden. I will cut you a bloom every morning. In addition to this, your safety in Pakistan will be assured, Dassah...if you marry me."

"Marry you?" Her neck and cheeks flooded with heat. "But I am already—"

"Shush," Tikah admonished her with a stern look.

"It matters not, revered Auntie." His eyes glistened at Dassah. "I am well aware that you must have been deceived and are not the legal wife of Cam Fraser. Since you were a young girl I have loved you, Dassah. You are as pure as the doves that flit in that tree behind you. To think that...that Englishman stole what could never be his is something *I* will never forgive."

The heat raging in her cheeks vanished. Numbness took over so that she hardly heard the rest of what Zakir said. "Become my wife, Dassah. You and your *amma* will be safe, and I will love your child as my own. Come with me to Baluchistan. It is sure to become part of Pakistan. And Karachi will be Jinnah's capital city."

Only 0700, and the sun glared white on the pavement and stone walls of Viceroy House. Cam waited in the portico of the north courtyard, the peak of his military cap shading his face. A filament of sweat trickled between his shoulder blades. Crowds were entrenched out front of the main courtyard, hordes of pressmen and photographers. A roaring filled his ears, not from the mob waiting for someone to leak a snippet of tomorrow's announcement, but from the blood rushing through his temples. Dear God, how would India react when it heard the death knell tomorrow morning?

Dad's vehicle motored through the security gates to be met by the guard in khaki. With briefcase in hand, Dad exited his car, and his driver drove on. In his role as ADC, Cam greeted Dad as he would any visitor, with a handshake, but today neither one of them could drum up any sort of lightness. Their handshake lingered longer than normal, the need for human contact heavy in the surety of what was to come.

"His lordship got back from London all right?" Dad asked as together they strode into the palace.

"Flew back day before yesterday, sir, with the approved amendments. He's been up since the crack of dawn. After a brief meeting with his staff and military, His Excellency will be in talks with Indian leaders. Most likely all day, since I doubt it will be easy to draw them into agreement."

Dad always worked hard not to show his frustration, but the sudden narrowing of his eyes gave him away. "The announcement is scheduled?"

"Yes. Simultaneously from London and Delhi. The secret almost got out a few times."

"So I see. The place is swarming with press."

Together they passed through the side door where the secretary escorted Dad down the long and vaulted corridor to the viceroy's study. Cam followed close behind. The secretary spoke in undertones but included Cam, who was in earshot. "Utterly maddening that Nehru rejected the original strategy of a British Dominion status for India. His Excellency had to rewrite the whole plan for division, with Nehru going over it with a fine-tooth comb."

"Today, we can only pray," Dad went on, "that all the Indian leaders agree on two self-governing authorities of Pakistan and India, and in addition to this, that they agree to all of this before anyone knows yet where exactly those new borders will be drawn."

The secretary gave him a knowing look. "Sir Cyril Radcliffe will be flown in to do the study and make those recommendations."

Dad shook his head. "A man who has never been to India in his life. God help us. God help India."

They reached the study. His stepfather took one of the seats set around the front of the large desk, joining the military advisors and the viceroy's staff. Mountbatten, in an impeccable gray suit, sat at the desk with a map of the world behind him. Cam, along with several other ADCs and military men stood at the rear of the study. Through the windows lay the large geometrical Mogul Gardens. The peacefulness of soothing water from fountains and channels contrasted with the frayed nerves in the room.

Mountbatten started. "As many of you know, I personally think Partition is absurd, but we're hemmed in with what the Indian leaders want. And they want it quickly. I simply can't crack Jinnah. I didn't realize how impossible this would be until I met the man. He wants his Pakistan, and while the Hindu Congress wants our assistance, Jinnah does not."

Mountbatten sent the group his matinée idol smile. "In a letter from His Majesty, he's assured me he and our British government know full well we are up at bat on a very sticky wicket. But gentlemen, we have got to pull the game out of the fire. The proposal I am to put before the leaders is that they accept two separate Dominion statuses for Pakistan and India under the umbrella of the British Commonwealth. The date our British Parliament has chosen for this to occur will come as a shock to some, but the Indian leaders are pressing for speed. We will have our work cut out for us."

General Pete Rees leaned forward in his chair. "This new date for withdrawal is atrocious. The Punjab is in crisis. Bengal equally agitated, all areas south of Afghanistan are on the point of explosion." Pete glanced at Dad. "Your thoughts, Geoff?"

Cam's stepfather spoke quietly. "Pakistan and India are to be violently carved out of one geographical area, out of a collective people—an impossible task to please all factions, no matter when this occurs. But this new date! In such a short time!"

The discussion continued. Cam, standing at the back of the study, watched all involved from the British standpoint, his stomach going sour. He glanced at his wristwatch and caught Mountbatten's eye. The Indian leaders would be arriving any minute. Today history would be made, and he could only implore God to see India…and Dassah…safely through the maelstrom about to begin.

The Hindu Congress and its leader, Jawaharlal Nehru who charmed Lord and Lady Mountbatten, were the first to arrive. Nehru was a handsome Kashmiri in his favorite white *achkan* coat that reached his knees, his narrow fitting pantaloons, a Gandhi cap on his head. Then the Sikh leader, Baldev Singh, arrived in western suit and Sikh turban. Soon after came the fastidious Muhammad Ali Jinnah. Jinnah, in his sophisticated English suit, greeted Mountbatten in the perfect Cambridge English he preferred but refrained from smiling as he entered the viceroy's study.

To Cam's thinking, Jinnah's cavernous features had to be the result of extreme ill health. The man didn't look like he had much longer to live.

As Mountbatten expected, the meeting went on and on, stopping now and then for the leaders to refresh themselves. The viceroy staff were run off their feet, going back and forth between the various leaders and their groups as the heads of their parties holed up in the study. As the day progressed, feelings rose and plummeted with each snatch of news that filtered through the corridors of the palace.

The Congress leaders, apparently, felt that only an immediate transfer of power could forestall the spread of violence and communal disturbances. A united India even if it was smaller in size was better than a bigger, disorganized, bleeding India. But Jinnah was forestalling as usual. He refused to agree to Mountbatten's proposal of Dominion status for Pakistan, claiming he had to discuss the proposal with the Muslim League members first. Mountbatten was insisting on a nod, only a nod from Jinnah, and he'd proceed with the scheduled broadcast on that.

Dad found Cam in the ADCs' room late in the day and insisted they walk in the gardens. They found a seat under a spreading banyan close to one of the long channels. From here they could see the windows of the study reflecting the setting sun, though not its illustrious occupants. Dad leaned an arm along the back of the bench. "I've known this day would come, but I had prayed it would come gently."

"It will not come gently."

"No, it will not," Dad said just above a whisper. "What will you do, Cam?"

"Look for my wife, even if it means leaving my post."

"Yes. Your first priority is to your wife."

Cam leaned over, his elbows on his knees. "You don't mind that I intend to leave the forces."

"Certainly not. If you need it, you have my blessing."

"Thank you."

"Your mother tells me you're doing well."

"More than six months sober."

The smile on Dad's face brought out the fan-shaped crinkles at the corners of his eyes. "I knew once you set your mind to it, you'd win the battle."

A smile worked its way on to his own face. "I certainly doubted. There were moments, I assure you, but with a mentor like Alan Callahan, and your exemplary example, something good had to rub off."

Dad turned to him, clearing a sudden roughness from his voice. "What does it matter if you and I don't share blood? You've been my son since you were three. I'm proud of you. Very proud."

"Even though I let you down."

"You had a dragon to slay, but you slew it, Cam. You'll make that bride of yours a solid, protective husband. What more can I ask of my son?"

"If only I'd slain this dragon before she left me. If only I'd listened to God's call on my soul earlier." His throat stung. "Dad, where the blazes can she be?

Where do I look?"

His father moved his arm from the back of the bench to grip his shoulder. "Through your recent ordeal, battling for your sobriety, you've leaned on the Lord like you never have before. Only he can help you find that pearl you misplaced. Trust in him—and you know I do not use those words as useless platitudes but as the foundation of my life."

Cam's tight throat made it hard to talk. "When the announcement is made tomorrow, and later when the new borders are drawn, the bloodbath we've seen up to now will be nothing compared to what will come."

His father's silence spoke for itself. He lifted his hand and pressed his thumb and forefinger to the bridge of his nose. In a tired voice he added, "I could tell you that your fears may have no substance, but you and I've been in India too long, not to mention seen active combat. Now of all times, a complete and neutral army is needed to keep the peace."

"Instead, our British troops will be on ships heading home, with the rest of the Indian Army split in two along religious lines." Cam's voice went ragged. "What of my wife then? Will Dassah be like the women I've seen in refugee camps? Or is she already dead?"

Twilight had dropped and night cloaked them without their notice. Sayed Ahsan, the tall Indian ADC, strode toward them. They rose to their feet to meet the distinguished Muslim officer.

Sayed murmured for their ears only, "Jinnah has given Mountbatten the nod. The new British withdrawal date will be broadcast tomorrow morning as scheduled."

Under the shade of a chinar tree, Dassah sat in the courtyard by the well, writing her prayers to Yeshu in her journal. Tikah had already left for her work in the hotel when Zakir bounded up the path. Without a word, he moved swiftly past Dassah and into the hut she shared with Tikah. She lifted herself from the lacquered cane chair—no easy feat—and followed him inside.

In the corner of the shack, he played with the radio switch. Tapping his foot, he crossed and uncrossed his arms waiting for the wireless to warm up. "An announcement has been made," he sputtered. "It is shocking, but...." He smiled. "Our land will belong to us sooner than I dreamed."

Moments later, the radio whined with static as Zakir searched for the All India Radio station. Crackling over the airwaves came an English voice. Zakir interrupted so that she could not hear what was being said or ascertain who was speaking. "The English Prime Minister Attlee, speaking from London."

"What is he saying?"

"Transfer of power has been pushed up to August fifteen. The British are going home. Because of this, the sooner we make our journey to Karachi, the better. Think of it, Dassah, I will plant you a rose garden in Karachi."

"August fifteen next year. What is new about this?"

"No, Dassah." He took her by the shoulders. "August fifteen *this* year. In only ten weeks, Dassah, they will be gone."

"Ten weeks? Gone?"

"Yes! Never again will you need to debase yourself before an English *sahib* or *memsahib*."

"Gone?" she repeated. The hollowness inside her grew to a dark expanse. The candle of her soul snuffed out. Her knees went weak. She groped for support. Zakir gently lowered her to the *charpoy* beside the radio.

*Cam...Cam...*soon they would not even share the same land. With a weak hand, she pushed away Zakir's hand of comfort. Soon Cam would not be in the same country as his own child.

27

July, 1947

The weight of her child eased only when she walked. Dassah paced the short veranda to the trellis swathed in jasmine. At least her baby's shifting to a lower position created more space below her ribcage. These past few days had brought easier breathing. With both hands she massaged her lower abdomen. Her little one would be born in a few weeks. Dipping her head, she released a long sigh. And then her child…fatherless…even before he or she took a first breath.

Since she'd awakened this morning, restlessness spurred her. The first sign of energy she had felt since the radio announcement two weeks ago, when life had gone dark. She paced to the end of the veranda encased in a climbing pink rose. Both Tikah and Zakir insisted she stay indoors or go no further than this courtyard, a pretty prison that held no allure. Even if she wished to go out, Zakir insisted she wear a *chuddar* in public. Safer, he said.

So far Dassah had refused. So far, she had also refused to journey to Karachi until after the baby was born and strong enough to travel. Thank Yeshu that Tikah supported her in this. Dassah also repeated her refusal to Zakir's marriage proposal. But in this, Tikah supported Zakir, and not her.

It made no matter. She paced to the jasmine bush. Tikah and Zakir could hope all they wanted for a marriage. Though Cam had abandoned her, was leaving the country, though the minister who married them was an imposter, she had made her vows in the presence of God. She would abide by her vows, though Cam's meant nothing to him. Though their child would be fatherless, and she not even a widow.

Her baby gave her a swift kick. She pulled in a sharp breath and paced the veranda once more.

When Zakir joined them in the evenings, they listened to the news. A lawyer had arrived from England, Sir Cyril Radcliffe. Apparently he would abide in a guesthouse at the viceroy's palace, sequestered from everyone, even from the viceroy, to study and draw up the new borders. But everyone wondered where these borders would be. Why could they not know where these lines would be before Independence Day? And why must Independence and Partition come so quickly?

The rioting had become worse. Rumors among the hotel staff bore more evil tidings than she could fathom. In their time off, the hotel employees who were not Kashmiri Muslims, but Hindu and Sikh, whispered in clutches, "Where should we go for safety?"

Even here in Kashmir unrest had been kindled. Her baby would be born in Kashmir before the transfer of power. After that? Where should she raise her child? India? Pakistan? She had no choice but to rely on Zakir's help. Yet her spirit churned.

Amma worked so hard, but she was getting older. Dassah would have to gain employment to provide for both Tikah and her child. For now it was a relief when Zakir purchased their food in the bazaars so they did not have to. Lately, he had repaired a number of broken sections to their roof, applying flattened kerosene cans to act as shingles. It was better to have a man to protect them. He was a good man. A strong man.

The churning in her soul gave her no rest. As an unmarried woman, she would have few resources. She must do something for the sake of her child. To save her little one from the life of a beggar, she must, she must—*oh, dear Yeshu, help me*—she must marry.

The words *in him, I live, and move, and have my being* slipped through her mind. Surely, her Savior would see that she and her baby found safe harbor. And Yeshu would not send her a husband who did not share her faith. Unless…unless Yeshu wanted her to help Zakir back to the faith in Christ he had as a child.

Lifting her face to the sun, she savored its warmth. For the first time since the announcement, she felt the sweetness of the Lord's presence, though the blue sky offered no answers, only the singing of a sparrow.

An intrusive sound of pounding feet disturbed the quiet. Parmindar, one of the hotel maids, raced up the path and stopped to brace herself with a hand on the veranda pillar. The girl heaved for breath. "You must come, Dassah. Out on the main street. The viceroy and his wife have landed at the aerodrome. Come quickly. They will be driving by. On their way to the Gulab Mahal." She giggled and waved her hands with feverous intent for Dassah to follow. "They are going to stay at the palace of the crown prince and the maharani."

With a tired smile Dassah waved the girl on.

"Oh Dassah, Zakir and Tikah are not here to stop you. What harm is there in going out to the streets to watch such goings-on? It is not good for your baby that you mope about this shack."

Dassah stopped her pacing. It had been a long time since something exhilarating happened in her life. Not since her wedding, but she thrust aside the memories that delivered pain and rejoicing in the same parcel. Parmindar kept up her cajoling. The young girl was right. Perhaps it would lift her spirits, for her baby's sake, to watch the viceroy's arrival.

Whisking a scarf from inside the hut, she dashed as quickly as she could to catch up to Parmindar on the street outside the hotel grounds. Throwing the gossamer veil over the top of her head to protect her from the sun, and from prying eyes as Zakir nagged her about so often, she pushed herself to as close to a sprint as she could manage. She held her arms around the bulk of her baby, but after only a few yards, she gasped from the pressure in her lower regions.

Crowds lined the wide main street. This road would take the state visitors to the Gulab Mahal on the other side of the lake, a view she had glimpsed many times on her honeymoon. Sunlight danced on the surface of her beloved, lotus-filled lake, where memories of her brief time as a wedded woman must remain buried in its blue and green depths. Memories of laughing in Cam's arms…of dancing on the houseboat deck…when they had read together. But then he had stayed away all night on that other boat.

Parmindar shook her elbow. "Look, Dassah, they are coming."

She forced a smile for the sake of the girl. No matter what upheavals took place, the people were eager to view pageantry. Even if the viceroy's decision gave the Indian people little time to prepare.

Standing on her toes, Dassah struggled to keep her balance as the growing crowd grew dense. People intruded between her and Parmindar, until Parmindar waved to her, a good ten feet away. Soon the girl disappeared within the throng.

Farther up the road, the happy crowd roared with cheers. Dassah strained upward to see the first of a line of black, shining cars with the royal emblem of the crown prince on their doors.

Elbows jabbed into her ribs as spectators shoved for a better vantage. Near her an old woman shouted, "Can you not see she is with child? You disreputable *badmashes*, may you be born an insect in your next life." The old woman hit several men on the head, but to no avail. The heaving crowd pulled the old woman away from Dassah so that they drifted apart like leaves upon turbulent waters.

Dassah's breath became rapid. She had been a fool to come out to the streets. Though the shouts remained cheerful, what if she fell, or was trampled? Anger, fear, anticipation of the past year raced through the hearts of this multitude. What if this crush turned to rioting? Her feet lost touch with the ground as she was partially lifted in the press. Sunlight blinded her as she looked for a way to escape…when she saw the car following the viceroy and his wife.

He sat in the back of that car. Her insides lit with a thousand candles.

Father God in Heaven…those features…. It could not be. But the peak of his military cap did not obscure the countenance she loved…that bridge of nose and line of jaw she had traced with her fingers…that mouth she pressed kisses upon in the night. *Janu*…beloved, the husband of her heart if not her life.

Her feet found the ground as the cheering crowd shoved past. She fell. Her knees and hands were scraped by gravel. Someone helped her to her feet. She knew not who, for they were swallowed up in the horde following the parade. Prodding elbows and bashing shoulders lessened as she shrank to the back of the crowd and leaned upon a balustrade close to the bridge.

All life drained from her. Cam, her beloved Cam...sitting at the side of kings. And she so poor. Of no importance. The candles of her soul snuffed out once more.

I am your refuge. In me you live and move.

Yeshu's words did little to assuage her heartache. Her child would have many better chances with his father. It would be better to relinquish the baby to Cam and to whatever woman he married. Pain drove deep and brought her to her knees...waves and waves of pressure. *Dear God...it has been months since I have bled.* She had been faithful at rest, until today. Her child was not due for another three weeks.

The sun shone bright, but her vision turned to night. Pain came and went. She sank to the pavement, holding to the stone balustrade. A long time later... minutes...a quarter of an hour, she could not tell. Voices shouted. Out of the shouting voices she recognized Parmindar's. Then Tikah's. Their voices came closer.

Tikah spoke softly at her side, out of breath. "I am here, beloved."

A man lifted her in his arms and began to carry her. Up, cradled close to his chest, she prayed that when she opened her eyes, she would see a miracle. *A miracle, please dear Yeshu.* Perhaps when Cam was driven past, he had seen her...Cam.... *Dear God let it be the husband of my heart who holds me. Let him be here for the birth of his child. Let him be here to help me...to protect me....*

When she opened her eyes, she saw Zakir looking down at her, and she squeezed her eyes shut. It was not Cam, but Zakir who was her protector.

Coming out from a gray fugue of pain, she looked to see the shack's pine walls. She lay on the *charpoy,* and Tikah loosened her clothing. In the background behind a curtain, Zakir murmured, "Does she need the doctor, Auntie?"

"Yes. Run! Her pains have come sudden."

It was hard to breath. Throbbing shards driving inward...downward. "Cam!" she cried when the pressure was more than she could bear. "Cam!" She could not bear that anyone else be her child's father but his true father. If she must go with Zakir for safety, then it would be better for Cam to take their little one.

Tikah took her hands. "Beloved, the baby is coming today."

She gripped *Amma's* hand. "Zakir must find Cam. He is at the palace. My husband is at the palace. *Amma,* we must give the baby to him. Better...better that he raise our child. And I will go anywhere with you and Zakir."

His Lordship and Lady Mountbatten attended the state dinner with His Royal Highness the Crown Prince Hari Singh at the Gulab Mahal that evening. It was arranged that Cam and another of the ADCs take their daughter Pamela out for some mild entertainment arranged at the home of the British Resident, advisor to the crown prince. To Cam's chagrin, he would have to see Phoebe tonight. She was acting as hostess on behalf of her parents, who were attending the state dinner. All Cam wanted to do was find Alan Callahan, but he'd have to wait until tomorrow. He'd sent a telegram to Alan letting him know he was here.

The city of Srinagar—with its meandering bazaars, tall chalet-like houses with elaborate fretted wooden verandas, and waterways leading to Dal Lake—was lit with streets lamps, lending a sense of a fairy tale as they drove to the Residency. Or was it that he would always associate this mountain lake and lush garden city with Dassah? Thank goodness, Pamela and her bodyguard nattered on in the backseat, leaving him in the front with the driver as he attempted to contain his rampaging emotions.

For a while Pamela and the bodyguard talked about the political situation, the immense workload that Pamela's parents had undertaken. All the while—as Cam always did no matter where he went in India—his eyes roamed the surroundings, hoping for a glimpse of Dassah. Praying she would stroll through this very bazaar, or cross one of the several bridges they drove over. As their vehicle came to the wide graveled drive and arched gates to the Residency grounds, he prayed, God forbid, Dassah would ever need any of the refugee camps he inspected with Lady Mountbatten.

A red-robed *chaprassi* with an impeccable white turban met them at the end of the drive and opened the car door for Pamela. At the top of the Residency steps, Phoebe stood in a blousy sort of frock to greet the honored guest. Inside the dim hall, they passed through to the large drawing room where the place was full of the younger set of assistant administrators, junior civil authorities, an assortment of lower military ranks, and female guests not much older than nineteen-year-old Pamela.

As soon as Pamela was formally introduced to all, the gathering relaxed and drinks, alcoholic and non-alcoholic, were distributed by servants. A gramophone was started up, and dancing began to the strains of a pre-war tune by Frank Sinatra. Phoebe made her way over to him, standing close to where Pamela sat on a chintz-covered sofa overlooking the garden, a glass of lemonade in her hand. "Cam, darling," Phoebe drawled, "it's been simply ages. Not since Eva's wedding. Naughty thing you, using the excuse of work not to visit me."

"Right you are, Phoebe." He smiled as he shook her hand before she had a chance to lean forward to kiss his cheek. Best not to give her an inch, and no sense arguing with her. Besides, she knew very well how dire the situation was. Her father as British Resident was up to his eyeballs working through the political situation with the crown prince.

She leaned close, grinning to beat the band, and spoke in an undertone. "The

Mountbatten girl's in good hands for the moment. I insist on stealing you for a few minutes."

It would appear churlish to decline, and he had no wish to embarrass Pamela with a fuss. "A few moments only, Phoebe."

"Would you like a drink first, a brandy and soda?"

His shoulder jerked infinitesimally. "No. Thank you, but no."

"Right. I forgot. I heard you were trying to nip the old drinking thing in the bud. Ridiculous if you ask me. In any case I think it's time we got back on track."

Not for one minute did he relish a tête-à-tête with Phoebe, but he followed her out the veranda to the extensive lawns and garden. She whirled to face him, all frivolity vanishing. "You've never rang me once or written, Cam, and I've written you reams. At your sister's wedding you gave me the brush off. Why, last August we were practically engaged, then not one word, one way or the other."

She turned her luminous cat eyes on him, but they did nothing for him. He wondered if they ever had. "My apologies, Phoebe, you're absolutely right. It was shoddy of me to give you no explanation." He drew in a breath, feeling clean and healthy enough to be making the right choice at long last, something his drinking in the past had hindered him from doing. "Phoebe, you'll make a wonderful wife for a chap who's on the upward rungs of political life, but I'm not that man."

She remained still. Perhaps still was not the word. Rigid was more accurate. "So that is that?" Her voice wavered.

Dash it all, he felt sorry for her. "Phoebe dear, you're a beautiful, vibrant woman. What do you want with a washed-up old military johnny like me?"

"Because you're an ADC to the viceroy. Cam, you could have an enviable career anywhere in the British Empire."

"With the relinquishment of India, there will no longer be a British Empire," he said quietly.

"You don't need to explain that to me. Daddy just received his embarkation orders, and we've begun packing. Like a lot of us British Colonials, we'll either squash into Ceylon or Kenya. And yourself?"

"Very soon I will no longer be part of His Majesty's forces. In fact the papers are being drawn up, and in the next few weeks I plan on leaving my position as aide-de-camp to Mountbatten."

"You're giving up your position?" Her eyes widened. "Why?"

"To look for my wife."

"Your wife? You can't mean that little Indian girl." She clapped a hand to her mouth.

"Dassah, yes." Her look of dismay made the back of his neck prickle. He wanted nothing more than to walk away from Phoebe and all her like.

"Cam," she whispered, lowering her hand to flop in her lap. "This is ridiculous. I don't understand."

He spoke through tight lips. "So it appears." She could wonder all she wanted. He refused to cheapen his love for Dassah by explaining.

She searched his expression, noting his jaw, probably guessing correctly that he gritted his teeth. "Cam, a man of your station doesn't marry one of the natives." She reached for his hand, simpering a little. "I can accept you had a bit of a dalliance with the girl. Quite normal for a healthy young man. But once we're married, I assure you, you will not wish to trespass ever again."

"Phoebe, I don't think you're hearing me. I am a married man. I asked Dassah to be my wife because I love her and one day I want her to be the mother of my children."

"I see." The thinning of her mouth proved she did *see* at last. "So, back in the autumn, that's what was going on, on your secluded little houseboat, something more than the usual seedy little affair."

He'd stayed too long and started to extend his hand in farewell. *Forever. Goodbye, Phoebe.* Time to get back to his duty of escorting Pamela Mountbatten.

"Don't be a fool, Cam. You're simply besotted with an attractive Indian chit. It's not the end of the world, or of us."

"Phoebe, there's no point in discussing this further. I intend to find my wife."

Something fluttered in her expression. A new gleam, a dryness to her tone. "You haven't found her yet then? Tell me, darling, why did the girl run away from you on your honeymoon of all things?"

"That is none of your business." His fists clenched. If Phoebe were a man... Then it struck him. "How do you know Dassah ran away while we were on honeymoon? I've only shared that with my family."

Her complexion turned pasty. "Look, I knew you were involved with the girl. Someone had to think sensibly since you obviously weren't, so when I ran into Dassah and that old woman the day after we partied on the lake, I took care of the situation. You should thank me."

It was as though a bucket of cold water were thrown on him. He attempted to slow his heart rate and spoke with crisp annunciation. "You'd better tell me, Phoebe. From the start. Do not leave out...one...single...detail."

His pulse swooshed through his temples, almost drowning out Phoebe's voice as she gave him her pathetic details. His hackles rose as he tried to ignore her British Raj attitude—*I am your mother and your father*—her high-horse assumption that she was doing Dassah a favor by getting her a job as a maid in a ski resort. And all along, this entire winter and spring, Dassah had been up at Gulmarg. But he was here now. Only twenty miles away. He started to leave. He'd beg Pamela's forgiveness but ask if he could return her to the safety of the palace, and take leave.

"Cam." Phoebe clutched his wrist. "Don't go. How can you be so frightful to me when you didn't tell a soul you'd married the girl, when actually by keeping it mum was the one sensible thing you did."

He cleared his voice. He'd borne more than a trace of that disgusting Raj attitude by keeping the secret at the start. Even afterward as he recuperated from his drinking, he'd not shouted to the world that he and Dassah were married.

"Keeping that ruddy secret is my greatest shame, Phoebe, but I must thank you. You've helped me see the light. I don't know why I didn't do this sooner, but I'll get my marriage announcement into *The Times of India* tomorrow."

A foolish grin must be spreading over his face, he felt as light as air. "I also want to thank you, for in your own way you showed kindness to Dassah by sending her up to Gulmarg. At least there she was relatively safe. All this time I've been worried sick she was in areas of the worst rioting. Now, if you'll excuse me." He brushed past Phoebe—not caring that her jaw dropped and her mouth hung open like a codfish—and entered the Residency.

It didn't take much to convince Pamela Mountbatten to return to the palace. In fact he could tell she found the whole thing a bore. With her days spent helping her mother, Pamela was far more interested in the social welfare of the Indian people than dancing to the crooning of Sinatra or Crosby. Pamela, Cam, and her bodyguard left the Residency, and Cam had no desire to look back even once at Phoebe. As soon as they reached the marble halls of the Gulab Mahal, he parted from his charge.

Relieved of duty, Cam hunted out one of the Indian soldiers he knew from years past, a soldier currently assigned to protect the crown prince. The man owned a Norton motorcycle.

As his friend walked him to the palace stables where all vehicles were kept, Cam went over his plans. Originally he'd planned on seeing Alan tomorrow. Not now though. Every fiber of his being wanted to ride out to Gulmarg straightaway.

Precious minutes ticked by as the Indian soldier led him to the stall where he kept his motorcycle. Cam waved good-bye and pushed the Norton out. When he reached the areas beyond the sentries, he swung his leg over the saddle, opened the throttle, and kick-started the engine. At first the engine coughed, then it turned over, and the bike took off with a roar.

Driving through the winding streets of Srinagar, with the wind whistling past his ears, and out to the road heading to Gulmarg, he spoke under his breath, "Hang on, Dassah. Stay where you are. I'm coming."

"Dassah, do not push until I tell you," Tikah spoke over Dassah's moans. The day had been so long, hours and hours of crushing waves, as though she was pressed by the crowds from that morning. A local doctor had come and gone. Before he left he said there was nothing to be done until her labor progressed, and from the size and shape, he felt the baby was not going to be born dangerously early. "In fact," he said in answer to her fears, "your baby may have reached full term. Perhaps you counted wrong."

Now it was night. Dassah lay on her back, her knees up, her feet flat on the *charpoy*. With each band of pain that tightened her womb, she clenched her fists and gritted her teeth. With the rising mountain of pain, squeezing, crushing all life from her she cried out.

Tikah took her hand. "Not yet, Dassah, do not push."

The mountain shrank away. The stone-like pain slowly dissolved…like waves seeping into tiny grains of sand. Her thighs trembled. She gasped for air.

Tikah planted a kiss on the top of Dassah's bare kneecap. "Hush, my precious daughter. Take a sip of water." Tikah supported her head and set the cup to her lips. Cool water brought blessed respite, but already the tightening returned. It built in force. Once more the mountain became granite ranges of pain. Ranges and ranges. Behind each other they marched forward, closer and closer with tightened fists. She gnashed her teeth. The pains changed to unbearable pressure. Of being torn…apart.

"Push, Dassah, now."

She pulled on the towels Tikah tied to the ends of the *charpoy* by her head. "Cam!" she screamed. Her vision went black. The mountain blocked all light as she pushed down…down to the center of her being.

"Push, Dassah."

Her sight grayed as the tearing numbed. A whimpering came from somewhere. The mountain grew smaller, dissolved as waves seeped, shushing like a lullaby into those grains of sand. The whimper turned into a wail. Her legs shook.

Tikah murmured, "All is well, beloved daughter. Your son is here."

A moment later Tikah placed a soft, squirming bundle on her chest. Though she ached and trembled, she raised her head to look down on the black hair plastered to his head. A good size, not too small as she had feared. Perfectly formed and breathing on his own, and crying with strong gusty cries. She laughed. *Oh, little one, it is all right. Cry, yell, show the world you are a strong man.* She had miscalculated? Perhaps this little one had been formed the very night of her wedding. *Thank you, Yeshu. Thank you.*

Wrapping her arms around his bare little body, she drew him to her breast and lifted one tiny hand with her finger. His skin was only a shade lighter than hers. His little hand opened like a starfish. Five small perfect fingers. His toes, she lifted those too. As she stroked the arch of his miniscule foot, he opened his eyes, and she gasped. Eyes like those of a Caucasian child—blue as the depths of Dal Lake—a little darker than his father's eyes.

Dassah must have dozed for a while. Her baby slept at her breast. He was clean, and so was she, Tikah had tended them both so well. The doctor returned and pronounced the baby healthy, a few days early, two weeks perhaps, but nothing to fret over.

It was close to midnight. A lamp burned in the far corner, and the radio hummed low. More news. More rioting in the various provinces, but she would not allow such sad news to rob her of her joy.

The world fell away, and there was only her son lying in her arms. She breathed in his sweetness, the purity of his skin the color of milky tea, but his hair held the same wave as Cam's. And the way he lifted his brows—surely that was the way Cam did too. She loved Cam with all her heart, but now that she held their child in her arms, what had she been thinking? She could never give him up. Even to his father. Even though she would name their son Cameron Geoffrey.

Zakir's voice mingled with Tikah's, but she paid little heed until Tikah's words, "She has just given birth, we cannot be moving her yet."

"We must get her away from Srinagar, Auntie. She saw *him* today. One glimpse and that brought her labor upon her. If she sees him again, she will feel compelled to give the child to him."

"She will not. Look how she holds the babe. Trust me, Zakir, I will not let her give my grandson away."

On her *charpoy*, Dassah held Cameron closer. How right her *amma* was. She would not give her baby up, though it cut deep to hear Zakir speak of Cam with such contempt. While her heart was awash with sadness that Cam was not part of her life, Zakir's jealousy did not sit right with her.

"But if we stay here," Zakir protested to Tikah, "the chances are high they will meet. If *he* talks to her, *he* will weaken her. You know the way of a man with a woman, what then, Auntie?"

Listening to them, Dassah might have wept but for the bliss of her son in her arms. She remembered too well the way of Cam with her, the elation of his touch.

Tikah tsk-tsked. "It is not safe to put her in a truck as you say. She will bleed—"

"She will bleed here too." Zakir's voice rose. "I am telling you, Auntie, it is not safe. Bad times are coming to Kashmir. Dassah and others like her will lose blood—you too—when the fighting starts."

A fist tightened afresh around Dassah's heart. She lifted up on an elbow, drawing her son closer. "What fighting are you speaking of? It is quiet in these streets."

Zakir strode to her *charpoy*. "It is fermenting. Trust me, as a soldier, I am knowing these things." He hunched down and touched the downy hair on her son's head. "Do you want to see him hurt, Dassah?"

Her scalp and spine prickled. "I will not listen to such unspeakable things," she rasped.

At the same time, Tikah marched toward him and pulled at Zakir's arm. "Do not frighten her in such a way. How can I be whisking her away at such a time when she may develop complications after delivery?"

His eyes swam with moisture as he stared at Dassah. "I say these terrible things to make you listen to me. I urge you to come directly from the birthing bed to keep you and your child safe." He took her hand. "We must leave tonight, so that I may protect your son. Be trusting me, Dassah. Me!"

She brushed her lips across her infant's downy head, the place that Zakir's fingers recently touched. All that mattered was that little Cameron be safe, that her tiny boy take his first steps in a protected place, to laugh and play and learn in all sweetness and innocence.

Zakir kept on. "I will hire a vehicle tonight. Steal one if I have to. Tikah, be ready to move her within the hour. If I drive carefully, you can nurse her in a truck box. I have a friend not far beyond the border of Kashmir. I promise it will not be too arduous a journey."

Dassah barely heard Zakir, her mind riveted on one theme, her baby's wellbeing. She raised her hand to take hold of the marble still strung around her neck in its leather webbing. Cam would be a good father to their son, but she could not give up her baby. That would tear her heart from her to the point that she would never recover. It had to be her who taught little Cameron to read *The Wind in the Willows* and the works of Kipling, the poetry of Tagore. It had to be her who taught Cameron to laugh and play and become a man.

With all that was within her—the Spirit of the Risen Christ—she would teach her son about Yeshu, even if it meant committing the contradictory act of marrying a Muslim to protect them, and living in Pakistan.

28

Before dawn the next morning, the bike nearly slid out from under Cam as the Norton fishtailed into the churchyard and skidded to a stop. He held back his overwhelming desire to curse. Racing through the night up to Gulmarg had been a blasted waste of time. He'd gotten there in the wee hours of the night, wakened the manager, wakened a good many of the staff, probably half the guests, and been frostily informed that Dassah and Tikah were no longer there. They'd left the employ of Nedou's a good month or more ago. The manager dismissed him, saying he hadn't a clue where they'd gone.

A month. Cam did curse this time, only to immediately send up a prayer asking forgiveness for his vulgarism. As a new man in Christ, he did not want to swear, even when the weight on his chest threatened to cut off his breath. But still, only a month. *Lord, have mercy.*

Ahead of him, the light in the darkened parsonage flickered, and thank God, Alan Callahan strode out the front door of his small bungalow, his hair awry, snapping his suspenders in place. "What blighted noise is this in the middle of the night? I'll not have you frightening the villagers."

Cam cut the engine. "She'd been up in Gulmarg all this time. Left there only a month ago."

Alan stared down his patrician nose. "And you know this how?"

"Phoebe Anderson, the daughter of the British Resident, found Dassah a job up at Nedou's Hotel there. I only discovered this tonight. Rode up there, only to be told..." His chest tightened.

The tall minister bent his head. "Praise God for his watchful eye."

"Will you come? I want to check all hotels in Kashmir. Seems to me, they may try to find similar work."

"What, on the back of that thing in the middle of the night? Let's consider for a moment before racketing off blindly. If she was working at Nedou's branch in the heights, the sensible thing would be to check with the manager of Nedou's here in Srinagar."

Cam went still, his only movement that of gripping and releasing the bike's handlebars. "If that's the case, why wouldn't the manager up there tell me?"

Alan looked at him askance. "Astounding, isn't it? No doubt you used the same suave diplomacy on him as when you first tried to convince me to marry you and your good lady."

The acidity of failure bubbled in Cam's veins. "Disappointed, Alan? All your prayers, all the insight you've shared, and I continue to act the wretch I've always been."

The minister's voice turned wry. "As we've discussed in our letters, while the salvation of your soul took but a moment when you surrendered in faith to Christ, the renewal of your person takes time. Why, the whole creation groaneth and travaileth in pain, ourselves also. The firstfruits of the Spirit waiting for the redemption of our body." His scrutiny of Cam turned to a chuckle. "Good gracious, do you think the Lord took only a few weeks to produce the exemplary man you see standing before you? Took a decade or more for me to grow from the drunken scoundrel I was to a man worthy of serving my current parishioners."

His voice softened further. "Look, I know the manager of Nedou's, and the sun will rise in an hour. I'll be with you in two shakes of a lamb's tail, then you may take me on that contraption to the hotel."

Still gripping and ungripping the Norton's handlebars, Cam waited, counting the minutes for Alan to get ready. *Dear God, have mercy. Don't let her slip through my fingers. Hold on to her tight for me.*

Barely twenty minutes later, Cam and Alan strode across the polished floors of Nedou's entrance hall with its floor-to-ceiling windows. A long-robed *chaprassi* with an imposing turban stopped them, but after hearing what they had to say, escorted them through the long-established hotel to the manager's suite. Already pots clanged in the kitchen in preparation of breakfast.

Though it was only dawn, the manager was at his desk, dressed in an English suit and going over the day's menu with the chef. Only after considerable encouragement from Alan did the manager agree to get his assistant in charge of the hiring. "Most of our staff are living in employee quarters," he said. "It would be prudent to check our employees first, and if the individual you are looking for is not here, then I will telephone my counterpart in Lahore. Perhaps they have gone there."

Alan remained calm, his pleasantness toward others in stark contrast to the razor-sharp reproofs he reserved for Cam. Yet Cam could think of no one else except for Dad that he would rather have at his side. This tall maverick preacher with his craggy face was a man of extraordinary courage and kindness.

And dear Lord, he needed Alan here to help him compose his nerve. It took all inner resources to keep from tapping his foot or pacing the carpeted office as the manager and his assistant sat at a wide mahogany desk looking down the lists of employees in a series of account books. How many employees did these hotels need anyway? Good gracious, hundreds and hundreds it appeared. Finally, the manager closed the account. "There is no one by that name, Hadassah or Dassah. It is not an Indian name. Nor anyone by the surname of Fraser, and of course this Hadassah you mention is like most Indian people—many do not have surnames.

"What about Tikah?" Cam swiped the hair off his brow. "Tikah, oh what was her last name? Akbar…right, like Akbar the elephant, that's how I remembered her name as a lad."

The manager flipped several pages and scrolled down. After an interminable length of time, his finger halfway down a page, he looked up. "We have a woman in the laundry by the name Tikah Akbar. She has rented a house in our employee section." The man's brows lifted. "She has her grown daughter living with her, who is unwell and incapable of work."

It seemed as though Alan at his side held his breath. Cam felt aware of everything. The guarded expression of the Indian men as to why he was looking for a native woman. The ticking of the clock on the manager's desk. The soughing breeze tapping the fronds of pepper trees against the windows. "Unwell? Incapable of work, you say? Where?" Cam croaked. "Take me there, please, this instant."

"Of course, *sahib*."

Cam and Alan followed the two hotel managers outside, through gardens laid out for the pleasure of paying guests, along a path that led to the back of the hotel to a rambling section of outbuildings. They strode to the end of the path to a courtyard surrounding a communal well and a series of shacks. They stopped at one with a veranda swathed in flowers and scratched at the rough plank door. No one answered. The assistant tapped and opened the door to speak into semi-darkness.

Cam pushed past and stepped into the one-room hut, whispering, "Dassah. Are you here, Dassah?"

The manager lit a lamp that illumined a lowly existence and confirmed the place was vacant. The hut of pine floors and walls contained only two string *charpoys*, a charcoal brazier, one low rickety table and a wireless. All clean except for a bucket in the corner that contained a pile.... He swallowed convulsively. A pile of bloodstained cloth. He whipped around to face the assistant. "Are you sure this is their room? You said the woman Hadassah had been ill. Of what? Someone must know? Where are they? Do their neighbors know anything? Had a doctor been called?"

The manager and his assistant rushed from the hut to presumably check with the neighbors while Cam turned to search the rest of the shack. So did Alan.

Was this really her quarters? Perhaps it was all a mistake. Aside from the metallic odor of blood and other human smells Cam couldn't decipher—a sweet but fetid odor—he caught a faint fragrance of jasmine and lilies. His gaze landed on the windowsill to a vase of flowers. Yes, she'd been here. Any woman could have arranged those flowers, but he knew from the artistic composition that Dassah's hand had created it. He raised his eyes to the rough ceiling beams and formed two fists. *Dear God, where is she?*

Alan had been rummaging around the shack, ran his hands along the towels tied to the end of the string bed, knelt to study the contents of wet and bloodstained laundry. He touched Cam on the shoulder. "I've attended more than my share of birthings in my vocation. Someone has had a child here—had a child, Cam, as in given birth—within the last few hours."

That sweet fetid odor, the bloodstained cloth, a newborn? The hairs on Cam's arms stood.

The manager stormed into the hut, trailing several employees, some currently on shift, others dragged from their beds. One young girl spoke to Cam over the yammering of the rest. "I am Parmindar. Why are you looking for Dassah?" She tugged at his arm.

He forced a soothing tone in her Kashmiri dialect. "I'm her husband. I'm worried sick about her."

"Her husband?" The girl's hands fluttered and clasped. "But I was sure she was a widow." Her eyes narrowed at him.

"Please believe me. I would rather die than bring harm to Dassah. If you are her friend, then I rejoice that she had such a wise and caring companion."

The girl peered at him for the longest while. "Are you the man who gave her the marble? The Christensen—"

"The Christensen Akro Slag." He grinned like a madman. "Yes, yes, the Christensen Akro Slag, I gave that to Dassah when she was a little girl."

"The man who gave her that was her husband. Dassah showed it to me many times. She said it was a gift from when they used to be in love."

Used to be in love. The girl's words nearly crushed him. "Where is she, please? Dassah is beyond the price of rubies in my heart."

She studied him a little longer. "You wear a uniform—did I not see you accompany the viceroy yesterday?" She didn't wait for an answer. "Dassah saw the parade too. That was when she collapsed." The girl took her time to ponder, but he dared not interrupt her.

A slow smile lit her eyes. "I am believing you, when you say that you would not harm her. But why would she leave when she must have seen you?"

"Because I am a wretched man who does not deserve her. I hurt her feelings. I did not hurt her in body, but I wounded her feelings."

She stared down at her clasped hands. "I am understanding now, I think. Though Dassah smiled much, she was very, very sad."

"Where did she go, Parmindar?" He softly put the question to her.

"You are a British *sahib,* you have the power to protect her. For this reason I am telling you. It is only because Dassah is a most kind woman that I want you to go after her." She hesitated, waggling her head. "I have not been liking this idea of them going off to the areas he thinks will become Pakistan. That is what her *amma* and her brother have been saying for many weeks—that they would be safer there."

Cam's heart stopped on two words. Pakistan and... "Her brother? Who?"

"Yes, Zakir." The girl chattered on, while in the background Alan and the managers talked with other hotel employees.

Alan took him by the arm and led him a short distance from the others. "Cam, it's confirmed—three people, Tikah, a man named Zakir, and your Dassah left these premises several hours ago. By truck."

Cam tried to turn away as adrenalin kicked in. His heart thudded to get on the road and follow, while the other side of his heart played a slow death dirge that she had fled from him ...with Zakir. How she must despise him.

Alan wouldn't let him turn away though. "That's not all, Cam." He shook his shoulder. "Get hold of yourself, man. Dassah gave birth to the infant that was born here yesterday evening."

He stared at the minister, his breath leaving him.

"Did you hear me?"

"I heard. And I can do the arithmetic. Eight months since I saw her last. Nine since our wedding night." Cam sank to the *charpoy* next to the radio, not knowing whether to laugh or cry like a baby himself. He was a father. Dassah had borne him a child.

Alan clasped him on the shoulder. "Your child is only a few hours old and on its way to the Punjab."

His child. There was no time to waste. He got to his feet. "These neighbors," he ground out. "Do they know what kind of vehicle? They must have gone down the road toward the border of Kashmir." Bile rose up his throat. So shortly after giving birth, his wife was in the back of a truck going through roasting hot villages, areas that were seeing the most horrendous carnage he'd ever heard of. Dassah, his Dassah, would be traveling through villages that could be razed, flattened by violence at any time.

Alan gripped Cam's shoulder in a more painful hold. "Now is the travail, Cam. Bear up under the fear and pain. Trust in God, like you never have before."

Cam's head swam. All these months he'd feared, he'd worried that she might be in those areas. But now, hearing that she was heading directly there. With Zakir driving her. Away from him. He steadied himself. "The baby...what...?"

Parmindar understood and stepped closer. "A boy, *sahib.*"

He raced out of the shack. Not sure if the footsteps following were Alan's, but it was Alan who swung onto the back of the bike. This wouldn't do. He'd need something bigger, a jeep, a truck, something that would take him down the winding mountain roads of Kashmir, down into the dust-filled plains of the

Punjab. Down into the very jaws of Hades to find his wife…and his son.

A coppersmith bird woke Dassah. Its metallic *tuk tuk tuk* call built in volume and repetition like that of a copper sheet being hit. It must be morning.

The quiet woke her. Inside the unmoving truck box where she lay, the canvas tarp trapped the sun. No longer did she smell pine and deodar forests, but parched dust. Dry heat stole even the sweat that broke through her pores. While she slept this past hour they must have passed the border of Kashmir and reached the sunbaked plains.

Tikah sat near her head, holding the baby with one arm and sponging Dassah's face with a tepid cloth. When she saw Dassah was awake, she placed little Cameron into her embrace and gave her a salt tablet and a drink of water from a flask.

Cradling little Cameron to her breast, Dassah sat up, listening to the stillness outside these canvas walls. The last time she woke, the vehicle had been bouncing over rutted roads. No matter what Zakir had promised back in Srinagar, the journey had been fraught with discomfort, as he had driven like a man possessed. Earlier in the night, after they left Srinagar, she had felt the swaying of the vehicle as it rounded the same snaking mountain roads that she had traveled all those months ago to her wedding with Cam. Where they had stopped to picnic. While she had dreamed of her wedding and of a red sari to proclaim her joy.

Now all was quiet and still, but for the coppersmith in a nearby tree. If only it were the little bulbuls that sang and played outside the houseboat of her honeymoon all those months ago. If only it were the frogs singing on the lotus blossoms instead of the breeze hissing in the sand.

She looked into her child's face. He arched his brows in contentment as he nursed. The skin of his hands, his tiny fingers unfurled like a flower, his little arms and cheek felt like satin and velvet to her touch. His eyes were sapphires when he opened them to lock with hers, and her heart overflowed its banks of love. Deeper than the Ganges. Wider than all India, higher than the mountains of the Hindu Kush was her love for her child.

"*Amma?*" she asked Tikah.

"Yes, beloved?" Tikah whispered.

"Where are we?"

"But fifty miles from Rawalpindi, Zakir is saying."

"Why have we stopped?"

Tikah's hesitation brushed a cold finger along Dassah's spine, and she sat straighter, clutching Cameron to her as he continued to nurse.

"Zakir was sure this village of his friend would be under the control of

Muslims," Tikah said. "He was sure Muslims were more prevalent in this area than Hindus and Sikhs."

"And that is not the case." That cold finger of fear crawled from Dassah's spine into her stomach. "Where is he?"

"Outside overlooking the village ahead."

Cameron stopped feeding, a trickle of colostrum trailing from his mouth as he fell into slumber. She kissed his dark silken head, placed him into Tikah's arms, and crept on her hands and knees to the tarp's opening.

"Dassah," Tikah whispered hard. "You will hemorrhage. Come back and lie still."

Though her insides ached with raw emptiness, she ignored Tikah and thrust the canvas opening aside. As her unsteady feet found the ground, white sunlight blinded her, bringing with it a wave of dizziness. Moments later her eyes adjusted to see bare, scorched hills quivering in waves of heat.

A grove of acacia hid them from view, but for how long? These thorny trees were not lush like chinar trees, but scrawny, casting little shade over the arid land. She scrambled low, clutching her abdomen that still throbbed, to where Zakir squatted near a thicket of chikri bushes. He held a rifle in his hands and shot a glance at her when her feet shifted a few pebbles. A low growl came from him. "Get back out of sight."

Hunching down beside him, she looked at a large village that sat in a gulley a quarter mile away. Only the small copse of trees hid their tan canvas-covered truck from the villagers on this barren hillside. A line of railroad track lay beyond the town. Like any other community in the Punjab, the houses were made of dun-colored brick. Cows and goats meandered down the main street that converged at the communal well under a large peepal tree. A patchwork of fields surrounded the village—mustard and squash, beans, irrigated by channels from a nearby river.

There was no sound from the one small mosque. Instead it appeared blackened by a recent fire, but a Sikh *gurdwara* appeared undisturbed, protected. So too did the Hindu roadside temple.

The town bustled. Children played in the dusty streets. Women drew water from the well. But their men stood wary, stationed here and there in the shimmering sunlight. Others were mounted on horseback with rifles in their scabbards. No Muslim prayer caps adorned these men. Only Sikh turbans and the rounded fez caps that Hindus preferred. Flags flying from electrical poles and houses were not the green flags with the crescent moon of Pakistan but the orange and green of the Hindu Congress.

Zakir cursed under his breath. "If I had but known this village remained under Sikh and Hindu control, I would have taken the other road. It is like this all over the province. Fighting is fierce over the farmlands."

"And you felt this was a safer place for my child?" She spoke through clenched teeth. "Can you not back the truck out the way you came and take another road?"

"They will hear the engine start up."

"If we remain here, someone will be coming to this grove, you can be sure." Fear for Cameron clawed at her.

Dust-filled lines scored deeply into Zakir's face as he turned to her. "Dassah, I will give up my life for you and your child."

"Yes, Zakir, but what power is there in your dying body to protect my son? Once you are dead, what then?"

Behind them came a crackle, as though someone stepped on a branch. They both swiveled on their haunches to look. At the same moment, her baby wailed from inside the truck.

She struggled to her feet. As she ran to the truck, she heard Zakir slide a cartridge into the chamber of his rifle. Her feet ground to a stop as she reached the vehicle, and she went rigid.

A man stood there. A tall Sikh wearing a crimson turban. A short, curved sword in his hand. A *karpan*, the Sikh's ceremonial dagger.

From where she stood outside the truck she could hear Tikah murmur to her baby within, and her little one's fretful whimpers. Her tiny child only wanted his mother. To be nursed. To be cuddled. *Yeshu, oh Yeshu, hear my cry.*

Behind her, Zakir's footsteps crept closer to stand beside her.

The Sikh's eyes narrowed on the rifle Zakir pointed at him. In Urdu the man spoke. "Be putting down your weapon, you fool. Are you not realizing that if you shoot it off the whole town will be upon you in minutes?" He opened his palms, beseeching, and slipped his *karpan* into the sash around his waist. "See, I am putting away my sacred knife. I will not harm you. Not all of us seek to kill and maim." He glanced over his shoulder. "My farm is over there. Come, I will hide you."

Dassah crept around the Sikh and to the truck's canvas opening but remained standing outside, listening to her baby whimper inside it. At the corner of her eye, she could see Tikah sitting near the edge of the truck bed looking out between the canvas flaps, her hands clenching and unclenching around the baby she held. All the while, Zakir kept his rifle trained on the man.

Zakir started to speak, but Dassah interrupted. "How can I be knowing you will not harm us, *sahib*?"

The tall, turbaned man peered down at her, his graying beard, his weathered features bespeaking many years—a grandfather perhaps? He lifted a helpless hand. "Please, little mother, be nursing your child. Evil times have befallen all of us, but do not let the babe go hungry." He glanced at the knitted prayer cap on Zakir's head. "I do not care what religion you are. My wife and I will not see you in danger, especially when you carry a child. Surely, these wicked times will end soon."

"These wicked times will not come to an end soon," Zakir said. "This area is sure to become part of Pakistan when independence is handed over. What do you plan to do, old man? Do you think your Sikh village will be safe then?"

The elder man's eyes glistened, and she detected a tremble to his hands. "I fear for my family. So many other villages have begun to march south, but we have held out. My ancestors plowed this land, these same furrows I plow. As Muslims fight for a land for themselves—Pakistan for Pakistanis—and Hindus fight for India, where are the Sikhs to go? Why could there not be a Khalistan for Sikhs?"

"You will not be safe here," Zakir interjected. "You must convince your people to flee to what is sure to be within Indian borders."

"And where will those borders be?" The old man cried, but a moment later his voice grew tired. "Perhaps you are right, young Muslim, but for the moment it is you who is in imminent danger. Lower your weapon and come with me. For the sake of your wife and child and old mother. Come! Quickly!"

Dassah stood, unable to move. "Shush, Zakir," she said when he started to speak. Only three things she knew. Her baby fretted to be nursed. Her blood trickled down her legs to pool at her feet in the dry grass. And it was not Zakir that she could put her faith in. Nor could she trust her beloved *amma* for guidance.

The coppersmith bird started up his rising *tuk tuk tuk* again, stretching her nerves.

And then in the distance came the twitter of an ordinary sparrow. The bird's sweet trill shimmered above the shifting waves of heat. She remembered telling little Ramesh and Padma last August during the Calcutta riots that not even a dusty sparrow could fall from the tree but that God saw. Only Yeshu had the power to die for those he loved and rise again. Only Yeshu had the power to catch his loved ones if they fell.

With her free hand, she touched the barrel of Zakir's rifle, pushing it downward, away from the old man. She signaled to Tikah to give her the baby. Seizing Cameron in her arms, she settled him under her shawl and let him nurse. Then, moving toward the Sikh gentleman, she whispered. "I believe the Almighty has sent you to help us. I am trusting in the one who created this world that you are as kind as you appear. Lead on, old father."

29

Their Sikh rescuer introduced himself as Narindar Dhillon as he guided them to his bullock cart on the road below the copse. Parched grass scraped at Dassah's ankles and shins. Under the merciless sun, what little strength she had seeped from her body. Her baby felt heavy in her arms...she, weightless. Spots of green and red dazzled before her eyes. She stumbled, reached out a hand. Zakir swooped to lift her while Tikah took the baby and followed.

At the cart, Narindar explained that he must take them on a roundabout trek away from the town to circle back onto his land. "This way you will remain unseen by the people of my community." Lines of sadness scored his face. "They are frightened and will not understand why I harbor people of Islam, when only days ago my people...Sikhs...did terrible things. In retaliation, you understand."

He had them sit in the cart box and covered them with a canvas.

Twenty minutes later, when the cart came to a stop and he removed the canvas, they blinked around them at the man's palatial home of sun-bleached walls. The house sat within a small fortress of outer walls and sturdy iron gates. Flowering creepers knit a pink and green pattern on the enclosure. Several cement staircases ascended to the roof of the main house, and to an older wing that appeared unused and engulfed with the flowering creeper.

At Narindar's instruction, Zakir carried Dassah into this older wing and through to a series of rooms surrounding a hidden courtyard. A soothing wash of blues and greens hit Dassah's eyes, greens from the sunlight filtering through flowering vines and melding with the chipped blue tiles of a large square. Though the heat burned outside, a sense of coolness washed over her. At the center of this tiled square, Zakir set her down. Through vision now graying with faintness, she peered around her.

Five or six people rested on a number of scattered *charpoys* and rugs. The men of this small group all wore Muslim prayer caps, some of the women were draped in *chuddars*, and their children stared back at her. One of the groups, a family, a mother and father held two little ones close. An older couple with a young boy about twelve sent tepid smiles to the newcomers, but fear tinged their welcome.

Dassah's eye stopped on a young woman in her late teens. Henna designs on her hands and feet had not yet faded—a bride, still wearing her wedding jewelry? A slender man with spectacles stood beside her, his hand on her shoulder. They smiled at her and little Cameron.

One of the Muslim women inched closer while her husband remained back with their two children. She knelt to help Tikah smooth a blanket on a vacant *charpoy* for the baby, making soft clucking noises at Cameron.

Narindar spoke in low tones for only those in this large courtyard to hear. "Three of my neighbors and their families are living in my home at this time." He called out in a more normal volume—not one shrunk by anxiety—and a handful of people rushed into the wing. Two young Sikh men in their twenties and women around the same age set up a cot in a room for Dassah to rest. "My children and their spouses," Narindar said. Moments later, he summoned his wife, Rani. An older version of one of the younger women came in, wearing a light cotton tunic and pantaloons, a diaphanous scarf over her shoulders.

While Rani smiled, she could not keep her hands from trembling. Her bangles jangled as she cast frequent glances at her husband. Whenever she seemed about to speak, Narindar held up his hand and murmured, "All will be well. Do not fret when it is only our neighbors we have known for many years." He began to introduce everyone—Tabish and his wife Sobia, another couple with children, Ali, who had been the teacher in this village, and his new bride Mahleeha.

But Dassah heard only the first few names before all sound took on a buzzing in her ears. A wave of heat tingled up her neck and down her arms, her surroundings blurred and faded to gray...and black as night.

Shafts of sunlight pierced the cold green waters that flowed around her. Dassah kicked her feet, spread her arms, and pushed the water behind her to move upward toward the sun-dappled surface, to a raging heat. The roar of water rushing past her ears grew louder.

Tikah's murmurs greeted her when she opened her eyes. "Hush, my daughter, be still."

The roar in her ears was not that of water, but from a train going past. Her skin felt hot as coals, and she shut her eyes against the throbbing in her head.

"You are in the throes of childbed fever, Dassah."

As the train passed and silence returned, she listened to pigeons cooing on the roof. Not the little bulbuls of Kashmir. Her discomfort had subsided enough to feel the sorrow that reached out like dark claws to drag her under again. She was not swimming in Dal Lake. Cam did not wait for her on the houseboat above the surface of the lotus blossoms. But there was her son in Tikah's arms, waiting to be nursed. Here was her reason to live and to rejoice.

Tikah settled the baby at her breast and cooled her brow with a wet cloth. "You have been in and out of delirium for two days, but Narindar is trying to get hold of penicillin."

Dassah's eyes cleared for a moment. High above her, bamboo *chics* covered narrow windows, tinting the whitewashed walls green. "Cameron...able to nurse?" she rasped.

"You had enough milk for the babe. Though you were only half aware, I have been able to get you to drink some water these last two days. Only twice have I had to feed him extra with boiled goat's milk." Her *amma* chuckled. "Such a little glutton. I am sure he has gained a half a pound already."

Outside the tall half doors that separated her private room from the rest of the hidden courtyard, Dassah could hear the sounds of life. Quiet conversation, a muffled cough, the steady pacing of individuals cooped up.

Heavier footfalls made their way closer, and the tall half doors to her room opened. When Dassah turned her head, her pulse sluiced through her temples like a flood pushing through too small a water gate, and she winced. Narindar and his wife rushed in with a small vial containing a few tablets. "Can you get her to swallow these?" he asked Tikah. "It is the penicillin."

Tikah nodded. "How did you get it?"

"I told our local physician that my daughter still suffers from milk fever as she did last week. It is well that we have another infant in our home, but I had to dissuade him from coming to the house to examine our daughter."

Dassah tried to sit up. "I cannot be taking medicine...what of my baby?"

Rani rushed to help Dassah lie down again. "Hush," Rani said. "The doctor assures us penicillin will not hurt our daughter's milk for her child, so it should not hurt your baby either. Here, take the tablet with some water." Between the two older women, Dassah settled so that Tikah could gently pull Cameron from Dassah's breast. The little one, satiated with milk, had fallen asleep. They turned back to Dassah to bathe her and dress her in fresh clothing.

Dassah grasped Tikah's hand. "Where are we, *Amma*? Are we safe here?"

Tikah brushed Dassah's hair from her brow. "This house is situated at the edge of the town overlooking the railroad station. From the courtyard, we can see trains arriving and departing, but you are too ill to move, so hush now."

Dassah's eyes grew heavy again, and the last she knew was her son tucked in her arm as new slumber embraced her, and she listened to the trains going past...where to, India or Pakistan?

Though still anemic and frail as a bird, Dassah recuperated enough to join the others in the hidden courtyard in the days that followed. As the next three weeks passed, she began to feel safe behind these fretted walls of stone and flowering vines. This fortress of a home with its green and pink enclosure and cool blue tiles was a haven during the hot days. In the evenings and night, the fragrance of frangipani and jasmine washed the troubles from her mind.

From twilight on, Narindar would sit on the rooftop of his house with his family, playing the gramophone and waving to his neighbors. Not only did he play the gramophone loudly because it lifted his neighbors' spirits, but the heightened volume covered up the sound of his secret guests.

One evening in early August, Dassah sat in the dark with Mahleeha and Sobia on the cool blue tiles, listening to the latest train departing, and Dassah played with Cameron. Light from the nearby train station gave them some illumination. Too young yet to smile, Cameron cooed up at her, so that her breath caught with amazement that he knew her as his mother. She was the center of his life and cared for all his being. Like Yeshu cared for her.

Sobia interrupted her thoughts with a strident whisper. "You have been telling us you are a Christian, but if you are a Christian, Dassah, you could tell this to the Sikh people of this town and they will let you go."

"No, she cannot be doing that," Mahleeha scoffed, on her knees, brushing her long dark hair. "Who will be believing Dassah is a Christian when she is accompanied by Zakir, a Muslim man? It is safer for her and her *amma* to hide with the baby here until all heads are simmering down."

"Or until our Muslim people overtake this village," Sobia added as she studied her fingernails with disappointment at their lack of polish.

"Shush," the younger Mahleeha said. "If our Muslim neighbors from other villages come here they will only be killing the Sikhs and Hindus. We can only hope that in other villages our Muslim people are doing what our Sikh friend is doing here, hiding those who are in danger even if they are a different religion."

Dassah let their discussion waft over her. She had already discussed this at length over and over with Tikah. For now, she rested in the safety Yeshu provided here in this house. Each day her heart filled to overflowing with joy over her child, and her own physical strength returned. She had her son and her *amma*. Light enough to see his sweet features. The warm velvet of night increased the fragrance of frangipani. Birds twittered in the foliage. Music from Navindar's gramophone floated down upon them.

She glanced over at Zakir, standing by the wall looking through a gap in the fretwork and foliage. So very romantic were these songs, sung by famous film actresses. While the lyrical ballad was pleasant to her ears, it did not have the same effect on her as it did on Zakir. He must have felt her scrutiny for he turned to meet her gaze. For a long moment, the song seemed to feed the hunger in his eyes for her, but for her, desire for what happened between a man and a woman died the day Cam left her alone on their houseboat.

Zakir must have noticed the cooling of her expression, for he turned to resume his staring through the gap in the wall. The slump of his shoulders brought her a pang of guilt. She had hoped with time something would grow between them so that she could keep her promise to marry him, but as the days passed, her confidence in that hope dimmed. Tikah came toward her. Leaving Cameron with her, Dassah got up to join Zakir.

Standing next to him, she peered through the stonework and foliage, out to the road, out beyond the single story train station of mud brick. Even from this distance in the moonlight, she could see refugees passing by in a long, silent column like they did many nights, their belongings in their arms, on bullock carts, or on their heads.

"Why do the Sikhs and Hindus not take the trains to safety?" she whispered to Zakir.

"Violence on the trains is becoming worse," he murmured. "Better to join those marching south, the same for Muslims coming north. If only I were not stuck here in this village overrun by Sikhs, I would leave and join my fellow Muslims. But I fear if I leave this house, the Sikhs will notice and come for you. Thinking of what they could do to you keeps the sleep from my eyes."

She took in the deep lines on his face showing his anxiety. It was such a bitter blow to him that he had not been able to be her gallant rescuer, but had so quickly been forced to rely on the good graces of this Sikh family.

They remained standing together until after the midnight train came and went, and then returned to the group now congregating in the square. Only after Narindar's neighbors and family went to bed, and after the passing of this latest train, would Narindar let his hidden guests stroll his outer grounds and sit under the acacia tree near the stone-lipped well. As they did every night, Narindar and his wife Rani came down to the hidden courtyard, bringing chickpeas, fried bread, and tonight, the luxury of halva pudding for dessert.

For a while there was the illusion of reality with the serving and partaking of the meal. As usual, the hidden guests praised Rani's cooking, and in the tradition of grandmothers from the beginning of time, Tikah held the sleeping Cameron in her arm while eating of her own food. Dassah smiled. She could be happy with these simple pleasures for the rest of her life.

After the meal was enjoyed by all, the Muslim children played in the dark soundlessly at a board game. Dassah felt the ache of their young bodies—how they must itch to run and play, but their parents hushed them to remain still. *Beloved Yeshu, let it not be long until the boys are free again.*

Narindar brought out that day's newspapers to share and in a woebegone tone, said, "The politicians are breaking our country into two pieces and will be saying to us in only four days' time, 'Happy Independence.'"

A chorus of murmurs from the men agreed with him.

Their Sikh benefactor had kept the gramophone playing on a low volume on the roof above, another of those romantic songs from a recent Indian film. As he lit a kerosene lamp on its lowest setting, in a corner where no light would show to those outside, Dassah glanced up to see Zakir staring at her with cow eyes. She made a mental note to ask Narindar to play some less romantic music in the future and dropped her gaze to the front page of the newspaper he held.

A grainy photograph in *The Times of India* showed the viceroy sitting in his study with the various Indian leaders and the countdown of the days on a large calendar behind him. Four more days to Independence. Nehru had asked Lord Mountbatten to remain in India for a year as its first governor general. She wondered if Cam in his role with Lord Mountbatten would continue, and if he would rub shoulders with the new president of India, Nehru. If she lived in the new India, she might see Cam again one day if she stood in a crowd and he drove by with His Excellency, but not if she and little Cameron made their home in Pakistan.

Did Cam think of her at all these days? Did he wonder how the new borders, when they were announced, would affect her?

Slightly raised voices pulled her from her thoughts and her eyes from the paper. Narindar was mildly chastising Zakir. What could this be about? From the way Zakir sharpened his shoulders as he stood, something disturbed him. He held a page he had torn from the newspaper.

Tikah clucked her tongue in disapproval over these bad manners. Dassah thought the same. How foolish of Zakir to annoy their protector. Narindar was nothing but kindness, and he enjoyed his newspapers.

With a gentle smile on his burnished and bearded face, Narindar held out his hand for the torn page.

Zakir remained standing, flicking glances at Dassah, but his hand remained clenched around the stolen sheet from *The Times of India*. "It is nothing, old grandfather. Nothing to concern this community."

The hot evening breeze blew cold on the back of her neck, the first she had felt in this haven of fragrant flowers and cool tiles. *Dear Yeshu, what is it? More death? Has another catastrophe followed us here?*

30

Zakir set the rest of the paper down and raced out of the inner courtyard to the grounds outside, still clutching the ragged piece in his hand. The baby was fine with Tikah, and Dassah slipped away from the others to follow him. What on earth did he not wish them all to see and discuss?

Catching up with him by the well, she whispered, "Zakir, if you care for me and my son as you claim, then I am insisting you disclose whatever is causing you such agitation."

He stood, his arms crossed, not speaking for the longest while, until he sighed. "You should have married me, Dassah, not the likes of Captain Cam Fraser." He practically spat the name. At last he turned to her, slender and handsome, his dark beard neatly trimmed. It would have been better perhaps if she could have loved him and not Cam.

But the truth hung in the night air, disturbed the dust at their feet, and quivered in the lacy boughs of the acacia trees. They had both realized it tonight with the romantic music coloring the dark canopy of sky. Though they had not spoken of it these past three weeks, the knowledge had been growing—she did not need Zakir to make her safe, and there was no other reason to marry him.

Somehow, being in the safety of this house with the threat of violence all around them, she knew that her life would always be like this with Yeshu. Even if she were truly married to Cam, life would have its challenges for them as a couple of mixed race. But married or single, no matter where she lived and moved, she was enclosed in Yeshu's protection, even if she died, even if she suffered. Sorrowful things happened to all mankind, but she could go anywhere in all the world, be with any people, and her dwelling would always be with the Son of God. His song as voiced by the sparrows, the bulbuls, the parakeets, surrounded her with a symphony of love.

"Zakir, it is only fair that I tell you now, I cannot become your wife."

"Because you are still besotted with Cam Fraser." Venom laced his tone.

A wave of sadness almost knocked her down. "You say Cam's name with such hatred, Zakir. Why do you hate him so? It is more than the fact he pretended to marry me and gave me a child that vexes you."

His answer issued like a dagger through clenched teeth. "The British have stolen too much from us. For two centuries."

Her recent compassion faded. "You are beating a dead bullock, Zakir. The British are leaving, and not all they did was evil. Do not forget the people who came to teach us, who paid *crores* of rupees to run the mission. Do not forget those who raised us in the mission."

"Indian women brought me up in the mission. Miriam, the mother of my heart, raised me. It was she who died that day of the massacre that I might live. Not some English *sahib*."

"Again I must remind you that Miriam would want you to view her death as a reflection of her life, a life based on the love and compassion of Yeshu. She died in rescuing you because she believed Christ spilled his blood for everyone out of love. Not like this shedding of blood all around us now that is born from hatred."

"As always, Dassah, you defend the British."

"And you conveniently ignore my reminders of what the mother of your heart stood for—not hate, but love."

"Well, I am telling you I hate the likes of Cam Fraser for taking what should never have been his in the first place. The Almighty never intended for people to marry those of other races and religions. You are a woman of India, Dassah. I cannot regain all that England has stolen from us, but I will take *that*...that which rightfully belongs to me—the Indian woman of my choice!"

"*That* which you speak of is me. I am not something to be bartered for. I am not a pawn for men to throw at the feet of their enemy."

The look he angled at her confirmed her suspicions. She was not the prize, only the weapon. No different than the men of her country who in this present evil plundered the wives, daughters, sisters, and mothers of their enemy to inflict pain. But it was the women who suffered, the children, the babies.

With a quick gesture to his brow, he made a half-hearted salaam. "So be it, Dassah. If you will not marry me, then at least I have the satisfaction of knowing *he* will spend the rest of his life lamenting over what he let slip through his fingers."

She turned to go back inside to join the others, but stopped at the entrance, keeping her back to him. "How can you know what Cam would feel?"

Zakir's silence hung like dust in the air.

"You have not spoken to Cam in years." She turned to him, but he avoided her eyes. "Have you?" She stomped her foot. "You are no better than the men of these lands. The anxieties in our country are turning you into villains and cutthroats. Thugs! You tricked me before, Zakir, telling me we would be safer to leave Kashmir, to come here. Tricked me into bringing my child here. I have known you from a boy, Zakir, I know when you are tricking me, like you are now. In time I might have grown to love you as a man, but because of this, I have known deep in my soul that I could never become your wife!"

He flinched as he looked away.

She stared at his back. "I will pray for you, Zakir, that one day you will remember who you were raised to be by the mother of your heart—a man who obeys the commands of Yeshu, a man who loves his neighbor…and his enemies."

Only the flinching of the muscles in his back told her that her words had struck a chord. He hung his head in heaviness, but she left him standing by the well. Trembling, she returned to sit with Narindar's family and the other refugees, and Tikah knew enough to not ask questions.

Close to two in the morning, the others went to their *charpoys* to sleep, as well as she and Tikah with Cameron. Wherever Zakir went, she did not know, or care. His journey was no longer entwined with hers. Only three more days, and Independence and Partition.

She tossed on her cot. Yes, only three more days. Still she did not know whether to stay, or whether to join the long columns migrating, and migrating in which direction? *Yeshu, oh Yeshu, show me.*

At dawn the next morning, Dassah ignored Zakir, though his glances were wracked with what she surmised was guilt…or sorrow? *Dear Yeshu let it be the sorrow that leads to a change of heart.*

Tikah swept the floor with a short twig broom while Dassah washed Cameron in a basin. She dangled her hair down for her baby to grab hold of. His small fingers tangled in her tresses, his gaze locked with hers, and she laughed as he kicked his feet in the water. Through the fretted wall, she heard the train pull to its normal stop outside the station. The hiss of steam rose from its pistons, and shouting rose above that—shouting far louder than the normal busyness of the station.

Clutching her bare and dripping baby to her chest, she silently sought Tikah's gaze and that of the others.

Zakir and the other Muslim men raced to the wall. Through a gap in the flowering vines, they could see what caused this outburst.

"A gang of fifty or more Muslim men have arrived by the train," Zakir whispered over his shoulder. "They are standing outside the station."

Shouting rose to a crescendo. Then she heard the clashing of swords as Muslims cried out in a musical croon, a mockery of the muezzin call to prayer, "Oh *kafirs*, you murdered our people in this village. You burned our mosque so we have returned to settle the score. Your people have raped and mutilated our women on the roads. You should have run away like people of other villages. Now, we have returned to take your houses and farms."

The once peaceful morning was ripped apart by screeches. Another and another. Zakir continued to peer through the wall, his stance like stone, but whispering loudly, "The few Sikhs standing guard at the station are now dead." His voice rasped.

Footsteps thundered down the staircase from the main house. Narindar's sons and sons-in-law were probably trying to sort out where best to defend their home.

The young bride cried, "I am Muslim, surely the men of our village have not returned to kill me."

"Of course not," Zakir whispered hard. "If we tell them we are followers of Islam taking refuge here in this Sikh house they will take us with them." He turned to Dassah. "If you want to live, you will have to come with me now. Join with the Muslims. If you do not, they will kill you. You and your Sikh friends are no longer safe in this place."

"You said that Kashmir was unsafe too." Her words came out deceivingly calmly. She gripped Cameron so tightly he whimpered, and she softened her hold. She spoke with her lips brushing her baby's head, and her little one leaned his forehead against her mouth. "Now you want me to leave this house, Zakir, and turn my back on the family that kept us safe these past weeks." She shook her head. "No! Scurry off like rats now that the other faction is here, but I will not come with you."

More screams passed through the stone scrollwork, the only thing hiding them from the goons trampling the ground around the train station and into the town. By now the Sikh and Hindu men were out of their homes, on their horses, or on their feet to stand their ground. Scattered gunshot sounded. The staccato of horses galloped past, but inches from their hidden courtyard. Fear ran down her spine like the tip of a knife slicing her skin.

Two of the Muslim men left the courtyard that had been their safe harbor. To her shock, Sobia's husband—the most peaceful of men—unfurled a green streamer that he'd kept hidden in his clothes, a green pennant with a crescent moon and single star. As he ran out of the Sikh's home, he yelled at the top of his voice, "Allah-O-Akbar," alerting the rampaging Muslims that he was one of them.

The Muslim women rushed to conceal their money and few jewels they had under their pantaloons and tunics. Along with their husbands they ran out also to join their fellow believers, but Mahleeha and her husband remained. Ali appealed to Dassah. "If we speak on behalf of Narindar's family to our Muslim friends, they may be protected. If we do nothing, there is every chance this house will be set afire and all within it burned alive. We have no choice but to join our people." In what felt like an instant, they too were gone.

From somewhere outside a man yelled, "We have spared you so far, but not today, *kafirs*, you unbelievers."

She heard a Sikh answer. "It is we who will send you to your eternal misery."

Zakir grabbed her by the arm. "See now. You cannot stay here with these Sikhs and Hindus, these unbelieving *kafirs*."

Her insides went dark. "Oh, Zakir, not you too. Is this how it happens? Because of the brutality of your neighbors you turn your back on those who have been kind. What will happen in a few years if I go with you? Will you one day call me a *kafir* because I do not follow Islam?"

With a long look, Zakir backed away from her, anguish creasing his face. "Dassah, come with me."

She shook her head. "Here in this dust, with my foot I draw a line in the sand. Here I stand and say I will follow Yeshu no matter where he leads me. I can only pray you will one day remember the kind of man Miriam raised you to be. Remember what Yeshu did for you. Zakir...remember!"

He hesitated as if he wanted to stay but backed away one step at a time. Wincing, he turned and followed the men. She felt no loss at his going, only numbness that one more tether from her childhood had snapped, and she held her baby tighter. Only in Yeshu would her future unfold...on one side of eternity or the other.

Tikah began thrusting their few possessions into a shawl. Dassah rushed to dress her baby, trusting in Tikah to gather all that he would require.

The clamber of fighting, the shrieks, screams, explosions multiplied in only minutes. Dassah smelled the burning odor of ignited petrol. Tikah came close to Dassah, who held Cameron. Tikah lifted the baby's tiny foot, caressing his satin toes. "Will they believe us if we tell them we are Christians?"

"I do not know, *Amma*. At this moment it makes no matter." Dassah drew her child closer while Tikah put her arms around the two of them. Together they trembled and waited.

Narindar stood at the doorway, blocking the light. He heaved for breath. Dust covered the tall Sikh. His turban sat awry upon his head, his two sons with him. Narindar's daughters and daughters-in-law clutched their children, who were pale with fright, and Rani clasped her youngest grandchild. Outside the gates, the violence clashed. "We must leave our homes and fields." Narindar dipped his head, hiding his tears. "We must leave our home."

"It is no matter, old father," Dassah said, but she quaked as severely as him. "It only matters that we live." *And breathe...and have our being...*

They stood, waiting for their previous Muslim neighbors to break through the iron gates. Dassah raised her face heavenward, holding her baby to her heart. It would be worse if she ran. The frenzied mob would be incensed further by the chase...would slaughter them in the scorched grass. Perhaps here—with the power of Yeshu to help—the thugs might stop and listen.

Her insides hummed with a thousand bees. Her teeth chattered as she sat down on the cool, chipped blue tiles. Tikah dropped to her haunches beside her, one arm around her and the babe. The others followed suit, squatting down, their hands together in a pleading manner for mercy. No one cried. All, too afraid to make a noise.

As if it were a film at the cinema, the mob burst through the gates, wielding knives and machetes. Filthy with dirt and blood, they swarmed into the old Sikh's courtyard.

"Yeshu," Dassah whispered continuously, having no ability to formulate any other word or prayer. Tikah did the same. "Yeshu, Yeshu."

The rabble raced into the courtyard, the house, yelling, "Allah-O-Akbar." Their voices came closer, closer. At last they reached the old wing. They were at the door…their arms raised, ready to strike.

Tikah yelled at the top of her voice, "My name is Akbar! My people are called Akbar from Baluchistan. I was born into an Islamic family. Do not strike these people!"

As though they ran into an invisible wall, the mob stopped. Staggered on their feet. Yet, still, their arms were raised, holding their weapons high. Ready at any moment to lower, to slash at their victims.

Dassah could not breathe. A heartbeat later, she struggled to her knees, the baby tight under her chin. "I am a follower of Yeshu," she said just above a whisper. Louder, "I am a Christian." Her voice grew stronger. "These Sikhs have protected Muslims here for weeks. Saved the lives of Muslims. Now I ask you to save your neighbor."

The muscles of the men in the advancing row twitched, but their faces remained masks lusting for blood. The reek of their sweat pervaded the room.

Dassah labored to her feet and stepped forward. "As a follower of The Holy Book, of the God of Abraham, I ask that you spare my Sikh friends and the rest of this village. I ask you to not spill blood in hatred."

One by one, Tikah's and Dassah's words passed behind the eyes of their attackers.

"Do not reward goodness with evil." She supported her baby's head with her hand. "Please, do not hurt the innocent."

One of the men—a leader, maybe—slowly lowered his machete.

No one in the group of frightened Sikhs behind her, or Tikah, seemed to breathe. Cameron sucked on his fist. All was quiet in this inner courtyard while outside the world was coming to an end. Many of the gang inside snickered, but soon the snickers ceased.

One by one, machetes lowered, so too did knives and clubs.

The man at the front with the torn shirt and small dirty turban sneered at her, his machete hanging loose in his left hand. "Perhaps we will not be killing you, and perhaps we will. For now you will be leaving this grand mansion to stay with the other infidels in the schoolhouse until it is decided what will be done with you." He ordered them to stand with whatever they wore on their backs and prodded them out of the old wing of Narindar's home.

Outside, the sunlight burned hot as a kiln, and Dassah pulled her scarf over Cameron's head to protect him. The little one slept now, trusting. *Yeshu….*

A few feet outside of Narindar's home, the group of hostages sidestepped a crimson stream that ran down the middle of the alley. Narindar's daughters started to weep. Dassah fought down a wave of nausea as the end of Rani's scarf trailed through the ribbon of blood.

Fighting continued around the well. A short distance away, people ran around, their hands in the air, shrieking. On the main street, many of the Sikhs' horses lay on the ground, deep slashes on their hides. So too did several of the Hindus' sacred cows. Houses and shops were on fire, and Tikah was the first to choke on smoke billowing black against the sun. Dassah covered Cameron's nose and mouth with her scarf.

They passed the train station. Rani and her daughters screeched the names of neighbors they recognized, whose bodies lay on the platform. In ditches, limbs twisted like broken, discarded puppets. One woman, lying face down in a ditch, her feet bloodied, her anklets and scarlet-stained pantaloons were all that Dassah could see. She swallowed hard.

As they passed the village well outside the schoolhouse, Narindar froze. Seconds later, he tried in vain to shield the eyes of his wife and daughters from the sight. But it was too late. They had already seen, and Dassah did too. Rani and her daughters wailed. Dassah blinked. She wanted to be sick. Flies buzzed. All around the well, blood seeped into the sand, over the lip of the well. In its depths they saw the bodies of many Sikh and Hindu females. Arms, legs, slick with blood, and overhead, the sun a white disc pulsing in the sky.

Had these women thrown themselves down…or been thrown?

Narindar's sons could take no more. In a flurry they turned on their aggressors, throwing them to the ground. Narindar called to his sons who were now a sea of arms and legs in the dust as the men fought, until a knife was drawn and blood spurted. A gunshot sliced the air. As the Muslims took back control, and as the crowd melted from around two of Narindar's fallen sons, Dassah saw too that Narindar slumped. His chest was a growing constellation of scarlet.

Time ground to a stop. Blazing heat sapped the last remnant of Dassah's meager strength. Tikah gripped her arm. Stars danced before her eyes as her *amma* took the baby. Shimmering white heat before Dassah turned gray. Before crimson starbursts on the white clothing of people turned to black.

Their attackers rounded up the few they wished to spare and by the pricking tip of swords, packed them into the schoolhouse. She managed to stumble inside, where a hundred sat. Or did her swimming vision trick her? Maybe it was a thousand or ten thousand who sat there, many nursing wounds, their white clothes now rust-red.

Villagers Dassah had never seen before reached out to Rani and her daughters. Her sons, her husband were outside. Alive? Dead? Women sobbed in mourning for their own. Dry whispers fluttered around Dassah like dust-covered leaves. "Did you hear, they have taken many to a field outside the town and killed them? With machetes. I heard them yell that by Independence Day they want no Sikhs or Hindus alive in this village."

They were given no water. So humid, Dassah could not breathe. All day she slipped in and out of faintness. The last of the sunlight seeped through her closed eyelids, so that the world turned crimson, scarlet—red as the wedding sari she had once wanted.

31

Cam's hair and clothes were stiff and gray with dust. He and Alan surveyed the passing column, five thousand strong in this group of Muslims going north. Not two hundred yards across a dry *nullah*, a caravan of Sikhs and Hindus equally as numerous did the reverse. The rains were late this year. Dust storms assailed these flooding rivers of humanity. Flies tormented them too.

When the people stopped to rest—here and there on the road, wherever they could find, under bushes, under bullock carts—they tried to live, tried to get on with the basics of life. That's all they had left to hope for, a place to sit down and eat, a place to close their eyes and sleep.

A few times these past weeks, he'd seen women give birth. The cycle of life didn't stop for political upheavals. Other women suckled their little ones where they could find a bit of shade…or none at all and sat under the cruel sun. Mothers and grandmothers struggled to find food to feed the children. Yes, there were men—old men, young boys—ordinary decent men for the most part. But Cam had eyes only for the women…the infants, the babies. In this mass, his wife carrying his child might be putting one weary, dusty foot in front of the other. *Dear God…*

For three weeks he'd been searching the Punjab by truck with two hired guards, both former soldiers, Jari, a Muslim, and a Sikh by the name of Tegh. And Alan Callahan.

Alan had insisted on accompanying Cam. "I feel responsible for this travesty of my clerical office." Before they left Kashmir, the minister's voice had resonated with a rich bass as if he preached from a pulpit. "To think a young woman married by me and not believing she is truly a wife before God and in the eyes of the law! Why, if I hadn't acted in such an unseemly hurry to get to my parishioners, I'd have made proper arrangements for the paperwork so your good wife would not have suffered this humiliation."

"If you remember correctly, Alan, it was me who pressured you into haste."

Alan's angular jaw stuck out. "I'll not disagree with you there. Back then you were a blighted scoundrel in need of a good ear wigging."

"And now, reverend?"

"You're becoming the man I caught a glimpse of those months back," Alan's tone wobbled. "With the power of Christ within you, you are starting to deserve your beautiful wife."

Heat seared Cam's cheeks. "Always the poet, aren't you, reverend."

Jari and Tegh returned from their separate ablutions, as impeccable as they could be in this interminable dust. Tegh preened his Sikh beard while Jari ran a thumb across his pencil thin military mustache. Dad had recommended them both, tall, fierce, honorable former soldiers who'd served in his regiment.

He and Dad had a system. At each town they stopped, providing the telephone or telegraph wires still worked, Cam would go to the local signal office and contact him in Delhi. For these past weeks, he'd reported no sightings of Dassah, or at least none that people could remember. Dad would relay what, if any, responses to the newspaper announcement he'd placed in *The Times of India*.

The reward of five-hundred rupees created a stir, a vast sum to starving people, but no true information had come through. Only hundreds of poor families hoping that if he did not find his wife, would he consent to taking their daughter to safety and a respectable life with food and wellbeing. But not one word of the true Dassah.

Can ran the ad for as long as the editor allowed but eventually was told over the phone several days ago, "No more, old chap. Do you realize how many people wish to put announcements in the personal columns looking for missing family? Thousands, Captain. After Independence, mark my words, those thousands you see in those migrating caravans will multiply into tens of thousands. Wouldn't be surprised if millions will be displaced."

The arrangements had worked, at least as far as communication went. As Cam and Alan stopped at village after village, town after town, they thanked God communication wires were still up. But for how long? Last night's briefing had taken place as Cam stood in a garrison depot one-hundred-fifty miles west of Rawalpindi. Dad told him then that the viceroy and vicereine would celebrate Pakistan's independence on August fourteen in Karachi and later that day fly back to Delhi for midnight, to celebrate Indian Independence from the very first moments of August fifteen. The fuse was being lit as they spoke. And the day after that, August sixteen, the new borders would be disclosed.

"Will Mother be joining you for the celebrations?" Cam asked over the telephone while looking at the dusty roads outside the depot, at another tributary of migrants flowing by.

"Not at all. She's still up to her elbows in disinfectant at the mission refugee camp. Jai's worried sick they might be facing cholera and typhoid epidemics. No, your mother won't leave Eshana until we're ordered home. The very last minute, if I know my Abby."

"You've received your embarkation orders, then?"

"Afraid so. September twenty."

Emptiness filled Cam's gut as he sank to an army-issue wooden chair and stared through the window almost obscured with dust.

Static hissed over the phone wire as Cam surveyed the tide of people streaming past. On the road, a young woman, far too thin, her pantaloons and tunic ghostlike with dust, a glimmer of emerald green beneath the film. Green... her favorite color. But then, she'd wanted a red sari to be married in. He'd failed her in that too.

"Cam," Dad asked him something he didn't catch. "Cam, are you there?"

The girl's long thick braid, a rope of dark silk, swung down to her waist. She carried a baby. Cam's heart did a somersault. He couldn't tell how old the child was. Tiny. But what did he know of infants? She turned. A smear of vermillion paste on her forehead wasn't completely caked with dust. A young Hindu woman.

Not Dassah. Not his child.

Emptiness yawed inside him, an emptiness that stretched forever, like this long column of humanity cutting the country in two.

"Cam, are you there?" Dad said on the other end of the phone. "Don't give up hope, God is faithful."

"But we both know, Dad, that there will be many men who will not find their wives when this all ends." He couldn't keep the bitterness from his voice.

It was his father's turn to go quiet. "Even then, son," his voice caught, "even then, God is faithful."

They hung up after that, with Cam's promise that he would telephone from another village tomorrow evening.

Next morning before the sun breached the hills, while Cam with Jari and Tegh were loading their sleeping and cooking gear into the truck, a police *jamadar* ran up to them. "*Sahib*, a telegram for you. Please be stopping to read your message. All night long, a General Richards in Delhi has been telephoning, telephoning, asking for someone to find you. We tried our best to locate you."

Cam snatched the message from the man, muttering a quick thanks.

DASSAH FOUND STOP GO IMMEDIATELY TO DAYAPUR EIGHTY MILES EAST OF RAWALPINDI STOP SIGNIFICANT RIOTING YESTERDAY

He passed the telegram to Alan and took off at a run for the signals office. It took several minutes, but the operator rang through to Delhi, to his father's office in the War Department.

"I got your message." Cam gasped for air.

"Thank God I caught you."

"Who supplied this information?"

"No name given, but last night Joe Milton from *The Times of India* telephoned after you and I hung up. He says the informant telephoned him from Dayapur. This person—a man—had details. Mentioned the mission in Amritsar...and a baby. This woman has a little one the right age, and an older woman that must be Tikah."

"What's the situation in the area?" An almost physical pain shafted through Cam to think of Dassah in the middle of this aggression.

"Not good. The informant said as of last night a number of villagers, including Dassah, are being held in a schoolhouse. Your guess is as good as mine if local authorities will hand them over for transport to refugee camps or..."

For several heartbeats neither spoke.

"How long will it take you to reach Dayapur?" Dad asked.

"Four, maybe five hours. Leaving now—"

"God's speed, son. God's speed."

Cam replaced the telephone in its cradle and turned to meet Alan, who stood waiting for him at the office door. Alan's black suit was filthy, his white clerical collar grimy from weeks on the road.

It was hard for Cam to form the words. "She's about five hours east."

"Then we'd better press on, old boy. All due dispatch and whatever else you military johnnies say."

"They're being kept in a schoolhouse, Alan. As hostages." Each word he issued was a dagger to his heart. *Please, God, please, let this separation, like the separation between you and me, end. Bring us together in your perfect love.*

He saw her dying a thousand times as the truck sped toward Dayapur. For the first half hour Tegh drove, but Cam couldn't bear it. He ordered the stop, changed places, and took charge of the wheel. Anything, everything, something, he must do something with his hands that would get him to her. Gripping this steering wheel, his foot on the petrol, attacking this ruddy long road. Four more hours. He shouted to the back to Jari and Tegh to prepare their weapons.

Three hours. At one point Alan gripped his forearm. "Have a care, would you?" The wheels on one side of the truck had almost lifted from the metaled road. "I'm more than willing to enter the celestial eternity," Alan said, "and greet my Lord face-to-face, but I'd as soon do that *after* we've rescued your wife."

Cam grunted, slowed...but only slightly.

Two hours more. Dust as hot as cinders blew into his eyes. His sweating hands slipped on the steering wheel. If rioting in Dayapur were still going on, then there'd be little or no time to reconnoiter the area. Best to bluff his way in. Even if things had settled down. Best to make them think he was a neutral British official.

He'd seen it in the eyes of refugees as he'd inspected the camps with Lady Mountbatten. He was no longer the enemy.

They'd come right up to Lady Mountbatten and Red Cross volunteers, so trusting—hurting, desperate people—weeping, holding out their hands for help. All these months in each woman's face he'd seen Dassah. And now, dear God, his child. People had come running toward those giving aid in trucks like this. Trucks for Red Cross business. The official Red Cross banner attached to its sides…a banner such as one in the back of this box. So too were a couple of small Union Jacks stashed.

He clenched the steering wheel so that his knuckles strained. He'd go in, all banners and flags unfurled. Surprise them.

And God willing, get her out of there before…before. A vice took hold of his chest. *Lord keep her alive. Keep them breathing. Keep them safe.*

They saw the smoke from several miles away as they neared Dayapur, a black cloud ballooning against a sky white with heat. Cam's heart ceased beating. *Think man, think.* According to the surveillance maps of the area, this was a farming community. A train station. Petrol tanks. A police station with weapons. The closer they came, the stench of the smoke thickened to an acrid stew of kerosene, scorched grass, burning rubber. A substantial clash had taken place here in the last twenty-four hours.

From a rise overlooking the town, they stopped. All four of them flopped to their stomachs on the ground and peered down into the small town nestled in a gulley. Several narrow streets. One main one…where yes, the police station took precedence. Train station beyond that. No train at the moment. At Cam's guess, maybe a thousand or so had lived here. From here, he could only see about fifty men about. Through his field glasses he could see outlying farms. The burnt remains of two larger buildings, one a mosque from the shape of the minaret, and a blackened Sikh *gopuram*. Smoke stained the sky.

His eyes blurred from sweat dripping from his brow. As he swiveled the field glasses over and over the town, he saw it. The schoolhouse. A small dun-colored building with a field out back, a swing roped to a tree, and a few soccer balls in the yard. Outside the building stood a guard, rifle in his hand. Cam's stomach turned to lead. It looked to be a police *jamadar*. Were the police protecting the hostages, or were they the aggressors?

At that moment, a pillar of smoke chuffed from half a mile down the railroad. A whistle shrilled. The train on its way to meet up with the main track going toward Rawalpindi was making its way into town. The train with five or six carriages chuffed into the station, and the shoe brakes ground. The train stopped. From its carriages and from the tops and sides of the train a number of goons got off. This gang of men carried weapons, machetes, rifles, and began to swagger from the station into the town. Was this the same gang who had done the damage yesterday? Had they returned to do more?

Time was up.

He signaled to the soldiers, and Alan followed suit. They unfurled the Red Cross banners they'd attached earlier. The British flags already adorned the hood. They got back into the truck. Alan sat in front with him, while in the canvas-covered truck box, Tegh and Jari clicked rounds into their rifle chambers. God willing, they'd get in and out without having to use firepower, but that was wishful thinking—four men against a crowd?

Gunning the petrol, the truck barreled down the hillside and roared into town, raising its own cloud of sand, just as the goons from the train reached the schoolhouse. At the sight of the Red Cross banner, the gang stopped on the road. Cam swerved the truck to a sliding halt not two feet from the mob. He and Alan darted out, leaving the two soldiers in the back, hidden for the moment.

Alan reached the rabble first, his hands upraised, waving a white handkerchief. "Friends," he said in Urdu, "we are come on humanitarian business. We will take these refugees off your hands. No need for more bloodshed."

Uneasy stillness shifted through the group. Cam could hear their muttering from fifteen feet away. He'd surprised them. Good, now to keep them off balance.

A rotund man in a soiled *dhoti* stepped forward. His hand clenched and unclenched the handle of his machete. "A pity you were not here last week, *sahib*." His tone turned nasal as his eyes went past Alan to Cam. The sneer was meant for him. "Last week many Muslims lived in this village and the Sikhs and Hindus slaughtered them. We are only doing what is right. These *kafirs* must pay for their butchery."

Alan met the man on the middle of the road. "Will murdering more people bring back those who were lost?" His voice rose to pulpit level more suitable for a cathedral than a small Punjabi village. He pulled back his shoulders and stared down his long patrician nose. "When this land is truly yours, will you want the sand so soaked with blood it will take generations to sop up?"

Good show, Alan. Half of Cam's mind took in this dialogue, the rest focused on the schoolhouse that whispered not a sound. Was she in there? Cam glared down the leader who continued to listen to Alan, but fixed his eyes on Cam.

The gang leader kept up the exchange with Alan. "I respect your position as a holy man, but it has dawned upon our thinking that we must spill blood in order to purge our land."

A small cry...a baby's cry...wavered, muffled from within, to reach outside. The sound turned Cam's knees to water. He swallowed deeply at the music of it, the fragility, and yet the strength...the sweetness of life.

Alan must have heard it too, but he gave no notice. He tilted his head at the Muslim man and smiled. "The spilling of blood in order to purify...what a noteworthy concept! At another time I'd thoroughly enjoy discussing this theological view—consecration by blood—a subject most dear to my heart. However." He paused for drama. "We'll be on our way as soon as we find the people we are looking for. We've been informed they are being well cared for in this schoolhouse. For which we thank you. Now step aside."

He almost had them. Cam could see it in their faces, utter confusion, swayed by the strength of Alan's articulation in their language. He strode shoulder to shoulder with Alan toward the schoolhouse doors, his soul thirsting for the sweetness of that child's cry.

A roar of voices stopped them. The Muslims took firmer hold of their weapons as the melee of shouting behind them increased in crescendo. Over the hill came a horde of men on horseback, others running behind them, Sikhs and Hindus, Cam recognized as they rounded the hilltop and poured into the gulley, brandishing their own swords, machetes, and guns, screeching the cry of war. In minutes the whole village would explode into another bloodbath.

His mind raced as he motioned to Jari to join him, and Tegh to keep the truck secure, leaving the locals to fight it out, just as in Calcutta last August. There was nothing he could do to keep them from murdering each other. His only thought was to save Dassah and his little one.

With Jari's back to them, his rifle trained on anyone who took a step in their direction, Cam tried the door. Locked. Though his heart galloped, he removed his revolver from its holster and aimed to shoot off the iron padlock. At the sound of the shot, as the stench of cordite filled the air, screeches came from within along with the sound of scuffling, as if people were backing away from the door. The padlock broke in pieces, part of it winged off, and Cam wrenched the door open and stepped within.

He listened to the throngs of men outside as they continued to battle. But inside this one large room, silence reigned as sunlight streamed through barred and shuttered windows and dust motes swirled. So many people in this one room, and all so quiet. Cam's voice failed him. The frail, elderly, or sick, sat pressed together on the floor, while those who could find a spare inch stood or squatted on their haunches. With the doors and shutters locked from the outside for who knew how long, the pitiful reek of humanity rolled out, and he barked an order for Jari to leave the truck and open all the shutters.

Alan entered the schoolhouse and immediately started to help people to stand and move outside. His pulpit voice issued strong and steady, so that the hostages listened to him and complied with tears and relief.

Cam stepped deeper into the room and looked over the small sea of heads. The back of the room was so densely packed. Was she here? He could make out Alan's voice as he gently escorted people out—those unable to walk, he and Jari lifted into the truck. Those who could walk they had congregate outside in the shade of the building, hiding them as best they could from those intent on murder on the main street.

An elderly woman with a thin muslin tunic and pantaloons sat on the floor in front of Cam. She straightened the scarf on her head. He reached down to help her up and passed her to Alan as she toddled out, when all he wanted to do was find Dassah...get her away...safe. And his child. Outside, a new volley of shots issued. Time was slipping by. They'd all be killed if they didn't get a move on.

Cam moved deeper into the building almost to the back and opened his mouth to call out for Dassah. Before he formed her name, running footsteps rushed up the stairs from outside, through the open door. A man whizzed past, jostling him. Cam reached for his weapon. Had one of the attackers raced in here bent on killing?

His mind spun as he watched the man clamber his way through the crowd of people stuffed into the schoolhouse, shouting, "Dassah!"

Cam froze. *Dassah.*

Zakir! That blasted man was Zakir.

The hairs at the back of Cam's neck stood. Where the blazes had Zakir been all along? In his Muslim garb, had he taken sides with those outside? Cam ground his teeth. And when had Zakir abandoned Dassah to her fate when it was he who had stolen her from Kashmir all those weeks ago? And now his blighted enemy had found his wife. Was seeing to *his* wife. Cam's hands clenched at his sides.

That tiny cry came again. He heard it even though the building was now full of voices, crying, arguing, begging him for help. "*Sahib, sahib....*"

The crowd parted as those who could walk began to help others who couldn't, so that Cam could see through to the back of the schoolhouse. Tikah and Zakir stood together in protective posture. From behind them that small sob was emitted once more. Not weak. It contained a trace of pique. The tightness in Cam's chest fluttered loose. His little one wanted something and was highly put out that he wasn't getting it.

He took the remaining steps to the corner where Tikah and Zakir had taken vigilant guard.

And time reverted. An arrow of afternoon sunlight shot through the barred window, blinding Cam for a moment. As he narrowed his eyes against the light, he recognized the veil, grass green in color that covered a woman's head, her green sari in the remnant of this crowd of frightened Indian people. Except that, different from that day last August, Dassah did not sit cross-legged, but stood. He couldn't move. Her skin the color of milky tea, her hair a thick braid of silk over one shoulder. Late afternoon sun set her awash in a glow of apricot. She looked down at the child she held, nursing now at her breast, so that all Cam could see was the line of her cheek, her brow.

His eyes smarted. His throat went dry. "Dassah," he thought he'd said, but nothing came out. At last he managed to speak. "Dassah."

Her hands fluttered. As light as the sensation in his chest. She clutched the child closer.

Then she shifted their son to her shoulder, freeing one hand. He thought she was extending her hand to him. But when she looked up, when her eyes met his, she held her mouth in a firm straight line, her expression serene…but with a fire in her eye.

She raised her hand, palm out. The universal language. Halt. Come no closer.

32

Gunshot crackled outside. People had gone mad, shouting, screaming in the streets. A whiff of coal smoke reached Cam inside the schoolhouse where he listened to the groaning of the injured hostages, whimpering children, weeping women. Only a few of the elderly men, their voices quaking, wondered what would become of them and their loved ones. Cam identified with them while most of the young men were either dead or outside fighting to the death. What was he going to do to help these refugees? He couldn't leave them to the crazed factions outside.

And the amber eyes of Dassah's in this scathing moment of brutality were wide, not with shock nor even despair, but with anger.

As she automatically adjusted the sari crossing her chest, the veil eased back from her forehead so that he could see the parting of her hair. She seemed unhurt, physically. Cam drew close, and she cradled the nursing infant—their little boy—that much closer.

Tikah and Zakir were both muttering something. Cam still couldn't look at them or listen to him. His gaze had stopped. His pulse had stopped...on Dassah and his child, and he was held hostage by the rage within her.

Behind him, Alan rushed up. "Cam, what about these peop—?" He went still at the sight of Dassah, standing firm as she nursed her baby with the sunlight bathing her in a halo, ready to grasp her freedom.

A Madonna and child, but not a placid medieval Madonna. An Indian mother and babe—Cam had never seen anything more beautiful, nor anything that paralyzed him more than the burning anger in her eyes. Though it felt like ground glass pulsing through his veins, he turned away, grasping the first coherent thought he could take hold of. "We'll take the hostages by train, Alan. Yes, by train. Keep these people moving. Down to the station platform."

Zakir took a step toward Cam and gripped his arm. "Good. The train is the only way to be getting her to safety. I have been praying for this all night."

What was Zakir nattering about? This wretched man who'd taken his wife from the relative safety of Kashmir to this place? Zakir, whom he'd begged to look out for her if he ever saw her, and pass on his message of love and fidelity? This traitor who had put his wife and child in danger? And where was he all the time Dassah was locked up in here? Collaborating with those outside tearing their neighbors to pieces?

Cam looked down at Zakir's hand that detained him, the impulse throttling through him to pull back his arm and land a fist in Zakir's face. Like the impulse to take a drink. That's what he'd wanted in the past—drink...take...do...whatever— to slake the craving of the moment. For a split second his hand clenched.

Zakir glared back at him, probably sensing Cam's desire to beat him to an inch of his life.

The muscles of Cam's shoulder tensed, drew back a fraction, and he grabbed hold of Zakir by the front of his shirt. He cursed silently. He'd learned how to conquer his impulses to drink a day at a time. A minute at a time if need be. A split second. *Lord, give me the strength, the strength to control this impulse too.* His fingers slackened. He let go of his enemy's shirt.

Zakir staggered back from the sudden release. It wasn't fear in his eyes, but an awareness, an unspoken understanding. "It seems in the face of death," Zakir said, "that perhaps you and I are learning at long last."

Cam flexed his fists. "As much as I want to give you the thrashing of your life, we're on the doorstep of a warzone."

Another fusillade of shots scattered outside.

Alan tut-tutted. "As usual your manly frankness is utterly charming, Captain, but do you think you two gentlemen could possibly assist with the job at hand?"

Cam shook out his hand, as if his fist had actually connected with Zakir's face. From the corner of his eye, he saw that Dassah watched him where she stood close to Tikah. Her brow crosshatched as she studied him and then Zakir, though she still had not spoken. Tikah patted the baby's back over her shoulder, putting Cam, Zakir, and the rest of the world in its place by ignoring them and seeing only to the child's needs.

Still mad as blazes himself at Zakir, he spat out the words to the tall Indian man, "Make yourself useful—help these people to the train."

A look of pain crossed Zakir's face, but he lurched into immediate action. Cam turned to ascertain the extent of the evacuation when he saw Zakir reaching to assist Dassah, and he jerked him back. "As a former soldier of the British Army, Zakir, I'm sure you remember what you were trained for. Those people over there need your assistance."

"Yes, Captain-*sahib*. As a man of honor—like yourself—throughout this dark night, I have done what I can for the safety of these innocents."

Outside, men's voices bawled out obscenities in Urdu and Hindi. Swords clanged. Glass shattered. Cam smelled the pong of smoke from a newly started fire. He'd been a fool wasting precious minutes bashing it out like a boy in a schoolyard. Later, when Dassah was safe, he'd give Zakir a piece of his mind, tear a strip off him, verbally. Beg Dassah for forgiveness. For now, he needed Zakir's skills.

"All right then, Zakir, I'll take you at your word." He spoke to Tegh. "Give this man your weapon. Arm yourself with another rifle, and tell Jari to load the injured into the truck box." He turned to Zakir. "You, get down to that train and stop the engineer from leaving. If my suspicions are correct, those goons are holding the train. Take a few able-bodied men with you."

Tegh thrust the loaded rifle at Zakir and darted out of the school.

Zakir stopped for a heartbeat. Holding the weapon in both hands, he squared his shoulders and lifted his chin. Gunshots sounded in the town. They no longer lived in the world of parade grounds, barracks of whitewashed stone, and flagpoles in flowerbeds. In the village of Dayapur, this had to be the first time Zakir held a weapon since the war. Though they were both dressed not in crisp uniforms but in soiled civilian clothing, and though they stood in silence and neither moved, in some invisible way Zakir came to attention. He might almost have saluted. Seconds later, he made a sharp about-face and did as Cam commanded.

Cam swiveled around to Tikah. Neither of them spoke. He did what Zakir had started to do, extend his hand to escort Dassah from the room, but she thrust her hand up again to block him. Her fingers trembled.

Janu...beloved...you are my wife.

Still, his wife refused to look at him and clutched their baby. Cam gritted his teeth. No time. No time. And then she stumbled. She wasn't as strong as she tried to project.

"Take the baby," he ordered Tikah. She nodded. Before Dassah had a chance to avoid him, he whisked her into his arms. Though she practically distained him earlier, she now put her arms around his neck. Was it simply self-preservation to hang on to something as he carried her, like she would cling to a rope if dangling from a burning building? Tikah came behind him with the child as he strode from the schoolhouse.

On the village street immediately outside, bodies sprawled at ungainly angles. Men, women, even children slumped in piles around the center of town at the well, blood drying poppy red on their clothes under the sun. Most of the fighting took place at the edge of town. A few goons from the train, with unforgiving faces, whipped around to him as he started out the short block to the train station. With Tegh's weapon trained on them, Cam ignored the gang members, walking out his gaggle of women and children, old men and boys. He trod the parched dust, holding his wife in his arms, daring those standing about to take one step toward him and his treasured cargo.

She'd been slight when he'd married her last autumn. She weighed so much less now, as light as the willow branches outside their houseboat on the lake. He could feel the fan shape of her ribs where he supported her body.

As Alan led the majority of those who could walk, Jari drove the truck with the rest toward the station. Tegh walked backward at the rear of their small column, shooting rounds at the ground close to anyone who approached. Gunfire rattled from the station. God willing, Zakir was holding hooligans off the train.

His *janu* didn't flinch at the noise. The baby in Tikah's hold wailed behind him, and Cam angled for a glimpse and saw a snatch of silky black hair atop a scrunched-up tiny face, a small, toothless mouth open in complaint. His son was no doubt angry at having his meal disturbed earlier. In the midst of this Hades, a smile tugged at Cam's mouth. The frail female form in his arms turned her head to listen too. He felt the brush of her cheek against his shoulder. As if from the very atoms of her body, he could feel her love for their son.

Her hand came up. This time she placed it on his chest. "I wish to walk on my own. To carry my son." He set her on her feet, willing her to return his gaze, but she fell back in line with Tikah and took her baby. Between Dassah and Tikah, they supported each other, and as much as it wrenched his heart, his job was to see that all got to the train.

He stepped back to view the entirety of the group of hostages, a good fifty or more, and he pulled his revolver from its holster, at the ready. The train came into full view as they entered the station. All six carriages seemed intact. A number of passengers cringed below the barred windows. From the locomotive at the front, Zakir stuck his head out the window, his arm raised showing off his rifle, a signal that he'd gained control of the train.

Alan reached the step of the middle compartment and took inside the first of the refugees from the truck and those who had walked. Tegh garnered a position near the corner of the station, close to the ticket booth, and continued to hold off anyone who approached. Jari jumped from the truck, opened the tailgate, and took up a position on the opposite corner of the station near the water tower, so that Alan could attend to the injured. Both soldiers held the station. The platform was clear. If there had been any passengers who had wanted to board from this station, they'd long gone.

Alan called out as Cam reached the train. "There's room in this compartment for your wife."

Cam ushered the group inside the train, refraining from assisting Dassah and Tikah. Sikhs and Hindus made up the majority of passengers who were on the train before its stop here in Dayapur. All clutched belongings wrapped in shawls or bundles, held their children near. No one spoke.

He watched as Dassah took her seat with no indication of relief or otherwise. Not a flicker of a glance his way. Her shoulders slumped forward as if under a great weight. *Janu, janu, look at me.* Only Tikah looked at him.

"Close the windows and shutters, if you would," he asked Tikah as he left the compartment. As he stepped down to the platform, he could feel her gaze on his back, but he heard next the sound of her closing the shutters as he'd asked. He called to Tegh to leave his position and move into this carriage. With Alan and Tegh, this car would be well protected.

He motioned to Jari to take up his position on the last carriage. They were almost ready to leave, and yet he felt in all the pandemonium as if two sets of eyes watched him. He glanced up at Dassah's window. Tikah didn't hide the fact that she stared out at him. But from the slightest of movements from Dassah—he wasn't sure—but had she been watching him...and turned away before he could connect with her gaze? As for now, she had set her profile to him.

There was no time to linger, and he then raced along the length of the train to the locomotive.

The engineer greeted him as Cam climbed aboard. "Oh, *sahib*, I am very, very glad that you are helping me get the train to Rawalpindi. Now that the British are leaving, we are missing their help. No one to help these days. No one upholding the law. All the country running amok."

Zakir and the stoker were the only others riding in the engine. Zakir was already helping the stoker feed the fire. When they opened the firebox, the roar of the blast muffled the clamor from the town. The engineer opened the regulator, and the wheels began to turn. Coupling rods clanked along with the slow woof woof of the blast as the train began to slide out from the Dayapur station.

"Is Dassah...your wife, is she well?" Zakir shouted across to him from the other side of the locomotive.

Cam positioned himself at the opposite window. "Well enough."

Under his feet, the steel footplates wove back and forth. Zakir stood at the other window as blood-crazed thugs swarmed into the station. Gunfire issued from Tegh and Jari at their specific spots along the train as it snaked out of the station. Including those shots and the shots he and Zakir got off, the four of them kept the goons intent on violence from climbing aboard. *More speed*, Cam prayed. *More speed.*

The stoker's face glowed red from the glare of the firebox as he shoveled in coal. The furnace breathed with roaring flames of violet. The firebox slammed, shutting off the hiss and growl of the fire. Steam hissed and shot up forty feet in the air as the engine passed under the signal gantry, and the train left town. Gradually the train's speed increased, but not quickly enough.

From Cam's stance at the engineer's window, he could see a number of men had jumped for the train. He let off a few more rounds. A ring of shots came from Zakir's side of the locomotive as well. Zakir stopped to reload. Soon, Cam ran out of ammunition and reloaded. Taking aim once more, he found his mark—two others hanging to the side of the train with swords in scabbards dangling from their waists. They fell to the ballast stones along the track. And the sick brew permeated Cam's veins, so familiar from the war—the relief of keeping those on this train safe, mixed with the corrosive anguish of taking lives.

Ahead lay a curved section of track. Cam looked back along the line of carriages. From the last car, Jari waved to him. For the moment the train seemed to be in their hands. God willing, they'd have no further trouble until they got to Rawalpindi and switched trains for Lahore where they could off-load these refugees to receive the aid they needed. The train passed over some switching points. Lights insides the train flickered, setting his nerves ajar as they thundered toward the next village twenty miles away. A village no doubt under Muslim control and in league with the ruffians they'd left behind.

Zakir yelled across the footplates. "Back in Dayapur I heard the station telephone ringing. Communication remains open between that town and the village ahead. You can be sure they have let their friends know to expect us. Can we not send a radio message and ask for British help?"

"Those days are past," he hollered back over the thunder of the engine. "The British are leaving. Entire regiments shipping out as we speak. We're on our own, trusting only in those Indian authorities who are managing to stay neutral."

The truth of the situation bore down on Zakir, plain to see in his stone-like expression. He shook his head, lifting a helpless hand and letting it fall to slap against his thigh. "I did not think I would ever wish for British help," he yelled. "And the only time I would ever wish it—it is denied me."

The truth of their so-called situation sickened Cam too. "I'm sorry, Zakir," he shouted. "I too wish our quitting India could have been done with more preparation, to ease the transition. This…this…" He spread his hand to encompass the passing Indian countryside. "This is not how I want to leave India." His throat thickened so he could hardly get the words out. "Can you believe me when I say I love India, that I love the Indian people, that they are my people?"

"Is that why you married an Indian woman? A trophy, a token of the great *sahib*'s passion for a country that is not his?"

At first anger cut through. But seeing the despair in Zakir's eyes pushed the anger aside. "You know me better than that, surely? You've known for months that I was looking for her."

The train clipped along at a good speed and reached banked rails. The engine leaned over the bushes, groaning and clanking.

"I can understand your love for Dassah, a woman beyond the price of rubies. Even up to yesterday, I wanted to steal her from you. Today I would rather see her live…as your wife…than be murdered."

"The lesser of two evils?" Cam couldn't help the smile that worked its way onto his face.

Zakir met his eyes. "It is Dassah who continually reminds me that not all the British have done is evil." He slanted a glance at Cam and hollered over the noise. "Surely you know *me* better than to think I sided with those unleashing rivers of blood in Dayapur. I did more than pray for your wife and son's safety last night."

Cam shouted back. "I suppose you were the one to telephone the editor at the *Times*. When all is said and done, and the lines drawn, that's what I would expect you to do."

A strange quiet broke over the locomotive, though the clamber and racket as the train went over its track points deafened.

Cam wiped his moist hand down the front of his shirt. "We did have some good times, did we not, Zakir?"

The Indian man stiffened his mouth in an attempt not to smile, but the smile emerged anyway, sun from behind a cloud. "I will admit only to being the better cricket player."

"While I had far more prowess as a raider in a game of *kabaddi*." Cam grinned back.

Zakir turned somber again, staring down at the moving footplates. "Dassah has been speaking much on what we learned as children at the mission." He glanced up at Cam. "Do you believe, like you did as a boy?"

"I do…now. For a long time though, I did not."

"Why did you return to your faith in Yeshu?"

"Discovered just how disreputable I can be without him. Not a pretty sight. My memories disgust me."

Zakir's gaze returned to the footplates. "As do mine. We both have much to be ashamed of…when hate smothers love."

The engineer shouted out over the roar of the locomotive. He pointed ahead to a ridge of hills, to a cutting through those hills for the track. But on those hills, above the straight cut walls of rock, any number of thugs could hide in preparation to jump on the roof of the train.

Cam hollered back to the engineer, "Don't slow! More steam."

He and Zakir took up their places by the windows again. The stoker opened the firebox and flung in more coal. His long handled shovel rang like a bell each time it clanked against the firebox. The roar and heat of the flames sucked what little moisture was left in their bodies. The train whistle screamed as they reached the hills. Jagged, reddish rock whizzed past as the walls of the cutting through the hills rose above the train by another ten feet. The grinding thunder of the engine echoed back at them, stopping the ability to think when a thousand screeches sliced the air like knives. The engineer tugged again on the whistle chord.

Feet jumping from the hills to land on the top of the train shuddered through the locomotive. Zakir leaned as far out his window as he could in an attempt to aim at the culprit now standing on the roof. Cam did the same from his side. In the narrow cutting, he could see nothing as the rock slid past in a haze of red only a foot or so from the sides of the train.

How many others had jumped to the top? He let off a round of shots, to no avail. But close to the end of the cutting, where the track came out of the hills to open plain, he caught a glimpse of a foot dangling down from the roof. The man above had slipped.

Reaching up, Cam grabbed hold of the foot in its leather *chappal* and hauled with all his might. The man fell. A scream came close to Cam's ear as the marauder was crushed between the rock face and the speeding train. Cam tamped down a shudder as the image of the man's death filled his mind with appalling detail.

They were out of the cutting now, out on open ground, and nearing the village a half a mile away. Without the noise of the locomotive bouncing back at them from the rock walls, he could make out the crackle of rifle fire. Zakir with him in the locomotive, Tegh in the middle compartment, and Jari at the end, were all doing their jobs. Cam viewed the entire train as it entered another curve to swing by the village and its station where another set of goons waited for the train to slow, so they could board. But those villains already on the train, who attempted to walk the roof, fell from bullet wounds, or the inability to keep their balance. And the train kept on, racing past the station, past those intent on violence.

Though he couldn't see Dassah within her carriage, he thanked God none of the villains remained, although gunfire continued, coming from the station and from men on horseback as they raced along the side of the train. Bullets ricocheted off the steel bulkheads. Gradually the shooting lessened as the flat plain of khaki scrubland stretched before them. The villagers were long behind them.

A white haze of heat wavered over the horizon. Cam slumped down to the footplates, pushing his thumb and finger into his dry eye sockets to ease the grit from them. They were safe, should now be safe all the way to Rawalpindi.

"*Sahib*," the engineer called to him over the stammering of the train's wheels hitting the track points. "*Sahib*."

He turned to the engineer, who pointed to the man crumpled like a sack on the floor. With a dirty rag, the stoker attempted to staunch the blood of the man who'd been hit. It was Zakir lying on the steel plates. Cam went numb. Blood seeped crimson over Zakir's shoulder and chest. Just above his heart. Red billowed like a shape on a map. Dropping to his knees, he pulled at Zakir's shirt to check the damage. A shoulder wound, only a ruddy shoulder wound, but from the amount of blood loss, the bullet must have nicked the artery. Minutes only.

Cam lifted his gaze and exhaled in sheer frustration. Why now? *Dear God, why now?* Heat poured upward from the steel footplates. From his seat, the engineer adjusted the regulator, his stoic face straight ahead as he understood the situation. The stoker, too, returned to shoveling the coal into the firebox. Hollow thunder and the ceaseless pounding of the locomotive seemed to tear Cam apart as he sat on the floor and held Zakir in his arms.

Zakir moved his lips. Cam leaned over to catch his words. "Tell her..."

"Tell Dassah...yes."

Zakir reached for his hand. "I...remember...Yeshu."

He squeezed Zakir's hand. "Hold on. In the name of Christ, man, hold on."

But Zakir went still. His eyes set on a horizon far beyond Cam's head, far beyond the roof of this locomotive engine as it hurtled along the tracks.

Flying cinders from the locomotive scorched the skin of his face and arms. He sat against the steel wall behind the engineer's jump seat. Heat burned through his shirt, but he couldn't move. The rocking of the train lulled him, and he shut his eyes.

Hot rays of the sun coursed through his closed eyelids. Memories encased in golden sunshine rushed in. He kicked his feet in the dusty *bagh* behind the mission. He waited for his turn to make a dash for the wicket while he and

Zakir shouted out instructions in Hindi. Days upon days scudded by, like clouds racing across the sky. Playing marbles on the mission balcony, sharing the treat of sugarcane in winter, mangoes in summer. His memories slowed.

It was twilight and he was twelve, just before he went off to England for school. The aroma of garlic and onions scented the dusty air in the *bagh* as they played on into the dark, until he heard Eshana or Tikah or his mother calling to them for the umpteenth time. Like two conspirators, he and Zakir urged the younger boys to go into the mission. And they remained outside in the dark, stars piercing the sky as they kicked the soccer ball between them.

Visitors in the *bagh* lit fires and sat around them. Telling stories. Singing songs. At last, arms slung over each other's shoulders, he and Zakir made their way out of the *bagh* and up the stairs into the mission to be welcomed by a soft cuff on the ear from Tikah or Eshana, a scolding from his mother. He couldn't remember now. Only the memory with Zakir stayed frozen in time.

India passed by as he held Zakir's body. India, the British India he'd known since a child, shimmered on the hot Indian rails, nothing more than a mirage. *Nullahs*, dry from lack of rain, villages, unchanged in centuries, huddled around distant train stations. Women washed clothes in ponds, gathered water from the communal wells. Men out in the fields with flocks of goats, water buffalos wallowed in the sun-dried slime of mud.

This place of brutality was no longer his home. He knew not where home lay, but by God's grace he would find a place that would bring smiles back to Dassah's eyes, a place somewhere in this world where he would never be parted from her again. A place where he would teach his son to be a man—a man who didn't judge others by their color, their skin, their culture, or hate a man because he didn't believe in his god.

Three carriages down, his wife sat in silence. She might never want to see him again. His baby cried the lusty cries of a healthy infant not quite four weeks old. Dassah might want him to stay clear of their son's life as well. She may wish him to go, be parted from her forever. He yearned to hold them both, to bridge the wide, blood-filled fissure between them.

33

Miriam shaded her eyes. The train emerged from the sun, a bloated orange disc melting into the horizon. As the locomotive glided down the Lahore track, it grew larger, blocking out the sun's rays that seemed to set everything aflame. The rains were late this year. And where would she be when the monsoons came?

Her brother opened a compartment door and braced himself as the train came to a gentle stop. He'd not had time to change. He was filthy, unshaven, had dried blood crusted on his clothes and a fathomless chasm of pain behind his eyes. There was no need for either one of them to go into the heartrending details. She'd received Cam's telegram that he'd sent from Rawalpindi yesterday.

She moved forward as he got down from the carriage, her voice a weakened version of the false bravado the British were famous for. "Hello, darling. Good gracious, Cam, you look ghastly."

"Hello, old thing." On cue, his voice strained for the right pitch. "You look ghastly, yourself. Are you all right?"

"We've all had our share in this recent unpleasantness."

"Still my gangbuster sister." With shaking fingers, he tweaked her chin as if everything was right as rain.

"And you, Cam, really?"

He flinched so slightly she almost didn't see it. "They're alive, old thing. That's all that matters at the moment."

Blasted tears sprang to her eyes, and she scrubbed them away with the back of her hand. "Right then. Let's stuff everyone into this fine vehicle. It's not the Silver Ghost we had for the wedding, but it'll do to get to Amritsar."

A man came up behind them who she'd failed to notice. Tall, gangly, past his prime, and as filthy as Cam, although he'd attempted to brush the dust from his clerical suit. "Alan Callahan," he introduced himself.

"Yes, of course," she said, shaking his hand. "Cam's mentioned you often in his letters to me."

"Cam," Reverend Callahan said without further ado, "will you help me assist the ladies from the carriage?"

Miriam went with them to the steps of the train, having the notion she would gather whatever belongings they had. Though, from what Miriam could see from the doorway, that was apparently nothing. Only Dassah sat by the window, looking out on the station, but her head didn't turn to watch the unceasing activity outside. For a moment Miriam feared. She'd seen women with posture like this every day for months.

Yet something in Dassah's quiet hands, the way she held her head, were not that of a frozen bloom. More like Eshana as Laine described her so often—a shaft of bamboo—strong, ready to snap back. For this moment in time, this beautiful Indian woman was bent and bruised, but not broken.

The minister helped Tikah, who carried the baby, down the steps to the platform. Miriam went with her, back out to the platform, longing to take the little one. She peered into the bundle of clean cotton to see a tiny face with fists clenched against his mouth. She couldn't help herself. With all the horror around them these days, she cooed like an idiot. Never thought she'd be the type, but here she was, making a fool of herself with funny faces for this newest member of the family.

At Miriam's inspection of the baby, Tikah pulled back at first, clutching the child closer. Then, ducking her head, she stared at her feet, holding the baby straight out to Miriam—like an offering, a stolen possession she was returning to its rightful owner.

Miriam took the baby, and a good long look at Tikah. Gone was the huge black shawl that used to envelope the woman from Baluchistan. The saffron skirt with its myriad of tiny mirrors hung in tatters around the hem. Tikah's features seemed a tad heavier, but her light gray eyes hungered on the baby as Miriam snuggled him close to kiss the dusky brow, the dark velvet hair at his temple. "Hello, darling nephew."

With the baby still in one arm, she grabbed hold of Tikah who started to turn away. "Not so fast, Tikah. Your grandson requires your care, and I will help my sister-in-law."

Tikah didn't speak. Her eyes connected with Miriam's, but Miriam vowed she could see a slight warming behind those gray eyes. Just a fraction. With God's help, one day this old biddy who'd stormed out of her rooms last September might cease seeing herself as some poor relation taken into the mission only to be abandoned and forgotten.

"Before I go to help Cam, Tikah, I want you to know that Eshana is waiting for you at the mission. I spoke with her on the telephone this morning. Laine's come up from Madras to help in the crisis. Both of them, my mother too, are rejoicing that you—*you*, Tikah—are coming home at last. By jove, they've started to cook the fatted calf and all."

The dour line of jaw softened. A crack appeared in that impenetrable façade of an expression. "The prodigal child returneth," Tikah said barely above a whisper.

"Apparently so. We share this little bundle of manhood, so I'm afraid you're stuck with us." Miriam placed the baby back into Tikah's arms.

She didn't stop to see what affect her words had. Miriam went to help her brother with his wife, get them to the mission. With these sour lemons life had sent them, *Please, Lord, it's about time we had some lemonade.*

As she reached the steps to the carriage it dawned on her—she didn't know what name Dassah had given the baby.

The following night, at midnight, the first few minutes of August fifteen, Miriam sat in the main room of the mission with Mother, Laine, the ever-so-erudite Reverend Callahan, and Cam. They listened to the wireless as the new President Nehru gave his speech, followed by a stream of other politicians blathering on. Jai and Eshana were busy in the surgery. Even at this hour they treated a number of poor wretches who'd straggled to Amritsar.

"I imagine there'll be fireworks tomorrow night," Mum said in a lackluster tone as she and Laine sat, knitting Red Cross regulation bandages. "Or I should say tonight, as the day has already begun."

"How can people celebrate," Miriam said to no one in particular, "when it's not until tomorrow, after the Independence celebrations, that the curtain will be pulled back to show the lines in the sand?"

"Pull back the curtain?" Laine murmured in refrain. "Lines in the sand?" Her tone turned brusque. "A rather poetic way to say that tomorrow the viceroy will open the safe and take out the documents that hitherto only Sir Cyril Radcliffe has seen, as he alone has determined where those blighted secret borders should be."

Cam remained stoic, staring out at the *bagh* lit by campfires around the refugee camp. He'd not spoken or glanced up for ages. Dassah and Tikah still kept to themselves in the prayer room at the top of the house. Miriam couldn't blame Cam. Let him seethe, poor lamb. He'd yet to hold his child, and yet to have his wife even speak to him. With that quiet strength Miriam recognized in Dassah, she worried married bliss might not be in Cam's future.

Alan, who'd been quiet during the speeches, steepled his fingers. Miriam waited for the next thing he would say. For the moment, he held his tongue and she smiled, fascinated by this man's need to weigh his words before expressing them. No wonder Cam enjoyed his correspondence and talks with this preacher. From Alan's conversation yesterday on the drive here, she'd learned it wasn't that he didn't joke—that all he said was like wisdom dripping from the fountain of knowledge—it was more than when Alan did say something terribly wise, it often had a zinger that left others speechless.

She'd thought he was going to keep his thoughts to himself now, when he repeated what Laine had said, "Pull back the curtain…." He shifted in his chair. "I have to disagree. Though the actual borders will be announced tomorrow, as of the stroke of midnight just past, much of the north of India as we knew it will become Pakistan. A country veiled…hidden in purdah. All to keep the free sharing of truth outside its floodlit barriers of barbed wire and ensure its citizens hold one mindset and one mindset only."

Laine uttered a small grunt in agreement and kept on knitting while Miriam and Mum shared a glance. Alan was right, of course. Father said the same thing on the telephone earlier from Delhi. Only Cam, his hands behind his back, kept staring out at the *bagh*. Almost as mute as Dassah, although he'd seemed all right at first, when she'd picked them up at the train station.

He'd chatted a bit in the front seat as Miriam drove from Lahore to Amritsar. Tikah had sat in the back with the baby and the Reverend. Dassah took up the middle, not frightened. Not in shock. Miriam knew shock when she saw it. Her sister-in-law was no wilting daisy, just speaking only when asked a direct question and then answering in as few words as possible. Resolute? Reflective? Angry?

Mum laid her knitting down and nudged Laine. "I've stayed up this long only to hear the announcement. I'm for bed. Tomorrow starts too soon."

"Right you are." Laine got up from her chair. "Will you check on Dassah, or shall I?"

Mum stopped for a moment, a hand to her head. "Let me. I'll check if she's sleeping all right, and even if it is past midnight, steal a moment with my grandson." She glanced at Cam, but he'd slipped out of the room unnoticed, perhaps outside to the patio.

After they'd gone, Miriam stood to turn off most of the lamps and the wireless. Alan remained where he was. The entire mission was quiet except for the low hum of sound coming from the clinic as Jai and Eshana continued surgery. For once, not even a child upstairs wailed or complained for a drink of water. But Miriam wasn't tired. Her mind clicked along rapidly, a train on its track…going where?

Alan moved in his chair and spoke, his low ecclesiastical voice adding to the quiet mood and not breaking it. "Have you decided to stay on?"

"What?" She jumped, not at his interruption but at the question.

"Now that most English are leaving or have left, will you return to Britain?"

She resumed her chair. "I think it's assumed that I will. And you—are you returning to England?"

"India is my home. My parishioners are my people. I wouldn't want to be anywhere but in the center of God's will." He issued her a shrewd look down his longish nose. He was certainly no matinée idol, not like Jack and his Peter Lawford looks.

"That's the stuff of life, being in the center of God's will," Alan continued. "And I've found the Lord especially attentive to our—shall we say—*emotional* needs when we step out in adventure with him."

"Adventure?"

"Some of us were created for quests, journeys of great purpose. None of the humdrum. Strike out with walking stick. Or in my case, the saddle of my horse, ride into the hills with the good news of Christ in my satchel. In your case a classroom…a lesson plan?" With his hands still steepled, he quirked an eyebrow in her direction.

"And your emotional needs?" She felt no compunction asking him such a personal question. "A partner in life to share—"

"To share the long, lonely nights?" This minister didn't bat an eyelash. "Share the bed of human love and partnership?"

"Yes. Quite." Normally she'd blush, but no heat seared her face. The man made her feel completely at peace.

"For myself, I have found the Lord's companionship enough. But you, Miss Richards…if the Lord created you for that particular form of human delight, then he will most certainly provide the substance, a partner equally enthralled with your…adventure. Your united mission in life will only add to the fullness of your passion for each other."

She remembered the night of the train derailment, almost an exact year ago. When she'd seen Dassah and Cam standing together for the first time in many years. Something invisible and bright had danced on the air between them. Something holy and full of a passion she thought at the time she would never understand. But she did now. And she wanted it for her brother and his wife, and for herself.

Alan leaned forward and rested his elbows on his knees. He really was terribly tall. Too tall for any sort of elegance, and if he were a woman, she'd had described him as plain. He needed a haircut, and his nose was overlong. His grin slanted off to one side, and he was the wrong side of forty-five, she was sure. But then she was attracted to Jack, and he was not much younger.

"One thing I will tell you," Alan continued on, and she wondered what she missed while her imagination had wandered. "Miriam, if you were created for the spiritual adventure of striking out into parts unknown—or parts already known—then you will never be satisfied with less. Nor will you be satisfied with a man who does not share your vision."

She released a knowing chuckle. "Has my brother been gossiping behind my back?"

The preacher looked at her as if she'd grown a second head. "Your brother would never do such a thing, so I fail to understand your question—gossip about what?"

So Cam hadn't spilled the beans that she was interested in another man. She studied the preacher Cam described as maverick. It was Jack who made her tremble with passion when he kissed her, but at the moment Jack was in Delhi. Soon his regiment would leave. And Jack…were his kisses enough? Were his embraces enough? Or was there something else she wanted to ignite her passion for a man?

It was almost six the next evening when the telephone rang. Miriam knew it was Jack even before Laine hooted out that the call was for her. She'd known in her aching bones from caring for the children all day that he would ring, though he'd not mentioned it in his last letter. But on this first day of Indian Independence she knew he would want to talk to her. Massaging the small of her back, she hurried to pick up the receiver in the main room downstairs.

"Miriam," his voice crackled over the wire. "I was worried I'd not be able to get through. My word, all of Delhi is going wild with excitement. What's it like up there?" Even over the phone lines she could hear the noise behind Jack, firecrackers, music.

"Much the same." Through the window, she peeked out over the rooftops, where the last rays of sunlight glinted off the domes of the Golden Temple of the Sikhs, the globelike spires of a temple to a Hindu goddess, a minaret poking up on the twilight skyline.

"You should have come with me, Miriam, like I begged you to."

"We've gone over all this before, Jack. I can't leave. Not now when so many people need a helping hand. Mother's still here, Laine too, but never mind all that, Jack. You sound wonderful. What's it like in Delhi? Father hasn't rung yet, so we've no idea."

"The crowds, Miriam, I've never seen the like. The cheering. The state carriage couldn't make it through the crowds to the flag raising. The viceroy and vicereine had to stand in the carriage and make their salute from quite a distance. The throngs, Miriam, a quarter million people all chanting *Jai Hind*."

She smiled, listening to him go on. "Miriam, darling, the crowds were so thick, nowhere to put a foot. People were afraid the infants would be crushed. Women were throwing their babies up in the air, catching them—it was raining babies, Miriam!" He seemed to run out of breath. "Marvelous, darling…if only you'd been with me."

Her eyes misted. She cleared her throat of roughness of what could have been for them as a couple. "It would have been wonderful to have seen all that with you."

"Darling…."

"Jack…don't…please."

"You've made your decision then." She felt his disappointment over the miles of wire. "I love you, Miriam."

"I love you too."

"Then why?" He muttered something that she was sure was taking the Lord's name in vain, and her heart saddened further for him.

"We're simply not going to the same places, darling."

"You're staying on."

"Yes, Jack, even though Kinnaird is sure to be in Pakistan, I plan to return to my students, those who are still there, and those who will come in the years ahead."

"How long do you think a Muslim state will allow you to practice your Christian faith, Miriam?"

"I don't know, darling." She wiped the dampness from her eyes. "I'm well aware there will be difficulties ahead. But those young women will need an education now more than ever."

"You're determined then."

Her throat closed so that she couldn't speak.

Though miles away, he seemed to know that. "All right, my love. No kitty claws today." His voice came across a bit strained. "You're amazing you know, utterly astounding. Put any decorated soldier to shame with your courage."

She giggled through tears and a stuffy nose. "Now you're being ridiculous."

"May I write to you?"

"Of course, dear, of course. Where can I send letters to you?"

"The regiment's been ordered to Palestine. Tomorrow we leave Delhi for the Bombay pier, taking the ship directly to the Near East."

In the background behind him, she heard the crackle of fireworks in Delhi. A moment later came the echo of fireworks here in Amritsar too. In spite of all the hatred simmering in the barricaded streets, behind the barbed wire separating people, some had found the energy to celebrate.

"Miriam, think of me in Palestine, as I'll think of you in Pakistan." With that he rang off.

Outside, fireworks shot off against the dark sky above Amritsar, reminding her of those red-hot cinders that flew like fireflies a year ago when the train derailed. That sense of loneliness came back, when she'd watched Cam and Dassah that night. When she'd hungered for what shimmered between them. Now hoping they would find it again. *Lord...Lord...I need a hug.*

The mission hummed with its normal level of noise. Children ran around playing or doing their chores. Older children were helping the younger ones to get to bed. Mother was seeing a small mob of them upstairs.

Now was not the moment in her life for romance or the sensuality of what her sister Eva had. *Oh Lord, I need a hug.* Now was the time to see to those who were hurting. In the meantime tonight, she'd hug some little tot who might be fretting, to ease the abrasions on her heart. And she'd pray about the adventure she knew in her heart the Lord had in store for her. Perhaps Alan was on to something there. A small joy swirled at the base of her spine. Alan was right, she could be happy single. In fact, the loss of Jack was moving away far more quickly than she would ever have imagined. It was as if he'd already boarded his ship, and the tether line had snapped and floated on the water, leaving her on the shores of her beloved India.

With a skip to her step, she started up the stairs, a hum under her breath. She'd almost made it to the next floor when a voice from the stairwell below stopped her in her tracks. "Miss?"

Miriam looked down on one of the teenage girls, a new girl. "Dharini, isn't it?"

"Yes, miss. May I be speaking to you for a moment?"

Miriam glanced upstairs, but Mother had everything under control. "Of course, what can I help you with?"

Dharini beckoned her to come all the way down, and then invited her to sit outside on the wall overlooking the *bagh*. For a while they sat in silence, taking in the sights and sounds of the relief center and all its turmoil, and Miriam began to wonder what on earth Dharini wanted.

"All the mission speaks of you, miss," the girl finally said. She licked her lips, keeping her gaze on the dusty ground below. "Perhaps it is selfish of me to be asking at a time like this, but I…but I have hopes for my future."

A tiny drumbeat started in the bottom of Miriam's frame. "What hopes do you have, Dharini?"

"I wish for an education. I wish to learn and broaden my mind, miss. Is that wrong for me to hope and pray for at a time like this? I would like to become a nurse."

The drumbeat inside Miriam strengthened, and she almost laughed. The passion that Alan spoke of last night was what she already knew she possessed. Her desire was to teach and broaden young minds like Dharini's. For a moment she almost expected to hear birds singing or a marching band break out with some triumphant piece of music. *Thank you, Lord, I'm excited to think of what you have in store for me. I wait in breathless anticipation.*

She tilted her head at the young girl. "So you want to become a nurse. That will certainly require education." As twilight ended and night began, she started to lay out the various options that, God willing, would soon be open to Dharini and girls like her. An hour passed, and the pleasure of talking to this young student filled the void that Jack's telephone call had created. Someone inside the parlor lit the lamps and strolled out to the patio not realizing she was in a private conversation.

From the corner of her eye, Miriam saw that it was the maverick Reverend Alan Callahan, and she smiled a small smile. Jack was not the man to share her dreams with. She was confident she could be happy as a single woman…but… perhaps there was another man, a man who loved India like she did, a man who would fight for the rights of Indian people and seek to protect the frail and needy. A man to share the good news of Christ with those Indians who wished to hear.

As Alan apologized for interrupting her and Dharini, he slipped back inside the mission. In an instant it had happened. He no longer seemed as unattractive as she'd thought him yesterday. In fact, there was something…yes, something about him.

Fireworks exploded. Sitting on the top step in the dim stairwell, Cam imagined the colored stars blazing the night sky. For him it was only another use of gunpowder, and he cringed a little at each blast, worrying how this noise, the shaking of the house might frighten his wife. Dassah was on the other side of the door he leaned against. Only a wooden door, an inch breadth of wood separated him from his wife. Not miles, not entire provinces, though it might as well have been. Since they arrived in Amritsar yesterday, she'd remained behind this door, in the room at the top of the house that used to belong to the founder of this mission.

Other than those few brief words she spoke to him when he carried her from the schoolhouse in Dayapur, she'd not spoken directly to him. This afternoon his mother had squeezed his arm as she passed him by, on one of her many tasks, while Eshana, Jai, and Laine worked unceasingly with the refugees outside.

"Give her time, dear," Mum had said as he'd stood at the base of the stairwell looking up at the closed door.

"Has she talked with you, Mum?"

"A little." His mother smiled. "We just sat together for a while, and she talked about the baby. It seemed all she wanted."

"And you're sure she's well?"

"Physically yes. She's seen some terrible things. Like we all have. She told me about some of it."

"And the baby's name?"

His mother's brow wrinkled. "She said she wished to keep that to herself for a while longer."

"I see."

She squeezed his arm again. "Give her time."

That was hours ago. Alan, the rest of them, Mum, Eshana, Jai, Laine, Miriam, and himself, along with a score of native Christians, worked and worked to dish out food, bring clean blankets, dole out water, try to bring some semblance of comfort to the devastated in the *bagh*.

It was late now. He should be getting some rest in order to help out again tomorrow, but he couldn't leave. If this was as close as she would let him come, he'd sleep out here, leaning against the door if he had to.

Footsteps from the bottom of the staircase started up. As the person rounded the last bend, he saw Tikah bearing a tray of *chapattis* and tea for Dassah.

"How is she, Tikah?"

The woman of Baluchistan stopped. They stood summing each other up in the dim light of the stairwell lamp.

"You are still sitting here, Cam."

A ripple of what felt like light ran down his spine. Tikah had said his name. "I'll wait all my life for her."

She stared down at the tray. "The minister has explained to Dassah and to me that she is indeed legally married to you."

"Dassah knows this?" Hope shot off inside him with the same explosive power of the fireworks. "But when?"

"The minister told her on the train from Rawalpindi, three days ago."

The skyrocketing hope fizzled to cinders and fell. If she'd known all this time that he had married her, then why...why? He glanced at the closed door. And why had Alan not said a word?

A long, ragged sigh came from the old woman. She stood on the stair, her brow creased, mulling something over. "So be it," she said to herself a long moment later. She held the tray out to him, gesturing for him to take it. Then opening the door she stepped aside. At first he didn't understand, but Tikah nodded for him to enter the upper room. When he did, she closed the door upon herself, so that he alone entered.

The fireworks stopped. From below, the sounds of an unsleeping city filtered up, the hum of many voices down in the *bagh*. Yet a breeze blew over the flower urns on the balcony in the dark. Somehow the smells of sorrow were dispelled by the perfume of roses, jasmine, and lilies.

He saw her figure lying on the *charpoy*. With the moon shining through the open glass doors, her silhouette lifted up on one elbow, and she seemed to peer into the darkened corner where he stood, breathless with hope, longing.

"*Amma?*" The almost musical pulse to her voice nearly broke his heart. "The little one is asleep at last. Although I despair I shall have enough milk for the little glutton."

He took a step closer, bearing the tray. "Tikah sent me in, Dassah, with your tea."

Her head shot up. Swiftly, she moved to a sitting position. In the dark he could see her adjust her sari.

"Dassah, may I bring your tea?"

She clasped her hands, her head dipped. "Yes," she whispered.

He brought her the tea, the fragrance of saffron wafting upward, mingling with the bouquet from the blossoms outside. As she sipped her tea, he stepped aside. In the dim light he made out the shape of his son lying next to her on the *charpoy*.

He stood aside, by the glass doors looking out at the balcony. Clearing his throat, he half turned to her. "Zakir, before he died, had a message for you."

She ceased sipping her tea.

"He said to tell you...well it was only a few words really. 'I remember Yeshu.'"

Her deep sigh reached him across the room.

"It's all right for Zakir, isn't it, Dassah?"

"He remembered what the mother of his heart taught him. He has returned to Yeshu."

His sigh echoed hers. They could both rest now over their brother. Silence embraced the darkened room. Only the soft feathers of breath from the baby could be heard.

She set the half empty glass on the small table of woven reeds. "Do you want to hold him?"

He nodded. She lifted the limp bundle. In his slumber he seemed to fold in two in Dassah's hands. She straightened the infant and stood to place him in Cam's arms. "Support his head...like this. Though he is much stronger at one month. He is lifting his head up to look around him when he lies on his tummy."

With the infant in his embrace, the waterfall of Dassah's words flowed over him. He brought the baby up close to his face and breathed in the sweetness of perfect, unblemished skin. Kissed the softness of the downy head, the silk hair. If they could talk of nothing else, to talk of their child might weave her heart toward him again. "You're a good mother."

Her hand came up to her mouth, as if she held back something she wanted to say. Or was it emotions she didn't know what to do with? Or did she not know the words to ask him to go?

"Everyone in the house is wondering what you named him," he asked.

She stood as still as time. "I was very sad not to tell your mother when she asked his name."

"Mother's all right. Bursting with pride over him. Laine too."

Her head dipped again. "Your mother is proud of him, and she told me how much she loves me. How delighted—"

"Both my parents are delighted, Dassah. They love you. They were so angry with me—"

"That you kept our marriage a secret!" Her voice sharpened. "Why, Cam, when we were truly married? Did you regret it afterward? Were you ashamed?" She waved a hand. "If so, then I will not remain—"

"No!" His loud voice brought a start out of the baby, but the babe only opened his eyes and stared up in the gloom at Cam. He nearly drowned in the depths of the child's eyes, until the little one closed them again and promptly fell asleep.

"I was a coward, Dassah," he whispered. "It's not easy standing up to bigots. I was afraid what people would say, afraid how they'd treat you, treat us. How they still might." His voice took on an edge. "And being the drunken sot I was, I didn't have the gumption to stand up and do what was right. But I'm changed, Dassah. I'm changed. I want to make up for hurting you, for the rest of my life. I want people to know how proud I am of you. Proud to be your husband...if you'll have me back."

She stood for the longest time. *Oh dear Father in heaven, help me. She's leaving me.* She walked away and stood looking out through the glass doors to the balcony and the urns of flowers.

Her whisper broke the silence of the room, overriding their baby's breath. "I am no longer a weak woman. No longer under your sway simply as a man with a woman, the way I was when I was seventeen and you came home from school. I am even stronger than I was in Kashmir during our honeymoon. I have grown strong in Yeshu, strong with his love, and it was his anger and despair flowing through me at the brutality and wickedness of my people as they hurt each other. I felt his weeping in my soul."

His throat closed. His heart cracked.

"But…" She turned back to him. "Just as I have become a new person, no longer weak but potent with the strength of Christ's love, I am seeing something new in you. Tikah told me last autumn that you were the image of your father." Her tone grew as soft as the breeze blowing over the jasmine and through the glass doors. "Now I see, you are no longer the son of your natural father, but the son of your *heavenly* Father."

Her voice broke as she inched closer so that there was no space between them, only their sleeping child. "As I live and breathe, for all my earthly days, I am yours, Cam. Is that not why I still wear the gift you gave me all those years ago when you were but twelve?" She pulled out the Christensen Akro Slag from the leather string around her neck. "Is that not the reason I gave your son the name of Cameron Geoffrey Fraser?"

His heart filled his chest, cutting off his breath. A joy so exquisite it sliced deep into the very marrow of his being.

"Nothing will ever separate us again," he rasped.

Holding his son close to his heart with one arm, he drew her to his side, feeling her willowy woman's shape yield to his solid stance as he supported her and held his son.

Her mouth reached up to meet his, and he murmured against her lips, "Nothing will ever separate us."

EPILOGUE

September 1947

On the Bombay quay, a kaleidoscope of color and humanity dazzled Dassah's eyes—women in saris of mango pink, peacock blue, lime green. Bengali clerks rushed here and there. On the dock, uniformed English soldiers joined the throng on their way back to England. So many people. The teeming press of millions. India, the land of her birth.

"So long…Christmas in two years…take care of yourself," Eshana, Laine, and Abby said between hugs and tears as they crowded at the base of the gangway. Tikah kept trying to lag behind, but Abby kept pulling her close. Jai, Geoff, and Adam stood aside from the three women, quietly saying their own good-byes. Miriam had already hugged her parents in farewell.

Not far from the gangway, Miriam, holding Cameron, stood with Cam and Dassah. "It'll be downright awful not seeing him every day. Getting a few snaps in letters won't do. Eva said the same thing before they sailed last week."

Dassah touched her arm. "I promise to have Cam take many, many photos to send you."

"It won't even do me any good to join Jai and Eshana and Laine and Adam when they visit my parents in Ireland two Christmases from now."

"Cam and I will be all the way around the world by then." A lump stuck in her throat as she watched tears swimming in Miriam's eyes.

"Why Canada, Dassah? If you wanted mountains, New Zealand isn't that far away."

"British Columbia in Canada seems to be a good place for us to call home. There are waterfalls, mountains covered in fir and cedar."

"But Ireland is cool and green."

Dassah let out a little chuckle. "There are more opportunities in North America."

Miriam broke down then, wiping her face with the tail end of Cameron's blanket. She put her arms around Dassah, and a moment later they both felt Cam's arm around them. "Cheer up, old thing. You'll soon have that entire squadron of soldiers weeping if you're not careful."

Miriam laughed. "I can't think why this breathtakingly beautiful woman consented to be your spouse."

Cam pulled himself up to his full height and puffed out his chest. A moment later, he released his breath with a chuckle and caught her eye. "Nor can I understand why she agreed to marry me. Makes no sense at all." He glanced at his sister. "Any chance of you entering the state of matrimony in the near future, old girl? I hear you've sent Jack Sunderland packing, but you've turned the head of a certain man of the cloth I know."

Miriam pursed her lips to one side. "Really? News to me."

"Well, write the chap a note up there in the wilds of Kashmir. You never know what may come of it."

"And you'd approve of such a liaison?" Miriam quipped.

His eyes grew tender, and Dassah's heart turned over at the love in his eyes for his sister. It was only a hair less than the deep love he had for her and their son. "Yes, clever puss," he said to Miriam. "The Lord knows very well you need a man who is more than a match for your intelligence. Be nice to attend another family wedding, see you decked on in finery like Eva."

"Not at all." Miriam winked at Dassah. "I'm more interested in your wife's style. Have I told you, Dassah, how gorgeous you are in that red sari?"

"Only six times since this morning."

"Red," Miriam said with a sigh. "The color of joy."

The love of Yeshu, remembering what he did for her in giving his life, was the only thing to restore her joy of wearing crimson. But it had taken some time, and much poring over the scriptures to bring the start of healing. A thought Dassah kept to herself.

An odd silence throbbed between the three of them. The time had come. Cam's parents and Tikah had gone aboard. Laine and Adam stood with Eshana and Jai on the pier. And Miriam handed Cameron to her and kissed her. Dassah returned the kiss and stood back for Cam.

Dassah watched as her husband's eyes glistened as he took his sister's hands. "So long, old thing. For now."

"Yes, love, see you in a few years. For a visit."

Then Cameron turned from Miriam, took Dassah's arm, and led her up the gangway. As they stood with the family on board at the railing looking down on the pier, light glinted off the tin roofs at the quay and bounced off the ground. Engines throbbed. Streamers broke as the liner pulled away from the pier. Miriam, Jai and Eshana, Laine and Adam, grew smaller and smaller. As the ship drew away from the shore, a loosened tether floated on the water, and Miriam waved to them.

They stood for a long time, gripping the railing. Cam's parents and Tikah had gone below with Cameron. Only Cam and she were left as the blue line of shore thinned to nothing, leaving only the great expanse of sea.

Her husband pulled her close. "Come away with me, *janu*."

She wound her arms around his shoulders as he lifted her chin and kissed her forehead, her cheeks, the tip of her nose. He lowered his lips to hers and murmured against them, "Come away with me, *janu*, the world belongs to us."brought him to dinner at the palace in the first place. I can't imagine social events like this are really the training he requires for taking care of his own matters."

Adam's laughter sputtered out of him. "I see your point. But I'm afraid I had other reasons for bringing him this evening."

"Well I was wondering. While I'm thrilled you brought Hector along, I'm not sure how he can help if your purpose was to woo me."

Adam slanted a lop-sided grin. "I thought if I flopped in the romance department—which was highly likely—then Hector would soften you up."

She let out a belabored sigh and leaned against him, placing her lips against the base of his neck. "And a good thing you did. That proposal of yours...all I can say is for a man with a First in literature from Oxford, you were sadly lacking in eloquence."

He lifted her face to his and touched his smiling lips to hers, muttered softly. "I know, shameful, isn't it? I'm sorry, Laine, I'll work on doing better in the future. I promise after we're married to quote poetry in your ear while we dance slowly every evening. Will that suit?"

The tiger cub leapt in the waves, and the moonlight shone over the Bay of Bengal as she wrapped her arms around Adam's neck. "Darling, your proposal was perfect. Couldn't have proposed better myself. I recognize the signs of the old flame, of old desire too, you know. But I give you fair warning, poetry, slow dancing, and kissing will do only for a start."

ACKNOWLEDGMENTS

I believe in happy endings. I believe in love and family and friendship. I believe in all of these things because I believe in a benevolent heavenly Father who wrote the wonderful story of salvation through His son, Jesus Christ for all mankind.

To see the final book to this series launched in 2014 is the happy ending to a fantastic stage in my life. This series started out in the midst of a painful time for me in 1999. Through the various drafts of Book 1, *Shadowed in Silk*, and later Book 2, *Captured by Moonlight*, I watched my four children, Lana, Kyle, Rob, and my birth-daughter Sarah, as well as my mother, my dear friend Rachel Phifer, and my husband, all go through some really tough times in their lives. But through it all I saw the faithfulness and tenderness of God working through those dark canyons of unhappiness and bringing my loved ones and friends out into a wide valley of joy.

And it was my brother Steve's and my sister Irene's wrestling and winning over their alcoholism that inspired Book 3, *Veiled at Midnight*.

I believe in happy endings because I see God make it happen all the time. So first of all, to God be the glory for this joyous occasion to see my British Raj series completed.

Thank you to my beloved husband David; my children Lana, Kyle, Rob, Sarah; my mother, Sarah; my brother, Steve; sister, Irene; my son-in-law James; daughter-in-law, Crystal; and grandsons, Zechariah, Keenan, Micah, and now little Ian.

And to my dear writing critique partner, Rachel Phifer, the award-winning author of *The Language of Sparrows*, a very special thanks. My writing would not be what it is without your wisdom and inspiration. Also thanks to my publisher David and Roseanna White and to the WhiteFire editors, Dina Sleiman and Wendy Chorot. Thank you so much for helping this series see the light of day. And let us all, writers, editors, and readers, trust in the Lord for a brighter tomorrow.

HISTORICAL NOTE

In this novel you will find a great many historical figures intermingling on the pages with my fictional characters. An easy one to recognize is Gandhi, the political savior to India. Also included are men greatly instrumental to Indian Independence and the creation of the country Pakistan, such as Jawaharlal Nehru, the first Prime Minister of India, and Muhammad Ali Jinnah, the father of Pakistan. Other politicians of that time are mentioned briefly throughout the book, but the two other figures who stand out predominately are Lord Louis Mountbatten and his wife Edwina, the last viceroy and vicereine of British Colonial India.

Much of the experiences of the people of India were taken from actual recorded interviews of individuals who lived through the dark times of Partition. But a light in the midst of all that hatred and despair was a Scottish missionary, Isobella McNair, who was the principal of the Kinnaird College for Women in the area that later became Pakistan. Kinnaird College was founded by the American Presbyterian Mission and the Church Missionary Society, and is still in existence today as a university for women in the city of Lahore in Pakistan. Although Kinnaird is no longer under Christian leadership, it remains a light of education for women in a predominately Muslim country.

That college and many other institutions of various faiths—Christian, Sikh, Hindu, and Muslim—as well as that of the British Government and the Red Cross, under the leadership of Lady Mountbatten, helped the suffering Indian people through the brutal partition of India in 1947. After the new borders were drawn, about 14.5 million people crossed the borders hoping to find relative safety with their religious majority. Low estimates of how many died are 20,000 with the higher estimate being that of 1,000,000. In the months after my fictional book ends, the War of Kashmir began and continues to this day to be an area of contention between India and Pakistan.

DISCUSSION QUESTIONS

1.   From the start of Book 1, *Shadowed in Silk*, the train system in India has been a metaphor for the British rule of India. In Chapter 1, can you project what this train metaphor foreshadows in the first chapter of *Veiled at Midnight* as Britain is scheduled to pull out of India in the chapters ahead?

2.   In Chapter 6 we read, *"Honestly, Miriam, the way you barge into Dante's Inferno you must think angels ride on your shoulder..."* We see here an aspect to Miriam's character. She's a heroic person in her own right, but does Miriam's inner strength come in its entirety from the Lord? Or perhaps a lot from simply the way she was raised?

3.   In Chapter 9 we read, *Cam laughed. "I'd say you're more the color of a creamed tea. But even if you were ebony, I'll thank you very much not to insult me with idiotic racial prejudice."* Racial and cultural prejudice is abhorrent to Christian thought. To find out how Christians are to treat others of different races read John 4: 7-26, Acts 10, and Galations 3: 26-29.

4.   In Chapter 13 we read what Tikah says: *"For a while I thought the mission was my home, that they were my people, that I shared their God. But I realized I had never really been a part of your family...Now I am a husk of an old woman."* Tikah's view of God is based on what she sees as her poverty-stricken circumstances. Is it possible your view of God's love may be marred by your understanding of your circumstances?

5.   In Chapter 17 we read, *Eshana implored Cam. "Tell me...why do I smell whiskey seeping from your pores, like it did from your natural father?" The truth hit him like an artillery barrage. He was just like his wretch of a father.* As much as Cam wants to emulate his stepfather Geoff, he wrestles with the character flaws he has inherited from his biological father. Read John 8:31-42. As Christians we want to follow in the footsteps of Christ, but we end up doing the same wretched deeds as our natural parents. But does God leave us in this predicament?

6.   In Chapter 23 we read, *a voice niggled at the back of Cam's brain. "You are a failure. There is nothing to hope for...all is lost."* Whose voice is niggling in Cam's mind? As the author I'll tell you—it is that of the enemy, Satan. He is the one who will constantly remind you of your failures and sins. What can you do to protect yourself from this bombardment from the enemy? You might find an answer in John 17, in Christ's High Priestly prayer for us, his followers.

7.   In Chapter 26 we read, *"In Him I live and move and have my being."* Dassah's theme centers around two of my favorite verses. One is Acts 17:28 that

is quoted in the scene above. Compare this with Dassah's understanding of herself as much more than a precious sparrow in God's eyes.

8.   In Chapter 30 we read, *The last of the sunlight seeped through Dassah's closed eyelids, so that the world turned crimson, scarlet—red as the wedding sari she had once wanted.* An underlying metaphor in this book is the color red that represents the spilling of blood. How could such a thing be positive? But think of Christ's innocent blood as He sacrificed Himself on the cross to save mankind. Such a horrible event, and yet as time unfolded we see it is the thing that saves us. Read Isaiah 1:18 and Ephesians 1:7

9.   In Chapter 33 we read, *The passion that Alan spoke of last night was what Miriam already knew she possessed. Her desire was to teach and broaden young minds like Dharini's. For a moment she almost expected to hear birds singing or a marching band break out with some triumphant piece of music. Thank you, Lord, I'm excited to think of what you have in store for me. I wait in breathless anticipation.* Do you really trust that God has a plan for your life, a plan that will fit you like a glove? Read and consider Psalm 37:3,4.

Twilight of the British Raj
~ Book 1~

Shadowed in Silk

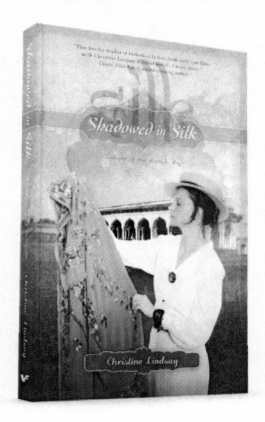

Twilight of the British Raj
~ Book 2~

Captured by Moonlight

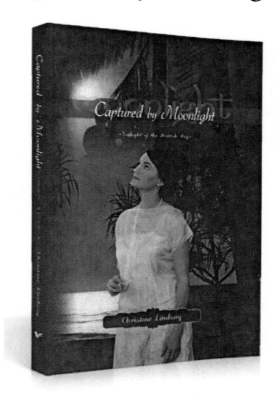

OTHER TITLES FROM WHITEFIRE PUBLISHING

Soul Painter
by Cara Luecht

Miriam paints the future...but can she change it?

Sweet Mountain Music
by Suzie Johnson

Chloe Williston will make a name for herself...no matter what beast she must track to achieve it.

A Soft Breath of Wind
by Roseanna M. White

A gift that has branded her for life.

Hidden Faces
by Golden Keyes Parsons

Four novellas bringing to life the unnamed women of the Gospels. Including *Trapped, Alone, Broken,* and *Hopeless.*

CPSIA information can be obtained at www.ICGtesting.com
Printed in the USA
LVOW12s0600311014

411299LV00001B/12/P